The

DARK
ASCENT

Tor Books by Walter H. Hunt

The Dark Wing
The Dark Path
The Dark Ascent

The DARK ASCENT

Walter H. Hunt

TOR®

A Tom Doherty Associates Book
New York

THE DARK ASCENT

A Tor Book
Published by Tom Doherty Associates, LLC
175 Fifth Avenue
New York, NY 10010

www.tor.com

Tor® is a registered trademark of Tom Doherty Associates, LLC.

Library of Congress Cataloging-in-Publication Data

Hunt, Walter H.
    The dark ascent / Walter H. Hunt.—1st ed.
        p. cm.
    "A Tom Doherty Associates book."
    ISBN 0-765-31116-X (alk. paper)
    EAN 978-0765-31116-0
    1. Human-alien encounters—Fiction. 2. Life on other planets—Fiction. 3. Space warfare—Fiction.   I. Title.

PS3608.U59D33 2004
813'.6—dc22   2003071141

First Edition: August 2004

Printed in the United States of America

0 9 8 7 6 5 4 3 2 1

This book is dedicated to the following people:

To my wife and best friend, Lisa, who continues to be first in my heart;

To my daughter, Aline, who knows the names of all of Dad's books already;

To my older brother, Raymond, whose interest in my writing career has brought us closer together; and

To my friend and fellow writer Rob Sawyer—thanks for all your help and support.

acknowledgments

Thanks to my editor, Brian Thomsen. His efforts have made my work better in every instance.

Thanks to Fred Iannelli, whose original vision helped me imagine what it looks like within the *gyaryu*.

And, in particular, thanks to Christine Aebi, who has been copy editor on *The Dark Wing, The Dark Path,* and now *The Dark Ascent.* The length of the manuscript has been the least of her problems: She's had to deal with alien languages and speech patterns, military terminology, and more details than I can keep track of. After her stellar work, you can rest assured that any omissions, inaccuracies, or errors in the final manuscript are due to my own oversight.

The Highspeech contains words that are used as modes of address between individuals. These words consist of two or three letters when translated into Standard. These words are called "prenomen" and indicate not only the status of the person being addressed (or referred to), but also the relationship of the speaker to that person.

Prenomen have two forms. One is used when the addressee or subject is alive, and the other when the person is dead. The prenomen used in the series are described below.

se, si.   This is the standard mode of address between individuals when they are of equal status or unknown to each other. *si* is used when referring to or addressing a deceased person. *se* and *si* are also used to address a person of lesser status.

ge, gi.   This mode is used to describe a lover, usually in a nonaffectionate or pejorative manner. It is also used colloquially to address a person of significantly lower status, such as a servant (or non-zor), though this form is archaic. This usage can often lead to duels and challenges.

ha, ha'i.   This mode is used when addressing a person of superior status (other than the High Lord or a person of equivalent status, such as the Solar Emperor). The person thus addressed will usually respond using the *se* form.

le, li.   *le* is used between intimates as a term of genuine affection. It is permitted only when a relationship is acknowledged by both parties; otherwise it can be cause for challenge. *li* is only used when referring to or addressing a dead mate.

hi, hi'i.   This mode is used when addressing the High Lord of the People. It has also been adopted for use when addressing the Solar Emperor, though the standard usage is with the prenomen and title, *e.g.,* "*hi* Emperor," rather than the given name. *hi'i* is used when referring to a deceased High Lord, and is generally accompanied by a wing-position of honor to *esLi*.

na, ni.   This mode refers to a Servant of *esGa'u*. It is used only rarely, often in literature. *ni*

ra, ri.   This mode, similar to the *na* form, is used to address important Servants of *esGa'u*, usually *Shrnu'u HeGa'u*. It is similar to the *ha* form. The *ri* construction is almost never used, as the notion of such a Servant being considered dead is difficult to encompass.

The

DARK
ASCENT

The starship *Trebizond* had just begun its eighth sweep of the volume near the Orionward jump point when its mass-radar registered something that defied description.

"What the hell—" Captain Richard Abramowicz began, watching the jump-echo resolve itself on his pilot's board. "Rhea, confirm that all systems are functional."

Rhea Salmonson, the watch helm officer, didn't turn around. She gestured over the console and an image of the surroundings appeared above, showing two huge jump-disturbances thirty thousand kilometers downrange. A dozen smaller ones appeared as she watched, mirrored in the board in front of Captain Abramowicz.

She looked at the board in front of her. "All systems are functional, Captain," Salmonson said.

"Beat to Quarters," Abramowicz said instantly, and ordered a course change, aiming the *Trebizond* for the gravity well.

Several more transponder codes appeared on the pilot's board. They moved in tight formation as they emerged from jump, tracking the *Trebizond*'s course and accelerating to intercept it.

Commodore, take a look at this."

Jonathan Durant, commander of Adrianople Starbase, looked

up from the engineering station. His exec, and the current Officer of the Watch, Arlen Mustafa, was standing beside the pilot's board; he'd focused on a volume near the Orionward jump point that hadn't been updated for several minutes.

The pilot's board for a starbase the size of Adrianople was several times larger than that of a fleet carrier. Instead of just keeping track of squadrons of fighters, a starbase board had to monitor the large amount of traffic transiting a planetary system. Adrianople was busier than most: It was an anchor for the Imperial Grand Survey.

"Have you run a diagnostic?"

"Nothing wrong at this end, sir," Mustafa answered. "The monitor station's deep-radar isn't transmitting at the Orionward jump point."

"Increase the range on adjacent sectors. We'll lose some resolution, but it'll give us coverage until we can get something out there to repair it."

"Aye-aye, sir," Mustafa said. "Switching." He gestured at the console and the volume display went blank and then slowly began to update.

"Let's get a tech crew out there next watch and . . . What the hell are *those*?"

As Durant watched, the display resolved to show two unidentified transponder codes. The mass-radar, registering the jump-echo and the distortion of local space, showed figures that made no sense. As he watched, the display updated to show at least twenty smaller echoes all moving at high relative velocities and descending into the gravity well.

"Who's on duty out there?" Durant asked, reading the figures. The two large echoes massed more than two million tons and more than three kilometers long.

"*Trebizond*, sir."

"Find her." Durant called up a display above the engineering station. Adrianople was expecting reinforcements shortly; a task force under the command of Admiral César Hsien was due within the next few Standard days, but there wasn't much on-station right now.

There hadn't been any need. Adrianople was a quiet posting; nothing but Exploration Service ships—certainly enough to fight pirates, but against something like this . . .

Durant had read Laperriere's report. Duke William, the First Lord, hadn't wanted to show it to him at all—"*part of the court-martial inquiry*," he'd said—but relented, finally, after sending Hsien along with most of what had come back from Cicero to Denneva for refit. Durant had found it just as hard to believe as the First Lord did. Still, it was clear that the High Nest believed it.

Now the High Chamberlain was gone; the First Lord was gone; most of Durant's operational tonnage was outsystem—with orders to return to base as soon as possible, to be sure, but outsystem nonetheless. The only recent arrivals had been a team of scientists from the Shiell Institute on New Chicago, here to look at the alien gear recovered from Cicero when Laperriere had gotten out of there.

Most of a century of peace had taught commanding officers to be cautious but not indecisive. Durant reviewed his assets, such as they were, and his options.

One thing he knew for sure: He couldn't do what Laperriere had done. Even if he were willing, he wouldn't have the chance.

"Arlen," he said, "set up a comm to every ship in the volume. *Trebizond,* especially, if you can locate her. Ten minutes. I'll be in my ready-room."

S**TILL TRACKING** us, Skip," Lieutenant Rhea Salmonson said. "The two big bogeys are still headed insystem." The *Trebizond* had been under way for twenty minutes; comm hadn't been able to reach Adrianople Starbase . . . some sort of broad-spectrum interference.

They were alone—except for ten unknown vessels following them as they moved across the outermost orbital. The *Trebizond* could bear on the nearest of its pursuers but probably couldn't hold out against all ten—and they were closing. Still, they hadn't opened fire. Abramowicz considered the possibility that the bogeys didn't have the range. If that were so, then it likely wouldn't be true much longer—and if it was not so, then it didn't make a damn bit of sense.

He looked aside from the pilot's board and saw his WS4 come down the ramp from the lift. *Trebizond* hadn't had a Sensitive on board until recently; Abramowicz had read the regs on Sensitives but didn't know much past that.

"Reporting as ordered, Captain," the WS4 said, saluting.

"Mr. Trang," Abramowicz said. "You're up-to-date on our tactical situation?" Vo Trang was a Regular Navy man who had turned up with Sensitive abilities. He'd been trained as a gunnery officer, Abramowicz recalled that.

"I am sir."

"Can you, er, *feel* anything?"

"I have . . . yes sir. Since we changed course, sir, I have been hearing . . ."

" 'Hearing'?"

"Yes sir." For the first time, Abramowicz noticed sweat on the other man's forehead. Some of the other officers on the bridge had looked away from their stations, attracted by the conversation between their captain and the Sensitive. The usual chatter had vanished, making the bridge suddenly quiet.

"Helm report," Abramowicz snapped, more to break the tension than anything else.

"Unchanged, Skip," Salmonson answered. "Nearest enemy vessel is twenty-two thousand six hundred kilometers downrange, still accelerating."

"What have you been hearing, Mr. Trang?"

"Voices, sir. I am . . . It—they—want me to listen to them. I can hardly . . ." He rubbed his forehead with the heel of one hand. "As they get closer it becomes harder to ignore them."

"What would happen if you listened?"

"Please don't order me to do so, Captain." Trang's eyes filled with anger—or fear, perhaps? Abramowicz couldn't tell. "No sir, I don't think that's a good idea."

"Why would that be?"

"I'm . . . I'm not sure just why, sir. But I'm not sure they'd let me go."

"You'd best explain yourself, mister."

Trang said nothing. He looked defiantly at the captain for a moment, and then down at the deck.

Abramowicz shrugged. "The voices are coming from the bogeys."

"I believe so, Captain."

"You're saying that whatever is aboard those ships . . ." Abramowicz gestured at the pilot's board in front of him, and the tac display dissolved to a representation of the nearest alien vessel: a big ungainly thing, irregular in shape, with an equally irregular defensive field signature. ". . . whatever it is, can project Sensitive abilities more than twenty thousand kilometers—enough to make you believe that it'd get hold of you and not let go."

"Yes sir."

"What would you estimate to be a safe distance?"

"Captain?" Trang turned partially away to look at the slowly up-dating image on the pilot's display.

"How far away do we have to be, for you to be safe?"

"I'm not sure, Captain. I think—"

Whatever it was that Vo Trang thought, however, had become im-material. As the Sensitive turned to face Abramowicz, whatever had been behind those eyes was abruptly replaced.

"Trang?" the captain of the *Trebizond* asked.

"It is easier for you to pronounce," Trang's voice said, "than the name I actually bear. This vessel resisted our *k'th's's* for longer than we expected."

"What the hell is a *k'th*—"

"Irrelevant," said Trang, or whatever was speaking with Trang's voice. "What *is* relevant, Captain, is that you listen carefully."

"And if I don't?" Abramowicz gestured toward the Marine ser-geant near the gunnery station; but he—like everyone else on the bridge other than himself and the Sensitive standing beside the pilot's seat—was immobile and staring off into nowhere.

Trang shrugged. "Then you will die and we will find another. You are not *important*, Captain Abramowicz. This meat-creature through whom we speak has value. You will merely be food for the *k'th's's*.

"Nonetheless, we have no orders to terminate you and will not do so if you listen carefully and do as you are told. You have one Standard minute to decide."

More than twenty holo-images hung in the air over Durant's ready-room table. None of them belonged to Rich Abramowicz—though Arlen Mustafa had located the *Trebizond* as soon as it came within detection range of another monitoring station. It was headed into the gravity well, with a fair number of hounds of hell behind it.

"I want your undivided attention," Durant said to the images. "Your mass-radar should show incoming hostiles. A couple of them are . . . Well, nothing in Adrianople System is a match for them. Nonetheless they're *here*. I've prepared and sent a comm-squirt to Denneva inform-ing them of our situation and sending our most current data.

"I've already dispatched *Eurydice* and *Aragon* toward the gas giant currently at opposition to the Orionward jump point. Their orders are to observe but not engage." Each of the three captains acknowledged with a gesture or a nod.

"What about *Trebizond*?" asked one of the other captains—Darrin Feng of the *Arcadia, Trebizond*'s sister ship.

"We haven't been able to establish comm contact with *Trebizond*. There's no indication of weapons fire, but clearly something is preventing her from raising us.

"Based on . . . what we know of the enemy, I am ordering all of you to stand off from *Trebizond*."

"And let her die?" Feng asked. Others muttered assent.

She may already be dead, Durant thought to himself. *And so are we.*

As they watched, the mass-radar showed *Trebizond* changing course and speed as her pursuers closed in. The ship's defensive fields suddenly dispersed, leaving her undefended.

Not a single shot had been fired.

As soon as Abramowicz had nodded his assent, Vo Trang collapsed to the deck. Suddenly everything was in motion; people all over the bridge found themselves doing whatever they'd been doing three minutes earlier, when Vo Trang had been . . . taken over.

"Dr. Ellis to the bridge," Abramowicz said to comm. "Helm, change course," he added, a chill in his voice. He named a new heading and speed. Rhea Salmonson spun to look at him, her eyes full of alarm, but he nodded. "Do it."

"Bridge, this is Hafner," came the voice of his exec. "I'm in Engineering—we're being grappled! Skipper, do you read?"

"Come up topside, Kit," he said. "I know we're being grappled. And we're about to be boarded."

"What the hell?"

"Topside, Commander. On the double—that's a direct order." *If you want to live*, he thought to himself, crouching down to check on his WS4. Trang was unconscious, but seemed to be breathing normally. Whatever had taken him, seemed to have let him loose.

"Drop your fields," Trang's voice said, though his eyes didn't open.

Abramowicz fell back in alarm, bracing his fall with one hand. "Captain—"

"Do it," Abramowicz said, gritting his teeth. "Drop the fields."

"Captain," Salmonson said, looking toward him, "we're in a hell of a crossfire. If we drop our fields we're dead."

"We're dead if we don't. Tell them," he said, grabbing the unconscious Sensitive by the shoulders and shaking him. "Tell them, damn it!"

Trang's eyes opened, and his lips formed into a half-smile. "Very well. You will be spared if you follow my instructions exactly. Drop your defensive fields and prepare to receive a . . . deputation."

Abramowicz lowered Trang to the deck. Somewhere within Trang's eyes, he could see fear and horror.

"Disperse the fields," Abramowicz repeated. His order was carried out. On the pilot's board, he could see one of the enemy ships closing to dock with his shuttle bay.

"When your deputation is aboard, will you let him go?"

"Since you are being so cooperative," Trang's voice said, "the answer is yes."

Trang's head lolled over onto its side, his eyes rolling up in his head. Abramowicz checked for a pulse—first at his wrist, then his neck—but there was nothing to find.

Eurydice's forward screen showed more detail than its captain truly wanted to see.

Amir Abu Bakr, whose uncle owned a quarter of Imperial Oahu (and rented it to courtiers at outrageous prices), had sought—and found—one of the quietest posts in the Solar Empire: captain of a Grand Survey ship near the Orionward edge. At least, it *had been* quiet—until the commander of Cicero Base had turned up with what was left of her command, then headed off on a zor starship for who-knew-what errand. Since then it had been drills and inspections, not to mention General Quarters every time the *Eurydice* was deployed.

Which had been damn near never. At least since Laperriere had come. And gone.

Until four hours ago, Abu Bakr had placed the entire inconvenience of it all at Laperriere's feet. Now, as he looked at the thing looming in his forward screen, he realized how foolish he had been.

Clearly, he thought to himself, *the commander of the* Aragon *must be thinking the same thing.* But *he* was not Natan Abu Bakr's nephew.

"How the hell are we supposed to fight something like that?" he said to no one in particular, leaning his chin on his folded hands as he sat in *Eurydice*'s pilot's seat.

"Our orders were not to engage," his exec reminded him.

"I know that, Peter," he snapped back. "But I don't think it's here just to refuel. Someone will have to fight it sometime."

The ship was irregular in shape, a shade over three kilometers from stem to stern; it had none of the streamlining of Imperial ships, no obvious port and starboard—it looked as if it had been constructed by pushing lumps of grayish clay together and jamming hardpoints on the outside. What they'd been able to gather from scanning suggested that the ship was in fact made up of a large number of small compartments.

"Captain," the comm officer said, "I've lost contact with *Aragon*."

"Well, reestablish it," Abu Bakr said without looking.

"I—I can't find her, Captain."

"What?" He looked from the forward screen to the pilot's board. He noted the *Aragon*'s last known position and was about to say something about it, when the icon turned from green to blue—indicating that the mass-radar data was stale, reflecting a projected position change based on its current movement vector.

"Captain!"

Abu Bakr looked at the forward screen again. An alien vessel—not the big one, but one more his size—was closing rapidly on their position. The pilot's board was already registering weapons discharge, and the *Eurydice*'s defensive fields were beginning to absorb energy.

"Target and fire!" Abu Bakr said, gripping the arms of the pilot's seat. "Come to new heading—" He named a course and speed, looking to put a limb of the planet between the *Eurydice* and the rapidly closing enemy. "Execute! And find *Aragon*!"

On the bridge of Adrianople Starbase, Commodore Jonathan Durant watched with horror as the *Eurydice* and *Aragon* opened fire on each other.

On the bridge of *Trebizond*, Captain Richard Abramowicz turned from the sight of two medical orderlies bundling up the body of Vo Trang, to see someone come through the lift doors. He wasn't sure what to expect, but a man in an Imperial Navy uniform wasn't it. Still, there was something not quite right about the man—something in his eyes.

This is your enemy, Abramowicz told himself.

The unknown officer scarcely looked aside as the orderlies carried the stretcher off the bridge. His attention was completely focused on Abramowicz.

"Save your energy, Captain," he said. "Your loyalty to the young man is quite noble, by human standards . . . but does very little for you now."

"I'm supposed to be comforted by that." Abramowicz exchanged a glance with Kit Hafner, his exec, and then returned his glance to the alien.

"It is not my role to comfort. There is something here I want, and I shall have it. The number of meat-creatures that die in the process is of very little importance to me. I believe I told you that already . . ." He crossed to the pilot's seat and sat in it, turning it around to face *Trebizond*'s captain. "And I do *so* hate to repeat myself.

"Believe me, Captain, your young Sensitive was having *very* uncharitable thoughts toward me, and I simply no longer needed him."

"And you need *me,* I suppose."

"Eventually not, perhaps. But in the meanwhile, I need what I came for—and you're going to take me to it."

"Where?"

"Adrianople Starbase. By the time we reach it, matters should be just about decided."

he transponder code for *Aragon* disappeared from the Adrianople Starbase pilot's board. The energy discharge had not yet registered visually; mass-radar operated on the same principles as jump technology, and over interplanetary distances, informational update was almost instantaneous. Any explosion would come no faster than the speed of light. *Aragon* had a few more minutes to live, though Commodore Durant knew the truth.

"What happened?" Mustafa asked, shaking his head.

"You haven't read Laperriere's report; I have: This has happened before. *Aragon* and *Eurydice* saw each other as enemies. They thought—" Durant leaned heavily on his wardroom table, feeling older than he'd ever felt. "I don't know. But the enemy . . . The aliens have the ability to make you see whatever they want."

Eurydice's transponder code suddenly winked out as well.

"What the hell do we do now?" Mustafa said. "Throw the rest of them into combat?"

"No, I don't think so. I think we only have one alternative."

"Surrender?"

"That's right. We can't escape, and I don't want to send more people out to die."

"Like the *Eurydice* and the *Aragon,* you mean." Arlen Mustafa clenched his fists. "You *knew* that would happen, didn't you?"

"No," Durant said, looking at his exec. "No."

Mustafa looked like he was going to say something else, but couldn't decide what it was. After several moments he turned away.

The door from the bridge slid aside. Durant turned to look and saw Dr. Edward Comeau, one of the Shiell Institute techs, enter the ready-room.

"Doctor," Durant began, "I don't have time for you now—"

"Yes, you do," the tech said. There was fear in his face. He took out his comp and gestured over it; the pilot's display over the table vanished and was replaced by a holo of the lab where the alien tech was being studied.

The alien equipment was a set of a dozen odd-shaped objects made of some unknown metal, with various indentations and protrusions. From the time a Marine squad had brought them aboard the starbase from the *Duc d'Enghien,* they had—as far as Durant understood—shown no sign of functioning in any way.

Now, in the holo, it was obvious that they were working—there were beams of energy connecting the twelve objects in a latticework that crisscrossed the lab. One of the Shiell Institute techs had evidently been standing in the wrong place when the equipment started working. He appeared neatly sliced in two just below the breastbone: His lower half was slumped on the floor, while his upper half, one arm thrown uselessly out, was sprawled on a table. The other techs were out of the way but were standing, immobile, looking aside emotionlessly.

In the center of the latticework was . . . something, or perhaps a holo of something. It looked like a tall rectangular pillar filled with iridescent gas, with a silver ball floating at the surface. A limb of light extended outward from within it to touch one of the alien objects.

"What happened?" Durant asked, after a moment during which he and Mustafa had stared at the scene, trying to make sense of it. He tried to read the expression in Comeau's face. "And what the hell is *that*?"

"The objects started interacting a few minutes ago," Comeau began. "Dr. Warren was killed instantly—at least, I hope to God it was instant. Then *that* appeared. It commanded me to come to the bridge."

"To find me," Durant said.

=That is correct, Commodore.=

Durant whirled to face the holo again. The voice he'd heard hadn't spoken aloud, but he'd heard it just the same; Mustafa and Comeau had heard it as well. It was like an abrasive, scraping noise inside his mind. It had no intonation; it remained at a steady pitch.

It came from the box in the middle of the latticework.

"Who— What are you? What do you want?"

=I am the Ór,= the box said. =I want, and will have, your complete cooperation.=

"For what purpose?"

=This system and this base will be secured. You will cooperate completely and instantly, or you will be terminated.=

"What does this 'cooperation' entail?"

=You meat-creatures require so much explanation for concepts that are childishly simple,= the Ór replied. Durant could feel the contempt in its remark, though the voice never changed. =The approaching vessels will take command of Adrianople Starbase and Adrianople System. You will surrender them at once.=

"Unless I choose to blow up the whole damn starbase, and you with it." Durant looked at Mustafa, with whom he'd been discussing surrender just a few minutes earlier.

=That is no longer an option, Commodore Durant,= the Ór answered. =The control and self-destruct pathways have already been blocked by the s's'th'r.=

Durant didn't know what a s's'th'r was, and wasn't in any hurry to find out.

"Then I only have one question."

=Ask.=

"If you're already in command of the starbase, why do you need me to cooperate?"

=My directives are to preserve life where possible. By cooperating you save more lives.=

"Like you saved the lives of the people aboard *Aragon* and *Eurydice*, you mean?" Mustafa asked, stepping toward the holo. "How did that serve your—your directives?"

=Where possible,= the Ór answered. =A necessary demonstration. Would you care to be another demonstration, Commander Mustafa?=

"Of what?"

=Of this.= A limb of energy leapt from the Ór and out of the holo to touch Mustafa amidships.

Mustafa turned away from the holo to look at Durant. Suddenly the anger on his face turned to horror as he looked at his commanding officer. "No," he said. "No, not—"

"What is it, Arlen?" Durant asked, looking from the Ór to his exec. "What are you showing him?"

=Something he fears,= the Ór said. =In thirty seconds the fear will cause a hemorrhage within his brain, causing his termination.=

Arlen Mustafa had fallen to his knees, his hands stretched out, his eyes wide, his mouth partially open and unable to make a sound.

=Twenty seconds,= the Ór said.

Durant shook his head. "No. Stop it. Turn it off!"

=Fifteen seconds,= the Ór replied. =It is a demonstration.=

Mustafa had fallen to hands and knees, his head hanging down, his legs twitching.

"You don't need to demonstrate any more! You— Your 'directives' are to preserve lives. Preserve *his*—I *need* him to manage this base. To manage it for you."

=Five seconds,= the Ór said.

As suddenly as it began, the limb of energy withdrew. Mustafa collapsed to the deck like a puppet with cut strings. Durant stepped to his side and knelt beside him.

=A lie,= the Ór said at last. =Still, a touching example of compassion. Most instructive.=

Durant felt Mustafa for a pulse and found one. His exec was breathing normally, as if he'd just passed out.

"I was supposed to let him die," Durant said angrily. "For your entertainment."

=Instruction. Do you require any further demonstrations? If not, prepare to surrender your base.=

The holo vanished and was replaced by the pilot's display. Durant looked up to see the two large alien ships approaching the base, and the *Trebizond* inbound, escorted by several smaller alien vessels.

As he watched the ships creep across the display, he hoped he'd made the right choice.

Ur ta'ShanriGar

PIERCING THE ICEWALL

PART ONE

chapter 1

WHEN THE ENEMY TOOK ADRIANOPLE, IT GAINED A BASE
WITHIN THE SOLAR EMPIRE, PLACING DOZENS OF IMPERIAL
WORLDS WITHIN JUMP RANGE. CICERO WAS THE FIRST
STRIKE—BUT ADRIANOPLE WAS THE FIRST, MOST SIGNIFI-
CANT STRIKE IN A LONG AND DIFFICULT WAR.

—Oren Kemal and Mya'ar HeChra
The Great War, volume I, 2429

"Five. I make it five." Dan McReynolds stood on the bridge of the *Fair Damsel,* scowling over the shoulder of the pilot at the display board. Raymond Li, the *Damsel*'s chief navigator, stood opposite, leaning forward on the board and looking up at the captain.

"So there are five ships with IN flags here. What's it to us?"

"I have to explain *everything* to you. Tamarind Station"—Dan gestured toward the forward screen—"is maybe forty parsecs from the nearest big naval base and we're only two jumps out of Crossover. Maybe it's a coincidence and maybe not, but we were carrying what might turn out to be a real important package."

"I thought that the—package—belonged to the High Nest."

"Look." Dan's scowl was enough for the pilot to stop what he was doing and look back at him. "The Imperial Navy takes care of its own.

I'll bet you a liter of the best whiskey we can buy here that the dock will be covered with bluejackets."

"I've had Tamarind whiskey, Skip, and I still won't take the bet. What've they got on us?"

"It's just a feeling I have. Five Navy ships . . . I don't believe in co-incidences, Ray."

As a matter of course, merchanters develop instincts about situations. In the days of ocean sailors, a captain might get a feeling sniffing the wind as it blew across his quarterdeck, or sense a change in the sky or the chop of the waves on the bow of his ship—certainly not *clinical* observations, but often more accurate than the poor instruments the captain might possess. Instincts were the difference between an experienced sailor and a dead one.

By comparison, space lacks many empirical clues. Wind, wave and sky have no convenient analogs; the sophisticated equipment required to navigate from star to star extends the scope and range of the senses. Perils and dangers can be perceived a long way off . . . Of course, death comes more quickly and more violently in space.

Still, at sea or in space there are certain things in common. Merchanters know to keep their heads down and listen to warnings wherever they come from.

As the *Fair Damsel* made its docking approach, Dan McReynolds got his first and only warning: He was not only expected, but there was someone waiting for him. The ship was committed and deep in the gravity well, and—as Ray Li had pointed out—nobody had anything on them.

Knowing that there was no avoiding it, Dan made himself very conspicuous on the dock as the *Damsel* began to unload its cargo. It only took a few minutes for uniformed Tamarind security to take notice of their presence, and a few minutes more for a deputation to make its way across the station deck to the *Fair Damsel*'s berth.

"Look at them swagger," Pyotr Ngo, Dan's chief pilot, said quietly behind him. "Tough guys."

"At least to the locals," Dan replied. People were deliberately making way for the half-dozen armed men and women making a beeline for his ship; he could see other civilians speaking furtively and looking in his direction, thinking, no doubt, *There but for the grace of God go*

I . . . "Get the Sultan," he said over his shoulder, without turning. "And hang close."

The group came up to where Dan stood looking over a cargo manifest. He deliberately tried to ignore them.

"You McReynolds?" asked the leader of the group, a tall, thin scowling woman in a well-decorated brown uniform.

"I'm *Captain* McReynolds," Dan said. Sultan Sabah and Pyotr Ngo took up positions behind him. "What's it to you?"

"Man wants to see you."

"Man got a name?"

"Imperial Navy," the woman answered with distaste. "Asked for you personally."

"*Me?*" Dan turned slightly to look at Pyotr and the Sultan. "You boys know why the Navy might want me?"

"Maybe wants you to reenlist," said the Sultan. "Scrapin' the bottom of the barrel for officer material, you ask me."

"I'm not interested in signing up." Dan turned back to the Tamarindi. "Tell the 'Man' that if he wants to talk to me he should send someone of his own. My papers are in order, and I've got work to do." He began to turn away.

"Listen, you—"

He rounded on the woman. "No, *you* listen to *me*. I've got a license to trade within the Solar Empire. I have my landing permit, my docking order, my permit to berth . . . and a published manifest that allows me to load and unload. Those are all you can question me on, Officer. If the 'Man' wants to talk to me, then the 'Man' had damn well better send his own messenger to talk to me rather than wasting my time and yours."

He turned away again and left the woman sputtering as the three crewmen of the *Fair Damsel* walked back into the cargo hold. After a moment, the woman took her cadre of guards back across the brightly lit deck.

"You think that was such a good idea, Skip?" the Sultan asked, looking over his shoulder at the retreating brown uniforms.

"Don't know. But I'm not going to be ordered around by some local tinhorn. I already did my time in the Service. Damn it, those papers are in order, too." He stopped at a stack of meter-high cargo cubes and sat down on one. "Give me that comp," he said to the Sultan, and began to query it for information.

"I'd better get the troops moving in case we have to bug out quickly," the Sultan said, turning his attention away from his captain.

"Wait a sec." Dan showed Sabah and Ngo the comp. "Says here that the biggest ship in dock is the IS *Pappenheim*, commanded by someone named Maartens. You guys know anything about either?"

"*Pappenheim*," Pyotr Ngo said, folding his arms over his chest and looking at the readout hanging in the air over the comp. "That's not a police cruiser—looks like a ship of the line, maybe Imperial Grand Survey or a perimeter squadron. The skipper's name doesn't ring a bell, though."

"The other ships here at Tamarind are all smaller ones. This isn't a battle fleet; it's more like a bunch of little guys that found a big skirt to hide behind."

"What are you getting at?"

"Unless I miss my guess, Pyotr, something big has started to happen, something that's gotten all of these ship commanders scared. Anything come to mind?"

"Sounds like a war," Pyotr Ngo said quietly. "Meaning—?"

"Meaning that whatever she got involved in"—and all three of them knew who "she" was—"has started."

"So . . . what are we going to do?"

"We go on with what we're doing, I guess," Dan answered. "And we wait for the 'Man' to come to us."

They didn't have to wait more than an hour. Dan had returned to his own quarters, leaving the Sultan in charge dockside; he was sitting at his cluttered workdesk when a private-channel message signal sounded on the internal comm.

"Captain here," he said. "What's up?"

"Personal base-to-base coming in for you, Skip," said the voice—Ray Li at the conn. "You want it patched through?"

"Where's it from?"

"*Pappenheim*," Li said, after a moment. "Imperial starship. It's docked down the way."

"Yeah, put it through." Dan gestured to the wall; a holo appeared on the opposite side of the desk. He whacked a spot on the wall with the heel of his hand and it flickered into focus. "This is Dan McReynolds of the *Fair Damsel*. What can I do for you?"

"Captain McReynolds." An older man in the uniform of a Navy

captain appeared, sitting at a ready-room desk. Near his left lapel there was an icon showing that Ray Li had marked it as "PRIVATE," so no one aboard—or on the station—could patch in. "I'm Georg Maartens of the IS *Pappenheim*. I sent a message to you earlier, asking you to meet me in the station command center."

"Yeah. Well, I thought it was local harassment, and I didn't like the tone."

Maartens smiled, which was unexpected. Dan had hoped to get a rise out of Maartens, who looked like a stiff-necked Regular Navy type. "I'm not surprised. Perhaps I can be more conciliatory. I'd like to invite you aboard for a drink, and to convey a message to you."

"A message."

"That's right." Dan noticed that the *Pappenheim* bridge was maintaining General Quarters, even though the ship was at dock. "Me personally. Mind telling me what this is all about?"

"This isn't exactly a secure channel. Perhaps you could join me at, say, 1600 Standard? If you'd like to bring your exec aboard, he's welcome as well."

"It doesn't sound like this is a yes-or-no question."

"Well . . . it isn't. But there's no reason that everyone on Tamarind needs to know that. I understand merchanter attitudes. I see no reason to show you up if it can be avoided. 1600 hours, then?"

Dan remembered the sights and sounds of an Imperial starship. It had been many years since he'd been aboard one, but the familiarity of "officer country" aboard the *Pappenheim* reminded him all too much of the *Torrance*. Even the cold antiseptic air in the corridors brought back memories of his time in service.

Pyotr Ngo—whom he had brought along primarily to provide a reality check—just looked nervous.

"What's with General Quarters?" Dan asked of the Marine squad leader as they stepped into a lift. They'd been escorted through the starship's corridors for almost five minutes; Dan suspected there might have been a more direct route, but perhaps Maartens sought to intimidate them.

"Sir?" the Marine squad leader asked, keeping his face unresponsive, not looking at Dan as the door closed; and, at the guard's spoken command, the lift began to rise.

"General Quarters. Why is the ship on alert?"

"I'm sorry, sir, I can't discuss security matters with—"

"With civilians. I know," Dan snorted. "I remember the regulation."

"Sir."

"Just thought I'd like to know what this Captain Maartens has in mind. What sort of fellow is he—can you tell me that? Or is it classified?"

"The captain is a fine officer, sir."

"I'd expect that. What's he like?"

"He's well liked and respected by the crew, sir." The Marine's expression never changed. "Captain Maartens has more than thirty years in service, and he's earned his bars. Sir."

This comment was aimed at Dan as a merchant captain; there wasn't much love lost between Marines and merchanters—or between Regular Navy and merchanters, for that matter. *Enemy territory,* Dan reminded himself. If the Marine had intended to anger him, Dan wasn't about to take the bait.

The lift reached its destination and the two merchanters were escorted out and along a few more corridors until they stopped in front of a door flanked by two other Marines. The squad leader executed a smart salute, and one of the guards gestured at the door without taking her eyes off of Dan and Pyotr.

"Come."

The door slid aside and the *Damsel'*s officers entered the room. Captain Maartens was sitting at a huge, neatly organized wooden desk, dominated by a slightly dented model of the *Pappenheim*. He dismissed the Marines with a gesture and pointed to three comfortable-looking armchairs in a part of the compartment set up as a sitting-room. He walked to a sideboard located under a framed portrait of the Solar Emperor and poured three small tumblerfuls of brownish liquid. He carried them on a silver tray to his guests and settled into an armchair of his own, extending his hand in a toast.

"Fair winds," he said, a traditional sailor's toast. They drank.

"Good brandy," Dan remarked after a moment. It was: Not the sort of stuff he'd expect a line officer to waste on a couple of merchanters. "How'd we earn this?"

Maartens took another sip of his drink, giving Dan a chance to look him over. The captain of the *Pappenheim* was deep into middle age, his hair gray and getting wispy, his eyes set deep in a face with history etched into it. The compartment reflected the comforts of a lifetime naval officer: wooden desk, armchairs and pile carpet . . . He'd been aboard this ship for quite a while.

"This is no ordinary shore call, as I'm sure you've guessed. My eyes and ears on-station tell me that all kinds of rumors are floating around, and I have to tell you that the worst one is true. The Empire is at war."

"With—?"

"Actually," Maartens answered, toying with his glass, "I think you already know who the enemy is. Most people don't, and won't, until we're deep into this thing."

"You must think I have pretty good connections."

"I know you do. Don't play dumb with me, McReynolds; I know where you jumped from and I looked at your crew roster." He paused—a moment of melodrama. "Tell me about Kearny."

"Kearny?" Dan's stomach lurched momentarily, and he wasn't sure if he'd let his face show it: His mind began to race as he tried to determine where this conversation was going.

"Kearny. Jackie Kearny. Engineer's mate. My best information says that she's not aboard your ship. Where is she, Captain McReynolds?"

"I don't see that it's any busi—"

"Oh, but it *is*. You're a reservist, Captain. Do I have to quote you chapter and verse on your current status? This is an emergency situation, and you're in a war zone. I'm empowered to call you to active duty. I'm doing it right now. By the same authority I can impress your ship and crew into Imperial Service. I can even appoint one of my officers to command that ship.

"But," Maartens continued, as he let it sink in, "I see no reason to take that last action. Nonetheless, Captain, as an officer under my command, you are obliged to follow my orders: And I am *ordering* you to tell me where I can find Jackie Kearny, engineer's mate, recently a member of your crew."

Dan took a moment before answering and exchanged glances with Pyotr, who looked stunned at Maartens' remarks.

"I don't know."

"I see." Maartens drank off the rest of his brandy and set his glass carefully on an end table. He leaned forward, elbows on knees, hands clasped in front of him. "Let me tell you why I have such a strong interest: I happen to know who she *really* is. And get this loud and clear, McReynolds: She's real important to me, and I take a strong interest in her welfare. Do you read?"

"I read you loud and clear," Dan replied.

"So, let me repeat the question. Where is she, and where is Ch'k'te?"

"I . . . don't know." Dan looked around the room, as if he'd be able to tell if anyone was listening in. "How secure is this room?"

"As secure as I can make it." Maartens spread his hands and leaned back. "That's why we're here."

"Last time I saw Jackie or Ch'k'te was at Crossover Station. They went ashore and didn't return. She told me to wait two days and then to bug out; I waited, then bugged out. I don't know if they're alive or dead, Captain, I really don't."

"I spent some time and cashed in a few favors to track her down." He stood up and walked to the sideboard, and began to pour himself another drink. "Let me tell you some things about myself, McReynolds. I'm fifty-eight years old, and I've been in His Majesty's Navy longer than you've been alive.

"When I was a powder monkey, a gunner's mate"—he finished pouring and walked back to his seat, tumbler in hand—"there were still stories told about Admiral Marais in the fleet.

"I'm the captain of a starship. Not the largest or best-built; God knows, not the newest. I was given command of the *Pappenheim* sixteen years ago, which puts me in the top ten or twelve in the fleet, in terms of time in service with one vessel. It's all I want to do, all I ever really wanted; never wanted to be a commodore, never wanted station or flag command. The *Pappenheim* is enough for me—as a ship captain, you understand that. I haven't got any axe to grind, never did. I'm Regular Navy, but not ramrod-straight; I'm loyal to the officers I serve."

"What's your point, sir?"

"Jackie Laperriere was an officer I served." Maartens took a long drink. "I was on-station at Cicero when the—aliens—took over."

"You were—"

"When she called, I came," he continued, his eyes now full of some difficult memory. "Picture this, McReynolds: First, most of the squadron goes haring off on some fool's errand beyond the border. Then what's left of it comes back with all of the Sensitives aboard dead. *Then* I get a call out of nowhere: 'Aliens have taken control of Cicero Down.' *Then* my exec, someone I've known for years, turns into—changes into—"

He took a long drink, and Dan thought he saw Maartens' hands shake. "Almost forty years, I've never seen anything like that. I turned . . . *it* over to authorities at Adrianople. I hope I never see another one.

"That's what we're up against, McReynolds. Aliens that can replace people we know. An alien replaced Jackie—well enough to fool me and everyone on the station. An alien replaced Bryan Noyes, commander of Cicero Op. But for Jackie Laperriere, I suspect that an alien might have replaced *me*. We figured that's what the aliens had in mind: infiltration of the Empire to gradually take it over, but by accident we—she—uncovered what they were doing. Jackie decided to evacuate Cicero, even though it cost her her career, but it saved a lot of lives."

"I wouldn't worry about her career. She's got a brand-new mission these days."

"Something to do with the zor High Nest, from the sound of it."

"I'd say so." Dan looked aside at Pyotr Ngo, who didn't comment. "The zor have boxed her into following some ancient legend, in order to recover a valuable item that they *let* the enemy capture. They knew it would happen, and they *knew* it would happen at Cicero—that's why they put a VIP in the path of the aliens."

"Torrijos."

"That's right, Captain: You look close enough, you realize that this accident was no accident, as seen from the High Nest. They saw this coming, maybe years ago, and they set it up."

"How did you get involved in this?"

"Old friendships." Dan smiled. "You've probably got the whole damn dossier; I go back a long way with Jackie, farther back and deeper down than you do. Another old friend called in an IOU and arranged for my ship to carry her and her caddie wherever the quest led them. I did it for a rather handsome fee, but I wouldn't have said no even if it was for free.

"The thing that burns *me*, Captain—and it should burn *you* as well—is that the High Nest saw all of this from beginning to end. They even foresaw what happened at Crossover—whatever *that* was—*and* where it all ends up. They even saw that they'd be alone *now*. Jackie and Ch'k'te are on their own, and it's fairly likely that's what the High Nest wants."

"Why?"

"Who the hell understands how a zor thinks?"

"I get the distinct impression, McReynolds, that you haven't told me everything."

Damn right, Dan thought to himself. *But you'd never believe it.* "I've told you what's relevant."

"All right, McReynolds. I could order you to submit to Sensitive examination, but there's probably no point to it." He stood and walked to his desk. He picked up a comp and carried it back to where Dan and Pyotr still sat. "Here are your orders," he said, tossing it into Dan's lap. "You have eight hours before we jump."

"Where are we going?"

"Look at the orders and get your ship ready for jump. You'll know soon enough. Dismissed."

"But—"

"*Dismissed,* Captain. We'll have plenty of time to discuss this, but not now. Get back to your ship, and prepare to bug out. You read?"

"Yeah." Dan stood up, turning the card over in his hands, as if he'd never seen one before. "Yeah, I read you, sir."

ᴡᴇʟʟ?" Dan asked Pyotr, as they crossed the deck from the *Pappenheim* to their own ship. "What do you make of that?"

"What do I make of it?" The chief pilot stopped walking and turned to face Dan, anger obvious in his eyes. "Do you remember when we started this partnership and bought the *Damsel*? Do you remember what you said when I asked if it was wise to purchase a bigger ship when it might tie us up with reserve commitments?"

"Pyotr, I—"

"*I* remember. Every damn word: 'Don't worry about it,' you said. 'There's no one for the Empire to fight against. How could they call me up?' "

"There wasn't any way of knowing—"

"No." Pyotr turned away from Dan and began walking toward their ship. "No, there wasn't any way of knowing, was there? So we're in the Navy now."

ᴛʜᴇ ᴏᴘᴇʀᴀᴛɪᴏɴ of a merchanter vessel of any reasonable size is a prohibitively expensive proposition. The costs of acquisition alone are such that few, if any, private individuals can ever afford to buy or build one; usually, only a corporate or government entity can come up with enough capital to do it. In the former case, large private companies build and staff fleets to conduct commerce, placing bonded captains in command at generous salaries but with no stake in the profits; in the latter, planetary, provincial and Imperial navies keep naval architects and shipwrights busy.

After a certain amount of time in a merchant fleet or service in a navy, skilled pilots, engineers or other hands want to acquire a piece of the action. As merchant fleets evolve, older ships that don't perform well are made available for their crews to buy out and go independent. In navies—especially the Imperial Navy—bigger and better ships are sometimes made available rather than just the oldest and slowest. In peacetime, when civilian governments don't want to foot the bill to keep them in service, navies often will provide ships in lieu of a mustering out bonus.

There *is* one significant difference. The navy will usually include a condition: that in wartime, the ship's captain and any other crewmembers are recalled from reserve status to active duty, placing the ship in military service. Since the last war had been Marais' war of conquest eighty-five years earlier, most people mustering out of the Navy were more than willing to sign, even given that condition.

This information wasn't welcome news to the crew of the *Fair Damsel*.

"Okay, pipe down, pipe down!" the Sultan shouted over the din in the cargo hold. Only Ray Li was absent; he was watching from the bridge. Everyone else had been assembled, most standing in the back of the hold or perched on cargo blocks or canisters. Dan and the Sultan stood facing them; the officers looked grim. The crew simply looked angry.

Eventually, order was restored and Dan looked around the room at the men and women that worked and lived aboard ship. Most of them were shareholders in the *Damsel,* which meant they'd put some of their own money into her, enjoyed the profits and suffered the losses. They had voting power to accept or deny a new shareholder, to decide on routing and the choice of officers. Dan, Ray, Pyotr and the Sultan held more than sixty percent of the stock and had already discussed strategy, so the captain wasn't worried about losing his job; still, there was no telling what most of the crew might think.

"You already know most of the facts, so I won't belabor them. In accordance with the indefinite lease contract under which the corporation bought the *Fair Damsel* eight years ago, the Imperial Navy has the right to recall us whenever a state of emergency is declared. They have now declared one, and I've received orders from the *Pappenheim* to jump from here"—he looked at the chrono on the wall—"in about five hours. Every crewmember with prior military service—provincial or Imperial—has been recalled to active duty, including me. The ship is now under my command, as a captain in the Imperial Navy. And I'm pretty damn far down on the seniority list, too." Some of the crew chuckled at that.

"The rest of you have two choices. The first choice is the easy one: Do nothing, keep your job, serve aboard the *Damsel* for the duration. Of the civilian officers, Pyotr has decided to do just that. Ray, the Sultan and I, of course"—he grinned a bit—"are stuck with the hand we've been dealt, as are several of you.

"The second choice isn't as pleasant, and I'm not really happy to suggest it, for good reason. The *Damsel* isn't armed worth a damn, and its hardpoints aren't really suitable for it anyway. They're not going to put us on the front line but we might see some enemy fire; we can't go where we want and, while they'll pay our way, we won't be turning much profit.

"Therefore, I'm prepared to make the following offer: I'm willing to buy out the share of anyone who doesn't want to come along. According to the corporate contract, that's worth a twenty-percent markup on the value of that share.

"I'm also willing to pay off anyone without a stake, at the usual markup for duress. It should be enough to get you off Tamarind.

"Captain Maartens of the *Pappenheim* has informed me that any key positions left vacant by such departures will be filled by Regular Navy personnel."

"How much time we got to decide?" asked someone from the group: Sonja Torrijos, engineer's mate.

"About four hours."

"What happens if we stay, and then want off later?"

"My guess is that there is no 'later.' I don't expect us to be calling at many civilian stations once we leave Tamarind."

There was some hushed conversation. Dan turned to the Sultan. "This really sucks," he said. "If I didn't want these people, I wouldn't have them aboard. But they didn't buy into this."

"They knew what they bought when they bought it," the Sultan answered, his arms crossed in front of his chest, a characteristic pose. "Everybody reads the contract; that's why we print it and get them to sign it."

"But they didn't expect to be mixed up in a war."

"Neither did I." The Sultan looked across the crew, now discussing the subject with some animation. "But you can't indemnify against it; they're here at the ass-end of nowhere for the same reason you and I are, Skip: to make money. Without the help you got from the Navy in the first place, they'd never have made the bundle they've made already."

"All true, Chief," Dan said.

"So why would they trade being dirtsiders for a chance at being part of a profitable operation when this is all over? Like you said, we're not going to be in the front line—how tough is this going to be?"

You have absolutely no idea, Dan thought. *Of course, it might not be any safer* off *the* Damsel.

Jackie, what the hell are we getting involved in?

"Is that the consensus among the crew, Chief?"

"I'd be surprised if you lost anybody, Skip."

While the discussion continued aboard the *Fair Damsel,* Georg Maartens sat alone in his cabin, sprawled in an armchair, his jacket tossed onto one of the chairs opposite. He let his arms hang over the sides of the chair and his eyes were shut; anyone coming in suddenly, would've thought the old man was asleep, but he wasn't—he was merely deep in thought.

What the hell are we involved in? he repeated to himself. *What kind of war* can *we fight?*

It wasn't Maartens' job to decide, of course. Fighting these aliens wasn't going to be like tangling with pirates or suppressing a colonial rebellion—the only types of conflicts he had experience with. On the other hand, the incidents at Cicero a few months ago had given him insight that was lacking in all but a few others in his position. There were only a handful who knew what was out there . . . *including Jackie Laperriere,* he reminded himself.

Wherever she is.

How do you fight an enemy that can change its appearance . . . that can take over your mind . . . that's way ahead of us technologically? The Admiralty hasn't let out information about the enemy, hasn't even admitted there is *an enemy—just "an emergency."*

He remembered an interview with Admiral Hsien, Maartens' new boss after leaving Cicero. The old man had told him in no uncertain terms that he was *not*—repeat, *not*—to discuss what happened there, since there was still a court-martial investigation going on. That wasn't the real reason, of course. Aside from McReynolds, who knew more about what was happening across the line than he'd been willing to admit, Maartens hadn't discussed Cicero with any of the other merchanter captains now under his command. He was leading them into . . . what? Their next destination, Corcyra, had had a naval research center, but now it was nothing but a ruin. There, most of them would get their first look at what the enemy could do.

He wasn't expecting to find survivors; but if there were any, his Sensitives would have to poke around in their minds before he'd let them aboard his ship. Cicero had made him paranoid. What would happen to squadrons led by commanders who were less suspicious, because they didn't know what they were facing?

As Maartens sat there, his eyes closed, thoughts racing through his mind, he realized the war had a good chance of being over even before it had begun.

chapter 2

WARRIORS OF THE PEOPLE IN THE VALLEY OF LOST SOULS
TRAVEL ON THEIR ERRANDS; THE DESPAIR OF THE DECEIVER
SETTLES ON THEIR WINGED SHOULDERS LIKE A LAYER OF
FINE, GRITTY DUST. THOSE AT THE OUTERMOST EDGE WHO
ARE MOST CAPABLE OF MOVEMENT AND THOUGHT, CANNOT
HELP BUT RAIL AGAINST THE LORD *ESLI* WHOSE ABANDON-
MENT OF THEIR SOULS TO THIS PERDITION IS CLEARLY IN
ERROR . . . IT CANNOT BE OTHERWISE: AS WARRIORS, DOES
NOT THE WORLD REVOLVE AROUND THEM? THE DESPAIR OF
ESGA'U GROWS HEAVIER AND HEAVIER AS THEY BROOD
UPON THEIR FATE, UNTIL AT LAST THEY SEEK THE SOLACE
OF THE CENTER WHERE MOVEMENT ENDS AND THOUGHTS
FIND THEIR REFUGE IN OBLIVION.

THERE ARE TWO WAYS TO ESCAPE THE VALLEY OF LOST
SOULS. ONE WAY IS VIRTUALLY IMPOSSIBLE: AT THE CENTER
IS THE PERILOUS STAIR THAT ASCENDS THE ICEWALL TO THE
FORTRESS OF *ESGA'U,* BUT ONLY THE RAREST HERO CAN LIFT
HIS HEAD TO SEE IT.

THE OTHER, NEARLY AS UNLIKELY, INVOLVES SELF-NEGATION:
RECOGNITION THAT EVEN THE GREATEST WARRIOR CAN BE
REDUCED TO NOTHING IF THE EIGHT WINDS BLOW A CER-
TAIN WAY, OR IF *ESLI* WILLS IT. STRIPPED OF EGOCENTRIC-
ITY, A WARRIOR CAN FIND A NEW INNER PEACE WITHOUT

SUCH FEELINGS. IT IS A RARE TRANSCENDENCE: ADMITTING
THAT CONTROL OF THE SITUATION BELONGS TO SOMEONE
ELSE — OR, PERHAPS, TO NO ONE. IT IS JUST SUCH A CHANGE
THAT SAVED THE PEOPLE FROM SELF-EXTINCTION WHEN *ES-
HU'UR* CONQUERED THEM THREE GENERATIONS AGO.

EVEN FEWER WARRIORS CAN ASCEND THE PERILOUS STAIR.
THOSE THEY LEAVE BEHIND CAN ONLY ESCAPE BY PIERCING
THE ICEWALL.

—Ke'en HeU'ur,
Ur'ta leHssa and the Icewall,
saLi'a'a Press: esYen, 2314

He remembered a starship hurtling across empty space. It approached in his peripheral vision, coming closer and closer and then striking him, impossibly, sending pain through every receptor. Then there was another instant of blinding pain from the other side, driving him into unconsciousness.

He could still see that ship flying at him, end over end, in slow motion. He had all the time in the world to trace its trajectory back to the origin . . . And trace it he did, watching it retreat like a vid image until it came to a halt in an upright position on a shiny, reflective surface.

Hands were around it in his mind's eye: two meat-creature hands, one of them bearing a circle of bright metal on one finger.

Two hands.

An Academy ring.

Suddenly, in the depths of wherever he was, he knew whose hands they were: They belonged to Georg Maartens, the captain of the Imperial starship *Pappenheim*.

Running the vid slowly forward . . . ever so slowly, so he wouldn't have to feel that pain again . . . he watched as Maartens picked up the ship, a heavy model of the *Pappenheim* itself, and flung it at him. He'd been distracted somehow—he'd turned away in meat-creature form to the door, to face Dante Simms, the Marine commander of the *Pappenheim*—and the model had hit him on the side of the head.

Where am I? he thought; followed immediately by, Who *am I?*

The first question had no answer. It was dark here, wherever "here" was: It might be a vat of *g'jn*-fluid to regenerate whatever parts he might have lost when . . . when—

The second question had an immediate response. *You are* N'nr *Deathguard,* he heard in his mind. *That is the most important fact. You are of the Ninth Sept of E'esh,* he added to himself, placing it at a distance, a color-change behind the first one.

N'nr Deathguard.

He knew where he was now—or at least what his current status must be: a prisoner of the meat-creatures, caught in their *k'th's's* somehow. It was impossible but it must be true nonetheless. The walls of his *n'n'eth* seemed intact, so his mind was unbreached; he didn't know how long it had been since the meat-creatures had struck him unconscious, but he must still be so. This emerging series of thoughts was clearly deep within his *i'kn*-mind, so whatever means had been used to keep him unconscious was beginning to wear off.

Soon, very soon, he would know where he was. If his *i'kn*-mind was beginning to function, his waking mind would emerge within a few *vx*tori* . . . all he had to do was wait.

He didn't have to wait very long. He became aware of minds in his vicinity: primitive, but still possessed of *k'th's's*—and too many to idly Dominate, particularly in his weakened condition. He let one eye open slightly, and saw a chamber. It was dimly lit and disturbingly square, with a higher ceiling than was comfortable; even his time aboard the starship *Pappenheim,* during which he'd accustomed himself to human habitation, had not completely eliminated his natural aversion to open spaces.

So. This was likely a zor habitation. That explained the *k'th's's,* then—the winged servants had far more powerful abilities than their wingless masters. It wasn't an encouraging thought—it meant they were aware of the threat he posed. His presence here also meant that the *Pappenheim* had escaped the digestion of Cicero.

To confirm his supposition, he saw two of the egg-sucking meat-creatures enter his field of vision. They were speaking in the High-speech; something was interfering with his ability to pick up stray surface-thoughts, so he was at a loss to understand what they were saying—except that it was likely about him.

One of the zor turned to face him. "You have awakened," it—he—said in Standard. "We have much to discuss."

" 'Discuss'?" he managed to croak. "I have nothing to say to you, m—"

" 'Meat-creature.' Yes, I know. Let us presume that we will dispense with the preliminary insults. My name is Byar HeShri. I will forbear addressing you as 'Servant of Despite,' and you can withhold your own pejoratives as well. Agreed?"

Byar HeShri took up a perch near where he lay. He opened his other eye and swiveled his head around to take a good look. He was lying on a large cot in some sort of examining room—an elaborate sickbay aboard a base or ship. He was physically unrestrained, but some sort of weak force field was being projected around the cot: It was like a hive-ship's defensive field, though obviously much weaker, but enough to disturb his *k'th's's* and prevent him from seizing this one's mind . . . though the winged servant did seem to be powerful in his own right.

A tiny amount of fear began to form on the outside of his thorax. He wanted to extend a tentacle and wipe it away, but he didn't want to call attention to it.

"You have left me little choice in the matter."

"There is always choice." The zor rearranged his wings. "For example, you may *choose* to cooperate with me and explain the objectives of your people . . . or you may choose otherwise. As you spent some time in the guise of a *naZora'e,* you might believe there may be some hesitation in extracting that information by force—but do not deceive yourself.

"You are far too dangerous for half-measures; you are also far too dangerous to be allowed where you might be rescued or left unguarded. Almost no one knows that you are even alive or in captivity."

"My own people know."

"I do not believe that they care very much about you at all," Byar answered. "From what we have been able to learn, there is a very low tolerance for failure among your people. And make no mistake . . ." The wings moved to another position. "At least for the present, *you have failed.* Cicero is in the possession of the enemy, but everything that could be removed from that place is beneath a safe wing."

"Except your precious sword," the alien answered immediately. "And you have chosen some egg-sucking zor warrior to try and fetch it back."

The zor's wings moved again; the alien thought it might possibly be in amusement, but had no way of being sure.

"Something of the sort."

I suppose there was no way to have avoided this becoming a media event, the High Chamberlain thought as he made his way through the closed-off terminal. Those privileged enough to have access to this part of A'alu Spaceport gave T'te'e HeYen a wide berth as he flew slowly and purposefully along, followed by his retinue, staying—as protocol required—two wing-lengths behind and one below. As the High Chamberlain went by, those he passed dipped their wings respectfully, assuming postures that communicated respect, awe or fear, in about equal proportions—all conveying what the situation required; all more or less ignored by T'te'e as he flew his path.

At the edge of his peripheral vision he noticed a 3-V camera crew tracking his movements: Without directly affronting him by close physical approach, they had deliberately invaded his vague sense of privacy—and some of his postures and expressions would be on the comnet a few sixty-fourths of a sun from now.

In an earlier time he would have cursed the crew to travel the dark paths of the Plain of Despite, but that seemed to be altogether too close and painful now; instead, he simply altered his direction slightly to stare directly at the crew-captain, whose wings had been arranged to convey a polite but justified defiance: *I have a right to be here,* it said. *An equal right to your own.*

At the High Chamberlain's glance, however, the anonymous tech looked away quickly, settling his posture into one of greater politeness.

That is better, T'te'e thought to himself. But the pleasure in winning the insignificant conflict was shallow, and the High Chamberlain despaired to think just how little his dignity meant anymore.

The spaceport named for the legendary first High Lord A'alu had grown to span a substantial area on Zor'a's main continent. A century ago, when the People were at war with the *naZora'i,* much of the activity at A'alu consisted of military craft; the Navy had commandeered several of the spaceport's terminals for its own use, arranging access-paths and lines of sight to make them inaccessible to civilian travelers. The traffic patterns around A'alu had been altered significantly to accommodate this usage, and in more than eighty years they had not completely shifted back.

After arriving in Zor'a System, the High Chamberlain had arranged for the shuttle to land on a field serviced by one of these terminals. He had come down to the surface separately and quietly, so that he could fulfill the ceremonial forms.

He perched on a narrow platform overlooking the field through a huge trapezoidal window. Below, the officials and press people were gathered, keeping an eye out for the approaching vessel. From time to time, one or another would ascend to get a better view, always careful to stay well below the High Chamberlain's level.

Some amount of irritation and impatience had already set in when the shuttle appeared on the flight path. T'te'e changed neither stance nor expression (cameras continued to record him, moment by moment), while the attendees below burst into a hubbub of action. The great, glass window prevented any noise coming in from outside, but the High Chamberlain's contemplations were interrupted by a fluttering of wings nearby; he turned to see Byar HeShri, Master of Sanctuary, coast gently to a landing beside him. The Sensitive teacher placed his wings in the Stance of Courteous Approach and waited for T'te'e to speak.

The High Chamberlain gestured to an aide who drew out a privacy-field cylinder and activated it. The slight humming that emerged was barely audible to the People on the platform but effectively masked the area outside it from prying microphones or attentive ears. Four of the liveried attendants placed clawed hands on their *chya'i* and began to make slow rounds of the elevated platform.

"I am pleased to have you nearby," T'te'e said at last, not looking away from the window, where a distant point of orange grew more and more distinct. "But your studies and preparations are surely of more importance."

"I wanted to see what we have wrought."

T'te'e turned to face him. Anger was scarcely repressed in his eyes. He did not allow his neutral wing-position to alter. "This is not of our making, *se* Byar. Were we not old friends and companions, I would feel it necessary to enforce that point with my *chya*."

"Eight thousand pardons," Byar answered, as his wings shifted to the Posture of Polite Indifference to emphasize the irrelevance of his apology. "Let me rephrase."

"Please do."

"This flight had no alternative but to come this way. *esLi* Himself alone knows how it shall end, but the *gyaryu* would be gone by this time. It is remarkable that the old man is alive after having lost it . . . but he knew the risks, as did we."

"Make your point."

"*ha* T'te'e, you know—as do I—that if the *Gyaryu'har* is not able to speak for himself, it is you who are answerable. So it is, with heroes: they must face the consequences of their actions, good or ill."

"Are you suggesting . . ." the High Chamberlain began angrily; but Byar HeShri simply raised his wings in the position of the Cloak of *esLi*.

"I suggest nothing except to assure you, Respected One and old friend, that you cannot cloak yourself with pain and guilt because our old friend returns in this condition. We knew that it was to happen. He is already lost to us, likely beyond all hope to recall. The People will have to do without a *Gyaryu'har* for a time. It is a blessing that they at least have a Chamberlain."

"*That* will not reassure them." T'te'e spread his hands, gesturing at the throng below, jostling and fluttering for a clear view of the incoming shuttle.

"It does not matter; we also lack the *gyaryu*. That will disturb them even more." Byar examined his claws, looking away from the troubled— and troubling—gaze of the High Chamberlain. "Can you tell me anything of what progress has been made in getting it back?"

"*se* S'reth was here an eightday ago. *esLi*'s Chosen One ascends the Perilous Stair alone, accompanied only by her spirit-guide. *si* Ch'k'te HeYen is beyond the Outer Peace now," he added, watching Byar's wings elevate briefly in surprise as Byar connected the last two sentences and drew the same conclusion he had drawn when S'reth had first told him. "The *esGa'uYal* know that the avatar of Qu'u still lives, and they have accelerated the pace of their attacks—as I am sure you are aware."

"Based on what I have begun to learn from the *esGa'uYe* we have in our custody, they understand less than you might think. But yes, Sanctuary is cognizant of this. Without our advance preparations, in fact, we would be far worse off . . ." He turned to look at the incoming shuttle, visible now, a glowing bird of prey descending toward the landing-field. "Still, you are aware of the stakes: Without the *gyaryu* to protect us, there will be little chance for Sensitives to withstand what is certainly coming. Without the Sensitives, there will be no Circle within which to stand."

"I am aware of that," T'te'e replied wearily. "I have no control—"

"That is the problem, *ha* T'te'e, is it not?"

"What?"

"That you have no control."

"I am not one of your students, *se* Byar. For a second time you come dangerously close to touching my honor. I let the first indiscretion pass. Are you seeking a confrontation?"

"No, I am not. Of course I am not. What I am seeking is your admission that this affair is no longer under anyone's *control.*" And he leaned on the word with additional emphasis. "Certainly not yours."

"What purpose does this 'admission' serve?"

"It pierces the Icewall, old friend. It pierces the Icewall."

T'te'e held the gaze of the Master of Sanctuary for several moments. To anyone watching, it would have seemed as if the two powerful Sensitives were engaged in a contest of wills; indeed, in their heightened state of Sensitivity, they could pick up stray thoughts from unprotected minds nearby: *What did the old one say to him? . . . the blade of* ha *T'te'e is singing, I can hear it! . . . Perhaps they are subvocalizing, maybe the lab techs can pick up something from the recording . . .*

The shuttle of the *Gyaryu'har* touched down on the landing-field. The High Chamberlain looked away from the Master of Sanctuary and let his hands drop to his sides. His wings slumped in a position of regret.

"With the High Lord in his present condition and the *Gyaryu'har* unarmed and indisposed, I am the ranking warrior of the People. Are you telling me that another climbs the Perilous Stair to confront the Deceiver and regain the *gyaryu* while I toil in the Valley of Lost Souls?"

"The will of *esLi* is His own business, as you well know."

"She is not even a warrior of the People," T'te'e hissed. "Even though I helped set her on this flight, I never thought we would rest the fate of the People on her alone."

"You are being disingenuous. You know the legend: You, of all people, must know the tale—and the outcome. What is more, the *es-Ga'uYal* are expecting—and looking for—one of the People. *se* Jackie may not be one of the People, but she is most decidedly a warrior."

T'te'e looked away from Byar and moved toward the edge of the platform. A cordon of guard-warriors formed around him. "It is time

for the Ceremony of Welcoming," he said, not exactly an acknowledgment of Byar's last comment. Without a further glance or gesture, T'te'e
launched himself into the upper flying-lane of the terminal.

So much dust gathers on his wings, Byar thought to himself, arranging his own wings in a posture of respect to *esLi. He must pierce the
Icewall or we truly* are *lost.*

The cameras recorded the Ceremony of Welcoming from a distance. While eight zor in the livery of the High Nest stood with
their *chya'i* drawn and their wings held in the position of Glaive of the
Hero, eight others performed an aerial exercise that had remained essentially unchanged since it was performed for the first *Gyaryu'har,* the
hero Qu'u, when he had returned from the Plain of Despite with the
sword of state. To the hundreds of billions of the People and tens of
quadrillions of humans that saw it—or would see it—the elaborate and
intricate dance held great artistic merit . . . but only the People understood its symbolic meaning, also unchanged since the time of Qu'u.

The Gyaryu'har *is home.*
The gyaryu *has returned.*

esLi forgive me, T'te'e told himself, as the grav-bed descended from
the shuttle airlock to ground level. He had his own *chya* placed in the
salute position, and his wings arranged in the Posture of Deference to
esLi; but his own Sensitive talent and the soft whine and snarl of his blade
made him realize that the Lord Over All had no forgiveness for his du-
plicity in welcoming back a *Gyaryu'har* who was essentially absent and
unarmed. The notion of *idju*—dishonor to the point of death—no longer
seemed to mean anything. It appalled T'te'e how quickly his most cher-
ished values seemed to have gone from paramount to inconsequential.

The *Gyaryu'har's* bed coasted to a stop almost directly under the
whirling pattern of airborne warriors. At a subtle gesture from T'te'e
they changed their motion to a slowly coasting circle. The High Chamberlain stepped forward to the foot of the bed where *se* Sergei lay,
arranged his wings in the position of the Cloak of Worship, and extended his *chya* out in front of him.

"'And the Lord *esLi* spoke to High Lord A'alu, and commanded
her, "Recite this in My Name.

" ' "Tell all of the generations of My People, alive and yet to come, that I have commanded this: That among the People there shall be one Lord, one High Nest and one High Lord.

" ' "Say to them: 'The Lord *esLi* has looked upon the works of His People, and has chosen in His grace to send them a sign whereby His will should be done—that a hero should be found. This hero should be of great and noble heart, and though young and not well-tried, he shall go forth to the Plain of Despite, and recover that which was lost, and which, with my assistance, he shall have regained.' " ' "

The awkward mixing of tenses had always made the passage difficult to follow, but ritual required T'te'e to articulate it just as it had been written in *The Legend of Qu'u* five-twelves of turns ago.

" ' "Tell them the hero has returned to them, and that he bears a sword I have reforged for him.

" ' "Tell them that by this sword shall My People become one People, and the Nest of the hero shall become the High Nest. This shall be the sword of the Nest, the sword of the hero that pierced the Icewall, who will stand within the Circle when the armies of the Deceiver come to the gates." '

"With these words the Lord Over All addressed the High Lord upon the return of the hero Qu'u, the first *Gyaryu'har* of the People. With these words we ceremonially greet the *Gyaryu'har* Sergei Torrijos, friend and Nest-brother, on his return—"

"Deception!" a voice shrieked in the Highspeech, cutting across T'te'e's address.

T'te'e's wings rose in a posture of defense, and he turned, with *chya* still drawn, to face the speaker just landing nearby.

Then, in an instant of reflex, T'te'e lowered his blade and bowed low, his wings pulled around him. "*hi* Ke'erl . . . I did not expect to see you here, High Lord."

Cameras recording the whole scene continued to run, following Ke'erl HeYen as he half walked, half flew, past his High Chamberlain to stand beside the bier of the comatose *Gyaryu'har*.

"Deception," Ke'erl HeYen whispered. "The Army of Despite advances as we speak—as we *recite, se* T'te'e!—and you seek to welcome back this shell, this—this container . . ."

"The *Gyaryu'har, hi* Ke'erl—"

"Is not here!" Ke'erl HeYen spread his wings in a posture that communicated madness, desperation and a sort of deep intensity that

T'te'e could not even properly perceive. "The *Gyaryu'har* is not here, T'te'e."

The High Chamberlain winced as the High Lord spoke his name, excluding even the least-honorific prenomen, but remained silent.

"His *hsi* is far away, in *Ur'ta leHssa.*"

The High Lord bent over his human sword-bearer: the old, old man who had served his grandfather and his father before him. More gently than a human observer might have believed, Ke'erl ran a clawed finger along Sergei's face, from his brow along his cheekbone to his exposed neck.

The High Chamberlain, for his part, looked on at this display of emotion, unable to act for a moment. Then it occurred to him that it was being broadcast across many worlds of the People and, in less than a sun, recordings of it would be available across inhabited space.

A gesture ended that: High Nest warriors moved to shut down the comm crews. The eight circling dancers from the Ceremony of Welcoming descended to land nearby, though they kept a respectful distance. Ke'erl continued looking down at Sergei, his wings held in a pose of sorrow.

T'te'e sheathed his *chya*. "*hi'i* Ke'erl."

The High Lord's arms dropped to his sides. He straightened and looked up at T'te'e. "Why do you disturb my contemplations?"

"It is not my intention to disturb you. I merely wish to prevent you from completely embarrassing yourself."

"I do not know to what you are referring." Ke'erl's eyes glittered with something T'te'e couldn't quite read: madness, lack of sleep, perhaps some kind of drug that could deaden the effects of the prescient dreams that were destroying the High Lord's sanity.

"Let me tell you to what I refer, *hi* Cousin," T'te'e whispered quietly. "I am referring to this foolish display you have just put on for *esLi*-knows-how-many of the People. se Sergei is far away, and both of us know why and how that came about. We could see the flight leading to this place from many turns in the past. Most of our people know only that *se* Sergei is sick. There was no reason to tell them otherwise."

"Why? Shall we wait until the *esGa'uYal* seize their *hsi*, too? They will not be listening *then*."

"That is not my intent."

"Just what *is* your intent, Cousin?" The High Lord's hand ventured close to the *hi'chya*, and T'te'e felt a thrill of fear: Engaging in blade combat with the High Lord would be a sure way to earn *idju* status, like it or not.

"My intent," T'te'e answered carefully, after a moment, "is to manage the High Nest according to your directions—or, rather, the directions you gave when you took an interest in the High Nest."

T'te'e looked around and noticed that the guards had moved the comnet crews well out of range. "That is my primary concern," he continued, his voice lower. "Attempting to guide the Nest from day to day. I am merely your servant, High Lord Ke'erl." His wings assumed the Configuration of Righteous Honor—not sure but that it would infuriate the High Lord, and not sure whether he cared anymore.

"Merely my servant," Ke'erl repeated. The High Lord's shoulders slumped, and his wings settled into an uneven pattern of disarray. "You serve emptiness, *se* T'te'e. The abyss stretches before you, and you bow to it." He waved his arms above his head, following their motions with his eyes for several moments. "You perform the Ceremony of Welcoming over it. Shrnu'u HeGa'u sits in the High Seat, *se* T'te'e, and commands that his servants attend."

Without a further word and without giving T'te'e a chance to reply, the High Lord took to the air and began flying sunsetward. The High Chamberlain gestured to four guards nearby, and they launched themselves after Ke'erl HeYen.

Emptiness, thought T'te'e, turning back to look at *se* Sergei. *You know about all of this, old friend. The abyss that yawns before the High Lord's mind's eye certainly exists, but we can hold it at bay with the* gyaryu. *I pray to* esLi, *the Lord Over All, that it can return to us.*

He watched Ke'erl HeYen receding in the distance, flying away from the shipping lanes with four High Nest guards escorting him. The orange sun of Zor'a dappled the High Lord's wings so that they appeared afire; he flew on, not noticing. It seemed fitting to T'te'e: a metaphor for the whole situation.

Hours later, when the scene had been replayed eights of times on the comnet and had begun to make its way outsystem, T'te'e was taking a moment's reflection at the entrance to *hi* Ke'erl's *esTle'e*. He had not ventured down the arbored path to see what the High Lord might be doing; *hi'i* Ke'erl might be asleep, or hurling himself against the roofdome of the place—it depended on the state of his madness this sun.

As the High Chamberlain stood quietly, watching the People of the High Nest move to and fro on their errands, he saw S'reth approaching. The ancient one walked with only a slight assist from his near-translucent wings, which were held in a posture that mixed amusement and genuine concern.

"*se* S'reth," T'te'e said. "I thought you had returned home. How may I assist you?"

"May we speak privately for a moment?"

T'te'e gestured to the arbor. They took several steps within, out of sight of the main concourse. T'te'e activated the privacy cylinder at his belt and the soft hum dulled the sounds around them.

"I am disturbed by the behavior of the High Lord this sun," S'reth said. T'te'e dipped his wings in assent. "I would be less disturbed, Younger Brother, if I had not heard something in his remarks: 'Shrnu'u HeGa'u sits in the High Seat, and commands that his servants attend.' "

"You ascribe meaning to that phrase. What do you think *hi'i* Ke'erl meant to say?"

"He perceives that something has happened. So do I."

"Where?"

"Adrianople."

T'te'e's wings moved into the Cloak of Guard. "Why do you think something has happened there? It is heavily guarded by an Imperial Fleet—"

"No, Younger Brother. It is *not*. It is *due* to be reinforced by one. But if the base has already fallen to the *esGa'uYal*, then that fleet will be flying into a trap."

T'te'e did not reply.

"I believe that *hi* Ke'erl sensed this, and my own contemplations tend to confirm it."

"I would be more inclined to give credence to this, *se* S'reth, if the humans would confirm it."

"They do not know yet. Indeed, they scarcely see the threat."

"What do you propose?"

"Allow me to travel to Adrianople," S'reth answered. His wings, rarely expressive, had taken on a position of respect. Normally T'te'e would have ascribed this to wry humor on the part of the old sage; but he perceived that S'reth really meant it—he considered it vitally important that T'te'e go to Adrianople.

"I would not willingly send you into *Ur'ta leHssa*, old friend."

"I do not intend to remain there, Younger Brother. But I do not wish a powerful force such as the one headed there to be trapped in the Valley. Send me and a few eights of Sensitives with strong *hsi*. This sun. *This* fraction." S'reth grabbed T'te'e's forearms with a surprisingly strong grip; there was emotion in his eyes. "I ask this favor of the High Nest that I have served so long."

His old wings moved to the Stance of Respect to the High Nest, and remained there for long moments. In the end, T'te'e could hardly choose other than to accede.

chapter 3

DESPITE HAS MORE ENEMIES THAN IT CAN COUNT. THE TRUE
WARRIOR KNOWS BUT ONE.

—The Legend of Qu'u

The food preparer beeped and cycled into inactivity. Jackie opened the door and pulled out her dinner, moving it from the warming tray to the small table opposite. She pulled down a cold drink and opened it and settled down to her meal.

Eat, she told herself, after dawdling for a while. *Never know when you might get another meal.* She forced herself to work her way through the food, chewing but not really tasting what she'd prepared. It was comforting to realize that she was still thinking like a soldier, but it didn't do much for her appetite.

Four days out from Crossover, and her mind was still back there: with Noyes, with Ch'k'te . . . It was almost as if that place *was* a crossing-over of sorts, like the ferryboat across the River Styx.

You are too melodramatic, she thought to herself, toying with the food in front of her. *Too many zor legends.*

"Too much talking to myself," she said aloud, testing it, trying to see what her voice sounded like. It sounded despairing, desperate, alone. No faithful friend to advise her.

On the other hand, she thought, *I still have my spirit-guide.*

She'd felt uncomfortable trying to talk with Th'an'ya since leaving Crossover almost four days ago: The way it had all come about, as if it were planned . . . It almost placed Th'an'ya in the same category as whoever/whatever had manipulated Jackie into this quest. She didn't know whether it was true, but she did realize that she'd become damned lonely in this little ship hurtling through jump.

"Th'an'ya," she said out loud, and concentrated on the image of the zor female who cohabited her mind. She closed her eyes; when she opened them, an image of Th'an'ya had appeared across from her.

"I am here, *se* Jackie."

"I need to understand some things. I— I don't even know where to start, really . . ." She let the sentence drift off, not knowing what to say.

Th'an'ya spoke: "When I was a teacher at Sanctuary," Th'an'ya began, "when I still held the Outer Peace—I conducted a training course for Sensitives. We used a technique to analyze a situation by reviewing the events that had led up to that situation, called 'flying the path.' Perhaps you should consider this method, to try and see how we have reached this point; and it may help you to understand what you must know next."

"May *I* make a suggestion?"

Th'an'ya's wings adjusted themselves slightly to indicate faint amusement. "Of course."

"*You* should 'fly the path.' Review for me how you—how *we*— reached this sun. I think I might find that useful."

"As you wish." She resettled her wings, assuming a more deferential posture. "It is appropriate to locate the event most distant from the present which bears directly on the current situation. That event, I think, would be a dream I had, nearly twelve turns ago."

"*Twelve* turns?"

"I was living on A'aen at the time." Th'an'ya laid her clawed hands on the table and looked down at them. "You know that I had gone to Sanctuary when my Sensitive powers began to manifest themselves. Once I gained full control, the Master of Sanctuary, *se* Byar HeShri, offered me a position as a guide and instructor there. For nearly two-eights of turns I worked either at Sanctuary or on loan to one or another Nest, but at last I decided that I needed a change of scenery. With Byar's permission, I went to A'aen as a gardener."

"A *gardener?*"

"A very relaxing job, excellent for strengthening the *hsi*. Not that I sought that; I simply wanted to be away from Sanctuary, on a different flight. Yet I was followed even there. I had a dream: Somewhere out in the void, the *esGa'uYal* had stolen the *gyaryu*, and the great hero Qu'u had gone out to find it.

"With regard to prescient dreams, it takes a skilled Sensitive to distinguish between imagination and a true precognitive impression. The best test is repetition—if the dream recurs, and is consistent, it is usually prescient.

"The dream recurred several times; each one more detailed and more disturbing than its predecessor. I finally had to return to Sanctuary. Within a few days of my return, several eminent guests arrived, including the High Chamberlain *ha* T'te'e HeYen, and—at last—the *Gyaryu'har*."

"You've met *se* Sergei in person?"

"Yes. They had come to Sanctuary to contemplate a most unpleasant flight: The High Chamberlain and others had attempted to make contact with the aliens out there." At Jackie's involuntary shiver—which was almost amusingly reflected in Th'an'ya's image—the zor female crossed her hands in front of herself. "I know what you are remembering, *se* Jackie. There were eleven Sensitives that tried to contact the aliens, and eight of them transcended the Outer Peace in the process.

"As you no doubt have been told, the High Lord is the most prescient Sensitive of the People. He had begun to sense the *esGa'uYal* even before the eleven tried to contact them, and he also had had a precognitive indication that the High Nest should pursue *The Legend of Qu'u*. It was the will of *esLi* that I go to Sanctuary, and at that point I became included in their plans."

"And what were their plans?"

"They concluded that the *gyaryu* had to be placed at risk somehow, but did not determine the way in which it could be done. At Sanctuary I had another prescient experience, linking the *gyaryu* with a young warrior whose face I did not know."

"Ch'k'te."

"... Yes." Th'an'ya wavered again. "I can sense your anger, *se* Jackie, for I know that you know what happened next. Yes, I did seek out Ch'k'te, who had just recently come into his Sensitive powers, and who was a young, impressionable warrior ..."

"You *used* him. Like I'm being used."

"You are so quick to judge." Her wings settled low on her back, indicating sorrow. "When I perceived what I thought to be the hand of *esLi* in this affair, I assumed that *li* Ch'k'te was to represent Qu'u. Still, I beg you to believe that I loved him."

"How much did you see, Th'an'ya? How far down in time did you perceive? Did you see your own death—and his? If you hadn't made him a pawn in this terrible game, he'd be alive now." Jackie's fists clenched. "How *dare* you talk about love."

"You understand us so little. You mind-linked with *li* Ch'k'te and felt the depth of his feelings for me, and you must sense that I tell you the truth about how I felt about him . . . *Feel*. Neither you nor I—even in present form—can ever know what flight *li* Ch'k'te might have taken, had I not sought him out as my mate. Yet I think that our *cle'eLi'e*—our 'mating'—strengthened his own *hsi* abundantly and made him strong enough to be the Ch'k'te that you knew."

"And loved," Jackie whispered.

"It is difficult for *you* to admit that."

"Of course it is—especially since I could never tell him." Jackie felt her voice growing husky and thick, and frowned. "Damn it, things used to be so simple, and now they've gotten so blasted complicated."

"Yes. Yes, of course. Love is a difficult emotion; it seems that your many human languages only make it more difficult." Th'an'ya's wings assumed an almost reverent position. "That you are not one of the People and yet were thrust into the impossible position of acting the part, makes *all* of this difficult to comprehend. I did love *li* Ch'k'te . . . and yet he was destined to play a role in 'this terrible game,' as you put it. I thought that he would become Qu'u, and so gave him most of my *hsi*."

"What does that *really* mean?"

"It means that . . . what was left behind, was only an 'image' of me. It functioned but was only barely a Sensitive. Given time, the *hsi* might well have been strengthened, but . . ."

"Did you . . . Did your death come about as a result of giving so much *hsi* to Ch'k'te?"

"I have no way of knowing, since this *hsi*-image"—Th'an'ya gestured to herself—"was not present at the moment of my physical body's death. I suspect, however, that the answer is yes."

"So you killed yourself to make him strong—and he killed himself to save me."

"There I think you err. I did not transcend the Outer Peace to make *li* Ch'k'te strong: I was flying the path that *esLi* had marked out for me. Similarly, Ch'k'te's death has meaning in the context of allowing you to continue holding the Outer Peace; but he died primarily for himself, *se* Jackie. In the greater scheme of things, his end was completely fitting, as he destroyed the object of his dishonor: that thing which had condemned him to life."

"You make suicide sound like an art form."

"Just so. To one of the People, the style of death *is* high art. You humans have an exceptionally parochial view of life and death, treating them as two essentially different things. They are merely different forms of the *same* thing. For example: Into what category do you place me? Am I alive, or dead?"

"Dead. But I see what you mean. How do you classify those unfortunate trillions who were not so clever to insert their *hsi* into unsuspecting mates?"

"If they are of the People, I classify them as within *esLi*'s Circle of Light. It is they whose wisdom and Inner Peace make it possible for some of our race to be poets, dreamers, artists . . . and, of course, Sensitives."

"*esLi* . . . is the composite of the People that have gone before? Is that a common belief?"

"Of course, *se* Jackie. We believe *esLi* to be the possessor of all the *hsi* of our race, since its beginning. It is the *hsi* that guides all of us, from the High Lord to the simplest warrior. It is for this reason that one of the People feels it so important to maintain the Inner Peace: to retain his honor. To become *idju* is not merely to suffer the contempt of one's own people, but to be separated from the guidance of *esLi* Himself."

Jackie took a sip from her drink and pushed aside the mostly eaten tray of food. "You . . . said that you saw this path when you were at Sanctuary; or, rather, that you dreamed of Ch'k'te"—she felt her emotion rising, and took a deep breath to fend it off—"in connection with *The Legend of Qu'u.* You sought out and found him, mated with him and gave him a large portion of your *hsi*. What happened after that?"

"What I know, subsequent to that, is only second-wing information and conjecture, *se* Jackie, since this *hsi*-image was submerged from the time of our *cle'eLi'e* until the moment when *li* Ch'k'te summoned me forth during our mind-link on Cicero. But I will seek to reconstruct it for you.

"After my death, *li* Ch'k'te grieved greatly for me and sought transfer from the naval service of the People to the Imperial Navy. As a distant clan-brother of the High Nest this was easily effected. Eventually he was posted to Cicero under your command. I cannot say for sure, but I can believe that the High Nest arranged to place him there."

"Then, Ch'k'te's posting to Cicero was no accident."

"Certainly not. The High Nest knew, or rather *sensed,* that there was something about to happen beyond the edge of the Empire; it also sensed that Cicero was at—or near—where the event was to occur. As the High Lord's madness progressed, the inner circle of the High Nest began to make preparations for the quest to be undertaken. *se* Sergei, the *Gyaryu'har,* was sent to Cicero when it became apparent that the sword should be placed into the possession of the enemy."

"Someone from the Envoy's Office explained that *se* Sergei had been sent to Cicero, but I never realized how far back it went . . ." Jackie stared into her drink-cup, looking at the face gazing back at her. "But, if all these people—including Noyes!—believed that Ch'k'te was Qu'u, how did *I* get mixed up in all of this?"

"I would conjecture that the *esGa'uYal* believe that Qu'u must be one of the People, since only a warrior of the People would be willing to transcend the Outer Peace to fulfill the Law of Similar Conjunction," Th'an'ya responded.

"Further, I could simply say it was the will of *esLi.* Even now, you might find that insufficient—insulting, even. I cannot describe in Standard *why* I recognized your *hsi* as that of the returned hero, but I knew it from the outset; even *li* Ch'k'te knew it, when you linked on Cicero. I chose to transfer my *hsi* to you at that time; my intuition was confirmed when you fought Shrnu'u HeGa'u during the *Dsen'yen'ch'a.* I helped you create the *hsi*-images with which you fought him; and he, too, saw . . . that you would fly the path of Qu'u.

"That ordeal was clearly painful for *li* Ch'k'te. He learned that I had moved my *hsi* into your mind. Like most Sensitives, he did not believe this could be done. He considered the idea of a *hsi*-image residing within a *naZora'e* mind as even less possible. When we spoke, in your quarters on Adrianople Starbase, I explained to him that despite my love for him, I existed for a specific purpose: to aid the avatar of Qu'u in regaining the *gyaryu.*"

"What must he have thought of me after that?"

"For a time I am sure he was angry at his fate—but you must believe that he had great respect and affection for you. You should not diminish his memory by thinking he resented your role, or his own."

"Did he resent *your* role?"

"He never really *knew* my role. But on the Plain of Despite, he was able to lift up his gaze."

"You think so." Jackie stood up, carried the tray to the disposal and tossed it in. "You think he was a true hero?"

"By all of the metrics we apply, yes: Ch'k'te was a hero, and his *hsi* now resides with the Lord *esLi*."

Jackie didn't speak for a moment. She leaned on the counter, facing away from the Th'an'ya-image still standing by the table. Jackie felt tension and emotion trying to overwhelm her as she stood there. She half expected Th'an'ya to have disappeared, when at last she composed herself and turned around, but the zor was still there, her wings arranged in a formal posture.

"It's getting easier to maintain that image," Jackie said to her.

"As we get closer to the *gyaryu*, it is only to be expected. You have become much stronger as a Sensitive, *se* Jackie, and your connection with *esLi* has grown."

"But I'm still not one of the People, and never will be."

"You say those words as if an apology were required. It is clear the wisdom of the Lord *esLi* is greater than our own, and He has chosen a human to be the agent of His will.

"You accepted the risks—you know the stakes. The High Chamberlain *se* S'reth—and even the servants of *esGa'u*—accept you as the avatar of Qu'u. As do I . . . as did *li* Ch'k'te. We must move on from that point."

"Where? Where do we go?"

"Consider this." Th'an'ya's wings moved through several positions, as if she were trying to decide on a direction. "The *esGa'uYal* have what we seek. It is clear that the closer you come to the *gyaryu*, the more your Sensitive talents manifest themselves; therefore you will have to rely upon signs of that increase, to locate it."

"I just wander around until my Sensitive talents tell me where the *gyaryu* is? Surely the aliens will know I'm coming and will be guarding the sword rather closely."

Th'an'ya's wings assumed the Posture of Polite Resignation: For a moment Jackie was painfully reminded of Ch'k'te. "You are right, of course," Th'an'ya answered, and it was clear she wasn't really answering the question.

"They could be waiting for me when we come out of jump."

"Perhaps. We have no control over that, but I cannot believe the Lord *esLi* would abandon us after bringing us this far. We can only hope that the *esGa'uYal* continue to await one of the People as the avatar of Qu'u and will not recognize you."

"They *must* know."

"The creature at the Center on Crossover Station did not know, *se* Jackie. If the *esGa'uYe* on Crossover was unable to communicate with others—and I suspect he had no time to do so—then the only ones who were aware of your identity would be *li* Ch'k'te, yourself . . . and the alien at Crossover. Two of those three individuals are now beyond the Outer Peace.

"This is the only advantage you—we—possess. We must make use of it. There must be information aboard this vessel identifying the alien and its role in *esGa'uYal* society. *You* must take its place."

"I wish I had such confidence in that advantage."

"Eight thousand pardons, *se* Jackie, but what choice do you have?"

Jackie didn't answer, since she couldn't conceive of a response. After a few moments of silence she felt Th'an'ya withdraw, unbidden, and she was alone again.

They had chosen Port Saud by consensus. It wasn't marked in the altered databases in the *Negri*'s navcomp, as Adrianople and Corcyra had been. It was outside the Empire—and was far enough away from trade routes to be worth no one's while to claim it.

The wars with the zor, at the opposite end of Imperial space, had made the place even less interesting. The Imperial Grand Survey didn't get to mapping it until 2372, and Port Saud hadn't been approached for annexation since then. Poor in minerals and other resources, thinly populated and far off even from freelancers' trade routes, Port Saud seemed an uninteresting target for would-be conquerors.

At least, that was the theory. Lieutenant Owen Garrett had picked the destination almost at random when they'd jumped from Center, with places like Adrianople possibly already in enemy hands. It could be a trap—but then, going almost anywhere could be a trap. *Negri*

Sembilan had to refuel sometime, and if there *were* aliens at Port Saud, they might not realize the ship had been recaptured.

*N*egri arrived insystem while Owen was off the bridge; they were only two hours away from Port Saud Station when he took the pilot's seat. It wasn't a surprise: There really was no need for him to supervise end-of-jump, as there were a dozen crewmembers aboard with more experience than he had. End-of-jump was timed to the millisecond. Owen's special skill would come in handy later, when they reached the port.

"A pretty sorry lookin' place, if you ask me," said Dana Olivo, vacating the pilot's seat as Owen arrived. Dana was one of the *Negri* officers who had escaped with them from Center. "But it's acknowledging Standard comm. We're lined up for the fuel queue at the gas giant in Orbital Five, then we've got an approach for temp berthing-space at Port Saud Station."

"Just like that."

"*Negri Sembilan* was here eight months ago," Dana said. "They may not know *Negri*'s current status."

"Meaning they don't know we've got it back."

"Meaning they may not even know that the bugs *captured* it. There's a mercantile council in charge of Port Saud. *Negri* is—was . . . *is*, really— an IGS vessel that pays courtesy calls once or twice a year."

"Do they know Damien Abbas here?"

"Sure enough. There's a merchant factor who's been a regular informant—guy by the name of Djiwara. The skipper would go stationside and visit Djiwara, toss back a few pints and get the latest gossip; he always seemed to know what was going on."

"Would he trust anyone but Abbas?"

Olivo gave Owen a look that said, roughly, *How the hell should I know*? "I guess," he finally said, "it depends on what story you give him."

*I*t was a place to start. Refueled and ready to make its next jump, the *Negri* was docked at Port Saud Station. The station originally had been built at half the size of Cicero Op. Owen learned from the *Negri*'s comp that the Port Saud Consortium—the governing oligarchy of Port

Saud System—had bought and boosted the thing from Far Macintosh System in the early 2200s, when that world had become a Class One world within the Solar Empire and earned itself a brand-new, Navy-built facility. Given the cost of orbital insertion from the planetary surface, even an inferior orbital station paid for itself in time, and the Consortium had added piecemeal to the original, orderly, wheel-like structure so that it now resembled the legs of an ungainly insect, spread out in a dozen different directions with no real order or organization.

Owen went aboard, his engineer's mate Rafe Rodriguez at his side. Owen wasn't sure if he could protect more than one other person; also, he trusted Rafe, the first man he'd met on Center when this strange new phase of his life had begun.

He and Rafe walked up an access corridor from the *Negri*'s berth, past stacks of cargo canisters and assorted construction materials.

"Dana's right. This station *is* a piece of crap," Owen remarked.

"Independent commerce in action," the big man answered. "But the universe is full of places like this. Everyone here"—he waved his hand around the wider corridor they'd entered, which was filled with activity—"is trying to make a living."

"Even in wartime?"

"I don't think it matters to them," Rafe said. "This isn't Center or Cicero. It isn't even Crossover."

"But it's still—"

"It's just a *place*," the engineer's mate continued. "It's been settled for more than two hundred years and it's never paid a single credit to the Imperial Government. It's never had an Emperor's Birthday celebration. Know what? They don't mind. And the pols in Sol System don't care. There are probably five hundred places like Port Saud System, and none of them is at war with the bugs."

"They're *all* at war with the bugs," Owen replied. "They just don't know it yet."

I⸑ ⱳⱥⱾⱖ'ⱦ hard to find Djiwara. He had offices on the main concourse, a wide-open area traversing the long axis of the station, close to the largest cargo docks. The great man himself—recognizable from an image stored in *Negri*'s comp—was standing outside the office, engaged in an argument with another merchant. The other man was getting the worst of it, and finally gave up and, with a few caustic remarks strong enough to peel paint, he turned his back on Djiwara and stalked off. Djiwara looked quite pleased with himself as he turned away.

"Mr. Djiwara?" Owen said.

The merchant factor trained a glare on Owen and Rafe. "J. Michael Djiwara at your service." He looked them over as if he were calculating their annual income. "Who wants to know?"

"I'm Garrett, of *Negri Sembilan*. This is Rodriguez."

"*Negri*?" His expression softened. "Where is my old friend Abbas?"

"He's . . . indisposed. He sent us instead."

"Really."

Djiwara made a great show of looking up and down the concourse, then beckoned them within his office. The room they entered was like a museum of curiosities, except it contained several rooms' worth of this junk jammed into an area no more than five meters across. Djiwara took a collection of plastic containers off of two chairs in front of his desk and gestured for Owen and Rafe to sit. He settled his own large form behind the desk.

"Thanks for taking the time," Owen said. "We—"

"Mr. Garrett." Djiwara held up his hand. "I have only one question for you: Where is Damien Abbas?"

"Mr. Djiwara, I—"

"Let me make it simple for you, Mr. Garrett," Djiwara interrupted again. "I have been in business on this worthless station for a number of years. While I have been here at Port Saud, my good friend Damien Abbas has visited more than twenty times—and each time he has sent a tightbeam message from the jump point telling me when the *Negri Sembilan* would dock and which vintage he would come and enjoy with me.

"Each time he has done this; each time except this one. Therefore I must assume something has happened."

Garrett exchanged glances with Rafe. When he looked back at the merchant, Djiwara had a pistol in his hand, aimed directly at Owen.

"Mr. Garrett, I would very much like to know *what*."

"You know," Rafe said, not moving a muscle, "some people might take that as being unfriendly."

"Not everyone is who he seems to be. You can't be too careful." The pistol remained pointed at Owen.

"That's true," Owen said. "But if we *weren't* who we seem to be, you'd *already* be in trouble, wouldn't you? I'd be willing to wager a liter of whatever swill they drink out here, that you could get a single shot off before the other one of us killed you."

Djiwara's frown deepened. Anger flashed in his eyes.

"What's more"—Owen said, adjusting himself in his seat; Djiwara's weapon followed the movement—"we wouldn't let it get that far. *If we weren't what we seemed.*"

Djiwara looked from Owen to Rafe and then back again. Owen never looked away, but tried to feign complete indifference with the weapon pointed directly at him.

"All right," the merchant said at last. He laid the pistol on the cluttered desk in front of him. "No hard feelings," he added.

"None at all," Owen answered.

"Right," Rafe said, breathing a sigh of relief. "Nothing like good old Port Saud hospitality."

Djiwara glared at him. "I still want to know where Abbas is."

"I don't know," Owen said. "Honest to God, I'd tell you if I knew—if it were up to me, he'd be sitting in this office right now. But . . ."

"But he's dead." Djiwara finished the sentence.

"No, I don't think so. Someone—some *thing*—has been impersonating him for most of a Standard year, but *it's* dead now. As for Captain Abbas . . . Look, you wouldn't believe me if I told you."

"Try me."

"A band of light swept him off the bridge of the *Negri* when we took it back from the bugs."

" 'Bugs'?"

"I think you know what I'm talking about."

"I'm supposed to have some insight into this preposterous story of yours." Djiwara's gaze traveled from Owen to Rafe and to his pistol. "You're right. I don't believe it—except that no one would make up something like that."

"Look, we need your help," Rafe interrupted. The merchant's gaze slipped back to him. "We need to know what's going on here."

"Here? On Port Saud? Nothing happens here. But maybe you can tell *me* what the hell is going on. I hear all kinds of things and most of 'em make no sense. Comm to Cicero is down—I suppose you know? There hasn't been any contact with it for nearly two months. Comm to Adrianople was down for several Standard days; it's working again—but there's something going on there, too.

"People pass through here and talk about fleet movements out at this end of the Empire. Then *you* show up and tell me—" Djiwara rested his hand on his pistol again. Rafe shifted in his chair; the merchant slowly and carefully moved his hand away.

"They're aboard Port Saud Station, aren't they?" Owen said quietly, knowing the answer.

Djiwara held Owen's gaze for a long time. "*Something* is aboard. There are people . . . not acting the way they should. People I've known for a long time." He leaned back again in his chair, like the weight of the whole of Port Saud Station was on his shoulders.

"You wouldn't believe me if I told you," Owen said again.

The lighting dimmed for just a moment. All three men looked up; then the lights came back to normal levels.

"The Solar Empire is at war," Owen said, his attention returning to Djiwara.

"Bugs," Rafe added. "Shapechangers. They've been replacing people—people you know. People like—"

"Abbas."

"Yeah," Owen said. "Like Abbas. He's been gone for several months, at least. The—alien that replaced him took over the *Negri Sembilan* and has been operating it outside the Empire. Its disappearance was the first indication we got that something was happening."

" 'We'—meaning . . ."

"The command at Cicero. Cicero belongs to the bugs. I . . . was stationed there." Owen's fists clenched. "Sounds like Port Saud belongs to them, too."

Djiwara scowled at Owen and Rafe again. "What the hell does this mean? If there are . . . bugs . . . on Port Saud, what do they want?"

"I have my suspicions," Owen said. "Believe me, this time you *don't* want to know."

They made their way back from Djiwara's offices on the main concourse; it seemed less crowded now. Still, there was activity at several docking-bays, and foot traffic alongside them. They had come aboard lightly armed; nothing to attract attention, but no one would go into a free port armed with nothing but a smile.

"Company," Rafe said, when they were several minutes along. He gestured above and to their left.

Owen looked briefly where Rafe had pointed. A station crewman in overalls was keeping pace with them on an upper catwalk. Owen concentrated, and after a moment was confident that their shadow was an alien.

"Fight or flight?" Rafe asked.

"There's nowhere to run," Owen answered. "Let's see what he does."

After a few hundred meters they had their answer. The one who was following them came down a ramp to meet two others. Together, the three aliens in human form turned to face Owen and Rafe as if they were waiting for them.

Owen felt the slightest pressure in his mind. He turned to Rafe, who was shaking his head like flies were buzzing around it.

"If you're looking for a fight," Owen said, from five meters away, "you'll get one."

"We have a message for your captain," the middle alien said, crossing his arms. "We don't have time to bother with you . . ." He lowered his voice and added, ". . . meat-creature."

The term the aliens used to refer to humans, chilled Owen but he ignored it. "Fine. Let's hear the message."

The alien smiled. "Tell your captain that the time has come to switch sides."

"Why would he want to do that?"

"Because his faction has already lost. Even her *N'nr* Deathguard will not protect Great Queen G'en in the end. He must know that."

"The captain keeps his own counsel," Owen answered, trying to sound like he knew where the hell this was going. "Besides, what purpose would it serve, to switch sides at this point?"

The three aliens looked at each other, then back at Owen and Rafe.

"Just deliver the damn message," the leader said.

"You know," one of the others said, "it only takes one of them to deliver the message."

Rafe clenched his fists. "There's just one problem. There's only three of you. I don't even need *this* guy"—he gestured at Owen—"to help me wipe the deck with you."

The leader didn't say anything, but looked up and to his right. Owen followed the glance to the catwalk; there he saw another tech watching the exchange. Owen's heightened senses, sharpened by his anger, made him certain it was another alien. He looked across the concourse at a group of cargo handlers: One of the group had stopped loading a canister and was watching as well; a few dozen meters farther on, a customs inspector stood, comp in one hand, the other resting on a sidearm. Both of them were aliens.

"Rafe—" Owen began, but the alien leader interrupted:

"Such audacity for a meat-creature," he said. "No. As entertaining as the idea might be, we have no instructions to disrupt your captain's mission." He turned to his two companions. "Let him go." He looked straight at Owen. "But you *tell* him."

Owen and Rafe walked forward and past the group, headed for the side accessway that led to their berth. All the way back to the *Negri Sembilan,* Owen felt eyes watching his every step.

chapter 4

THE LEGEND OF QU'U (continued)

WITH THE VALLEY OF LOST SOULS LEFT BEHIND, THE
HERO MADE HIS WAY UPWARD ON THE PERILOUS
STAIR. THE STAIR WAS A TREACHEROUS PATH,
SOMETIMES NO MORE THAN A SET OF HANDHOLDS   [The Perilous Stair]
BARELY WIDE ENOUGH TO ACCOMMODATE HIS TALONS;
ELSEWHERE, THERE WERE PLACES HE COULD STAND
AND EVEN WALK FORWARD AND UPWARD. BENEATH THE
TALONS OF HIS FEET, HE WAS CHILLED BY THE INDIGO
ROCK OF THE ICEWALL.

AFTER QU'U HAD CLIMBED SOME DISTANCE, HE
PAUSED TO REST. THE WINDS TORE AT HIS WINGS AND
THREATENED TO PULL HIM AWAY FROM THE STAIR,
AND THE CHILL OF THE PLAIN OF DESPITE MADE HIS   [Winds of Despite]
BODY SHIVER AND HIS TALONS CLENCH. HIS *CHYA*
REMAINED SHEATHED: THERE WERE NO ENEMIES TO
FIGHT, AND HE NEEDED TALONS ON BOTH HANDS AND
FEET TO MAINTAIN HIS PURCHASE.

THOUGH IT PAINED HIM TO DO SO, QU'U FLEW THE
PATH OF HIS QUEST: FROM THE FIRST APPEARANCE OF
THE SERVANT OF QU'U, TO THE JOURNEY WITH HIS
FRIEND HYOS TO THE FOREST SANCTUARY, TO THE

ENTRANCE TO THE PLAIN OF DESPITE. AS HE RESTED,
HE WONDERED IF HE COULD GO ON.   [Flying the Path]

... EVEN THROUGH THE ENCOUNTER WITH
ANGA'E'REN, HE REMEMBERED HIS ONE TRUE ENEMY:
THE SORCERER WHOSE FORTRESS LAY FAR ABOVE,
HIDDEN IN THE SHROUDING FOG.

BELOW HIM, ON THE PLAIN OF DESPITE, THE WAR
CONTINUED BETWEEN THE CONTENDING FACTIONS OF
THE *ESGA'UYAL.*

SOMETIMES THE FOG PARTED, ALLOWING HIM TO
VIEW THE BATTLES: THERE WERE SCENES OF VIOLENCE
THAT FAR EXCEEDED THE BATTLES BETWEEN E'YEN
AND THEIR ENEMIES IN U'HERA.

Years of business partnership with Pyotr Ngo had made Dan McReynolds intimately aware of his friend's moods, particularly the bad ones. Without a word being exchanged, he could read the expression on Pyotr's face as the other man stood at the engineering station.

I don't want to be here, either, Dan thought. Pyotr could read that response, too, but it didn't change anything.

Fair Damsel was twenty seconds from jump transition. Their destination was Corcyra System, a wealthy colony-world that was probably only a few years from buying its own Class One status as a full member of the Solar Empire; it made the finest crystal anywhere, the sort that graced wardroom tables of the best-furnished starships in the Imperial Fleet. The emperor drank his best vintages from Corcyran goblets.

One jump from Adrianople; one jump from Tamarind; one jump from Cicero—*Fair Damsel* was horribly, dangerously, exposed to an enemy that might take any of those places. Cicero was already theirs, and there might be a battle for Adrianople anytime.

It made sense to go there: for *Pappenheim* and *Tilly* at least, and for the little carrier *Bay of Biscay* ... But, for Dan's ship, and fellow merchanters *Reese* and *Oregon*, it was the *last* place they wanted to go. Still, orders were orders.

Dan glanced at the chrono, which had already counted below ten seconds. *Damsel*'s defensive fields, such as they were, and her meager weaponry, were ready to go online directly after transition.

He nodded to Ray Li, sitting at the helm. Pyotr continued to scowl at the utterdark in the forward screen, waiting for the silver streams that accompanied transition from jump.

"All right, everyone," Dan said. "Here we go."

The pilot's board sprang to life as the darkness faded and stars appeared. *Pappenheim* appeared first, about two thousand kilometers downrange; it was two minutes ahead of the *Fair Damsel*.

"Oh, crap," Ray said. "Jump-echoes. Big ones."

"What's our status?" Dan asked, watching the other ships register on the board. It showed four enemy IDs, a third of the way around the circumference of the system.

"Fields up, weapons online. Looks like everyone's here." Ray highlighted the icons for *Pappenheim* and the other five ships under Maartens' command.

"What are the bogeys doing?"

Ray didn't answer right away. As Dan watched, two of the IDs vanished, and in short order the third and fourth ones did as well.

"They left."

"They were on their way to transition?"

"Looks like."

"Comm the flag. We register four bogeys headed outsystem. What are your orders? *Fair Damsel* sends."

The message went out to *Pappenheim*. Dan drummed his fingers on the arm of the pilot's seat. He was a few years out of starship command, but old habits died hard; he thought about what he'd do if he were sitting in Maartens' chair.

Jump is a tricky business. It would've been possible for the bad guys to abort their jump if they'd noticed the arrival of the Imperial ships; but if they didn't notice, or didn't care, a jump outsystem would send them to their destination—and it would be a few days, at least, before they, or anyone they'd tell, would return.

Given the firepower of this little squadron, Dan would want to be far gone by that time. So—whatever they were here to do, they'd better do it damned quickly or plan on getting out now.

"Scan for hostiles in the system," Dan said.

"We're not registering anything here—friend or enemy," Ray said. "Nobody here but us."

"What about system defense?"

"Nothing." Ray spun in his chair to face Dan. "No defense boats, no traffic control. Nothing on civilian or merchanter frequencies, either."

That statement echoed for a moment on *Fair Damsel*'s bridge. Corcyra was an industrial world with lots of commercial traffic. A quick comp check showed the population at a bit under two million.

The comm board signaled. "Incoming from *Pappenheim*," Pyotr said, looking at the board. "We're ordered to proceed into the inner system."

Pyotr Ngo's face was pale and drawn as he turned to face Dan, looking away from the display that showed telemetry scans of Corcyra's changing surface. Dan was unaccustomed to seeing his exec so upset; the pilot's board was already indicating that Maartens expected his report.

"Pyotr?"

"The world doesn't match the Grand Survey data at all, Dan. I mean, we're not equipped like an Imperial starship, but it's pretty damn clear that something . . . extraordinary has happened down there."

"I'll ask you what Captain Maartens is going to ask me: What do you mean, 'extraordinary'?"

"I mean that there's considerable atmospheric activity—the sort you'd associate with explosions or firestorms. All comm frequencies are jammed. But that's small-scale compared to the map data. It's almost as if the continents have changed."

Dan looked at the board. "Corcyra Four does have a high degree of vulcanism, so there are earthquakes and volcanoes. Could there have been some sort of . . . I don't know . . . *tectonic* event?"

"Not in this timescale. The Imperial Grand Survey mapped Corcyra most recently twenty years ago. Tectonic plates don't shift more than a few centimeters in twenty years even on a world as unstable as this one. What's more, there were almost two million people living on this world. Surely they'd have noticed if their continents were moving at high speeds . . ."

"Is there any sign of them?"

"Any sign of the people?" Pyotr looked down at the deck. "Nothing. It's as if they were never there."

"That's impossible. There must be something, some evidence—"

"Here." Pyotr pointed to the displays as Dan leaned over his station. "Look for yourself."

●   ●   ●

Ten minutes later, when Dan made his report to Maartens, he had to admit the same.

"Nothing. Look at the scans, Captain: It's a wasteland down there."

"I spent some time in Exploratory, McReynolds, did I ever tell you that?" A vague outline of *Pappenheim*'s ready-room showed near Maartens' holo, sitting in an empty area of *Fair Damsel*'s bridge. Maartens sat leaning back, his face fairly impassive. "Five or six years ago I did a tour outside the Empire with the Grand Survey. Corcyra was an analysis site for Survey data; I must have visited here at least ten times.

"There were labs, factories, homes, restaurants, bars . . . This was a *living* world, McReynolds. I remember it. A hundred years ago, people with our jobs saw what happened when the zor attacked human worlds: they burned, they bombed, they killed people. But they left something behind: foundations of buildings, ruined highways, corpses . . .

"They left *evidence,* McReynolds. But this isn't anything like what the zor did. We probably watched the bastards jumping out of here.

"Let's set aside the question of *how,* since it'll take intel and tech analysis to determine the answer. What about *why?*"

"You want my opinion." Dan McReynolds didn't move, holding his commander's eye. But inside, he felt himself squirming, trying to decide what the older man was getting at.

"Sure," Maartens answered. "Favor me with your opinion."

"Well . . . First, by obliterating every visible trace of what caused this destruction, and returning the world to something like its natural state, they've made it more difficult for us to fight back."

"Makes sense." Maartens noted something on a comp in front of him. "What else?"

"The zor were more interested in human deaths than in destroying equipment; they went after civilian targets whenever they had the chance. During the wars we even scavenged from places like Alya and Pergamum. There's nothing here left behind to scavenge. But I don't really think that's the reason this was done, sir."

"All right, McReynolds. Why *was* this done?"

Dan folded his hands in his lap and took a deep breath. "They mean to scare us, Captain. They want us to know that they can do this."

"But what—?"

"Think of it, sir." Dan let his gaze fall to the physical map of the world, rotating slowly on the pilot's board in front of him. It showed no cities, no roads, no structures of any kind. "That's Corcyra down there, but it could be New Chicago, or Mothallah, or Shipley, or Dieron. Or Terra.

"The enemy wants us to *know* they can destroy us, completely and utterly—as if we had never been. *That's* the sort of fear they want us to carry around."

The shuttle began to settle slowly toward the tarmac. The ocean stretched, blue and pristine, occasionally dotted with whitecaps, for as far as he could see beyond the rim of Molokai. Off to his left he could just make out the long stretch of Shipwreck Beach on Lanai; while through the window he could pick out the hundred-story arcologies—self-contained cities of a hundred thousand or more—along Hanauma Bay on Oahu. Beyond Hanauma was Diamond Head, the dormant volcanic crater that formed the Imperial Palace enclosure.

Randall Boyd hadn't made many visits to the Imperial presence and hadn't been here since the message from High Lord Ke'erl HeYen revealing the dark path to the Solar Emperor. This time, he was sure, his summons to the emperor's presence was likely due to the performance of the High Lord on broadcast 3-V. The Imperial ambassador on Zor'a had been called in and given a briefing on the High Lord's medical condition but the High Chamberlain, who had given the briefing, had been carefully and deliberately vague about the actual pronouncements.

The reason for this was simple. Once it reached diplomatic ears on Zor'a, rumors would fly in all directions. Obviously the emperor believed there was more to the story and that it could be kept under wraps somehow here on Oahu. The High Chamberlain's instructions on the point had been succinct and vague: *"Tell the emperor all that he is able to comprehend."* It was about what Boyd would have expected from *ha* T'te'e.

The overhead light went off, indicating that the shuttle was secure. He stood and moved toward the exit, briefcase in hand.

As Boyd floated toward the tarmac he was struck with the balmy, humid air of Hawaii. It was a marked change from the damp and chilly rainstorm he had left behind in Genève. At the bottom, Mya'ar HeChra, the High Lord's *esGyu'u* (literally "talon"; but, in translation, "ambassador") to the court of the emperor, was waiting for him.

"My old friend," Boyd said, followed by a ritual greeting phrase in the Highspeech. Mya'ar extended taloned hands to grasp Boyd's forearms.

"Good health to you, *se* Randall," Mya'ar replied. They began to walk across the tarmac toward the domed entrance to the Imperial enclosure.

"So, *se* Mya'ar. Bring me up-to-date."

"Ah." The zor let his wings flutter a bit. "As you can well imagine, the emperor is most disturbed by the remarks of the High Lord, and his . . ."

". . . indiscretions."

"I suppose you might call them that, yes. The broadcast was closely scrutinized and a close advisor to the Throne has made a rather astute observation: that *se* Sergei was unarmed when he returned to the High Nest. The explanation of the High Chamberlain was rather obtuse, at least by *naZora'i* standards. I am not sure why, but I expect *ha* T'te'e has his reasons. Your visit to Genève and your summons to the emperor's presence will only compound the uproar."

Randall smiled; Mya'ar had not meant it to sound so much like an accusation. "It didn't seem like the sort of thing best broadcast for anyone to overhear. What's more, I don't think *ha* T'te'e cares very much about what sort of uproar he causes."

"If the emperor receives you in open court, *se* Randall, and begins asking questions, the answers will be on the 'net in a few sixty-fourths of a sun.

"I do not expect the emperor to do this, but I am sure you will be interrogated just as I was. I was questioned at length about *se* Commodore Laperriere, *si* Commander HeYen and the Cicero matter. I had little to report and no specific orders regarding the path I should fly. I assume you are better informed."

"I have the whole story," Boyd said, patting his briefcase.

"What will you tell them? The emperor will ask you to reveal everything, since you are, after all, a human first and a servant of the High Nest second." Mya'ar's wings changed configuration, revealing a note of irony in his comment.

Boyd smiled. "They will not like what they hear."

"Will that change your story, my friend?"

"No, I don't think so. Someone's got to tell the emperor what's going on; that's why there's an envoy."

"And an *esGyu'u*."

"And an *esGyu'u*," Randall agreed.

The ⊔⊓⊏⊏ brought them down to a large sunroom set into the cliffs of Diamond Head. The room was constructed on a gentle curve, sweeping over several dozen meters, and was tiled in a cream-colored marble. The permaglas windows gave a breathtaking view of the Pacific Ocean. The rays of afternoon sun honeyed the tile and cast a long shadow from the man waiting to receive them.

"*hi* Emperor," Mya'ar said, inclining his head.

"Your Highness," Randall added. He glanced beyond the emperor; there were several servants hovering at a respectful distance, but a small glowing pin on the emperor's lapel indicated that a privacy shield was active—sound and vision were blurred beyond a few meters.

It meant the emperor was concerned about the subject to be discussed, and that he had absolute trust in the two people with whom he would be discussing it. Both facts sent a message.

"So good of you to join me," the emperor said at last. "I'm sorry I haven't been able to speak with you recently."

"I thank Your Highness for his time," Boyd replied.

"I understand that there is some explanation for the incident we recently witnessed at A'alu Spaceport," the emperor said, directly to the point. "Perhaps you can elucidate."

"I'm . . . not sure where to begin, sire."

"We are at war, young man, and the High Nest is our ally . . . I presume?"

"Very much so, Your Highness. We have a common enemy."

"The . . . *esGa'uYal*, I suppose you would say."

"The aliens, sire. They are one and the same."

"And they have the zor sword of state?"

"Yes, sire, they do."

"Ah. Now we progress." The emperor looked out across the ocean. The sun dappled his features. "I assume that the *Gyaryu'har*—Mr. Torrijos—is in his present condition because of the absence of this talisman?"

"That is correct, sire."

"And it was taken while he was at Cicero?"

"Yes, Your Highness, when the aliens took control of Cicero Down."

The emperor turned and fixed Boyd with a glance, a frown deepening on his face. "Then answer me this, Envoy. I am aware that Torrijos was sent to Cicero—'placed upon the dark path,' I believe the High Lord said at the time—because of a dream. But if Torrijos is important to the High Nest and the sword is important to Torrijos, then why in the hell was it left in harm's way long enough for it to be actually *captured*? It doesn't make any sense to me. I am ready for my explanation now."

Boyd took a breath and considered the answer he would give. He had known this question would be posed; it was a matter of deciding how he would respond.

"The High Nest chose to send the *Gyaryu'har* to Cicero precisely so this would happen. It was expecting that the sword would be taken, sire—indeed, the High Nest did not expect *se* Sergei to survive at all."

"They sent him *to die*?"

"He is a warrior, Your Highness."

"He is in a *coma*, Envoy. This entire matter is insane. It's some part of an insane plan from an insane High Lord."

"I wish it were that simple, Your Highness."

The emperor turned away from the High Nest envoy to look at the zor who shared the private interview. Mya'ar stood unmoving on the perch.

"Enlighten me."

"Insane or not, Your Highness, the High Lord Ke'erl knew *with certainty* that there was grave and imminent danger. It was felt there was no one who would accept this information . . . considering its source."

"I have . . . read the reports of the commander at Cicero, and reviewed the Admiralty investigation. I believe this information has been released to the Envoy's Office and to the High Chamberlain."

Boyd nodded in agreement.

"Does all of this correspond to the knowledge that the High Lord possesses?"

"It confirms a number of things, sire. It portrays the aliens as inimical, both to mankind and to the People. It shows them to be powerful Sensitives with abilities whose strength and scope far outweigh ours— they can portray or perhaps even assume the form of other beings.

There's every reason to believe this has been done already."

"Meaning—"

"There might be aliens disguised as humans or zor already within the Empire. Perhaps even here at court or in the High Nest. There is no way to know."

The emperor paled at that statement, as if the full understanding of its meaning had just descended upon him.

"Already."

"The High Chamberlain believes that to be the case, sire. If the infiltration of Cicero had not been accidentally discovered, this might never have even been suspected."

"We are already lost," the emperor said softly.

"Not if Qu'u returns," Mya'ar interjected. It was the first comment he had made during the entire conversation, and it caused both the emperor and the envoy to look at him.

"I assume," the emperor said, after a moment, to Boyd without looking away from the zor, "that *you* understand what he means."

"The hero who will recover the sword placed in the possession of the aliens is the only hope for both races. It is why the sword was allowed to be captured: The High Lord believed that circumstances would call forth a new hero, a new Qu'u."

"And has this happened?"

"The High Nest is satisfied that it has, sire," Boyd said.

"Who would this 'hero' be?"

Boyd told him; and as the emperor sat and listened, he seemed overwhelmed by the complexity of the thing. The envoy, for his part, felt it necessary to clarify the process by which the choice had come to pass. Boyd thought that hearing a description of the sequence of events from the zor point of view must seem surreal; it was as if the emperor's hold on the whole situation had been uprooted and set adrift, with nothing to hang on to. Gambling the entire Empire as well as the People on a single toss was no less unnerving, especially since the emperor himself had no consent in, and no control over, the outcome.

Six hours later, a high-priority shuttle arrived at Honolulu Port from halfway around the globe. It was met by a 'copter at a private pad, already mostly occupied by a human and a rashk. The rashk, a lizard with six limbs, was wearing something that looked like a tent-sized purple silk bathrobe with the Imperial Intelligence emblem over the breast; he spread across two normal human-sized seats and had to incline his head to fit his two-meter-high frame into the compartment.

After the briefest of greetings, the prime minister—who had come all the way from Genève at his emperor's summons—boarded the 'copter, which took off and flew toward the 'Iolani Palace in central Honolulu, a few flying-minutes away.

"Thank you for responding so quickly, Ahmad," the prime minister said, when the 'copter was in the air. "I'd rather have you here in person than just on comm."

"It's blind luck." The director of Imperial Intelligence, a portly, middle-aged man, was not as familiar a face as the prime minister—most citizens on the street wouldn't have picked him out of a crowd of Imperial bureaucrats. Which was, of course, just as he wanted it. "If M'm'e'e Sha'kan and I weren't already in New Los Angeles instead of out at Langley, David, comm is all you'd have gotten."

The rashk, M'm'e'e Sha'kan, said nothing but sat stolidly, his four arms slowly weaving some pattern. In fact, he seemed to be asleep, head bent toward his chest—except that his middle eye was cracked slightly open, as if following the conversation.

"I think it'll be best for us to brief the emperor together."

"Meaning you'd be just as happy not to do it alone."

The prime minister didn't answer.

"By the way, David, I agree. Do you know what the representatives of the High Nest had to say to the emperor?"

"It was a private conversation." The prime minister folded his hands and looked out across the Pacific Ocean at the glorious sunset. *Beats the hell out of the sunsets over Lac Lèman,* he thought.

"My question remains."

"Yes, of course I know. It told us very little we don't already know—the High Nest arranged for the sword to be taken away, but has sent the Cicero commander to retrieve it."

"An unlikely choice," the director said.

" 'Of the ocean, a wave a part only is,' " rumbled the rashk. Both men turned to look at him.

"Rashk proverb," the director explained.

"Meaning—"

"Meaning is," M'm'e'e Sha'kan said, stopping the movement of his arms, "that we not the entire pattern perceive can; says not that there no pattern is. For zor People, water deep is, ocean wide is." Two of his arms landed with a slap on his thighs, muffled through his hydrating robe.

"Still," the director said, "we've been working on this since Cicero was evacuated. It's clear that the zor have an end in mind—but we just can't see what it is."

"His Highness won't be happy with that answer."

"David, *no one* knows how the zor think. They—"

"Zor know, how think zor," M'm'e'e Sha'kan said. "Time it is, *them* to ask."

"The *emperor* asked them," the prime minister said, turning on the rashk. "Do you know what they said about our commodore? 'She climbs the Perilous Stair.' What in *hell* does *that* mean?"

"In legend—" M'm'e'e began, but the prime minister held up his hand. Both of the rashk's left hands rose to mimic the gesture.

"No," the prime minister said. The rashk's pairs of arms began to move in weaving patterns again. "In the *real world,*" the prime minister continued, "they know where she is—where is it?"

"Some data available is," the rashk answered quietly.

"Oh?"

"We know that Laperriere was aboard Crossover Station," the director said, "and that her exec—"

"Hyos," M'm'e'e interjected.

"Ch'k'te HeYen," the director said, frowning. "Her exec was killed aboard the station and Commodore Laperriere left somehow. She was clearly *not* afterward aboard the merchanter that took her there."

"And we know that because—"

"Because, David, that ship has been recalled to active service and is part of Admiral Hsien's command. Laperriere is *not* aboard."

"Has anyone thought to ask the captain of this merchanter what happened?"

"I don't believe anyone in Hsien's command is aware of Laperriere. She and HeYen boarded the ship under assumed names."

"A human and a zor traveling together might attract some attention, you'd think," the prime minister said. He looked out the 'copter's window; they were just crossing the Nimitz gevway by Aloha Tower— 'Iolani Palace was not far away.

"They were both gone by the time this ship was called to service. Laperriere is gone—and honestly, no one knows where she is."

"The emperor isn't going to like that answer, either."

The 'Iolani Palace was just ahead; the 'copter was beginning its descent toward the pad on the roof.

"Then we'll have to come up with some more questions," the director said.

M'm'e'e Sha'kan said nothing, but merely waved his arms in pairs, his face reflecting the last light of day.

Two hundred and fifty parsecs away, the High Lord felt the configuration of the Plain of Despite begin to resolve into a new pattern.

As he dreamed, the tiny shred of self that had not been consumed by the madness of knowledge fought to hold on, talons extended, wings forming the Stance of Defiant Anger. The *esGa'uYal* were beginning to stir.

chapter 5

THE LEGEND OF QU'U (continued)

STEP BY STEP AND ONE CLAWHOLD OVER ANOTHER,
THE LONE HERO QU'U CLIMBED THE LAST SEVERAL
SIXTY-FOURS OF WINGSPANS, COMING AT LAST IN   [Cloak Against Despite]
SIGHT OF THE FORTRESS OF DESPITE. LIGHTNINGS
CASCADED ACROSS THE TURRETS, HIGHLIGHTING THE
PROFILE OF THE BATTLEMENTS WITH FIERY LIGHT.

QU'U DID NOT BELIEVE THAT HE APPROACHED   [Eyes of *esGa'u*]
UNNOTICED. THE ENCOUNTER WITH *ENGA'E'REN* HAD
CONVINCED HIM THAT SERVANTS OF THE DECEIVER
WERE EVERYWHERE IN THE PLAIN OF DESPITE.

INDEED, HE THOUGHT TO HIMSELF. *HOW CAN I HOPE
TO PREVAIL IF DESPITE CAN COMMAND SO MANY
ALLIES? WHAT WILL CONFRONT ME NOW?*

The esGa'uYal are beginning to stir, the voice in Jackie's mind said, as
she drifted between sleeping and waking.

"I don't want to hear it," she said, and burrowed farther beneath the
blanket. Her voice seemed to echo across a great distance, as if she were
on the top of a high mountain. The words were broken apart and carried away by the wind . . .

• • •

The wind blew around her, whistling through the holes in her cloak where, if she were one of the People, her wings would have gone. From where she stood she could see the ghoulish shadows of the rocky, icy Plain far below. The huge mass of the Fortress of Despite towered above her; the glow of her *chya* seemed almost feeble by comparison. Ch'k'te, his ethereal, almost transparent body hunched against the extreme cold, and Th'an'ya, her aura glowing faintly blue, stood by, as if waiting for Jackie to take action.

"We have come so far, *se* Jackie," Th'an'ya said over the sound of the wind, though she did not seem to be raising her voice. "You must complete the legend."

It was incongruous: Jackie knew that on the Perilous Stair, Qu'u was alone—in the legend, he spoke of being the "lone hero."

"I *must*?" She held up her *chya* and even Th'an'ya stepped back. "We have gone through all kinds of hell for that damned sword. I have followed my instincts and my abilities; I have been as close to Qu'u as I could be: I have faced demons and shadows. I have climbed the Perilous Stair and now you're telling me that I have to . . . I have to 'transcend the Outer Peace'? I've come all this way to commit suicide?"

"In the legend," Ch'k'te said, the wind almost taking his voice away, "Qu'u knows that it is his duty to confront *esGa'u* the sorcerer and take the *gyaryu* from the Fortress." He gestured toward the castle. "It is why we are here. *esLiHeYar, se* Jackie."

"If we're correct," she heard herself say, "we're really standing outside the fortress of the leader of the aliens, Ch'k'te. She'll drop us back into reality, whatever the hell *that* means. Then she'll rip my head off.

"You're already dead and Th'an'ya is no more than a *hsi*-image in my mind, so you two have nothing to worry about. Qu'u was made immortal by the Lord *esLi* because he was willing to let *esGa'u* rip *his* head off. I have no guarantee that the Lord *esLi* will do the same for me."

Th'an'ya's sharp intake of breath was audible even above the storm.

Keeping the Fortress visible in the corner of her eye, Jackie made her way along the ledge to Th'an'ya's glowing form. "What is it, Th'an'ya? Does my lack of faith disturb you? Did you think that searching for the *gyaryu* would truly transform me somehow? I may be the heir of Qu'u, but I am *not* Qu'u himself. I may serve the People in this quest, but I am not one of the People. I *cannot* be one.

"I will not walk in there and destroy myself for no purpose. One of the People might be willing to do that, but I am not."

As the three figures watched, the lightning illuminated the great Fortress in pale light, and it seemed in that moment to resemble nothing less than a huge caricature of the aliens she had met at Crossover and at Cicero. As she looked at it, unable to turn away, she saw the great hinged doors of the tower opening, revealing a ghastly cerulean light that surrounded—

The broken hilt of Ch'k'te's *chya* was in her hand and held up in front of her as she sat bolt upright in her bed, with no sound but the regular crooning of the ship's systems and the beating of her own heart.

She looked around the room, viewing the scene as if for the first time, like some sort of 3-V documentary. She kicked the bedcovers away from her feet and swung her legs over the side of the sleeping-pallet, keeping the hilt at the ready.

Nothing happened. Slowly, she let her mind concentrate on the dream that still echoed in her mind.

"Ch'k'te," she said, and then cursed, placing the vivid image of her friend crouching in the storm beside the terrible sight of his corpse on the deck at Crossover. For just a moment, she felt the slightest additional warmth from the grip of the *chya* but then it was gone.

She laid it on the bed beside her and quickly dressed, discarding the idea of further sleep. As she was pulling on a boot she became aware of someone else in the room and looked up to see Th'an'ya watching her.

"You don't even come when I call now. You just appear."

"I come when I am called," she answered.

"But I—"

"I come when I am called." Th'an'ya perched on a low stool nearby. "The servants of Despite are stirring, and all-out war is not far away. This part of our journey, also, is nearing its end; the *gyaryu* is very close."

"We're still in jump."

"At the moment, we are. The ship's chronometer indicates that we have less than half a sun before we emerge."

"Where?"

"Near the top of the Perilous Stair, *se* Jackie."

Th'an'ya said it matter-of-factly, though Jackie knew that she must have shared the dream. She shrugged and pulled on the other boot and then stood up, absently tucking the *chya*-hilt into her belt. Her mouth felt as if she'd swallowed a liter of polymer lubricant and her head still echoed with the wind from her dream.

"I wouldn't go up to the Fortress of Despite in the dream, Th'an'ya. I refused, even though you and Ch'k'te—" Her voice wavered for a moment. "Even though you and Ch'k'te told me that I must. What does it mean? Will I be unable to complete this quest after all of this preparation?"

"No one can answer that question, not even you. It is therefore pointless even to ask it at this stage."

"Great." She walked past Th'an'ya's image into the main compartment, glancing at the forward screen for a moment. It displayed *anGa'e'ren*: the utterdark of jump, with no features or interruptions. "So now I'm even denied access to self-doubt."

She ordered something to drink from the autokitchen and turned to the galley table to sit down. Th'an'ya was already perched opposite, her wings held in a position that denoted a slight confusion.

"What's the matter?" she asked the zor. "Can't read my wings?"

"Your mood is difficult to understand. It is clear that there is great danger approaching, scarcely hours away, yet your mind does not appear to be focused on the quest."

Jackie looked up, half smiling. "I think even Ch'k'te would laugh to hear you carp like that. I've read the legends. From what I can see, the great hero Qu'u didn't spend a lot of time 'focusing on the quest.' He and his loyal companions just bumbled around like *artha* in the mist, waiting for the next test of their courage or strength, until they found themselves divinely guided to the object of their travels.

"This time it's different somehow because I have this cryptic pattern to follow. 'What are we doing?' I ask. 'Going to the Plain of Despite to recover the *gyaryu*,' you answer. 'How do we get there?' 'We go to the Center.' Then, once we do that and I manage to defeat the guardian of the Stair at the mere cost of the only living being I can completely trust, I am mysteriously able to escape onto the next talon of my quest, the path neatly laid out for me. I hurtle forward, waiting for the next test of my courage or strength, until I find myself divinely guided . . .

"Beginning to get the idea? I mean, *really*, Th'an'ya. I'm angry, I'm depressed, I'm full of self-doubt. I'm not sleeping well, I feel like I have a hell of a hangover, and I don't know whether I'll even know what to do when the time comes. I may not even know it if it hits me over the head. As helpful as you've been to me, you still talk in riddles. I don't know if I completely understand them.

"How in *esLi*'s name am I supposed to get focused? I don't have an 'Inner Peace' to concentrate on, wings to speak with . . . I don't even have a damn *chya*." She took the broken sword from her belt and tossed it onto the table—finely hewn metal clattering on plastic in the silence—as Jackie rested her chin on her folded hands and looked up at Th'an'ya's image.

You will know, the voice within her mind said.

"All right," she said, standing up suddenly and pushing her seat back. "I've had just about enough of *that,* too."

Th'an'ya backed away slightly, her wings arranged in a defensive posture.

"While we're being so blasted honest, it's about time the origin of that voice revealed itself." She strode out of the kitchen area into the main cabin and held her arms wide. She turned around and faced away from the forward screen. "Come on. If Th'an'ya can show herself, so can you."

Th'an'ya faded into existence beside her. "The voice is not a *hsi*-image within your mind, as I am," she said softly.

"What is it, then?"

"Concentrate," Th'an'ya answered. It was really no answer at all.

Jackie looked from her to the blank wall and then back again, as if considering the word, and what she meant by it.

Jackie closed her eyes, and let her arms fall to her sides. *All right, then,* she thought. *Whoever you are, whatever you are, I'm listening. I've been listening since you first spoke to me at Cicero, when Bryan Noyes tried to take me apart.*

Show yourself. Man or zor, rashk, otran or alien, I want to see you now.

She heard a sharp intake of breath beside her. Slowly she opened her eyes to look at the blank wall. An image hovered in midair. It was not a person but rather an object: one she had seen before, stretched across the lap of an old, old man visiting her in her quarters at Cicero.

It hung point-down, its hilt at about the level of her forehead. It was black like a piece of obsidian, and chased with *hRni'i* too delicate and too faint to read from several meters away, but it glowed with an inner light that seemed to highlight the decorations and drown out the internal illumination of the ship's compartment. The image of the *gyaryu* was not completely opaque: She could make out the far wall through it, as if it were a hologram projected from some distant location.

She took a step forward and then another and another, until it was at arm's length: She could reach out and touch the image if she wished but she didn't dare, fearing that it might suddenly vanish.

It was quiet other than the sounds of the ship. The image of the sword hovered like a taunt; then it faded away entirely. She waved her hand in the space where it had been, but it had left nothing behind.

Jackie slumped into a seat and ran a hand through her hair.

"It's the sword," she said to herself. "The voice has been coming from the sword itself—ever since Cicero. Ever—since—Cicero." She balled her fists. "Now, the ten-thousand-credit question: Did the High Nest know this would happen, too?"

Th'an'ya did not answer. Jackie stood and walked slowly to her image, which stood quietly in place, her hand gripping the polished wood staff, her wings raised politely.

"Tell me you knew about this, too."

"I did not," Th'an'ya answered. "We did not foresee that the *gyaryu* itself would communicate with you. When you revealed that a voice was speaking with you—one well versed in our culture—I thought—I assumed—"

"*esLi.*"

". . . Yes, *se* Jackie. I thought that you might be receiving messages from the Lord of the Golden Circle, and I thought . . ."

Jackie turned away from Th'an'ya and ran a hand through her hair again. "I'm walking into the Fortress of Despite, Th'an'ya. I've read and studied what we know about the alien that used to drive this rig. There is *no* chance that I can replace him. *It.* Whatever."

"There is no choice, *se* Jackie. If you can convince others that *you* are R'se—"

"And what's the chance of *that*?" She turned to face Th'an'ya again. "R'se was . . . Let me see: a 'Deathguard.' That rated him pretty high up in the hierarchy. He was some kind of independent operative, reporting directly to the High Queen."

"*Great* Queen."

"Great Queen." Jackie corrected herself. "R'se had come to Crossover to get Qu'u. To get *me,* except that it thought Ch'k'te was Qu'u. After all, he was the Sensitive, and he was one of the People." She picked up the *chya*-hilt from the table and looked at it as if she'd never seen it before. "We're betting the entire future of both races on the thin hope that R'se wasn't able to fire off some sort of message. Because if he did, there'll be a welcoming committee for me when this bucket comes out of jump. If we're wrong, I'm dead, or worse. And so are *you*." She pointed at Th'an'ya's image; her zor companion's wings rose slightly in alarm. "This is a hell of a chance you're taking, unless you know something you haven't told me."

Th'an'ya did not answer.

"Damn it—you *do* know something."

"No," Th'an'ya answered. "I do not know anything that is pertinent to this discussion. I believe that *esLi* protects us, *se* Jackie, and His talons have guided our path thus far. He would not have placed your foot upon the Perilous Stair without a reasonable chance of success against the Lord of Despite."

"Have faith, you say. *Very* comforting. I'm betting my life on your faith."

"I have already bet *my* life on it, *se* Jackie. You need not remind me of the stakes. Recall what you were told in *Ur'ta leHssa*: Once you have set your foot upon the Perilous Stair, there is no way to turn back. When this vessel reaches its destination, you must take the role that circumstances give you."

"Whether I want it or not."

"Most certainly. I will be here to help you as long as I can."

"Until . . ."

Th'an'ya looked past Jackie to the empty wall where the image of the *gyaryu* had been. "Until the will of *esLi* determines otherwise. I cannot see the end of this flight, *se* Jackie."

A comm-squirt is transmitted using essentially the same technology that permits ships to travel over interstellar distances: The data packet is transmitted across normal-space and then is transitioned to jump in a given direction for a given amount of time, after which it emerges at its destination. Since its mass is effectively zero, the speed of transmission is significantly higher than that of a jump-capable vessel.

The comm-packet that Commodore Jonathan Durant sent out from Adrianople was aimed at Denneva, the closest Imperial naval base. While there was no way to reach Admiral Hsien in jump, the warning of events at Adrianople should have been enough to bring reinforcements to relieve the base from the aliens.

Except that the squirt never left Adrianople System. Disrupted, dispersed and deserialized, it dissipated into interstellar space and was never launched into jump at all.

Gibraltar emerged into normal-space just a few milliseconds ahead of the rest of Admiral Hsien's command. It was not a lack of precision—jumps were timed down to the microsecond, after all—it was a desire on the part of *Gibraltar*'s commander, Dame Alexandra Quinn, to always be *leading* when she carried the admiral's flag.

Admiral César Hsien stood motionless on the bridge, watching the pilot's board record the incoming vessels and register the transponder codes of ships already in Adrianople System.

"Have we received clearing from traffic control?"

"It's just coming in now, Admiral," Captain Quinn said.

"Fine. Keep me informed," he said, walking into his ready-room. There was no need to supervise *Gibraltar*'s progress into the gravity well; the officers and crew could handle the mundane details while he reviewed reports.

Hsien often found himself pausing and imagining the universe as he had first seen it as a young ensign fifty years ago, when his honored grandfather was still making speeches in the Imperial Assembly. Grandfather Tomás had been a bit shocked but still mostly pleased to have a scion of his family attend the Naval Academy; he would have been duly impressed that young César had risen to the rank of admiral.

For the admiral's part, he believed he'd grown accustomed to it but had never really lost the wonder associated with travel among the stars.

He could see it now as he laid down his stylus and closed his eyes: the long streamers of silver resolving themselves into points of starry light, the transponder racing to catch up with the insystem traffic, the navigation station giving location while helm got control, the ship raising its defensive fields as a precaution against some surprise attack lurking near the jump point—

His reverie was interrupted by a comm signal. He opened his eyes and said, "Yes?"

"Incoming comm from Adrianople Starbase, Admiral. Commodore Durant."

"What does he want? We've been cleared to enter the gravity well, correct?"

"We have, Admiral. The commodore did not give a reason for his comm."

"Very well," Hsien said. "Put him through." He gestured to the ready-room table and displayed a small version of the pilot's board over it; to its right, a holo faded into view, showing the command bridge of the starbase. Jonathan Durant sat in his chair—*a bit nervous,* Hsien thought to himself. He didn't know Durant well. *Couldn't be afraid of an admiral, now, could he?*

"Durant," he said. "What can I do for you?"

"I'm just checking in, sir," Durant answered. Behind him, officers moved to and fro, attending to the business of the base. "I hope your jump was uneventful."

"On time and precise, Commodore. Fair winds and calm seas." None of that applied, of course—it was airy metaphor.

"Good. Glad to hear it, sir. I . . . assume that all of your command has arrived within Adrianople System as well."

Hsien looked irritably from Durant to the pilot's-board display. *Gibraltar* and her seven sister-ships were all clustered in formation, headed into the gravity well; and there was another marker from a ship that had just recently transited from jump. The transponder code marked it as a zor ship, which struck Hsien as strange.

He leaned forward to comm the bridge of the *Gibraltar* to ask about it; but as he did so, his eyes traveled across the display to notice two other ships boosting toward the position of his squadron.

"Durant," he began to say, as he noticed the mass signatures and indicated sizes of the vessels—bigger than anything in his command; indeed bigger than anything he'd ever seen before—when, all of a sudden, the strangest feeling came over him.

The room seemed more dimly lit than he liked. The chair itself was uncomfortable, forcing him to sit upright, a posture to which he was unaccustomed.

The squareness of the hatchway doors struck him next. Rather than being round and smooth, worn from the passage of countless bodies, they were angular and much bigger than they needed to be; indeed, the entire chamber was large, with altogether too much room for a single . . . a single—

A single individual, he felt himself prompting.

But the admiral, raised on the huge empty grasslands of western Canada on Earth's North American continent, was disturbed by the images coming forth in his mind: They consisted of many bodies rubbing close together in the narrow confines of a single chamber, one chamber among thousands, all of them sharing each other's workspace and yet cooperating harmoniously because they shared each other's surface thoughts—

Oh

—In comparison, his mind seemed to reel at the idea of such open expanse under a dim, cold yellow sun, though the idea of Alberta's sunny plains had always been comforting to him while traveling deep in space—

Oh my

—And the isolation of his mind from the hundreds of others aboard the *Gibraltar* and elsewhere in the fleet made him suddenly lonely and afraid, even though the sharing of minds never seemed to have been a priority before—

Oh my God Oh my God Oh

We are here, Admiral Hsien, a voice hissed in his mind; and he felt powerless to reply. *We have need of your primitive equipment for information. We are prepared to terminate you all* . . . (Actually, his mind reported calmly, the word "terminate" seemed to imply the concept of feeding to the young, usually while still alive.) . . . *if you oppose us, and to treat you with at least minimal respect if you cooperate.*

Choose now, Admiral Hsien.

He reached to gesture at the comm but found that he could not move. He tried to cry out but found himself unable to do so. His eyes fixed forward, looking at the face of Commodore Jonathan Durant on comm; he could not look even from side to side.

How pitiable a creature, the voice said. *Why should we even bother? Better to use our* k'th's's *on more pliable targets.* His enhanced understanding gave him no image of what a *k'th's's* might be, but he wasn't anxious to find out.

Hsien found himself watching and listening as the captain of the *Gibraltar* changed its course toward the two huge enemy ships. He heard his own voice giving similar commands to the other ships in the fleet.

Suddenly he felt a presence in the room and a faint stirring, like a breeze blowing through an open window. He could not raise his head to see, but he felt, and heard, something gliding across the deck toward where he sat, immobilized, feeling like a fly trapped in the spider's web, waiting to be consumed . . .

Ann Sorenson, His Majesty's Consul on Cle'eru Four, turned away from packing her office when the door chimed. With staff already gone, there was no one to filter visitors; but Security was still on duty, so it would not be anyone dangerous.

"Come," she said, returning to the onerous job of separating useful from useless.

Hansie Sharpe stepped into her office, one hand holding a handkerchief with which he was mopping his brow. "Beastly hot," he said to no one in particular, darting his eyes from place to place in the room and taking in the whole scene.

"I'm afraid the Imperial bureaucracy puts little emphasis on personal comfort," the consul answered. She took her seat behind the desk, stacked with piles of documents. "I can offer you a drink, though, Hansie."

"No, quite all right," he answered, taking a chair opposite. He looked nervous and on edge. "It's true, then."

"What's true?"

"The Empire is pulling out of Cle'eru."

"I wouldn't exactly say that. It's more a question of changing to wartime status."

" 'Wartime status.' And with whom are we at war?"

"You know I'm not at liberty—"

"Ann, my dear," Hansie interrupted. "Do me the courtesy of dropping diplomatic pretense. We've known each other and—I thought—been friends since you came to Cle'eru six, or was it seven, years ago?"

"Six."

"Six, then. I think you would have to acknowledge that I am among the leading citizens of this world, and as such have a right to know at what risk the colony is being placed."

"I suppose you do." She folded her hands in front of her on the desk. "However, I am under orders not to volunteer any information. You're not looking to set our longtime friendship against my duty to His Imperial Majesty, are you, Hansie? Because you must know my choice."

"I . . . accept that, Ann. On the other hand, if you could confirm or deny information I already possessed, you wouldn't be violating your orders not to volunteer anything, would you?"

"Well, I . . ."

"I thought you might see it that way," he said, beaming as if he'd scored a debating point. "Now, Ann, dear, you needn't tell me anything—merely answer yes or no. Fair?"

"I . . . suppose so." *It'll be the easiest way to get him out of my hair,* she thought.

"Now." He adjusted his sprawl in her chair. "We are presently at war, correct?"

"Yes."

"And our opponent . . . is not some faction within the Empire, nor is it bandits outside our borders. It's someone—no, *something* else. A new alien race."

". . . Yes, though I'd like to know your source."

"Ah." Hansie gave a carnivorous smile. "That would be telling. May I continue?"

"Please do."

"Our zor friends have their wings all aflutter about this business and I understand they knew something about it long before it began to happen."

"Yes," she answered.

"Excellent." He sat forward and placed his carefully manicured hands palms-down on her desk. "Now, tell me, Ann, my dear: Isn't it true that the naval officer that passed through here only a few weeks ago—Commodore Laperriere—is wrapped up in this, too?"

The question was so out of character with the previous line of inquiry that it caught her completely by surprise. She remembered the woman as well: a career-officer type, Regular Navy . . . except that she was working closely with the zor. Ann had had a bit of an exchange with her.

Hansie knew something. What was it?

"That's classified, Hansie. I'm afraid I can't go into it."

"I knew it. I knew it!" He flopped back into the chair. "I *smelled* something." He tapped the side of his nose. "Never fails, my dear. All right, let me take this a step further. Even the old zor sage S'reth is gone, bag and baggage. We both know how insular the zor are here and how proud they are of their development"—he jerked a thumb in the air—"up there. S'reth has been here practically since the world was settled, more than seventy years ago, and it looks like he's not coming back.

"Everything I hear says that S'reth is not the only such zor to have departed this planet. Most of the ones that left seemed to be heading for the zor Core Stars, clear to the other side of the Empire.

"I know for a fact"—he tapped a finger on Ann Sorenson's desk—"that Laperriere met with S'reth less than three days before she left. Now *she*'s gone, *he*'s gone, and *you're* going home as well. Something's going to happen here on Cle'eru, isn't it? There's going to be some kind of attack."

"I don't know that to be true."

"Ann, my entire *life* is here. Everything I own is here. Everything I *am* is here. I must know.

"Are we going to be attacked? Is Cle'eru safe?"

"Hansie." Ann looked away, at a pile of papers—anything to not meet his eyes. "I don't know if Cle'eru is safe; I don't know if *anywhere* is safe. We're—" She looked at him then, a pained look in her eyes. "We're all in danger."

"What are you telling me?"

"More than I should. Look here, Hansie, I have a lot of work to do—"

"What about the defense squadron, Ann?" Hansie stood up, turned away, and then seemed to round on her. "They jumped out of here. Where did they go? Has the Empire abandoned Cle'eru already?"

"I can't tell you where they've gone."

"Can't? Or won't?"

"I don't see as it matters. That information is classified, Hansie, and you knew that when you came in the door. If your sources are so damned good, maybe *you* should tell *me*. Now, I really do have work to do and I don't have much time to do it." She returned her attention to her desk.

"Not much time."

She looked up at him. She didn't really know what to say to Hansie Sharpe; she'd always been a gracious host, pleasant company on a distant posting. She wanted to reassure him somehow, even though it was annoying to have to deal with him at all. Ann didn't really feel she owed him anything, but still . . .

"No. Not much time at all."

Hansie looked down at the floor and seemed about to reply. He started, stopped again and finally said, "Well, I suppose some information is better than none. I suppose I have a lot to do, as well."

chapter 6

The navcomp guided the small ship into Center System. The ship's ID was recognized by traffic control without Jackie's intervention; it slid into the surprisingly busy pattern headed into the gravity well. The majority of the vessels were small ones moving at high g—clearly robot ships—doing mining and materials transport in the outer system. It fit with what she'd read in the ship's database about Center: a society based on the veneration of mechanization and automation. It explained why there were so many ships in the pattern.

As the ship found its way into the inner system, she could feel a dark and hollow rhythm: presences, powerful and malign, lurking just within perceptible range.

The esGa'u'Yal *are here,* she thought. *The ones who took Cicero.* *Minus one.*

The navcomp gave her a good fix on the location of the primary; she was somewhere over two hundred parsecs from Sol System, and at least thirty from her departure point at Crossover. Right ascension and declination placed her near the galactic equator, a quarter-turn spinward from galactic center. From Sol System, Center's star would appear in the constellation of Orion. She could locate Betelgeuse, Alnitak, Rigel, Alnilam and other bright stars in that constellation; Center was just another anonymous, dim star as seen from Sol System—or Dieron System, for that matter.

It is on the Perilous Stair, the voice admonished her.

Oh, shut up, she told it, as the ship descended into the gravity well.

The ship was able to enter the atmosphere and had landing clearance already approved; it was clearly expected. Navcomp informed her that this had been its last port of call before departing for Crossover nine days ago—four days before R'se and Ch'k'te had both died there.

She was expected, and right about now.

The ship settled onto the tarmac. An accessway extended out from the terminal and secured itself to the airlock hatch.

"What now?" she asked Th'an'ya.

They are expecting R'se, Th'an'ya answered, without appearing as if she had been expecting the question. *They will assume that you are the* esGa'uYe *who slew* li Ch'k'te.

"How do I convince them of that?"

There is a way, Th'an'ya answered. Jackie heard the outer airlock door cycle as the pressure equalized. *If you are feared, none will question. I will help you.*

I thought Sensitives didn't like to do that, she thought in response.

The need is great, Th'an'ya said, with a brief image of a wing-position that corresponded to a zor's shrugging of the shoulders. Jackie remembered a scene from Cicero Down, which seemed a century ago: a young Marine feeling the fear that Ch'k'te had projected.

It's not going to work, Jackie answered. *They'll see right through it.*

They will see what they expect to see, se Jackie.

The airlock door slid aside, and a man entered the main compartment of the little ship. He was a tall, thin man with deep-sunken eyes and long arms, who seemed to be wearing clothes that hardly fit him. He made a gesture to Jackie with both hands, touching each thumb together and spreading the fingers wide, and inclined his head.

"Honored One," he said. He looked around, as if expecting to see something—or someone—else. "I am K'na, of the Ninth Sept of E'esh. Your choice of guise is . . . curious."

Arrogance, Th'an'ya reminded her.

"My guise is no concern of yours," Jackie snapped. "The other one was no longer of any use."

"And the prisoners . . .?"

"Are also none of your concern."

"They are on board, I presume?" The man looked around, bowing again. "If I can be of any assistance—"

"The attempt was unsuccessful."

The man smiled—rather unpleasantly, Jackie thought—baring his teeth ferally. "I don't expect that First Drone H'mr will be happy with that."

"He will not have a choice. The situation did not develop as I expected. H'mr will have to accept it."

"I'm sure he will. You'll get a chance to explain it to him yourself when he arrives."

"He's coming . . . here?"

"In a few *vx*tori*," he answered, making a sort of glottal choke-swallow sound in the middle of the alien word. "I imagine you'll have time to arrange your *n'n'eth* before he comes. You'd better: H'mr is not patient with failure, as you know. *Especially* among *N'nr* Deathguard."

She shot an angry "Iron Maiden" look at him and he visibly cringed. "The *N'nr* Deathguard generally judge their own," she ventured. "I will remind you of that. I'm sure that H'mr is not patient with meddlers, either."

That retort seemed to work. "I meant no offense, Honored One," K'na replied, "I—"

"I will need accommodations while I am here," she interrupted him. "Can you arrange this, or must I find a *capable* functionary?"

If the man actually had been human, Jackie suspected he would be flushing with anger. Instead, whatever resentment he felt, simply came out in his voice.

"No, Honored One," he hissed. "It will be arranged." K'na made the gesture to her again, then turned away and walked toward the airlock. He looked over his shoulder once, as if he intended to add something but thought better of it, and stalked away and off the ship.

When he was well away, Jackie let out a long breath, grabbing hold of the nearest wall for support. "I've made an enemy," she said.

If I am correct, se Jackie, Th'an'ya answered, *you have not earned the enmity of anyone of importance. What is more, he believed you to be R'se.*

"For the moment."

Thus is the Perilous Stair climbed: one step at a time.

"Thanks for reminding me."

"*se Admiral.*"

Hsien's eyes were closed, but he felt his nose wrinkle at a faint antiseptic smell, mixed with a musky, sharp odor. But even the prenomen before his rank—indicating that a zor had addressed him—failed to prepare him for the first sight he had from a bed in sickbay: an ancient zor with nearly transparent wings perched on a stool beside the bed, its wings held elevated and partially encircling a tiny, frail body. He also noticed a sword at the creature's belt, though it seemed somehow different than any zor blade he had seen.

"Who—?" he managed, and realized his throat was as dry as a deck-plate. The zor reached over to a side-table and picked up a squeeze bottle, placing the straw to Hsien's lips. Despite his reluctance, the admiral drank. After a few moments he felt better.

"Who the hell are you?" he asked in a whisper.

"Your distaste for my kind is as great as rumor suggests," the zor answered. His face betrayed no expression, of course, and the admiral couldn't make much of his tone of voice, either. "Nonetheless, I would have expected a trifle more civility toward the one who has saved your life. I am S'reth. There is more to my genealogy but I suspect that you would not be truly interested at this time."

"Saved—"

"It was the will of the Lord *esLi* that our ship arrived insystem before the alien aboard your vessel was able to crush your mind like a *cthi*-fruit, *se* Admiral. With Sensitives trained to combat such attacks, we were able to force—*it*—off the *Gibraltar* and allow your ship and several other vessels to jump outsystem."

"What about . . . Adrianople?"

"I do not completely understand the question."

"Did we abandon Adrianople?"

"It makes no sense to attempt to defend something already lost, *se* Admiral. There are no friendly vessels at Adrianople System, including this one, if that is what you ask."

"That was . . . the biggest starbase on the Imperial frontier."

S'reth rearranged his wings. "It is proper to use the past tense, *se* Admiral."

Hsien tried to sit up but was overcome by a wave of vertigo and nausea so strong that he was forced to lie back. He waited for the room to stop moving and then looked at the zor again.

"What happened to it? What happened to *me*?"

"You were overcome by superior force. On your orders, your squadron launched an attack on the alien vessels in Adrianople System."

Hsien was about to protest but a memory formed in his mind: sitting motionless in the ready-room of *Gibraltar,* hearing his own voice giving orders to close with the enemy. More fleeting scenes of destruction and death began to hurtle through his consciousness like reflections in a fractured mirror, half-formed and sharp-edged. He closed his eyes but the images continued to come, swirling around him as he lay immobile, as frozen as he had been in the ready-room—

"*se* Admiral."

His eyes snapped open. "It was not—I did not—"

The old zor fluttered down from his perch. "I shall obtain something warm to drink for both of us, *se* Admiral. Your ordeal has been difficult and unpleasant; but if we have any chance of defeating the *esGa'uYal,* we must learn as much as we can from you."

Without further words and without waiting for a reply, the zor walked out of his line of sight.

Admiral Hsien's colloquy with the old zor sage lasted three Standard days. He was being lodged in a residential-looking two-room hospital suite in the medical wing of Oberon Starbase, fifteen parsecs from Adrianople. After the first few sessions and some restless sleep, he found himself more able to get up and move about. It was difficult to admit failure: Even given what he knew about the events at Cicero, Hsien had trouble bringing himself to confront the possibility that there was an enemy he couldn't fight.

There was nothing to rely on but the experiences of those who had actually fought the aliens. Accordingly, he sent for someone who had just arrived insystem and had survived the escape from Cicero.

Anything that provided respite from the careful recollection of the incident at Adrianople was welcome. Collecting his thoughts, Hsien positioned himself at a workdesk in the outer of his two rooms and beckoned to the orderly to admit the officer.

"Admiral Hsien. Captain MacEwan of the carrier *Duc d'Enghien* reporting as ordered, sir."

"MacEwan," Hsien said. "You were a part of Cicero Task Force, weren't you?"

"Yes sir." Barbara MacEwan stood unmoving opposite him; Hsien detected the slightest change of expression, as if she had not been expecting the question.

"What is the status of your carrier, Captain?"

"We are at eighty-five–percent strength, sir. Our fighter wings have suffered minor casualties and I have not yet been assigned replacements."

"I see. Tell me, MacEwan: Do you have any experience fighting these"—he gestured vaguely—"these alien ships?"

"No sir. We did not engage the invading force at Cicero, Admiral."

"I have read the report of your former superior—Commodore Laperriere. She indicated that engaging the invaders there would have been suicidal . . . Do you concur, Captain?"

"I . . . would not contravene the commodore's assessment, sir." MacEwan appeared to be choosing her words carefully.

"Very well." Hsien folded his hands in front of him on the table. "I need to have a clear understanding.

"Laperriere made a command decision several weeks ago to abandon Cicero Base. Whether that decision was justified or not, is up to her court-martial to decide, but in any case it was clearly in response to an enemy attack, perhaps similar to the one we just experienced at Adrianople." Hsien observed MacEwan carefully, but she betrayed nothing. "As I recall, the official report indicated that Commodore Laperriere redeployed the task force to Adrianople with all possible speed, contrary to established regulations regarding defense of sister ships. Have I gotten the measure of the situation to that point?"

"The commodore . . ." MacEwan looked away as if she were upset with herself. "Yes, Admiral, you are correct."

"You arrived in Adrianople short one fighter wing. Is that also correct?"

"Yes, Admiral." She was looking at him straight-on again, her eyes angry.

"Yet you followed the commodore's orders—you did not engage the enemy as you withdrew from Cicero. How did you come to lose this fighter wing?"

"I . . . They flew out of range, Admiral. They got in too close to the enemy, and . . ." MacEwan seemed unable or unwilling to continue.

"This is very important, Captain. The fighter wing flew out of range. What happened then?"

MacEwan stood roughly at attention. "I lost nine combat fighters in total, sir, including an entire fighter wing—and might have lost the

Duc d'Enghien itself—if Commodore Laperriere hadn't ordered me to stay on course and leave them behind. While I watched, the fighters in one of my squadrons turned their weapons on *each other,* and blew each other out of the sky. All but one."

Hsien let the moment of silence stretch out after she said this; then he quietly asked, "What happened to that one?"

"It went off the deep-radar. I believe it was brought aboard an enemy vessel."

"Did Commodore Laperriere expect this to happen?"

"I—I suppose she did, sir. She knew the capabilities of the aliens firsthand, Admiral, and knew that we couldn't fight them. I didn't believe her at first, and was prepared to bring the *Duc* about to—"

"Your defense of Commodore Laperriere is most touching, Captain, but—"

"Begging the admiral's pardon," MacEwan said quietly, but forceful enough to stop Hsien in his tracks. He looked up at Barbara MacEwan, standing straight upright again. "If the admiral pleases, there's something I would like to clarify."

She seemed intent on clarifying, whether it pleased him or not. He leaned back in his chair, his arms crossed in front of him.

"Go ahead, Captain."

"I'm aware, sir, that the commodore risked her career and her reputation by electing to withdraw from Cicero. At the time, most of the officers in her command questioned the wisdom of just picking up and leaving. Still, when she gave the order we assumed that she knew port from starboard, and executed it.

"Well, sir, as we were pulling out from Cicero she gave the order that no one was to change course or even come to the aid of another ship in the task force, *even* if we received contrary orders—*even if they came from her.* She had just come face-to-face with aliens capable of taking her place, capable of taking *anyone's* place. A handful of these aliens had infiltrated Cicero and came very close to taking control of it, and *no one noticed.* The High Lord's Champion, or whatever he is, was there, and they *still* managed to take control. I still don't know how she knew what to do, or how she managed to get control of Cicero long enough to evacuate it; but she saved several of His Majesty's ships and a few thousand of his subjects because she was willing to sacrifice her career to do it.

"The career and maybe even the life of Commodore Laperriere may not mean a damn thing to you, sir, but I give you my solemn oath as an officer in His Majesty's Navy, that the commodore is the reason I and my command are present at all to follow your orders. If it pleases the admiral."

The last sentence conveyed the impression that Captain MacEwan didn't really give a damn whether it "pleased" the admiral or not. It was clear she was both convinced and committed; and her willingness to stand up to the Admiral of the Red was evidence that he should take her story seriously.

Given his recent experience at Adrianople, he couldn't do otherwise.

Hsien took a long time to look her over. At last, he said, "Your comments are noted, Captain MacEwan. Given your experience at Cicero, then, how would you advise we proceed, now that Adrianople is lost?"

"I wouldn't venture to say, sir."

"*Off* the record, Captain. *I* have to defend the Solar Empire. How would you suggest I do it?"

"Sir." MacEwan again stood up straight, and looked Hsien in the eye. "If my experience is correct, Admiral, I would say we cannot defend anywhere, and that if the enemy came insystem, we might do no better than to cut and run. *Sir.*"

"If we run from here, won't they simply follow us?"

"I suppose they will, Admiral."

"Then, what you're suggesting makes no strategic sense. It's not an alternative."

"Then I thank God I am not an admiral, sir."

C aptain on the bridge."

Following habit, Georg Maartens glanced at the chrono above the pilot's board as he came down the short gangway to the center of his bridge. It showed end of jump to be just under two minutes away. His ship was about to emerge, as ordered, at Thon's Well System. Thon's Well was a dim red primary with no habitable worlds and four large gas-giants; its only importance was its location, at convenient jump distance from two large naval bases at Denneva and Oberon.

Other than its location, there was very little to recommend Thon's Well System; Maartens didn't remember ever being there before. He had no idea why his command had been ordered there, but he knew enough to follow orders—and here they were, or nearly so.

"All systems at optimum, all hands at Quarters, sir," his new exec said, as she handed him the current status comp. He took the pilot's seat and glanced quickly at status then took a moment to give *Pappenheim*'s first officer a long look.

Commander Suzanne Okome had proved herself to be an able officer during her first months aboard his ship, but Georg hadn't quite gotten used to her yet. A new second will always put his or her stamp on the departments under an XO's command—duty rosters, battle readiness, ship discipline—and Okome had gotten right to it, quickly winning the respect and trust of the ship's other officers and crew. It had been a good choice, though one he'd have rather not made . . . except that his former "first" had turned out to be—

Best not to think about that, old man, he told himself.

"Is there something wrong, Captain?" she asked.

He realized his expression must have betrayed something, and forced a smile. "No, nothing at all, Commander. Everything looks shipshape."

"Jump minus a minute-and-a-half, Skip," his navigator said, without turning.

"All departments report."

"Engineering reports green," the watch engineer answered.

"Comm is green."

"Helm is green, awaiting normal-space control."

"Nav is green; reporting jump target within oh–point–oh–oh–oh–three of designated destination space."

"Gunnery online and ready, Captain," Okome added, standing at his side.

"Good." It was a formality; he would've had warning well in advance if some system was amiss, but the pre–end-of-jump report was part of regs, especially during wartime.

With all that was happening, regs were at least something to hang on to. "You may proceed."

The chronometer counted down. There was tension on the bridge, as always: Faster-than-light travel was still imperfect and there was always a chance that the ship could emerge in a gravity well, or in atmosphere, or even fail to emerge at all—but, with the knowledge that the Empire was at war with an enemy of unknown power, entering a system where the enemy might already be present, made the tension even worse.

No one aboard the *Pappenheim* had ever seen war until just a few weeks ago. Just before they left Corcyra, Maartens had received orders for his little squadron to jump to their present destination—Thon's Well, a small outpost system fifteen parsecs from Adrianople, where they'd originally been headed. There was a conclusion to be reached, but Georg Maartens didn't really want to reach it.

"Half a minute, Skip."

"Defensive fields powered up and ready to come online, sir."

Maartens looked aside, nodding at Okome as she said it; they would go up as soon as the *Pappenheim* made transition.

The last seconds ticked away. The navigator, having received the go-ahead, began transition to normal-space; the utterdark gave way to silver streams that rapidly resolved themselves into stars. The pilot's board began to make sense of incoming signals and the comm officer worked double-time to sort out broadcast traffic.

"All squadron vessels reporting arrival, Cap'n," the comm officer said.

"Will you look at that?" Maartens said, to no one in particular, as the board began to fill with transponder codes.

In addition to four capital ships at each of the two jump points, each of the four gas giants had a small orbital station that managed traffic through the atmosphere. A squadron was deployed at each station, and *Pappenheim*'s pilot's board recorded the names of the capital ships and IDs for the support vessels.

Orbital Three: the *Prince Rupert*–class carrier *Xian Chuan,* the same class as the *Duc d'Enghien;* with two top-of-the-line *Mandela*-class starships—the ship-of-class *Mandela* and the *Nasser;* and four *Broadmoor*-class starships, the *Admiral Anderson, Edgerton, Casian* and *Tsing Liu.* The flag was aboard the *Mandela*, with Admiral Kevin Stark, based at Denneva. He was the senior officer on-station, as the *Gibraltar* did not seem to be in Thon's Well System.

Orbital Four: four *Emperor Ian*–class starships—the *Emperor Cleon, Emperor Alexander, Empress Patrice* and *Empress Louise.* This was the newest sixth-generation ship design being built at Mothallah shipyards, mostly replacing *Broadmoor*-, *Malaysia*- and *Wallenstein*-class ships. *But not all,* Maartens thought to himself: *Pappenheim* was a

Wallenstein-class ship. The *Emperor Ian*, the ship of its class, was Erich Anderson's ship; his many-times-great-grandfather was the famous Admiral Kerry Anderson who won at Aldebaran during the Six Worlds' Revolt. Anderson's command was out of Oberon.

Orbital Five: three *Hang*-class ships—*Xun Hang, Su Hang* and *Fei Hang*—and a half-dozen zor ships. Maartens didn't recognize the classes, but the tonnage info made them out to be the equivalent of sixth-generation starships. *Fei Hang* had the squadron flag; Maartens didn't recognize the name of the commander, and wasn't sure where it was based.

Orbital Six: several more zor ships. And among them . . .

"Lieutenant," Maartens said, turning to his comm officer. "Confirm that ID." He jabbed a finger at a point in the air where the transponder showed the name *Nest HeYen*.

A twenty-centimeter cube near Maartens' finger went blank and then redrew; *Nest HeYen* code appeared again. "That's accurate and correct, Cap'n."

"That's the zor fleet flagship, and it's showing a Twenty-one." "Twenty-one" meant a representative of a head of state—it corresponded to the number of guns for a salute, or the number of sideboys needed to receive someone from that ship. The High Lord of the zor— or someone representing him at a very high level—was aboard that ship.

Maartens rubbed his chin, wondering what it meant. "Comm the flag. Request permission to approach for refueling. *Pappenheim* sends." He looked at the pilot's board: His command had formed up—*Tilly*, his sister ship, was a few hundred kilometers to port and a few ship-lengths behind, while the merchanters *Oregon, Fair Damsel* and *Reese* had taken up positions in a ragged clump aft. His tiny fighter platform, the IGS exploratory carrier *Bay of Biscay*, brought up the rear. *HaKale'e* and *Kenyatta*, two of the four first-raters occupying the volume near the Adrianople jump point where he'd just emerged, hung nearby, menacingly large.

"We're directed to Orbital Six, Cap'n."

"Where *Nest HeYen* is?"

"Aye-aye, sir. And there's something else on incoming comm." The comm officer looked back at his board and then turned to face the captain. "I have a Priority Twenty-one message for you, sir, directly from *Nest HeYen*."

Maartens swiveled his chair around. "I didn't quite read that, Lieutenant. Did you say that we had a *message* from the flagship?"

"Aye, sir. The message has an official comm-seal with the cadency
mark of the High Lord himself."

"What does the message say, Lieutenant?"

"It's an invitation to come aboard as soon as we reach our anchor-
age, sir, for an interview with the High Lord himself."

"He's aboard the flagship in person?"

"That's what the message says, Cap'n. The High Chamberlain requests permission to come aboard *Pappenheim* to brief you."

"*Me?*"

"Yes sir. The message requested you by name."

Maartens rubbed his chin, wondering what to make of it. "They're
awaiting a reply, I assume."

"Yes sir. I haven't acknowledged receipt yet, if you want to hold off."

Maartens flexed his hands and then formed a pyramid. "No, that
won't do any good. Acknowledge receipt and invite the High Chamberlain aboard. Commander"—he continued to Okome without pause—
"assemble the right number of sideboys and get an honor guard to the
shuttle bay. Get clearance for our ships at Orbital Six, and let's get our
dress blues on and find out what the High Lord wants."

He stood, and he and his exec walked toward the lift. "You have the
conn," he said to the engineering watch officer already headed for the
pilot's seat.

The question of why *Pappenheim* and Maartens's command was
receiving this honor was still hanging in the air when the High
Chamberlain of the High Nest came aboard. His gig traversed the short
distance from the Orbital Six station to *Pappenheim*'s hangar deck as
soon as Maartens' ship achieved parking orbit. *Nest HeYen* was
nowhere in sight, but the board showed her under way toward the Adrianople jump point.

The High Chamberlain was accorded twenty-one sideboys, acknowledging the honor with alien dignity by altering his wing-position
slightly. He and the four other members of his entourage waited for the
ceremony to be complete, and then followed the captain and his exec to
the ready-room without further explanation.

"I am curious, *ha* Chamberlain," Maartens said, settling himself into his chair. Okome remained standing to his right, comp in hand. "To what do I owe the honor of an interview with the High Lord?"

"You have . . . some knowledge of our current situation."

"I can't imagine what."

"I am sure you *can*," T'te'e HeYen said, placing his wings in a different position. He sat at the end of the conference table in *Pappenheim*'s ready-room on an extruded perch; the four other zor formed a sort of honor guard and stood behind him. "You have had some experience with the *esGa'uYal*."

"The vuhls."

"Just so."

"Very well," Maartens said, placing his hands before him, palms down, on the table. "I will help in any way I can."

"The High Nest appreciates your cooperation."

"Perhaps you can answer a question for me: Why have we been ordered here to Thon's Well System?"

"That is easily answered. The High Lord has concluded that the *esGa'uYal* will attack the fleet here, *se* Captain. After many months of skepticism, even the Imperial Admiralty has begun to take such pronouncements seriously."

"Why would the enemy be interested in Thon's Well, *ha* Chamberlain? There isn't anything here worth attacking."

"At the moment there is, *se* Captain: several eights of ships."

"Only because the High Lord and the emperor ordered them *here*. If they hadn't come, the enemy wouldn't attack here."

"Or . . ." the High Chamberlain answered, letting his claws extend for a moment and then quickly retracting them as if he'd suddenly taken notice, ". . . the reason they will attack here is because we have *given* them a reason."

Maartens took a breath. "You're playing chicken with them."

"We are drawing them to this place, if that is what your metaphor signifies. Yes we are—and it is part of a pattern the High Lord understands but I do not. The Eight Winds blow where they will, *se* Captain, and I cannot alter them and neither can you."

"No, but I can't help but telling you, sir, that I consider it foolhardy at best. We would be better suited to defend something"—he waved a hand—"something like a naval base."

"Such as Adrianople?"

"Such as Adrianople," Maartens agreed.

"Adrianople has fallen to the *esGa'uYal, se* Captain. The walls of that fortress were insufficient to keep the invaders out. Five days ago a squadron arrived there and was nearly transported to *Ur'ta leHssa.*"

T'te'e HeᵞeΠ let that sink in for a moment. The human captain had been in transit when the fleet of Admiral Hsien was nearly captured at Adrianople; obviously he had only just now heard that the base was taken.

Knowing what the enemy could do was little solace. *esLi* regarded the ignorant more gently, who did not know how they would die . . . Except that this *naZora'e* was not of the ignorant ones: he had faced the *esGa'uYal* with the avatar of Qu'u.

The consequences of the *esGa'uYal* seizure of Adrianople were clearly going through the captain's mind. *If Adrianople cannot protect against the Deceiver,* he would be thinking, *what place* can?

"*ha* Chamberlain," Maartens said after several moments, folding his hands before him on the table. "I can't hope to understand the grand pattern of things, but I'm prepared to do my duty here or anywhere else His Imperial Highness sends me. But forgive me for being curious."

"Curiosity is a trait beloved of *esLi, se* Captain."

"Then you wouldn't mind answering a further question or two before I meet with the High Lord."

"It is my purpose for being aboard the *Pappenheim,*" T'te'e replied, hoping he'd rendered the ship's name sufficiently well to avoid giving offense—though he knew humans tended to place less stock in such things than the People did.

"Excellent," the captain replied, placing one hand palm-down over the other and leaning forward. "*ha* Chamberlain, tell me about Qu'u."

The Chamberlain's wings changed position as Maartens said the name. The other zor shifted his own position nervously.

A hit. Maartens thought to himself. *A palpable hit. Send a "Well done" to Gunnery Section.*

"Qu'u was a legendary hero of the People," the Chamberlain answered, after a moment. "You are a student of our culture?"

"No sir, not hardly. But it seems as if I've heard quite a bit about the legend recently. And I don't mind telling you, *ha* Chamberlain—and I won't mind telling the High Lord in person—that I don't much like seeing a friend of mine mixed up in that legend against her will."

"I do not quite understand your meaning."

"I suspect that you *do, ha* Chamberlain," Maartens answered. "I am certain the High Lord wishes to consult with me on just that subject. Do not dissemble with me: I have too much data now.

"Point: Jackie Laperriere, a friend and commanding officer, experiences first contact with our alien enemy—'the servants of the Deceiver,' as you would say." He extended a single finger, pointed down toward the table, and added a finger for each point.

"Point: Before the Imperial Navy can court-martial her for doing the wrong but smart thing for abandoning her post, she gets transferred to your authority.

"Point: She next finds herself aboard a merchanter named the *Fair Damsel*, which, incidentally, is now under my command. She gets as far as an open port outside the Empire, called Crossover. That's the last anyone's seen of her.

"From what I understand, she's following some ancient legend involving Qu'u and the sword called the *gyaryu*. Since it was taken from Cicero several weeks ago, I can only assume that you've sent her off after it, somehow convincing her that she is Qu'u.

"And my last point, sir—" Maartens took a deep breath before continuing; the High Chamberlain's wings moved ever so slightly, as if he knew where Maartens was going with this.

"Jackie Laperriere is too damned levelheaded to follow this legend, especially considering its ending—which I've read, sir, right to the last stanza. I'm guessing she has, as well. She's not suicidal, *ha* Chamberlain; she knows how the legend turns out by now."

T'te'e settled his wings into the Posture of Polite Resignation. *Again,* he thought. *Again you have underestimated a* naZora'e. *You underestimated se Jackie and now you are ill-prepared to deal with this Captain Maartens.*

You have dealt with envoys and diplomats too long. The naZora'i *understand so little of us and we know so little of them. The* esGa'uYal *are counting on that: If we cannot choose the same flight, we will be destroyed each in detail.*

"In the legend," T'te'e said at last, "the hero Qu'u ascends the

Perilous Stair to the Fortress of Despite. There he sees the *gyaryu* awaiting him, unguarded and seemingly unprotected. Without the spiritguide or his faithful Hyos to advise him, he takes up the sword and achieves *esHu'e'Sa,* the Dark Understanding."

"And *esGa'u* points his talon and blasts him into next week."

"... Yes," T'te'e answered, reasonably sure that he understood the captain's unusual expression. Diplomatic training had not prepared him for the onslaught of colloquialisms with which he had been bombarded. "Because of the attack of the Deceiver, the great hero transcends the Outer Peace. Yet his willingness to undergo the journey alone, to face the challenge of *esHu'e'Sa,* to have the courage to transcend the Outer Peace on the Plain of Despite—within the Fortress itself—causes the Lord *esLi* to extend His mighty Talon and draw him from out of Despite to come within His Golden Circle."

"*esLi* saves him."

"That is what I said," T'te'e replied, working to keep annoyance from his wings.

"You believe *esLi* is watching out for Jackie. Have you convinced *her* of that, as well? Does *she* think that He will save her at the crucial moment?"

The High Chamberlain assumed the Posture of Honor to *esLi.* "I do not know, *se* Captain. I do not know what *se* Jackie believes. She is a warrior, and will take the warrior's part.

"Eight thousand pardons," he added, after a moment. "I follow only the orders of *hi* Ke'erl in this matter. I do not believe he takes into account that you and the other actors in this drama are not of the People. You cannot reasonably be expected to accept things as they are, merely because the High Nest directs it."

"I didn't ask for an apology, *se* Chamberlain," the captain said, "only an explanation."

"You deserve both."

Maartens nodded.

T'te'e assumed the Stance of Contemplation and continued: "Your friend ... our champion, for such she is ... was foreseen many years ago. She has been sent to retrieve the *gyaryu.*"

"*se* Sergei's sword."

"The sword that he carried, yes. It is a powerful talisman and dangerous in the talons of the *esGa'uYal.* She is alone now: Her companion was slain in her travels."

" 'Her companion'—Ch'k'te?"

"*si* Ch'k'te m'Sath's *ehn* HeYen." The High Chamberlain's wings descended to a posture of sorrow. "He has transcended the Outer Peace."

"Damn." The High Chamberlain sensed a great disquiet in the human captain. "Where is Jackie now?"

"On the Perilous Stair," T'te'e answered, and realized immediately that the answer would not suffice. "She is— She is very close to the *gyaryu,* perhaps on the same world."

"What world?"

"I do not know, *se* Captain. It is not within the scope of my wings."

"ᚺᚪ ᚛ᚢᛖᛖ." Maartens leaned back in the chair. "I have one more question before I go to see the High Lord. How critical is Jackie's success? Does this upcoming battle even matter if she fails—if she's captured or killed?"

"She must not fail."

"That's not an answer, damn it. Tell me, *ha* T'te'e. Is this lure for the enemy anything more than a diversion? If she fails and we somehow win the battle, is it meaningless?"

"She *must not* fail, *se* Captain. That is all I can say."

"Then I would suspect that this interview is done. I—"

Maartens' final reply was interrupted by a bosun's whistle. "All hands to Quarters," said a voice from comm—the Officer of the Watch. "Captain to the bridge, acknowledge."

"Maartens here," he said, exchanging glances with Suzanne Okome. "Report."

"Enemy vessels near Adrianople jump point, Captain. Incoming orders from Admiral Stark."

"I'm on my way. Maartens out." He stood and looked at the High Chamberlain. "It looks like you'll be our guest for a little while longer, sir. Would you care to come to the bridge?"

T'te'e HeYen turned, in a single, fluid motion. "I would be honored."

chapter 7

IN WAR . . . THERE ARE ROADS WHICH MUST NOT BE
FOLLOWED, ARMIES WHICH MUST NOT BE ATTACKED, TOWNS
WHICH MUST NOT BE BESIEGED, POSITIONS WHICH MUST
NOT BE CONTESTED, COMMANDS OF THE SOVEREIGN WHICH
MUST NOT BE OBEYED.

—Sun Tzu,
The Art of War, VIII:3

Between Port Saud and Cle'eru—where the officers of the *Negri* planned to reenter Imperial space—there was an argument. The argument was regarding the identity of the *Negri Sembilan,* and whether it was a good idea to retain that identity even after the ship was back within the Empire.

Those who had decided the *Negri* should change its name—a court-martial felony—believed that the bugs had infiltrated the Empire and would be waiting for the ship when it turned up again. Rafe Rodriguez belonged to this group; the experience on Port Saud Station had spooked the big man, and he argued that the last thing they should do would be to turn up anywhere and advertise that they were there.

Owen was in the other camp. His time on Center and Port Saud had convinced him of two important things: First, that the news of their seizure of *Negri Sembilan* hadn't gotten much beyond Center; and second, that it was fairly clear the bugs weren't all on the same side. There wasn't much chance that any of the factions were in any hurry to side with the Solar Empire—much less the crew of *Negri Sembilan*. In the end, they decided to leave the ID alone.

It took three days for *Negri* to go from the Port Saud jump point to Cle'eru transition. They had chosen Cle'eru because it was within the Empire but under the administration of the zor High Nest; a defense squadron and an Imperial consul were there, but the communications between the Admiralty and the High Nest were such that they might not be aware of the recent history of the *Negri*. The proximity of Adrianople Starbase might offer some protection, as well—it was unlikely that Cle'eru had fallen to the bugs. Still, no one aboard the ship was taking any chances; as *Negri* approached jump transition, all hands were at battle stations, and the ship was ready to deploy defensive fields and execute an emergency jump to get out of there.

Transition was uneventful. To their relief, comm picked up system traffic control right away; Cle'eru System had a complex navigational profile—two asteroid belts and lots of cometary and meteoric debris. *Negri* was guided to a station at the jump point.

"And we're going there *why?*" Dana Olivo asked.

"To take on a local pilot," Owen said. "Check the *Negri*'s comp. Just about nobody flies into this gravity well without help, except maybe a ship of the line. We're not equipped."

"The comp says that Cle'eru has a defensive squadron. The pilot's board doesn't show anything bigger than a defense boat, and there are no military IDs at all, human or zor."

"Yeah, fine. Point taken. Our info is out-of-date. We're taking on a local pilot to guide us into Cle'eru System."

"And then—"

"And then, I guess, we find the consul and we hand over the *Negri*, and this whole adventure is over. What we've seen should be pretty valuable to the Admiralty."

The local pilot was a zor, which was no real surprise. He was crippled: His wings didn't seem to move properly, and they didn't settle perfectly over his shoulders. Instead of the usual fluid grace, the zor walked with a slight limp; he slowly came onto the bridge and stopped, as if he were sniffing the air.

Owen was standing near the pilot's board looking at the holo of Cle'eru System. Even with *Negri*'s navcomp, he wouldn't have wanted to navigate the place without a local pilot.

"*se* Captain," the zor pilot said, making his way slowly down the ramp to the pilot's seat. Owen considered correcting the title, then thought better of it and just stepped out of the way.

"Welcome aboard," Owen said.

"I am K'ke'en," the zor answered, giving Owen only the merest glance and then focusing his attention on the board. "We can get under way when you are ready."

Just like that, Owen thought. "As you wish, Pilot."

K'ke'en gave a heading to the navigator. "Ahead one-quarter, *se* Helmsman," he added. The ship began to move off toward the inner system.

"So tell me," Owen said. "Where's the squadron?"

"It is gone," the zor answered. His wings moved slightly, as if he wanted to enhance his comment with some gesture, but couldn't quite finish it.

"Gone? Where?"

"Outsystem. The squadron went to help."

"To Adrianople?"

"No," K'ke'en said, looking at Owen for a moment before returning his attention to his task. "No. Adrianople is said to have fallen. It was not possible to defend it."

"Why?"

"The Eight Winds blow where they will," K'ke'en answered. "This news seems to come as a surprise to you. I do not know why, but curiosity is a trait beloved of the Lord *esLi,* so I will ask: Did you not know of this, *se* Captain?"

"I did not."

"Ah." K'ke'en looked at him again. "*Negri Sembilan* has been traveling through the Plain of Despite for some time, has it not?"

He said it matter-of-factly, as if it were self-evident. Owen wasn't sure what the term meant exactly, but it seemed obvious what the zor referred to.

"We have been cut off for some time."

"Do you search for the Perilous Stair as well?"

" 'As well'?"

"The High Nest chose a champion to search for the Perilous Stair and to ascend it. Do you search for it as well?"

"I don't know what you mean."

"Do you seek the recovery of the *gyaryu*?"

"What's a *gyaryu*?"

"The Talon of State."

"The sword? The one that the old man carried?"

"Yes."

Owen looked across the bridge at Dana Olivo, who was standing at the engineering station, his arms crossed in front of him.

He shrugged his shoulders at Owen.

"No, we aren't looking for it. Who's this 'champion'?"

"A *naZora'e* warrior. She was here, but now she is near, or perhaps climbing, the Perilous Stair."

" 'She' . . ."

"She was accompanied by her Hyos."

Owen looked baffled; he hadn't the faintest idea what a "Hyos" was.

"*se* Ch'k'te HeYen," the zor added. "The name of the *naZora'e* is beyond this Nestling's ability to pronounce."

Owen had already reached a conclusion, as soon as he'd heard Ch'k'te's name. "Laperriere. You're talking about Commodore Laperriere."

K'ke'en didn't reply, but inclined his head very slightly.

"That doesn't sound like the commodore to me," Owen said.

" 'That the sound is alien is the fault of the ear, not of the voice.' Much has happened while you traveled through the eternal war. What was fixed is now changed."

"That's almost cryptic enough to be meaningless. If you have something to tell me, tell it." Owen was more upset with his own impatience than anything else.

K'ke'en didn't speak for several moments, then he settled his wings as best he could and said, "The language used to convey information is chosen according to the subject. In matters of legend, it is easiest to use the context of the legend to explain it—this is simply the Law of Similar Conjunction. The legend is why your commodore was here. It is why *you* are here."

"I still don't understand."

K'ke'en shrugged. "Perhaps it is not intended that you should. But your commodore does; she has chosen the flight of Qu'u, to seek the sword taken by the *esGa'uYal*. Her path led her here to Cle'eru to ask the advice of my Master; she then departed Cle'eru System in pursuit of her quest. I assumed she had remained aboard her original vessel, but I was later told that she and her Hyos had joined the crew of a merchanter. I never spoke with her, though she was only a few meters from me as I piloted the vessel out of Cle'eru System."

" 'Master'? Who is your master?"

K'ke'en spoke a course correction to the helmsman. "The sage *se* S'reth," he said, after a moment. "I understand that he will not be returning."

"Why not?"

"It is because . . ." K'ke'en looked at Owen, his eyes full of emotion. "*se* Captain, on the Plain of Despite there is a place called *Ur'ta leHssa*, or the Valley of Lost Souls. The Deceiver will send People to that place, where they are condemned, trapped forever without even knowing they are trapped. Cle'eru is soon to become a part of the Plain of Despite, and Master S'reth did not wish to be here when it happened."

"What about you? Don't you want to get out, too?"

K'ke'en leaned forward, enough to partially raise his wings. It was a further mockery of the grace with which zor usually expressed themselves. "I am here to convey knowledge to *you, se* Captain. Master S'reth instructed me thus: That the one who would come to Sharia'a would find his way to Cle'eru System, and that it was my honor to help him along his way.

"This is *my* place," he added. "If it is on the Plain of Despite, so be it. The Lord *esLi* knows where I am. But *you* should not remain here any longer than necessary."

None of it made much sense to Owen. "I'd hoped to speak with the Imperial consul," he said.

"Indeed." K'ke'en's shoulders sagged, as if the weight of his wings was far too great. "I regret to say, *se* Captain, that she, too, saw the wing of *esGa'u*—the consul closed her offices and departed several suns ago. I suspect that she, too, will not be returning."

ꟽass-radar across Thon's Well System was registering three enemy ships of immense size, and a number of smaller ones.

For those that had survived the contact at Adrianople, the scan data was frighteningly familiar: huge, compartmentalized vessels with immensely powerful energy-output curves and extensive weaponry. Their course and heading indicated that they had jumped from the direction of Adrianople.

Maartens reached the bridge with T'te'e HeYen beside him. The watch crew seemed surprised by the appearance of the High Chamberlain and his escort, but took it in stride; Maartens took the pilot's seat and looked over the board. *HaKale'e, Samos, Decatur* and *Kenyatta*—the four capital ships that had been deployed at the jump point when the *Pappenheim* had transitioned to normal-space only hours before—were nowhere to be seen.

Admiral Stark had already issued orders to the ships on-station. *Xian Chuan* was under way on an intercept course; *Mandela* and *Nasser* were on the same heading, with the four *Broadmoors* seconds behind. They were deepest in the gravity well and accelerating at high speed toward the Adrianople jump point: Fortunately, the third-orbital gas giant was currently at opposition. The Emperor Ian–class ships, led by Erich Anderson's ship, were just leaving orbit; they were a quarter of an orbit away and had almost as far to travel as the carrier and its escorts.

The *Hangs* were beginning to form up at the fifth orbital but had the farthest to travel, as the planet was in conjunction with the jump point and they would have to cross Thon's Well System to engage.

The ships at the sixth orbital were in the teeth of the invaders, as that gas giant was directly at opposition to the Adrianople jump point. There were seven other zor vessels nearby, along with the *Pappenheim* and the other ships under its command.

Nest HeYen was already at turnover, decelerating toward the jump point alone.

Maartens hadn't received orders to move, just to deploy defensive fields. He wasn't ready to put the *Pappenheim* or anything else under his command in plane-of-battle; a *Wallenstein*-class might take on the smaller vuhl ships, but he was in no hurry to do so.

Maartens looked at the High Chamberlain and then back at Suzanne. It was quiet on the bridge of the *Pappenheim*.

The *Nest HeYen* crept closer to the incoming vuhl ships.

"You have an explanation for this, *ha* T'te'e," Maartens said, without looking at him.

"I do not know, *se* Captain. I am not surprised that the *esGa'uYal* have appeared, but . . ."

"But you didn't expect *Nest HeYen* to take them on alone." Maartens gestured at the pilot's board. "The carrier is more than an hour downrange; the *Emperor Ian* and her pals might be ten or fifteen minutes behind.

"Nav, how long before the zor flagship is within firing range?"

"Two minutes," the navigator said.

"Two minutes before they're in range of the vuhl ships, one against three. No one will get there to back them up. *What the hell is going on?*"

Maartens swung his chair around to face the High Chamberlain, who had taken up a position a few meters to Maartens' left. Suddenly T'te'e cried out and reached up to his own head. His talons were extended; he crouched, his wings rising around him. As Maartens watched, the High Chamberlain's *chya* flashed from its scabbard and was out in front of him, giving off a perceptible glow.

Maartens was out of his seat in a few seconds. The zor guards were faster: They encircled the Chamberlain and had their swords drawn and pointed outward before the captain could take a second step. Maartens found himself in front of a zor, the business end of a *chya* pointed at his chest.

"What's—" he began, but he stopped as he heard, or seemed to hear, a loud humming or buzzing sound. It was obvious that others on the bridge heard it as well, and that it was rapidly rising in volume and strength.

"Comm, shut that off!" Maartens shouted, covering his ears.

"It is not on comm," the High Chamberlain said, as he stood upright again, seemingly with some effort. Two of the zor stood by and supported him. He held his *chya* tightly out in front of him. All of the zor weapons had taken on a pale glow that seemed unchecked by the phosphor lighting on the bridge.

As the swords began to glow with even greater intensity, the sound reduced. At last the blades were like lances of orange fire and the bridge was nearly silent.

"We . . . are . . . under attack," the High Chamberlain said softly.

"Mental attack," Maartens said. The High Chamberlain bowed slightly, his neck-muscles bulging as he did so. *Of course it's* mental *attack, you old fool,* Maartens told himself. "How can I help?"

"It seems impossible that . . . such force could be—projected across this great a distance, but . . . perhaps we have . . . underestimated our adversary. Send—to Admiral Stark to . . . warn him."

"What about *Nest He Yen*?" Maartens chanced a look at the pilot's board: *Xian Chuan, Nasser* and the admiral's flagship, *Mandela,* were at turnover and starting to decelerate toward the battle zone.

"It climbs . . . the Perilous Stair."

The four guards nearest to Maartens adjusted their wings as T'te'e said this.

"It's *all alone*."

The three vuhl ships had begun to fire on *Nest He Yen;* it was returning fire but already starting to show energy buildup in its fields.

"Report from sickbay, Skip," the comm officer said. "Dr. Callison reports that all ship's Sensitives have been brought in, either raving or comatose. He wants to speak with you—"

"Tell him to stand by." Maartens returned his attention to the zor dignitary. "*ha* Chamberlain, is there anything we can do to fend off this attack?"

"It . . . is possible that mod— . . . modulation of the ship's defensive fields might have an effect." The Chamberlain's blade flashed for a moment. "We have experienced . . . changes in Sensitive abilities when . . . a ship changes course or speed."

"Comm," Maartens said without turning, "send that information to *Mandela*. Helm, begin evasive maneuvers. Begin sending a random energy fluctuation to the field travelers."

"Aye-aye."

Maartens looked at the pilot's board again. *Mandela* and *Nasser* were starting to veer away from the firefight between *Nest He Yen* and the enemy vessels. The *Broadmoor*-class ships had passed the point where they should have corrected their course; they were on a vector that would send them out of Thon's Well System at high speed.

Emperor Ian and her sister ships had begun to decelerate. The *Hang*-class ships were still moving, but were far out of range.

"They're attacking—"

"They are attacking the . . . fleet," the High Chamberlain gasped out. "They are not all so . . . well defended."

The bridge was completely quiet now. The High Chamberlain stood slightly straighter and his attendants stepped aside for him, though they remained on guard.

"We have very little time," the Chamberlain said. He still seemed to be straining as he spoke. "You must inform the rest of your fleet that—"

"Excuse me, Skip," Okome interrupted. "Take a look at this."

Maartens and the Chamberlain stepped closer to the pilot's board, where Commander Okome pointed.

Nest HeYen had continued its line of travel: It was on a collision course with the middle ship of the three vessels now lashing it with furious energy.

"The High Lord is aboard *Nest HeYen*," the High Chamberlain said. "He—" His wings rearranged themselves, and then again. He turned to face the captain. "I must speak with the High Lord."

"Comm," Maartens said, unwilling or unable now to look away, "hail *Nest HeYen*."

Several moments passed. *Nest HeYen* crept forward, its icon on the pilot's board moving ever closer to the three main invaders.

"Channel open, Skip."

"*hiL'le HeYen*," the High Chamberlain said, and then spoke rapidly in the Highspeech. There was an instant audio-only reply and the zor communicated for some seconds while *Nest HeYen* crept nearer to the three alien ships that seemed to be converging.

"What's happening?" Maartens said, at a pause in the conversation.

"*esLi*'s Golden Light," the High Chamberlain said. "In the name of *esLi*'s Golden Light."

"What the hell is—?"

A racket of random static, explosions punctuated by the occasional scream of what might have been a zor voice, poured out of the comm channel—

The forward viewscreen was polarized almost to opacity by a huge detonation thousands of kilometers away—

And there was something else, like the sudden termination of a chorus of voices that had previously been inaudible: a sudden silence that drowned out all other sound . . .

In his chamber in esYen within the sprawling High Nest compound, Sergei Torrijos screamed in his sleep. Healers were present night and day; the one currently on duty flew immediately to his bedside and began checking the old *naZora'e*'s vital signs. Torrijos tossed back and forth a few times but then was silent; his body returned to its original torpor.

The eyes never opened but the face took on an expression that, to other humans, conveyed pain and sadness. Only later did the reason for such an expression become clear. As always, without wings to convey deeper meaning, the *Gyaryu'har* remained, at least in part, inscrutable.

In a guarded chamber on the fourth moon of HaKeru—Zor'a's outer gas giant—a *N'nr* Deathguard writhed in pain against a sudden, violent assault on his *n'n'eth*. He knew where it was coming from: The most powerful Sensitives among the winged meat-creatures were feeling some unimaginable release of *n'n'eth*-energy.

He changed his form to the one he had worn for several months, an Imperial naval officer named Christoph Kim whom he had consumed with his *k'th's's*, but it had no effect—the assault continued, wave after wave, preventing even the simplest thoughts from emerging from his *i'kn*-mind. Finally it overwhelmed him like a black wave too powerful to withstand, leaving him a lifeless husk.

Maartens' question was left unfinished and unanswered. The High Chamberlain crumpled to the deck and was attended to at once by a guard. The transponder indicator for *Nest HeYen* winked off the pilot's board, along with all three of the enemy vessels.

Maartens stepped back into the pilot's seat.

"We're recording antimatter explosions, Skip," Suzanne Okome said. "Four of them."

"Comm, get *Nest HeYen*," Maartens said, already knowing the answer. He glanced at the deck, where the High Chamberlain half lay, half knelt. "And get Dr. Callison up here."

"She will not answer," the High Chamberlain whispered.

"Comm?" Maartens said.

"I have a large packet of transmitted data from the *Nest HeYen*, Skip, but I can't raise the ship. It's gone, sir. Also, I have an incoming message from the Flag."

Maartens looked from the High Chamberlain to the forward screen and then back again. The comm channels were clogged with messages, and his comm officer was struggling to filter them out. "Let's have the message from *Mandela*."

"Channel's open, Skip."

"Captain," said a voice almost drowned in static. "This is Admiral Stark aboard *Mandela*. Is the High Chamberlain still aboard your vessel?"

"Yes sir," Maartens answered. "He's—a trifle indisposed at the moment. We have just recorded a large explosion, likely involving *Nest HeYen*."

"Consider it confirmed," Stark answered. "*Nest HeYen* activated its self-destruct sequence within a few dozen kilometers of the enemy ships. It . . . seems to have had the desired effect."

"I'm not sure I understand, Admiral."

The High Chamberlain had gotten to his feet somehow and was now standing beside the pilot's seat.

"The High Lord has transcended the Outer Peace," the High Chamberlain said.

"*ha* Chamberlain—" Maartens began, but the High Chamberlain's wings altered their position slightly.

"Dead, *se* Captain. Along with everyone aboard *Nest HeYen*. Along with the intruder vessels, it seems."

Maartens could not directly answer.

At last the navigator said, "Confirmed, Skip. There appears to be a great deal of debris moving at high relative velocity from the blast area. No sign of either *Nest HeYen* or the bogeys."

Maartens clutched at the arms of the pilot's chair as he grasped the impact of what had happened and what it meant. He'd been shocked by enough things in the past few months, but *this* was something else.

"What was the sound we heard?" he asked the High Chamberlain.

"*Chya'i*. It was the sound of thousands of *chya'i* and their bearers giving their *hsi* back to the Lord *esLi*, all at once." T'te'e's wings settled almost onto his shoulders. "It does not take a very powerful Sensitive to register that.

"My *chya*, too, should have been consumed in that explosion."

Maartens had no reply.

chapter 8

THE LEGEND OF QU'U (continued)

AS QU'U ADVANCED INTO THE FORTRESS WITH
CHYA BEFORE HIM, HE FELT AS IF SIXTY-FOURS OF
SIXTY-FOURS OF EYES WERE GAZING UPON HIM.
THE FOG ON THE STAIR WAS LEFT   [Uncloaked Before the Deceiver]
BEHIND, AND THE ANGRY SKY ROARED ABOVE,
LIGHTNINGS CRASHING UPON THE BATTLEMENTS
AS IF DRAWN THERE.

BEFORE HIM, HE COULD SEE AN OPEN COURTYARD,
SWEPT BY WIND AND DRENCHED BY RAIN. THERE WERE
EIGHT STATUES PLACED THERE, EACH SHOWING A
WARRIOR OF THE PEOPLE HORRIBLY WOUNDED. THEY
SEEMED TERRIBLY LIFELIKE; QU'U WOULD HAVE PASSED
THEM BY WITH NO MORE THAN A RESPECTFUL
WING-GESTURE, UNTIL HE REALIZED THAT THE   [Tortures of the *Hssa*]
STATUES WERE NOT OF STONE OR CLAY—BUT WERE
INSTEAD *LIVING WARRIORS,* TRAPPED IN THEIR FROZEN
POSITIONS BY SOME SORCERY OF DESPITE. THE
PLEADING EYES CRIED OUT TO HIM, BUT THE WINGS
COULD NOT MOVE TO FORM A PHRASE. LIKE THE
WARRIORS TRAPPED IN THE VALLEY FAR BELOW, THEIRS
WAS A PRISON WITH NO ESCAPE.

They lodged Jackie in a high-rise apartment block in Center's biggest metropolis to await H'mr's arrival. It was an automated city, in what seemed to be a constant state of urban renewal. Robotic construction equipment was visible from her window forty stories in the air, at every stage of work from bulldozing to construction to finish work. From what she'd been able to learn about the world, it fit: Center had been founded by a religious group dedicated to the veneration of technology; the group had arrived there late in the twenty-third century, equipped with nanofactory equipment, and had set about converting the planet's rich raw materials to industry and transport networks and cities. For a century the planet had grown in population, extending civilization across its surface, and across Center System . . . And at the end of the following century the vuhls had arrived and taken it, seemingly without firing a shot—what they'd intended to do at Cicero as well.

K'na didn't turn up again, either at Jackie's apartment or in the city center when she went out for a look around. It was eerie: She'd found her way to Center—the Perilous Stair. Jackie had managed to pass the first test just as Qu'u had done; and she was on the Stair without Hyos, just as Qu'u had been.

In fact, she wasn't sure just what to do next. She argued the point with Th'an'ya, who assured her that *esLi* would provide. Jackie wasn't quite so sanguine about the outcome. It was a matter of survival for both of them.

Th'an'ya was now with her almost continuously, though she was rarely visible except by way of a sidewise glance in a mirror or in one of the polished metal or glass surfaces that proliferated in the city.

The voice of the sword was there as well, whispering phrases from zor legend, as well as encouragements such as, *Come claim your heritage. Come to the Center.*

She ignored it, not knowing what to make of the comments, not sure how to proceed. It was as if she, like Qu'u, were waiting for something to happen to permit her to stumble into the next adventure.

She didn't have long to wait.

Three nights after her arrival on Center, she was preparing a meal when the apartment door chimed. This was a surprise; only residents could enter using passkeys, or admit guests through a code entered into the apartment comp. She knew no one, either within the building or outside. The most likely visitor—First Drone H'mr—probably wouldn't have to ring.

Setting her preparations aside, she reached for her coat and pulled out her pistol. She gestured at the 3-V monitor that showed the outside hallway.

Standing outside her door was a familiar figure, one whose face she'd seen perched atop a zor body and then, more recently, melt into the image of Bryan Noyes on Crossover—before he had become something even more frightening.

This is some kind of trick, she thought. *This is a vuhl.*

I do not sense the hsi *of an* esGa'uYe *outside the door,* se *Jackie,* Th'an'ya answered from within her mind. *This seems to be a* naZora'e.

As she watched, Damien Abbas looked up and down the hallway, stepped back from the door for a moment as if to examine it, then rang the doorchime again. He looked more worn and aged; but he had the same stocky frame that she remembered.

She waved at the door-release and the door slid aside. She kept the pistol pointed directly at it. Damien Abbas, former captain of the *Negri Sembilan,* had an expression of pure joy on his face when he saw her, but it melted away when he caught sight of the weapon.

The door slid shut behind him. He slowly spread his arms wide, away from his body.

"I'm unarmed."

"I can see that," she answered. "Move very, very slowly to the armchair."

He did so, not taking his eyes off her. The armchair faced the apartment window and overlooked the night-lit city; he sat in it. She could see his reflection against the darkness and her own reflection behind him, the weapon pointed out in front of her.

"I hope it wasn't something I said," he remarked at last.

"What are you doing here?"

"I could probably ask you the same question, but you've got the gun."

"I'm a little short on humor, Damien. How did you know to find me here?"

"I followed you home, ma'am. I saw you on the street—" He began to swivel the chair, but she took aim with the laser: Her reflection did the same and Abbas froze.

"You stay where you are." She gestured with the pistol. "Let's have a few answers to a few questions first. What are you doing here?"

"I told you, Commodore, I saw you on the—"

"On *this planet*. Why are you on this planet?"

"That's a complicated question."

"No, it's a simple question. Do you have a complicated answer to it, Captain?"

"Yes ma'am, I do." He brought his hands together and Jackie tensed; but he just cracked a couple of knuckles and she relaxed. "There are parts of it I understand very well and there are others I don't understand at all."

"Let's start from the beginning. What happened to your ship?"

Abbas didn't answer, but cracked a few more knuckles.

"*Answer me*. At Sargasso—what happened at Sargasso?"

"Bugs," he said. "They took *Negri*, with the help of the Sensitives. They took it—and they took my place. I know it's hard for you to believe—"

"You'd be surprised what I'll believe, Captain. Go on."

"The bugs took *Negri*, ma'am. You know about the bugs, I suppose."

"Intimately."

Abbas looked at the reflection of Jackie Laperriere in the window. "The ones who took the place of the chief officers . . . including me . . . took out *Gustav Adolf II* when it came to investigate."

Jackie felt a lump in her throat and a sinking feeling in the pit of her stomach. "Continue. What happened next?"

"They dumped us here. Twenty or thirty of us—from *Negri*, the *Johore*, a few other ships. I'm not sure why—no one was in any hurry to tell us. From what I was able to learn, the other ships had been captured when some admiral came out after us."

"Admiral Horace Tolliver. Most of his ships didn't come home at all."

"So I gathered, ma'am." Abbas turned to face her, but her pistol didn't waver. He looked at her almost pleadingly, but at a slight gesture turned away again to face the reflecting window. "We found each other here on Center. Fellow prisoners and all. They put us to work—I drive an aircar down at the port."

"And now, I suppose, you're the leader of the secret underground."

"Not hardly." Abbas looked down at his hands; perhaps he had run out of knuckles to crack. "Can't make much of a secret underground with only one person."

"But you said—"

"The secret underground . . . got away, ma'am. On the *Negri Sembilan*."

"How? How'd you fight the—the bugs?"

"We had our secret weapon."

"Which was—?"

"Garrett."

She thought a moment, trying to place the name. "Garrett? You mean *Lieutenant* Garrett? The pilot from the *Duc d'Enghien*?"

"That's the one. Had the Imperial tour of a bug ship, from what he said. Then he turned up here—claimed he'd walked some kind of rainbow bridge from there to here."

"That happened *ten days' jump* away. You're telling me that he 'walked' through *jump*?"

Abbas didn't answer. Instead, he stood up from the chair and began walking toward Jackie. She aimed her weapon directly at his chest but he didn't waver. He didn't make any sudden moves, but he didn't hesitate, either.

"You're not going to shoot me," Abbas said. "And I'm not a bug, and I'm not your enemy, and I'm tired of looking out the damn window."

Jackie lowered her pistol, but didn't set it down.

"I'm trying to tell you what Garrett told *me*. He . . . remembered having been scooted off a bug ship with the help of a bunch of colored bands of light. They talked to him, told him they were helping him to escape so that he could teach."

"Teach who?"

"Not sure, ma'am."

"Teach *what*?"

"Don't know. But I have my suspicions. Garrett had this ability—he could tell when someone was a bug in disguise. It was the damnedest thing—he didn't know how he did it, but it worked . . . The bugs knew something was up: They were spying on us; they'd decided he was dangerous."

"Did they know why?"

"Not as far as I know, Commodore. They were just watching him."

"So Garrett's on the *Negri* now?"

Abbas looked at her as if he wasn't sure he could answer the question, then he looked down at his feet. "Yes ma'am. And I have no idea where the ship has gone."

"And why the hell aren't you with him, then?"

"I *was*. The last time I saw him, we were both on the bridge of *Negri*. So were a few dozen of His Majesty's loyal officers and crew. With Garrett's ability, we'd been able to take control of a gig and then take the ship back. There were only six bugs on the ship—it was almost too easy."

Almost too easy, Jackie thought. *Where have I heard that before?*

"But something happened."

"And I have no idea what it was. I was with the group that took the ship—and there was a bug that looked just like me. He and his two friends . . . got to most of us. Then the lights went out, and—"

" 'And'?"

"And then the lights went on again and I was sittin' in The Shield with a drink in front of me. I was in a goddamn bar with a drink." His hands had made fists. "And I was all alone."

" . . . How long ago did this happen?"

"Several days ago, ma'am."

"And *Negri*—"

"It's gone from Center System, that's for sure—with everyone else on board. No one else has turned up. They must know I'm here, but days have gone by and . . . nothing. No bugs. It's like I don't even matter."

"You helped steal a ship—killed, what was it, six of the bugs? How could they just leave you alone?"

"Commodore, I swear to God I don't know. I don't know why the hell I'm not on the bridge of my ship. I don't know why I'm still alive. I don't know why I get up each morning and go to the port."

A sign, the voice said to her from within her mind.

"And I don't know why I'm here, either," she answered, after a moment. She looked into Abbas' eyes, trying to reassure him. "I think you're a pawn in this game, whatever it is. Owen Garrett probably is, also.

"I'm sure *I* am."

"So . . . why are *you* on this planet, ma'am?" Abbas asked. "Garrett said you'd evacuated Cicero so that the bugs wouldn't take it. What got you to Center? Are you undercover?"

She began to answer and then stopped. *No,* she thought. *I can't volunteer any information. This is a trap.*

This is a shNa'es'ri, a crossroads, Mighty Hero, she heard in her mind. *A step away—or a step forward. It is up to you to choose.*

They were the words the Abbas-zor had spoken to her when she stood at the base of the Perilous Stair.

I got it, she thought. *Abbas is here, I'm here. If you're so damned smart, why don't you help me out on this?* she asked the voice, angrily. *Tell me what I'm supposed to do. If this is really Damien Abbas, then maybe he can help get me closer to you.*

She let her eyes close for just a moment, trying to extend her perception. She wanted to reach something she could not identify, something she could hardly understand.

It is up to you to choose, the voice repeated.

She opened her eyes to see a look of surprise on Damien Abbas' face, bordering on terror. His hands were clenched at his sides.

What the hell? she thought.

"I am here for a specific purpose. It's probably best you don't know any details," Jackie said.

"All right," he agreed. "Then I guess . . . I'm reporting for duty."

"I'm not sure where this is leading. I—" *I have to go alone,* she thought to herself.

"*In the final analysis, Mighty Qu'u,*" the guardian of the Perilous Stair had said, "*you must be alone. It is your destiny.*" And he had worn the face of Damien Abbas.

"Damien, I can't promise you—or myself—anything. I'm almost completely in the dark, feeling my way along."

"At least you're moving, Commodore. I'd rather be moving than standing still."

She set the laser down on the counter. "I can't answer right now. Come back tomorrow and I'll know what I want you to do. In the meanwhile, don't even think about me, about this meeting or anything related to it. If the Overlords realized who I was, where I was—"

"I understand."

"You'd better go. I've got a lot of work to do."

As if suddenly released, Abbas stood quickly and made for the door. "Tomorrow," he repeated.

"Be prompt," she added.

"Aye-aye ma'am," he said, and threw her a quick salute. The door slid open and he stepped through and out.

She looked at the window after he was gone and saw Th'an'ya's image there beside her reflection.

"I either took a step closer to the *gyaryu,* or gave myself over to the Deceiver," Jackie said. "Or maybe both."

"The *gyaryu* is very close, *se* Jackie. The appearance of Captain Abbas is a sign that you are upon the Perilous Stair and that you have passed the *shNa'es'ri*. Now you are climbing on the Stair. The Fortress lies at the end."

"In my dreams," Jackie answered, turning away to lean on the counter, "I refused to complete the legend. I wouldn't go into the Fortress. I believed I could not do what Qu'u had done: face certain death, believing that *esLi* would save him in the end.

"I'm still not one of the People, damn it." She turned to face the window again. Th'an'ya's image had disappeared.

"And I'm not Qu'u," she added, to herself.

In the final analysis, Mighty Qu'u, you must be alone. It is your destiny.

On the jump from Cle'eru to the naval base at Stanton, Owen Garrett interrogated *Negri Sembilan's* unexpected passenger: the Confederated Press reporter Ian Kwan, who had convinced him that it was worth their while to transport him back from Cle'eru to a more civilized part of the Empire. Kwan had been left behind on the zor colony with no way to get home, and had bargained for his passage with the only currency that made any sense: information about the progress of the war.

"I've got a nose for news," he said to Owen, a day into jump. "I've just run into a little bad luck."

"That," Owen answered, "is an understatement."

They were sitting in the main galley. It could have been the wardroom, but Owen didn't feel like entertaining as if he were really the captain of *Negri Sembilan.* Even if he had, Ian Thomas Kwan wasn't the sort of person he wanted reclining there. Something about him bothered Owen—he wasn't sure if it was Kwan himself, or reporters in general.

Owen took a sip of coffee. Kwan toyed idly with his comp.

"I *thought* I had a ride," Kwan said. "I was planning to travel with Hansie Sharpe, but the little bastard took off without me. There wasn't a merchanter left in the system and I didn't expect to find space on a naval vessel. I appreciate it, I really do."

"We're a bit . . . out of the ordinary."

"Oh?" Kwan sat forward. He was recording the session, Owen was sure; rather than object, he knew that he could just make sure the comp met an untimely end if something got in there that shouldn't have.

"Tell me what's happening," Owen said, changing the subject.

"You've heard about Thon's Well, of course."

"Tell me more." Owen couldn't place the name—it was a solar system, but he had no idea where it was.

"You *don't* know." Kwan's eyebrows went up. "You must've been pretty far outside the Empire, then."

You don't know the half of it, Owen thought, glancing at the comp on the table. *And you're not going to.* But he said nothing.

"Apparently, the enemy," Kwan continued, "whatever it is, attacked a major fleet deployment there. After Adrianople fell"—Owen's stomach jumped, and he tried not to show it—"the Admiralty sent a large part of the fleet to Thon's Well. Why the hell the fleet was there, I have no idea, but there they were. Apparently the zor flagship—with the High Lord aboard—was destroyed at close proximity to the enemy. Took 'em all out."

"The High Lord was *killed?*"

"I should say so. Of course, they say he was crazy—maybe that's why . . . Well, when the old man, the sword-bearer—"

"Torrijos."

"That's the one." Kwan held Owen's gaze for a few moments, perhaps a bit surprised that Owen knew the name. "Anyhow, when the old man's body was returned to the zor homeworld, the crazy High Lord made a fool of himself on 3-V. At least for a while—it was cut off. The High Lord said that the aliens were going to roll right over us and destroy us . . .

"What do *you* think?"

"I don't have an opinion on the subject."

"You must, Captain. We're at war—we haven't had a war since Marais' fleet went after the zor. I thought you military guys would be all kinds of excited about this. Take that commodore who passed through here a few weeks ago—she was thick as thieves with the zor, and it seems like this is a war they've been expecting for a while."

"That commodore?" Owen thought. "You met Commodore Laperriere?"

"At one of Hansie's parties. She didn't have much to say—to me, at least."

"Meaning—"

"Nothing." Kwan sipped his own coffee. "She wasn't talking to the press that night. I tried to give her some friendly advice . . ." He spread his hands wide.

"The commodore doesn't take much advice," Owen said; adding, to himself, *At least from people like you.*

"I got that impression. You know her well?"

"I'm serving under her," Owen said. "Right now."

Kwan looked at him curiously.

"I'm going to give you a little piece of advice of my own," Owen said quietly. "This war has started to get very serious, Mr. Kwan. It's likely to get worse before it gets better. You should probably figure out who your friends are—and who your enemies are." He leaned forward across the table; Kwan seemed to shrink back. "You should make sure Commodore Laperriere isn't one of them."

condemned to life. A TERM USED TO DESCRIBE ONE OF THE
PEOPLE WHO HAS BEEN DECLARED *IDJU,* OR DISHONORED;
BUT WHO, FOR SOME REASON, IS NOT PERMITTED TO TRAN-
SCEND THE OUTER PEACE—I.E., TO TAKE HIS OWN LIFE.
USUALLY THIS PERSON MUST COMPLETE SOME SPECIFIC TASK
AS A WAY OF EITHER EARNING THE RIGHT TO SUICIDE OR TO
BE READMITTED TO THE SOCIETY OF THE PEOPLE.

—Dr. Ariana Sontag,
Dictionary of Zor Sociology,
New Chicago University Press, 2314

"*se* S'reth."

S'reth heard his name being spoken as if from a world away. *an-Ga'e'ren* lay lurking outside the hull of the orbital station that hung above the homeworld. S'reth felt it like a shroud at the edge of his consciousness, but he kept it at bay.

"Honored One, I ask eight thousand pardons, but I must speak with you."

S'reth cast aside the curtain of contemplation for a long-enough moment to open an eye and examine the other. Rh't'e HeNa'a, Speaker for the Young Ones, stood on a nearby perch; his wings were held in the

Posture of Polite Approach. It was close enough to be intrusive, but far enough away to avoid offense.

He had come back to Zor'a just a sun earlier. His time with the fleet had tired him more than anything in eight turns, at least—even more than flying to the top of the *esGa'u*-cursed chamber to speak with the High Chamberlain, which had been his fate when he last visited the homeworld.

The viewing lounge aboard the station was barely occupied. This suited him: Most of its inhabitants had kept their distance from him during his short time here—some, he knew, held him in low esteem and perhaps even contempt, while others had some sort of reverence that S'reth found equally inappropriate.

"I should know better than to sleep in a public place," S'reth said softly, finding his voice after a moment. "The respect of Younger Brothers is such that none would interrupt, ascribing great solemnity to what is no more than the onset of senility."

"Honored One, I—"

"Pah. It is nothing, *se* Rh't'e. How can this old one help you?" He used the "*se*" prenomen without thinking; the Speaker for the Young Ones deserved "*ha,*" but S'reth couldn't be bothered anymore.

Perhaps this is the Dark Understanding, S'reth thought to himself. *It is no worse an explanation than has been offered in the last sixty-four of sixty-fours of turns since the story of Qu'u became legend.*

"Advice, *se* S'reth, nothing more."

"Advice should be accompanied by *egeneh*. Come closer, *se* Speaker." S'reth noted that Rh't'e's wings communicated some trepidation. It made him wonder where the other's feelings lay: in contempt or in reverence. He guessed it was the latter and dismissed it as foolishness, a false mystique he admittedly had done nothing to deter.

"Let me order some refreshment." The Speaker descended gently to the floor and spoke a request. S'reth followed, slowly and carefully, his inner ear accounting for the slight spin in the orbital base as he did so.

The legend was almost complete now: It had all come to pass, just as they had believed it would. The servants of *esGa'u* traveled abroad through the World That Is, and Qu'u was near the top of the Perilous Stair, having finally passed the *shNa'es'ri,* just as in the legend.

As for the terrible destruction of Thon's Well System: *hi'i* Ke'erl's sacrifice was reminiscent of a passage in the story of *seLi'e'Yan,*

"Standing Within the Circle." General *ha'i* Ge'el e'Yen—after the destruction of the Legion of *esLi*—transcended the Outer Peace while releasing the *hsi* from many eights of *chya*. Despair had driven *ha'i* Ge'el; S'reth wasn't sure what had caused *hi'i* Ke'erl to resort to such an extremity, but he might have had that legend in mind.

"You came here to speak of *seLi'e'Yan* and the *anGa'riSsa* of *ha'i* Ge'el, *se* Rh't'e?"

"It is difficult to broach the subject, *se* S'reth. Paralleling *hi'i* Ke'erl to *ha'i* Ge'el . . . There are some in the Council of Eleven who suggest that our High Lord's madness brought him to believe that he must transcend the Outer Peace thus. So many *chya'i*—such a waste."

"A waste, *se* Rh't'e? I am not so sure. It may have bought Qu'u valuable time."

Rh't'e contemplated this for a moment, and S'reth thought to himself: *Of course it is a waste, you old* artha. *It follows the legend exactly, but . . . such a cost.*

"Patterns within patterns, the weave of destiny, the palest shadow of *esLi*'s Golden Light," S'reth said into the silence. "It does not surprise me, not now. We cannot do other than accept."

"I must ask you a question, Honored One. Both Byar HeShri and the High Chamberlain do nothing but dissemble, but I am confident that you will answer." The Speaker's wings oriented themselves in the Stance of Respectful Expectation: He awaited a direct and truthful answer. "Did you know that it would come to this? How long have you known?"

" 'Come to *this*'?"

"The death of the High Lord. The coming of the *esGa'uYal*, the loss of the *gyaryu*, and, particularly, the choice of a *naZora'e* to rescue it. No one in the Council knew of this last. They—we—were aware of the enemy lurking in *anGa'e'ren*, but no one knew that the *Gyaryu'har* would be thus risked.

"So here we are—"

"Where the Eight Winds have blown us," S'reth interjected.

"So here we are," the Speaker repeated, his wings settling into the Posture of Polite Annoyance, "with a new High Lord, no *Gyaryu'har*, and no *gyaryu* unless *esLi* wills that the *naZora'e* is able to recover it. Where *does* that leave us, *se* S'reth?"

"It leaves us where we expected, Younger Brother," S'reth replied. "*seLi'e'Yan*. 'Standing Within the Circle.' We still await Dri'i, the one who will teach the Shield of Hatred to the heroes of Sharia'a."

S'reth sighed, feeling the dust of *Ur'ta leHssa* heavy on his wings. "To answer your question: Yes, this was foreseen. Prescience is not always accurate, *se* Speaker." The door chimed and slid aside; an *alHyu* stepped into the room with a tray bearing *egeneh* and cups. The servant settled them on a side-table and departed rapidly.

"Why were we not informed of this?"

"Would it have changed anything, Younger Brother? I have been where you are now. I know what the Council of Eleven does, how it functions. *se* Byar knew, *ha* T'te'e knew. I knew. A few others as well. *hi'i* Ke'erl—may he dwell within *esLi*'s Golden Light—knew that this sun would be reached and he might not be here to see it."

"And *ha* T'te'e—"

"Yes?" S'reth took up the pitcher from the tray and poured steaming *egeneh* into two unadorned cups and the shallow saucer left on the side. He dipped one extruded talon into the saucer and raised it, dripping, to draw the sign of *esLi* in the air. Both he and Rh't'e placed their wings in a posture of reverence for a moment; then he took up the cups and handed one to the other. "*esLiHeYar,* Younger Brother. Now drink."

They drank. S'reth felt the beverage course through him, making his shoulders and thin wings shiver for a moment.

"My old friend *ha* T'te'e rightly believes that it would be most harmonious to his Inner Peace to have been by his lord's side when *hi'i* Ke'erl transcended the Outer Peace and conveyed his own *hsi* to *esLi*. If there is anything his training and the past few years' experience should have taught him, is that it simply was not meant to be.

"He will be troubled for many suns, Younger Brother. Then he will realize that *hi'i* Ke'erl knew in advance how important his presence would be while Qu'u climbed the Perilous Stair. That is why he has been condemned to life."

" 'Condemned to life.' " Rh't'e shook his *egeneh*-cup slightly, making the liquid swirl in a circle.

"Let me set your mind at ease on another point, *se* Speaker." S'reth placed his cup on the tray and turned to face the Speaker directly. "Before the High Lord destroyed *Nest HeYen,* and the *esGa'uYal* with it, he sent a transmission to the High Chamberlain. You should review this transmission carefully, *se* Rh't'e.

"*hi'i* Ke'erl held the Inner Peace when he transcended the Outer Peace. He knew what he was doing; he was not trapped in *Ur'ta leHssa*.

"In short, *se* Speaker, the High Lord did *not* die insane. Pursued by demons, yes. Seized by the truth; faced with the reality of the World That Is; burdened and perhaps crushed by leading the People through this *shNa'es'ri*—yes, all of those things—but not insane.

"*esLi* give us strength," S'reth said softly, his wings again in a position of homage. "*esLi* give us the will to fly such a path with the courage that *hi'i* Ke'erl possessed."

The Speaker for the Young Ones seemed to consider this for a moment, testing the breeze with his wings.

"The humans will not understand this."

"The easy answer, my friend, is to say, 'Let the humans think what they will.' However, it is that sort of approach that will allow the *es-Ga'uYal* to destroy us. The only alternative, I am afraid, is to try and explain it to them.

"They *must* know. They *must* understand that *hi'i* Ke'erl's action was not just an expedient; it was truly a sacrifice.

"It was what *esLi* willed."

Stanton System had been colonized in the early twenty-second century by the overpopulated Terran country of India. A deputation from the Indian parliament, accompanied by a group of Indian religious leaders, had boarded a ship and visited a dozen Earthlike planets recently opened for colonization. While the government officials took water and atmospheric samples, examined shipping lines and space hazards, and evaluated sites for new cities, the Hindu priests traveled upcountry to determine whether the world had the elusive qualities required to support the culture that would be settled on it.

They finally settled on the seventh world visited: the fourth planet of Iota Cancri, a yellow-and-white double star sixty parsecs from Sol System. There were abundant mineral resources; the oceans were stocked with edible creatures; the system had few navigational problems and stable jump points . . . and the main continent had a long snaking river that emptied into the sea through a wide, low delta: It was a new Ganges, uncountable kilometers from the original one. Over the course of three years, three-quarters of the two billion inhabitants of the Indian subcontinent migrated in huge ships that moved them, bag and baggage, along the two-week jump from Sol System to Stanton System. It was not without incident: A terrorist insurgent group almost destroyed one of the ships—and two hundred thousand Indian migrants with it—but was thwarted, barely in time.

By the time the migration was complete, Stanton was one of the most populous worlds in the Solar Empire.

Almost three centuries after a group of Indian dignitaries had laid eyes on Stanton System, the crew of the *Negri Sembilan* got its first look at New India. A native voice hailed them in Standard and guided them toward the naval facility, where several ships were already on-station. As *Negri* approached, the pilot's board began to identify ship signatures.

"I'll be damned," Owen said as he watched the configuration grow in the forward screen. "I think that's the *Duc*."

Rafe had come onto the bridge a few minutes before. He glanced at the pilot's board, and then at Owen standing at the front of the bridge. "I won't even ask how you know that," he said. "But you're right."

Barbara MacEwan, captain of the *Duc d'Enghien*, was waiting on the hangar deck when the gig from the *Negri* touched down. Her most experienced Sensitive, Gyes'ru HeShri, was beside her. There were Marines on the catwalks above—armed; but it wasn't obvious.

He'll know, she thought. *Don't think he won't.*

A dozen of her fighter pilots had assembled on the deck, against her orders. Ever since the hail had come from Owen Garrett aboard *Negri* a few hours earlier, every pilot's mess aboard *Duc* had talked about nothing else. Barbara turned and fixed another glare at the pilots, who stood all in a row; but they were used to it and refused to wither. Besides, her new wing-coordinator, Van Micic, was standing with them.

"Karen would've kept these clowns in line," she said to no one in particular, but didn't really believe it. Her former coordinator, Karen Schaumburg, had recently gotten her own command as the captain of the light carrier *Montgomery;* Van was an acceptable substitute, but Barbara was set in her ways and knew it.

She shrugged her shoulders and turned back to face the gig. Owen Garrett descended on a grav platform. He saluted her as it reached the deck level and Barbara returned the salute, trying to keep her face impassive.

"Permission to come aboard, ma'am," he said, coming to attention.

Barbara glanced at Gyes'ru, who inclined his head. "Granted." She extended her hand and took his. "Damn, it's good to see you. It takes so damn long to get you fighter jockeys trained up, I hate to see it go to waste." The fighter pilots all chuckled. Normally, Barbara would've turned around and let them have it, but she let that go, as well.

"Thank you, Captain. It's good to see you, too." Owen looked up at the catwalks and then back at Barbara. "You had to make sure."

"You bet I did. Especially with you. Last time we saw you . . ."

Owen shrugged. "I'm sorry that I took so long to report back for duty."

"How'd you know to come here?"

"We took on a passenger at Cle'eru, ma'am. He briefed us on the . . . on Thon's Well; and told us he'd heard that some of the fleet had redeployed to Stanton System. I'd been looking for a safe port to bring back *Negri*. We heard that Adrianople wasn't the place to go, and it was blind luck that we wound up at Cle'eru."

"The zor world?"

"That's right, ma'am."

Barbara turned away from Owen. "Commander Micic, dismiss these reprobates, on the double. If they don't have duties, find them some." As the little assembly broke up, she took Owen by the elbow and guided him toward the exit.

"Did you happen to see . . ." Barbara looked back toward the gig and then back at him. ". . . Commodore Laperriere? She jumped for there aboard a zor ship, and that's the last I've heard of her."

"No ma'am. I heard that she left Cle'eru System aboard a merchanter named *Fair Damsel*."

"Where'd you hear that?"

"A system pilot told us. He'd guided the ship to the jump point a few weeks back."

"Damn. What's she up to?"

"Ma'am?"

"Nothing." Barbara made a fist with her right hand and rapped it on her thigh; then slowly, deliberately, unballed it. "She and Ch'k'te have been pulled into some sort of 'legend' by the zor High Nest. I don't know what the hell it's all about."

"I get the impression, Captain, that her quest is the only thing that's important—it doesn't matter what we do, whether we win or lose battles. It doesn't even matter that we managed to get *Negri* back into friendly hands."

Even before he finished the sentence, he realized he'd touched a nerve. Barbara MacEwan stopped walking, put her hands on her hips and glowered at Owen.

"Now, hear this, Mister Garrett. You listen carefully, because I'm only going to say this once.

"*Everything* we do matters, from fighting battles at Thon's Well to guiding one of His Majesty's ships back to a safe harbor. This is what we get paid for. Maybe the crazy quest the commodore is on trumps everything that happens at the Imperial Court, or in the Assembly, or at the High Nest, or here in the fleet, but that doesn't mean we shouldn't be doing it.

"A thousand Standard years ago and more, my ancestors were fighting wars in the Scottish Highlands against the invaders from the south. The English had the arms, they had the ships, they had the numbers. They had *everything* but the ability to overcome the Scots. The English did everything they could to defeat them: They sought to divide them, they committed acts of terror and reprisal, they played politics.

"And even so, it took hundreds of years before the Scots and English swore loyalty to the same monarch; and by the middle twenty-first century, the Scots went their own way again."

"Ma'am, I—"

"I'm not finished, mister. The soldiers who serve in any war have an obligation to do whatever they can for crown and country. That's particularly true for soldiers who swore oaths as officers, like me. And like you, too. I have *no idea* what in hell is going on with my friend and former commanding officer. Maybe she's the key to this whole war, and maybe if she fails it doesn't matter in the end whether we win a hundred battles or bring a hundred ships back safe—but in the meanwhile it matters *everything* to me. That's why I wear this uniform." She plucked at a sleeve, turning the sword-and-sun emblem on her jacket to face him. "And as long as I do, I'm going to do my duty.

"Do you read me, Lieutenant?"

"Yes ma'am."

"Good. Now, you come with me. Before you get turned inside out by Admiral Hsien and his staff, I'm going to pour you a little libation, and you're going to tell me what in the hell happened to you."

chapter 10

Nest HeYen crept forward on the display; its icon was almost on top of the three IDs showing the monstrous, huge hive-ships that had been dropping from the jump point into the gravity well of Thon's Well System. A haze of enemy IDs hovered nearby, mostly aft of the three great ships. The pattern of Imperial ships had begun to break up into disorder: some clearly approaching too fast to decelerate in time; others moving on the wrong vector to even approach the battle zone.

Seconds ticked by on the chrono, hanging in midair, below and to the left of the display.

Then, suddenly, *Nest HeYen*'s signature vanished. Less than a second later, the mass-radar echoes of the three ships and a dozen other smaller ones vanished as well.

The chrono kept advancing steadily. A half-minute went by; *Emperor Ian* and its flankers had straightened their course and were closing on the remaining enemy vessels. Now it was *their* turn to be in disarray: Some were trying to maneuver around the irregular zone of destruction caused by the death of the four ships, one zor and three vuhl; others were accelerating toward the jump point. The four *Broadmoor*-class starships—the *Edgerton, Casian, Tsing Liu* and *Rainier*—had managed to execute a turn that would bring them there ahead of the ships trying to escape.

The chime rang at the ready-room door.

"Halt replay," Georg Maartens said. The chrono and display froze in position. *Edgerton* and *Casian* were just opening fire on the foremost vuhl ships straggling toward the jump point—caught between the *Ians* and the *Broadmoors,* they all would be destroyed.

He'd seen it several times already. "Come," he said. The door slid aside and T'te'e HeYen came through the door.

The High Chamberlain offered a slight bow to Maartens, who began to stand up. "Eight thousand pardons," T'te'e said, gesturing toward the display. "I did not mean to interrupt."

"No, not at all." Maartens began to gesture the display off. "It's something to occupy my mind until we reach Zor'a. I still have a report to write."

"Please," the High Chamberlain said. "A moment." He took a step forward and pointed at the mass-radar disturbance near the center of the current view. "This . . . is the place."

"Where *Nest HeYen* was destroyed," Maartens said.

"Where the High Lord"—T'te'e's wings moved to another position—"caused the ship to activate its self-destruct sequence."

"That's right. The matter/antimatter explosion engulfed the nearest hive-ship, and the subsequent disturbance destroyed the other two."

"Yes." T'te'e let his hand drop to his side. For a moment it rested on the hilt of his *chya* and then started away, as if the sword were of molten metal and had burned him.

"It is a great loss," Maartens managed, after a moment.

"It was a great victory." T'te'e looked away. "The High Nest will honor *hi'i* Ke'erl for his sacrifice. It was an *anGa'riSsa*—a ritual blood-letting."

"When you came aboard, *ha* T'te'e, you spoke of the High Lord's dreams." Maartens ran a finger along the dented surface of the *Pappenheim* model on his desk; it reflected the display that hung above it, pinching some parts, distending others. "His vision brought us all to Thon's Well; his vision told him that the vuhls would attack there.

"He had this maneuver in mind all along, didn't he? He meant to destroy *Nest HeYen* at that worthless place, taking as much enemy firepower as he could."

"I . . . would venture to say so."

"But you didn't know it was coming."

T'te'e's talons came out of their sheaths a centimeter or so. Very slowly and carefully, the zor crossed his arms across his chest and the talons retreated.

"No, *se* Captain. I did not. If I had known, I would have been at the High Lord's side, as would have been proper."

Suddenly Maartens understood something that had evaded him since the battle. At the High Chamberlain's request, Admiral Stark had detailed *Pappenheim* and its command to escort T'te'e to the zor homeworld. During the few days they'd been in jump, the High Chamberlain had kept almost exclusively to his quarters, politely refusing the courtesies of the captain's table and the officers' wardroom.

Now the captain knew why.

Maartens gestured the display off. He stood up and walked to a cabinet in a side-wall of the room. Reaching into an inner pocket in his uniform tunic, he withdrew a metal key and opened a small lock. He pulled out two glasses and a flask of *h'geRu* and carried them to the table.

Without a word he took the flask and poured two fingers of the bluish, almond-odored liquid into each glass and handed one to T'te'e, taking the other one himself.

"Drink," he said.

"*se* Captain," T'te'e began, "I—"

"Drink," Maartens insisted.

The High Chamberlain looked at the glass and then at *Pappenheim*'s captain over it. He dipped a talon into the *h'geRu* and made a small sign in the air, and then downed the glass and set it on the table. Maartens took a sip from his own glass and set it next to the empty one.

"Need your torpedoes armed again, *ha* T'te'e?" he asked.

"Thank you, no."

"I'll leave the bottle out if you change your mind." He took the Chamberlain carefully by the elbow and steered him toward a pair of armchairs on the opposite side of the room, under a frowning portrait of a man dressed in ancient costume. With a gesture, a perch extruded from the floor. Maartens sat in one of the chairs and indicated the perch for the zor.

"I feel as if I am about to be instructed," T'te'e said, his wings adjusting as he stepped onto the perch.

"You're damned right," Maartens said. "I hope you enjoyed the taste of that *h'geRu*. It's almost a hundred Standard years old; it was presented to me by a zor officer who served under me a dozen years ago. I don't take it out except for special occasions that I share with persons of honor.

"And what's more, sir, I don't serve it to dead people, no matter how high their rank or station. Make no mistake about it: If you'd been aboard *Nest HeYen,* you wouldn't be getting that drink from my century-old bottle of *h'geRu,* the first booze that man and zor ever shared together."

"I am not sure what you are implying."

"The High Nest has just lost its High Lord, *ha* T'te'e. Don't you think it's a good thing that it didn't lose its High Chamberlain as well?"

"I was meant to be at the High Lord's side when he transcended the Outer Peace, *se* Captain."

"Georg. I also only drink with friends, sir."

"*se* Georg, then. I fear that the High Nest has lost its Chamberlain as well, since I am certainly *idju* for my negligence."

" 'Negligence'? For surviving the suicide of your High Lord? Your *insane* High Lord, who killed—what was it—three thousand of his best servants? You consider yourself dishonored because you weren't one of them?"

"His sanity is not the issue."

"I agree. He did what he did for whatever reason, but that goes for *all* of his actions. Don't you concur?"

"I fail to see your point."

"Let me clarify it for you. You obey the directions of the High Lord, correct?"

"It is my duty."

"If he commands you to die? If he commands you to kill?"

"Of course."

"And what if—" Maartens crossed one leg over the other, letting himself smile just a bit. He folded his hands over his knee. "What if he commands you to go across to a human ship to provide an intelligence briefing to a commander?"

T'te'e thought about it for a moment, and his wings moved to one position and then another.

"I . . ." he began, and then moved his wings again. "Are you suggesting that *hi'i* Ke'erl sent me to *Pappenheim* specifically to *keep* me from transcending the Outer Peace?"

"I am suggesting, *ha* T'te'e, that the High Lord realized he had to do this terrible thing—this ritual bloodletting—and that he would die in the process. He knew your place was at his side, and that if he ordered you to remain behind with no explanation, it would be a matter of honor for you to refuse or lose face.

"He knew that you would follow his orders regardless of what they were . . . even if it resulted in your own death.

"He also knew that if he did nothing—if he kept you by him—that the next High Lord would have no one with your skill and wisdom to provide advice and guidance. So he chose another path: He dispatched you on an important mission, preserving your life.

"And, I might add, preserving your honor as well."

"A fourth course," T'te'e said. "Your argument suggests . . . that I should not consider myself *idju* at all."

"Of course not." Maartens uncrossed his legs and stood up. "Would I waste hundred-year-old *h'geRu* on someone who was dishonored?"

T'te'e stepped forward and grasped Maartens by the forearms. After a moment, *Pappenheim*'s captain returned the gesture. There was emotion in the zor's eyes; Maartens didn't know exactly what to make of it, but felt that something important had happened.

"I believe, *se* Georg," T'te'e said, after a moment, "that I should like another drink."

From the fortieth floor of her apartment building, the storm was still impressive. Jackie had been out earlier, exploring the city, and had had to make a dash of a few meters to get to the front doorway. It had been enough to soak her to the skin. It wasn't as if she had anything better to do—until H'mr arrived, she was no more than a VIP on leave. On any other night but this, she'd have been glad to sink into a tub and let the day's tensions seep out; but she was expecting a visitor tonight.

After giving herself a moment to be dwarfed a little bit by the majesty of nature, she gave over to a few quick minutes in the shower. Then she pulled on some dry clothes, thinking about what she'd dreamed the previous night.

She had stood at the top of the Perilous Stair again, her body shaking in the cold as the wind blew through the holes in her cloak where wings should be.

This time, though, there was no audience for her to complain to, no

Hyos for her Qu'u—she was alone. At her belt was an empty scabbard, and overhead, the lightnings cascaded from a sky impossibly high above. Off in the distance, across the Plain of Despite, she could make out the towers of Center's capital city.

The Icewall lurked behind, menacing, a physical presence that seemed ready to topple onto her at any moment.

"Now is the time for the *shNa'es'ri*, Mighty Hero," the voice said from an immense distance. "One step forward, to stand within the Circle."

"How did I come to be here?" she shouted against the wind that swirled around her.

"The Stair," the voice answered. "You climbed the Stair, for you had no wings to fly."

"Don't remind me, damn it!" She pulled the cloak closer around her, feeling the broken *chya* in an inner pocket . . . warm, almost alive. "This image, this construct—how is it represented in the real world?"

"This *is* the real world, Mighty Hero. This is the World That Is."

"This is the Plain of Despite!" she answered quickly. "The Plain of Despite isn't in the World That Is!"

"When the *esGa'uYal* walk the earth, when the High Lord has given up his *hsi* to the Lord *esLi*," the voice replied, "how will you distinguish them?"

"Answer my question!"

"The path you choose will lead you here, Mighty Hero."

"Any path?"

"The path you choose," the voice answered. "The path to the Fortress."

⊓onight's storm seemed to resemble the terrible one in her dream; lightning emerged from the clouds over the distant mountains almost a hundred kilometers away. In her mind's eye she filled in the backdrop of the Icewall beyond it, extending from the unseen horizon to the zenith of the sky; its substance formed from the blue-black clouds illuminated by intermittent flashes that fought for position through the angry storm.

In a way, the scene before her apartment window was more surreal: more like a scene from a book than the view she'd had in her dream from the top of the Perilous Stair. A zor sage like S'reth would no doubt have some cryptic aphorism at this point, like the insistent voice of the *gyaryu* that haunted her, awake and sleeping.

She wanted it to be over with. Being alone with the burden of the legend had pushed her forward, but made both her career and her life seem small and insignificant in comparison—feelings incompatible with her personal and professional self-esteem. Somehow, a resolution, even a defeat, seemed preferable.

While she stood there, the door chimed. She glanced at the outside monitor and saw Damien Abbas, or at least someone who looked like him.

Is that him? she asked Th'an'ya.

She waited for the familiar response for a moment.

Th'an'ya? she asked again. The door chimed again. Her mental voice seemed to echo, as if down a long corridor, but she heard no response from Ch'k'te's soul-mate.

Instead, the inner voice answered: *It is beginning, mighty Hero. Like Hyos, E're'a is trapped in* Ur'ta leHssa.

Trapped? Jackie could not help but repeat. E're'a was the spirit guide from the Qu'u legend. To her surprise, the voice answered her directly.

Only the hero can complete the ascent of the Perilous Stair, it said. *The hero must go alone. You knew that from the beginning.*

Jackie thought about the image of the Valley she'd experienced back at Crossover when Ch'k'te was still alive: the large, spread-out *L'le* with the despairing zor trapped there, the burden of the Valley settling heavy on their wings. In the inner region, there had been an octagonal town square, where hundreds of zor had been rendered immobile and lifeless.

Ur'ta leHssa: the Valley of Lost Souls. Somehow *esGa'u* had plucked Th'an'ya away and . . . trapped her there. Jackie had to remind herself that this was not like the human perception of Hell: The Lord of Despite could trap anyone in the Valley, regardless of merit—it was not as a punishment for evil deeds. Only the will of *esLi* could rescue someone from there.

The door chimed a third time; from the monitor, it was clear that Damien Abbas was very nervous. He had no Th'an'ya to consult—and now, neither did she.

She stepped to the control and opened the door. Abbas quickly darted inside and the door closed behind him. "What's wrong?" he asked immediately.

"Something's happened," she answered. She grabbed her jacket, feeling for the familiar broken *chya* and her pistol.

"What—"

"It's hard to explain. Do you have your aircar?"

"It's parked on the roof. I don't know how long it'll be before it's missed."

"Do you think you can reach those mountains?" she gestured toward the distant range, illuminated by a sudden crash of lightning. The light from outside cut a hawklike mask on Abbas' face.

"In this weather? I . . . I guess so. The fuel tank's full, but if there's too much turbulence, we might have problems."

"But it's possible."

"It's possible."

"Let's go, then." She took his elbow and steered him toward the door, suddenly forced into motion. *This is it,* she thought. *The path to the Fortress.*

Abbas turned out to be an expert pilot. Despite the wind and driving rain, he fought the little craft into the air, and presently they were above the city, heading toward the mountains. He reached cruising altitude with the tank gauge still reading near full.

"I suppose you have a plan," he said.

"I've got something in mind. Tell me more about the bugs."

He looked forward through the windscreen and then back at her. Lightning flashed close by, near enough to make them both flinch. When it passed, his face was framed again in strange half-shadows.

"The bugs can appear human, but we've seen them dead in their native form." Abbas gritted his teeth, not looking away from the controls. Jackie didn't inquire as to how he'd seen a dead bug.

"The ruler is called the Great Queen. She's off-planet somewhere, farther out in space where the Empire has never explored, Orionward. Her representative here on Center is someone called the Second Drone, though everyone just calls him 'the Governor.' The Drones are some kind of elite warrior class. They seem to be constantly jousting, forming alliances and trying to outwit each other.

"There's a First Drone—he's also off-planet, and everyone's afraid of him, including the Governor. There are also Third and Fourth

Drones and a whole host of lesser ones, as well. There are also some scary folks called 'Deathguard'; they're also involved in the political struggles somehow. From what I hear, the First Drone is supposedly coming to Center soon, on some kind of inspection tour."

"I know." *H'mr will not be pleased,* she remembered. *I can well imagine.*

Abbas looked at her, unsure how to respond. He looked away and made an adjustment to the aircar's course and speed, checking the fuel.

"The Great Queen had apparently hoped to invade the Empire a little bit at a time, taking ships from us, seizing control of stations, taking . . . taking the place of—" Some memory seemed to frighten him and he turned his attention back to piloting for a moment. "They took Cicero but somehow they showed their intentions."

"That's right." Jackie felt her fists clench in her lap and she forced her hands to relax. That was a lifetime ago, an eternity ago.

"They're waging a war that they can't help but win," he said matter-of-factly. "They're too far ahead of us, their Sensitives are too powerful. They can change shape, take anyone's place."

"That doesn't mean they'll win," she said, realizing how it must sound. "My mission—"

"What is it, ma'am? Why are you here on Center?"

"I—"

Suddenly there was a brilliant flash of lightning, seemingly right outside the cabin of the aircar. The light was bright enough to blind her for a moment; but not before she caught a glimpse of some sort of rainbow, like a series of colored bands, scoring through the cabin. When her vision had cleared, she found that she had Ch'k'te's broken *chya* in her hand.

Opposite her, Damien Abbas was still looking at her, his eyes open, his expression caught somewhere between surprise and fright.

She looked at the *chya* and then back at him again. He did not seem to be moving at all. To her inner hearing, there was an afterecho of a terrible word, something spoken to her companion that she could not hear . . . that would have ended her life if *she* had heard it instead.

Someone—some *thing*—had turned Abbas' mind off, like a power switch.

Just like John Maisel.

Alone, the inner voice said.

The aircar, lacking its pilot, began to respond to the storm, tossing this way and that, bucking in the wind, headed for the ground.

•   •   •

Dan McReynolds and Georg Maartens stood at the end of a long arbor on the ground floor of the huge main hall of the High Nest, while zor of all descriptions walked and flew above them. It had been an eight-day jump getting here. After arranging the High Chamberlain's reception at the Zor'a orbital base, Maartens had inquired for orders, only to learn that the High Lord had asked for the two of them personally.

McReynolds rocked slowly from foot to foot, impatient to get on with whatever was about to happen. Maartens, equally impatient but damned if he would to show it, stood at parade rest, observing the zor who were glancing toward the humans. After a moment, they would give up the challenge: it crossed language and race boundaries, and though the human was the alien here, he seemed able to hold his own.

"The High Lord will see you now," said a voice, and the two humans turned to face a younger zor. He adjusted his wings—as zor constantly, inscrutably did—and beckoned for McReynolds and Maartens to follow.

They walked under the arbor after the zor, who wore a red-brown sash, as had every official they'd met thus far. "The High Lord sends her apologies," he said, after a moment. "She was in contemplation."

Maartens looked at McReynolds, who returned a similar glance. *"She"? "Her"?* he thought, knowing McReynolds was thinking the same.

Moments later, Maartens would have had to admit, if pressed, that he would not have been able to tell the difference: The zor—perched at the center of a vibrant, growing garden with deep-blue sky overhead— seemed the same as all of the others he'd met in the course of his career. Perhaps the wings were darker or lighter, the head a bit more angular— but there was no obvious physiological difference, no change in costume or stance, to indicate this zor was female.

"hi Sa'a," he said, when the young servant gestured for them to step forward, to stand before the High Lord's perch. *"esLiHeYar.* It is a pleasure."

"Captain Maartens," the High Lord replied. Her voice was different in some fashion Maartens could not place. "It is a pleasure to make your acquaintance as well. And you must be Captain McReynolds," she said to Dan, who looked even more nervous.

"Dan McReynolds," he said, extending his hand; then, realizing this might not be appropriate, he began to withdraw it. But before he could do so, the High Lord had come down from her perch and gently grasped his forearms with her taloned hands. He smiled faintly, not knowing whether he'd done something right.

Her wings settled. "There are many questions I would ask," she said. "But I forget my duty as host. May I offer you refreshment?"

"Sure," McReynolds said, and let his hand fall to his side.

A pair of chairs already conformed to human shape were present, along with a table set out with *h'geRu* and *g'rey'l*. Toasts were offered and drank to.

"*hi* Sa'a," Maartens said, after a pause, "I don't exactly know why we're here."

"You are here at my request," she said, as if that were news.

"I understand that, ma'am," he answered. "I'm not sure we can add any information to what you already know."

"I do not require any additional information," the High Lord said. "I only wished to meet the companions of Qu'u. Of *se* Jackie. I have never met her, myself."

"I haven't seen her since Crossover," Dan answered.

"No, but you know her well."

"Not as well as I thought I did." Dan ran a hand through his hair and rubbed his neck. "Look, *se*—uh, *hi*—Sa'a, do you know something we don't? . . . No, that's not quite the question." He set his glass on a table. "Obviously you know more than we know. Do you know where Jackie is?"

"Outside the Fortress of Despite," the High Lord answered at once. "Very near the *gyaryu*."

"I mean in real life."

"You make a distinction that I do not understand."

"What planet is she on?"

"I do not know. Does it matter?" The High Lord's wings changed position again. "If you knew the answer to that question, what would you do?"

"'Do'?" McReynolds looked at Maartens. "I guess I'd try to get her out of there."

"She is there for a purpose."

"*Your* purpose," Dan said, finding himself growing annoyed. "Not *her* purpose."

"I must differ with you, *se* Captain." The High Lord's head turned to one side, as if she were listening to something far-off and remote. "This is another distinction I cannot appreciate. She *is* Qu'u now, and

Qu'u stands before the Fortress of Despite. She will confront the Deceiver shortly."

"And the Deceiver will destroy her, if legend holds true," Maartens said.

"She will obtain the *gyaryu* first."

"And then he will *destroy* her, *hi* Sa'a," Maartens persisted. "Is there nothing we can do? How can we . . ." He set his glass down. "How can we just sit here, powerless, while she—"

"*se* Captain. We *are* powerless. Qu'u must confront this final challenge alone. Honored Cousin *si* Ch'k'te has transcended the Outer Peace. The spirit-guide is trapped in *Ur'ta leHssa*, the Valley of Lost Souls. The guardian of the Stair showed the way, and now she is alone."

"Wait a sec," McReynolds said. "You said that the spirit-guide is trapped in the Valley of, uh, Lost Souls. How can that be? Has she lost Th'an'ya?"

Maartens looked at him, his expression a query. "Th'an'ya? Who's Th'an'ya?"

"Yes." The High Lord answered McReynolds. "*si* Th'an'ya is lost in the Valley."

"Who the hell's *Th'an'ya*? McReynolds, you've been holding out on me."

"You'd never believe it, Captain. I didn't believe it until I saw it."

"Saw what?"

"Ch'k'te's mate. She was a powerful Sensitive, and her spirit—her *hsi* . . .?" He glanced at the High Lord for a moment, seeking confirmation.

The High Lord inclined her head.

"Her *hsi* got into Jackie somehow. She's Jackie's—I don't know—advisor or guide or something."

"Got '*into*' her?"

"Into her mind. Double occupancy. Jackie made Th'an'ya appear like a 3-V projection aboard the *Fair Damsel,* just before she went aboard Crossover Station with Ch'k'te."

"If she's gone, does that mean the aliens have taken over her mind?"

Both humans turned to look at the High Lord, as if expecting an answer.

"It is in the talon of *esLi* now," the High Lord said. "She stands before the Fortress of Despite," she repeated.

"Has she been *taken,* damn it?" McReynolds stood, causing the

High Lord to lean backward. Almost too fast to see it, another zor was standing before him with *chya* drawn and pointed toward his chest. McReynolds didn't move, not counting on his own reflexes to get him out of the way of being skewered, but his hands had formed fists. "Tell me what it means. Explain it to me. *Has* she been taken?"

"I cannot answer."

"You *can* answer! Tell me, High Lord. *Tell* me."

"Sit down, McReynolds," Maartens said, looking at his human companion and then at the zor guard, who stood ready to defend the High Lord.

"No." McReynolds didn't flinch. "No, I won't sit down, Captain. We're here now at the center of things, with the High Lord. The *new* High Lord. All the answers we're ever going to get are available now, if we can just come up with the right questions.

"I don't know anything about fortesses, or stairs, or swords, or 'Qu'u, really. All I know is that someone I care about has been left alone to follow a quest shaped by dreams of madness, and now she's *alone*. If she's alone, then something's happened to her mind. *Has* she been taken by the aliens?

"And if so, *is* it over? Everything we've seen—the destruction of the zor flagship, all of it—does it all amount to nothing?"

There was a long, uncomfortable silence. Finally, the High Lord spoke. "My dreams tell me that *se* Jackie knows the secret to resisting the *esGa'uYal*. She has not been taken, but she must still confront the Deceiver. *esLi* alone knows the outcome."

"The dice haven't been rolled yet?" McReynolds asked.

The High Lord looked at McReynolds and then had a brief exchange in the Highspeech with another zor.

"No. The confrontation has not yet occurred."

"Will you know what happens?"

"I expect so. It is imminent, and we will know."

"Well." McReynolds took a step backward, and settled back down into his chair. "I guess we'll just wait."

Owen Garrett was en route to the zor homeworld as well. His uniform jacket had brand-new lieutenant-commander's shoulder-boards on it—a field promotion awarded him by Admiral Hsien for having recaptured the *Negri Sembilan*. Garrett was not the only veteran of the *Negri* to have received a promotion for his efforts, but he was the only one on his way to Zor'a.

Going to the zor Core Stars hadn't been his idea. Given the choice, he would rather have gone back to Green Squadron aboard *Duc d'Enghien;* it had been his home for most of the time he'd been in His Majesty's Service. After Center and the wild ride as commander of the *Negri,* it would've been something comfortable and familiar.

But it wasn't to be. Captain MacEwan had told him while they drank two-hundred-year-old whiskey in her ready-room: There weren't going to be any more missions in Green Five.

"It's the only thing I've ever really done, Captain," he'd protested, when she broke the news to him.

"It's off-limits now, Owen," she had said. "The last thing we need, after all you've been through, is for you to get turned into plasma. You have some sort of skill." She held her tumbler up to the light, casting reflections on the table. Owen reached for the bottle; Barbara took it up first and poured him another drink. "What's it like? What does it feel like?"

"Seeing an alien? It's . . . hard to describe. It's as if everything stops: all the sound, all the movement; it's all damped down and quiet. And all of a sudden I can *see.*"

"How does it come about? Is there something that sets it off?"

"No . . . Yes. There is." *They killed each other: Aaron Schoenfeld, Devra Sidra, Steve Leung, Anne Khalid, Gary Cox.* He remembered it, and he felt his anger grow.

Suddenly it was interrupted; Barbara MacEwan was carefully prying his fingers off the glass he was clenching.

"These tumblers have been in my family for six centuries. Do you realize how many MacEwan ghosts would be kicking my ass all over the Solar Empire if I let you break one?" she said. "Now. What sets it off?"

"Anger. Hatred. I remember—at Cicero . . . I remember the others from my squadron, how they were forced to—"

"I remember it, too." Barbara reached for the bottle now and carefully poured another small amount of the fiery stuff into each glass. "But *I* can't see aliens in human suits."

"But *you* haven't been aboard a bug ship, and you haven't walked through jump on a rainbow path."

"I don't know why the bugs—the vuhls—would give you the ability to see through their disguise."

"They wouldn't. But there's another player—someone else. Some *others*. Bands of color. What the zor would call . . . *esGa'uYal*."

"I thought the vuhls *were* the *esGa'uYal*. That's what Commodore Laperriere and the zor from the High Nest called them when we were at Adrianople."

"No." Owen took up his own glass again, admiring the crystal, letting the light play off the amber liquid within. " 'Fair winds,' " he said—a sailor's toast—and drank, feeling it burn down his throat. "No, the bugs aren't the ones who gave me this power . . . this ability. This is a weapon that is aimed at them, and they want me to teach it."

"To whom?"

"I don't know. Maybe to you." Owen smiled. "No offense meant, ma'am, but I could imagine teaching *you* to use anger to fight the aliens."

Barbara's eyes flashed with fierce emotion for a moment. Owen tensed, waiting for the famous MacEwan temper to lay into him; but instead she laughed. "You've got guts, Garrett, I have to admit that," she said, drinking off her whiskey. "You've earned another drink," she added, "if you want it."

He'd wanted it. Several hours later, when he'd been grilled by Admiral Hsien aboard *Gibraltar*, he wanted a few more. But the orders had come while he had still been aboard the admiral's flagship. Owen's gear was transferred from cold storage on *Duc* to *Counselor Rrith*, and off he went.

Behind him was everything he'd ever known since he'd entered Officer Candidate School; ahead was a place he'd never seen—a zor place called Sanctuary. Somewhere beyond the end of this jump was the person, or people, who he was supposed to teach . . . *what?* How to be angry? How to hate—and how to be able to recognize bugs disguised as humans?

He wished he knew. Whatever Owen was headed for—however he was being aimed at the bugs—it was out of his control. It was out of Captain MacEwan's control, out of Admiral Hsien's control . . . and the same was true for the emperor, the High Lord . . . everyone and everything except six bands of color he'd only seen and heard in his dreams.

The *esGa'uYal*.

He hoped like hell that "Sanctuary" would be able to explain it.

chapter 11

THE LEGEND OF QU'U (continued)

THE *GYARYU* WAS A FINE SWORD MADE OF SOME BLACK
METAL, CHASED WITH INTRICATE *HRNI'I* THAT QU'U
COULD NOT READ; IT SEEMED TO BE DRAWING ALL OF
THE LIGHT IN THE ROOM INTO IT, SO THAT IT GLOWED
WITH OBSIDIAN LIGHT. FROM WITHIN HIS MIND,
QU'U—WHO HAD NEVER SHOWN A HINT OF SENSITIVE
POWER—HEARD THE *GYARYU* CALLING TO HIM.

"IT CALLS TO YOU," SAID A VOICE. QU'U WAS DRAWN
AWAY FROM THE SWORD TO THE SOUND OF THE VOICE,
WHICH WAS COMING FROM THE SHROUDED PERCH.
THE VOICE WAS DEEP AND [Turning Away from *esLi*]
SONOROUS, YET COMPELLING AND STRONG. HE
KNEW IT TO BE THE VOICE OF *ESGA'U*, THOUGH HE
WAS NOT SURE *HOW* HE KNEW.

"I HAVE COME TO RECEIVE THE DARK
UNDERSTANDING," QU'U SAID. "I AM READY TO USE MY
CHYA TO OBTAIN IT."

"YOU DO NOT NEED A *CHYA*," THE DECEIVER SAID
TO HIM, STILL WITHOUT REVEALING HIMSELF FROM
THE SHROUDED PLACE WHERE HE PERCHED. "IT IS

THERE FOR YOU TO TAKE UP, MIGHTY ONE. NO ONE IS
STOPPING YOU."

"YOU HAVE TRAPPED IT, LORD OF DESPITE," QU'U SAID
CAREFULLY.

"IT IS NOT OF MY WORK," *ESGA'U* REPLIED. "YOU HAVE
COME FOR THE DARK UNDERSTANDING, WARRIOR
QU'U; I HAVE WATCHED YOU AS YOU TRESPASSED IN MY
DOMAIN, AS YOU TOUCHED YOUR
CRAWLER-BLESSED TALONS IN THE MOUNTAINS   [Plain of Despite]
OF NIGHT, AS YOU ASCENDED THE PERILOUS STAIR.
WHY WOULD I PLACE A TRAP UPON THE BLADE? YOUR
COMING IS NO SURPRISE."

"I DO NOT UNDERSTAND."

"TAKE UP THE SWORD AND UNDERSTAND."

The aircar fought her for several kilometers. The fuel gauge showed near empty, even though the vehicle had only reached the foothills. There'd been a malfunction—perhaps as a result of the lightning strike, perhaps not.

A small part of Jackie's stomach felt sick thinking about Damien Abbas, whose body was slumped on the floor of the aircar, eyes open, expression unchanged. It was as if his part to play were done, and he had been discarded.

Now she felt even *more* manipulated. It was clear there was only one way to go now—*forward*. She would force the aircar as far as she could.

It wasn't very far. Her onboard comp showed a landing-platform in front of a small villa. The building was silhouetted against the backdrop of a high cliff that reminded her of the Icewall. She couldn't get the aircar above the cliff. In its lee, the wind at least abated, making the landing easier. Just as the aircar touched the platform, the engine quit.

Pulling her jacket close around her, feeling the familiar bulge of the broken *chya* against her side, Jackie left the aircar behind and approached the open doorway of the villa.

As she stood in the front hallway—dark but illuminated by lightning flashes—she could see a figure sitting in a side-room. He was looking directly at her.

So much for stealth, Jackie thought.

"You might as well come in and sit down," the seated figure said, gesturing toward a comfortable-looking armchair across from him. The *gyaryu* sat near him on a carved sword-rest. She could hear it calling to her in an almost audible voice.

Despite the invitation, she remained in the doorway. Looking back toward the long, dimly lit hall, with its polished floors and vaulted ceilings, she could see hiding-places but no obvious avenues of escape. With her aircar disabled and the storm continuing to howl outside, it was obvious she was trapped.

She couldn't even communicate with Th'an'ya, but she wouldn't have done so anyway, since the vuhl (she assumed him to be a vuhl, despite his human form) would surely detect it. There was an outside chance that they still didn't know about her spirit-guide, and Jackie didn't feel like giving that information away.

Welcome to the end of the line, she thought to herself.

"Allow me to pour a libation," the man said, totally at ease. He rose and walked to the sideboard near the window, where there was a carafe and a set of goblets. Lightning again split the sky and peals of thunder followed close behind: The storm was very nearly overhead.

He turned, after a moment, holding two fluted glasses with pale-brown liquid in them. For an instant, as the lightning flashed behind, Jackie got a good look at him. He was not overly tall and had a spare frame, almost emaciated. He wore a uniform, though not one she recognized—it looked something like an Imperial naval uniform, but was a century out of style. There were no emblems or indications of rank.

"What makes you think I'm going to drink that?"

"Oh, really, madam. Don't be droll." His silky-smooth voice seemed designed to set her at ease, but instead it merely made her more edgy. "You are on a world controlled by powerful Sensitives, and you are here"—he made a sweeping motion with one hand—"because I have arranged for you to come. That should rule out the possibility that I have drugged or poisoned the contents of this glass.

"I truly bear you very little ill will, considering the trouble that you and your kind have caused me. Indeed, though I imagine you would not possibly believe me, I have brought you here to help you."

"To help *me*." She stepped into the room, still on edge, gauging the difference between herself and the other. "How do you propose 'to help'?"

"Why, with the object of your quest, of course." He extended one hand, offering her a glass. She took it from him, careful not to touch his hand. He gestured with the now-empty hand toward the sword-rest holding the *gyaryu*. "You need not dissemble about *that*, either— the sword is the reason why you are here. It is also the reason I am here, though I expect to take my leave shortly.

"You see"—he reached out with his glass and gently touched it to hers, producing a single, crystalline sound—"I am here to deliver it to you."

"At what price?"

" 'Price'? You misunderstand me, dear lady. There is no cost involved, other than what you have already paid. The *gyaryu* is yours to take." He took a sip from his glass and seemed to contemplate her over it.

"Who are you, to give the *gyaryu* to *me*? Are you with some rival to the Great Queen?"

"Who am I?" He returned to his seat and settled back into it. He smiled up at her: two rows of perfect teeth, like some kind of predator. "You can call me Stone."

The name didn't mean anything to her. "And what's your agenda, Mr. Stone?"

"For quite some time I've been an advisor to the Great Queen, though she'll be getting along without my counsel from now on. And it would be *extremely* simplistic to call me her enemy, though it certainly wouldn't be the first time I've been accused of such a crime.

"No, I've got other employers. They've been watching this affair play itself out, Commodore, and it is their consensus opinion that it is best for their interests that the *gyaryu* be placed in your hands."

"These . . . 'employers.' They believe in the Qu'u legend?"

"They wrote it."

She shrugged this off as bravado, although the offhand way in which Stone said it disturbed her. She came over to stand behind the other chair.

"So, you're going to let me take the sword away, out from under the Great Queen's—"

She had wanted to say "nose," but she couldn't remember if vuhls really had noses, in their natural form. Before she could finish the sentence, however, Stone smiled and cut through her train of thought.

"Far more than that. It has been decided to place the *gyaryu in your hands*."

"I don't understand the distinction."

"Take up the sword and you will understand." He stood up and stepped away, allowing her to come close to where it lay. She knew how the legend ended: Qu'u found the *gyaryu,* unguarded, in the Fortress of Despite; he took it up and experienced something called the Dark Understanding . . .

And then *esGa'u* destroyed him.

And then *esLi* saved him.

Would Stone play the part of *esGa'u* here? And was *esLi* standing by on comm, waiting to extend His Talon to rescue her?

And what the hell *was* "the Dark Understanding"?

She set the goblet, still untouched, on a side-table and reached out for the sword, keeping one eye on Stone.

In a comfortably appointed room near the High Lord's Chamber of Meditation, the comatose form of the human *Gyaryu'har* lay in repose. It was constantly tended to by healers and functionaries looking for some sign that the old man might either recover from his terrible affliction, or transcend the Outer Peace and thus end his suffering.

It came as a surprise to them when, suddenly, a broad, beatific smile spread across his face. Attempts were made to rouse him then, to no avail.

"*se* Jackie."

Sword in hand, Jackie turned toward the source of the voice and watched Stone and the villa room fade out like a 3-V that had just been switched off.

A man was walking toward her out of the darkness. She didn't recognize the form or the gait, and held the *gyaryu* out in front of her. Instead of snarling, as a *chya* might do for an enemy *esGa'uYe,* it seemed to warm in welcoming.

"Welcome, *se* Jackie," the man said, coming into view.

"*se* Sergei?" She was shocked to see him: He was younger, perhaps seventy or so, and seemed strong and healthy. It almost seemed as if her memory of the old, old man that had come to Cicero was some sort of caricature of this person.

"Not exactly in the flesh, but that's me. Welcome to the *gyaryu.*"

"Welcome to . . ."

"You've visited a mental construct representing the Plain of Despite; this construct is very similar and almost as old. This is the *gyaryu,* the Talon of State of the People." Sergei smiled and came up alongside her. "Of course, you'll require a guide."

"You."

"Tradition. Or so I understand it." Sergei began to walk forward.

She walked with him, still holding the sword in both hands.

"What tradition is that?" she asked.

"Do you know the history of this sword?" Sergei asked her, instead of replying. "Several thousand Standard years ago, it was used literally and symbolically to unite the People on the Homeworld under the leadership of the first High Lord, A'alu. It has been wielded—and carried—by hundreds of servants of the High Nest, each one epitomizing the ideal of *esLi*'s servant in the World That Is."

The place they were in seemed somewhat less dim now; she could make out the floor—a hard, black, unyielding surface covered with whorls and symbols; intricate *hRni'i.*

"Eighty-five years ago, when we were poised to utterly destroy the People, the High Lord *hi'i* Sse'e HeYen placed the *gyaryu* in the hands of Admiral Ivan Marais, naming him both 'Dark Wing' and 'Bright Wing,' destroyer and renewer."

She held the sword in a parry position ahead of her. She looked past its point and could see another figure walking toward them: a dignified older man, his hair graying at the temples. His face was startlingly familiar; it looked back at her with the hint of a smile and piercing gray eyes.

"Admiral Marais," she whispered.

"Admiral," Sergei said to the figure, as it came up to meet them. "May I present to you Jacqueline Laperriere of Dieron, commodore in His Majesty's Imperial Navy."

"A pleasure," Marais said, extending his hand.

Jackie had no real choice but to lower the sword. Not knowing what to do with it, she sheathed it in a scabbard that hung at her belt. She shook the hand of the famous Admiral; it seemed warm and alive, though she knew the man had been dead more than sixty years.

"Your reputation precedes you, sir," Jackie said, not sure just what to say.

"That can be a curse or a blessing," the Admiral replied.

They began to walk together: Jackie in the middle, flanked by Marais on her right and Sergei on her left. "For example, I know a great deal about you, madam, and yet I do not feel that I know you at all. There are some . . ." He smiled and stopped, looking Jackie up and down, seeming to look right through her. ". . . some that have already made a decision about you based entirely on your performance so far."

"I didn't realize I was on trial."

"The quest that has engaged your attention as you progressed here has been a trial." They began to walk again, and Jackie noticed they were approaching a place bathed in faded orange light. "Though your effort has been most special—given the circumstances—you are by no means the first to be tried thus. You are not even the first human."

"Present company . . ."

"You begin to understand." The light ahead was growing brighter; it appeared as if they were emerging from a dark tunnel into a spacious open area. In the entryway stood a zor warrior, *chya* in hand, his wings arranged in the Stance of Respectful Challenge.

The *chya* and the sword hanging at Jackie's belt seemed to communicate with each other. At last the zor lowered his guard-weapon and sheathed it.

"Kale'e m'Shan *ehn* HeRri'i," he said, placing his wings in the Posture of Reverence to the Warrior.

Jackie inclined her head respectfully.

"You would be Commodore Laperriere." Despite the difference in speaking apparatus, the older zor seemed to do fairly well with the name, as if he'd been practicing.

"*si* Kale'e perished in a battle during the war," Admiral Marais explained. "He was the last one of the People to bear Qu'u's sword. When I met with the High Lord some days later, *hi'i* Sse'e presented the sword to me, rather than settling it on another."

"Now it is being settled on you," Kale'e said. "You will be the new *Gyaryu'har.*"

Jackie looked from Sergei to Marais to Kale'e. The wing-position of the zor, and the solemn, understanding expressions of the two humans, confirmed Kale'e's blunt assertion.

"Now, wait a minute. I know how this legend turns out, and I'm not ready to check out yet. And I'm *not* in line for a job change. Besides, that title belongs to you," she added, to Sergei.

"*Did.* I am old, *se* Jackie; my predecessors are all dead, though some of their *hsi* remains here. Even the *hsi* of the Admiral, though he is human."

"I thought *hsi* returned to *esLi* when its owner died."

"Not always, *se* Jackie."

Jackie whirled to see Th'an'ya approaching from out of the darkness. The humans and the other zor seemed to recognize her. They also seemed to be unsurprised at her appearance. "For example, I have not given all of my *hsi* over to the Golden Light of *esLi,* since it was needed to aid you in your quest." Then, as if in answer to her unasked question, Th'an'ya added, "Now that you have achieved it, I am able to emerge here.

"Also, a warrior of the People surrenders the smallest part of his or her *hsi* so that the *chya* he or she bears, may function. That is why such blades must be ritually destroyed, since that *hsi* remains even after the warrior's death. As for the *gyaryu*"—she spread her wings in a posture conveying a revelation of understanding—"it is the *hsi* left behind by its hundreds of bearers through the centuries that gives the *Gyaryu'har* understanding and capabilities second only to those of the High Lord. The wisdom and knowledge of each bearer is available to the current one, to guide him—or her—on the proper path."

"It was your path to fly all along, *se* Jackie," Kale'e said. "This was a path of revelation, and it needed to be flown so that the High Nest could have a new *Gyaryu'har* to combat the *esGa'uYal.*"

"The High Nest *has* a *Gyaryu'har,* damn it," she retorted, pointing a finger at Sergei. "I understand that you're old. I also understand you brought about the attack on Cicero specifically to put the sword into the hands of the aliens, so I'd come to the surface to go and get it. But I never intended anything but to return the sword to you, wherever the hell you are now."

"Zor'a," Sergei said. "But it is no longer necessary to return it to me."

A noise like a sighing breeze through leafy branches wafted through the air. Jackie felt goosebumps down her arms and on the back of her neck.

The High Lord Sa'a HeYen had been flying across a dream landscape of battle and destruction, earnestly trying to lift her head to see the Fortress, impossibly far above. She had struggled for what seemed an eternity; then, suddenly, as a blinding flash from an explosion lit the land below, she looked upward to see the menacing structure for the first time . . .

•   •   •

The physician by the bedside of Sergei Torrijos placed his wings in a posture of reverence to *esLi* and drew the sheet over the face of the corpse.

You—"

"I have transcended the Outer Peace, *se* Jackie. You shall bear the *gyaryu* back to the High Nest on Zor'a, but it will not leave you again."

"And if I refuse?"

"It is always within your power to refuse," Th'an'ya replied quietly, her wings assuming a posture of resignation. "There was always the possibility that you might choose a course other than to accept the burden of the office. You are not one of the People, and *idju'e* cannot be used as a stick to coerce your cooperation.

"Before you refuse to take up the *gyaryu*, bear this in mind: Many ships belonging to the servants of *esGa'u* are within the Empire at this moment. Without the *gyaryu*, all of it is at risk of Domination. The *esGa'uYal* will continue their attacks and show no mercy. With the *gyaryu*, at least some of that space will be protected, since the servants will not dare approach. Even Shrnu'u HeGa'u could not defeat Qu'u when he took up the sword."

"I still have to get off this world."

No one answered her, as she looked from face to face. Sergei and Admiral Marais stood side by side, their faces full of understanding but betraying no emotion. Kale'e's wing-position was one of reverence to *esLi*. Th'an'ya, half in shadow, stood in a posture Jackie hadn't seen before: *a'Li'e're*—Choosing the Flight.

"Decision time," Jackie said, to no one in particular. Sergei nodded.

She looked down at the *gyaryu* hanging in its scabbard at her waist and then reached in under her coat and drew out the hilt of Ch'k'te's broken *chya*. To her surprise, it still felt slightly warm to her touch.

"You told me that a *chya* is ritually destroyed when its owner dies. What happens if it breaks?"

"The *hsi* that it held, remains within," Kale'e answered. "The warrior does not truly reach *esLi*'s Golden Circle until it is freed."

"That means Ch'k'te is still in here. It's a damn lucky thing I picked this up," she said, glancing at Th'an'ya.

"Indeed," Th'an'ya replied.

"Is there enough of Ch'k'te's *hsi* to call forth a *hsi*-image?"

"Here on the *gyaryu*," Th'an'ya answered, "I would expect so." Her wing-position changed again and Jackie could read her emotions clearly. It had probably taken considerable will for her to keep from suggesting to Jackie that she do so.

"How . . . do I do it?"

"Concentrate."

She concentrated, disregarding her tenuous position in the real world, her fears about the *gyaryu* and her future and the plots that had made her so crucial to the completion of the quest. She remembered Ch'k'te—

The sighing breeze seemed to lightly jostle a windchime, off in the dark distance somewhere.

"I am here," she heard, and turned to face Ch'k'te—his eyes full of life, his wings in a posture of reverence. "I cannot remain long, *se* Jackie."

She embraced him, somewhat to the surprise of the other humans present.

"I don't know what to do," she said at last.

"We are all bound by duty," Ch'k'te answered. "From the time I took up my *chya*"—he gestured to the stump in her hand—"I followed the duty that my Nest and my People placed upon me. As an officer in the Imperial Navy, I also had a duty. When you chose to take up the role of Qu'u, I knew that I had another duty."

He looked across at Th'an'ya, whose wing-position had not changed. "At last, on Crossover, when the *esGa'uYe* released its hold upon me, I performed my final service to you, and duty to myself.

"What you are offered is an honor, but it is a duty, also. Remember that the High Chamberlain told you that you could do what neither he nor the High Lord nor, perhaps, what any one person could do. Now you are on the verge of having done so.

"Qu'u was not the eldest, nor the greatest, warrior in his Nest. But he was the one that the Lord *esLi* chose.

"As are you chosen, to stand within the Circle while the *esGa'uYal* carry out their destiny."

"Some 'destiny.'"

She handed the broken *chya* to Ch'k'te and placed her hand on the hilt of the *gyaryu.* "In the legend," she said, "Qu'u reaches the Fortress of Despite alone. He appeals to the Lord to take them from the Valley of Lost Souls, where *esGa'u* traps them after Qu'u begins to ascend the Perilous Stair.

"Then, if I *am* Qu'u," she said, "I'd like to appeal in kind to *esLi* to do the same for you. I'm truly sorry that I didn't know to do this before. And Th'an'ya," she said, turning to her, "I have held your *hsi* here"—Jackie tapped her temple—"for long enough already. I will miss your company but I feel honor-bound to release you."

"*se* Jackie." Th'an'ya stepped forward and extended a taloned hand. Jackie took hold of it. "When I chose this flight, I did not know if it would succeed, nor indeed what would happen to my *hsi.* I did not expect that I would ever go to *esLi.*

"*li* Ch'k'te spoke of duty. I, too, have taken upon myself the duty of readying you for this decision. I would not want you to become *Gyaryu'har* at such a crucial moment without whatever meager guidance I might continue to provide."

"I think," Jackie replied, half smiling as she looked over her shoulder at Sergei, Marais and Kale'e, "that I am well provided-for. Go now. *esLiHeYar.*"

Th'an'ya and Ch'k'te both arranged their wings in a posture of deference to *esLi* and then they both changed to the Posture of Respectful Affection.

Then they took flight and receded into the dark distance, a flash of golden light from somewhere dappling their wings until they vanished from sight.

Jackie turned again to face the three others.

"I'm ready," she said.

Kale'e bowed to her and gestured that she step past him into the light. As she did so, she found herself in a lush and verdant garden. With Kale'e by her side, she walked along a carefully manicured path. Out of the corner of her eye she could see that several . . . then several more eights . . . then a few sixty-fours of zor . . . were following her as she approached the center of the garden. At last she came into a large open area with a perch. On it stood a zor with ceremonial garb, his wings held in the posture called the Cloak of Worship.

" 'And the Lord *esLi* spoke to Lord A'alu e'Yen, and commanded her, "Recite this in My Name.

" ' "Tell all the generations of My People, alive and yet to come, that

I have commanded this: That among the People there shall be one High Nest and one High Lord.

" ' "Say to them: 'The Lord *esLi* has looked upon the works of His People, and has chosen in His grace to send them a sign whereby His will should be done—that a hero should be found. This hero should be of great and noble heart; and though young and not well tried, he shall go forth to the Plain of Despite, and recover that which was lost, and which, with my assistance, he shall have regained.'

" ' "Tell them that the hero has returned to them, and that he bears a sword I have reforged for him.

" ' "Tell them that by this sword shall My People become one people, and the Nest of the hero shall become the High Nest of My People. This shall be the Sword of the Nest—the sword of the hero that pierced the Icewall, who will stand within the Circle when the armies of the Deceiver come to the gates." '

"As it was said unto me, *se* Jackie, so do I say it unto you. To you is given the *gyaryu*, the Talon of State, recovered from the Plain of Despite many five-twelves of turns ago. You are *naZora'e* just as your two predecessors were, but you are heir to my legacy.

"I am Qu'u.

"I name you *Qu'uYar:* the Recoverer, the Piercer of the Icewall. By your own will you are *Gyaryu'har,* the One Who Stands Within the Circle. Your predecessors will always be here to assist you. May you walk in Light, *se* Jackie Laperriere. *esLiHeYar.*" Qu'u executed a stance that seemed to bow so low, that for a moment Jackie thought he'd fall off the perch.

Instead, he—and indeed the whole scene—seemed to become watery and dim, fading from view, until at last she found herself again in the sitting-room, the *gyaryu* in her hands.

Stone was still in the place he had been when she had last seen him. She reached inside her coat pocket and found the *chya*, but it was just a cold, inert piece of metal.

"Gone to *esLi*," he said, raising one eyebrow.

"I suppose you witnessed all of that."

"No, actually not." He twirled the stem of a goblet between thumb and forefinger. "I have a reasonable idea of what happened . . . but no, I didn't pry.

"So now you have the *gyaryu*. I presume you have 'the Dark Understanding,' as well—whatever *that* might be."

"Don't you know?"

"I don't really care," Stone said, smiling faintly, in a way that chilled Jackie. "Now that you have the sword, it remains only to get you to put it back to use."

"How do you plan to do that?"

"The simplest possible expedient." He gestured toward the hallway. As she watched, the dark was interrupted by several parallel bands of brightly colored light; they seemed to stretch out the door and into the night, beyond her range of vision.

"What the hell is that?"

"You are wasting *time,* madam," Stone answered. "What it *is,* would be far too difficult to explain. Suffice it to say that it will bring you back to Zor'a. I'll shortly be using similar means myself."

"I don't understand—"

"My dear commodore." Stone smiled again, showing the perfect teeth. "It is not required for you to understand. Soon . . . very soon, if I'm not terribly mistaken . . . several Drones who report directly to the Great Queen, including First Drone H'mr, will be arriving here. They will deal with you first and then with me. I don't intend to be present, and I strongly advise you to depart as well. As one who has experienced Domination in person, I should think you'd need very little convincing."

"Zor'a is hundreds of parsecs from here."

"You'll be there before you can work up a sweat. *Come on,* Commodore. It's not as if you have a choice."

She backed away from him, sword at the ready, until she could see brightness all around her. Through the luminescence, she could see another path beginning to form, from the sitting-room, in the opposite direction.

"Don't step off the path," he said; and then he began to walk his own route. After scarcely a moment, he receded into the distance.

She felt the familiar pressure of approaching vuhl Sensitives. Rather than wait to see who would show up—and realizing that she didn't really have a choice—she turned and began to walk along the rainbow path.

Soon there was nothing but blackness. She kept the *gyaryu* drawn, and *anGa'e'ren* kept its distance.

Excerpted from the final transmission by the flagship *Nest HeYen*, under the personal sigil of Ke'erl HeYen, High Lord of the People; received by IS *Pappenheim* at Thon's Well, 14 January 2397:

> . . . This is not a false seeming. The hero Qu'u travels alone now, with no direction from the sage, unaccompanied by Hyos, the spirit-guide trapped in the webs of *Ur'ta leHssa*. The hero climbs toward the Fortress of Despite.
>
> The People and the *naZora'i* together face an enemy that *esGa'u* would have wished us to face alone. Eights of turns ago, the Deceiver sought to keep the People and the other races apart, but the will of *esLi* was stronger, and brought us *esHu'ur*, who was also *esTli'ir*, though many wings and many more wingless ones did not see the weave of the Golden Circle, nor perceive its wisdom . . .
>
> Beyond the edge of our perceptions the *esHara'y* lurk, no longer waiting, but acting upon the direction of their Master. They are led by a Queen, who has an advisor—an *e'gyu'u* the equal of our *Gyaryu'har*—who has granted them dominion over all they sought to conquer, as long as the advisor lives. Many races have fallen under the talons of these *esHara'y*, and we who oppose them are their next flight. We cannot stop them from their conquest. Yet if *gyaryu* and hero return to stand within the Circle, something may be

preserved for the bright generation to follow. This *a'Li'e're* may well be one that the *naZora'i* will not desire to make.

The one who comes to exact blood-price for the deeds of the *es-Hara'y* of this generation will be sharp-taloned and terrible, and in his wake the ones who follow will turn against each other when the *shNa'es'ri* is passed.

I say to the People: The Eight Winds are calm now in my soul. To transcend the Outer Peace is to join *esLi* within the Circle; it must be thus, so that the hero who stands before the gate of the Deceiver may recover what was lost. The hero shall defend that Circle while the *esHara'y* rake their talons in the ashes of what we have built.

esLiHeYar . . .

I⊏ had taken a long time for Second Drone H'tt to accustom himself to the wide-open spaces that the meat-creatures favored. Standing on an observation balcony overlooking one of the docking areas of Adrianople Starbase, he forced himself to look up and down and side to side. It gave him more than a slight amount of vertigo; he forced the feeling down and away, pushing it into his *i'kn*-mind where it would bother his dreams but not his ability to function.

He had spent many twelves of *vx*tori* in human form—which he held now as well. Even though the meat-creatures at Adrianople had seen his other form, he found it just as easy to command their obedience by wearing the appearance that disturbed them less—but he always had problems with the open spaces.

Agoraphobia. It occurred to him that some clever primitive might identify the trait with his race, letting a disguise be penetrated. But it seemed that the humans, at least, often suffered from this (and other) perverse fears, so there would probably be lots of false positives if that were the litmus test they chose.

He turned from the dizzying vista to see the human commander of the base approaching. Durant had not changed much in the few weeks he had been here; he was careful and guarded, particularly around H'tt, but always seemed to be barely leashing his anger.

H'tt shrugged his human shoulders. It was something he would no doubt have to address. *Eventually,* he added, to himself.

"Commodore," H'tt said.

"You asked to see me," Durant said. He walked to the edge of the balcony and looked down at the concourse, where the business of the starbase proceeded, a few twelves of meters below.

Extraordinary, H'tt thought. *No fear.*

"We will be receiving an important visitor soon," H'tt said. "First Drone H'mr is on his way to Adrianople."

"Your superior."

"In a manner of speaking. He will be inspecting this facility and evaluating our progress. I trust . . . he will find everything satisfactory."

The sentence seemed to end with an unspoken "*. . . or else.*" Durant turned to face the vuhl master of the base. "When is the First Drone expected?"

"Within the next several Standard days. He is conducting a tour of occupied systems. He has matters to deal with elsewhere and then he will come here."

"I see."

"I expect the cooperation of your staff. It could be most unpleasant if anything improper happened during his visit."

"I understand."

"But you do not approve."

"I am not here to approve, sir," Durant said, looking away again. "My base is in your . . . hands because it was the best way to save lives. I remain a subject of the Solar Emperor."

"Meaning?"

"I won't dissemble with you. I expect that although you may need me now, there will come a time when I and all of these people"—he gestured toward the concourse—"will be superfluous. Don't expect me to be happy with that."

"Commodore, I believe you operate under a misconception."

"Is that so."

"Yes, it is so; and I believe that if I correct that error, you might find this easier to accept.

"If we intended to kill all of you, be assured we would do so—indeed, we would have done so already. I hope you realize, there might be a different outcome."

"If we cooperate."

"Just so. If you cooperate. Your race . . ." H'tt resisted using the term "meat-creature," but it crossed his mind just the same. "Both your race and the zor could survive and benefit from a relationship with ours."

"As slaves."

"As *clients*," H'tt said. "We have many technologies that could ben-efit your peoples; you, in turn, have capabilities that could help First Hive."

"I'm so glad to hear that our welfare is your concern. I suppose that's why you let Hsien's squadron go."

H'tt's *i'kn*-mind raged at Durant. It was all he could do to restrain it. "Your sarcasm is touching."

"Your perception of human emotions improves by the day, I see."

"Are you trying to enrage me, Commodore?"

"Why would I do that?" Durant turned to face him again. "You could kill me with a thought. Your . . . technology has nearly shattered the mind of my exec. One would think it mighty dangerous to goad you, sir."

"Quite correct. I'll remind you to keep that in mind." H'tt gestured toward the concourse. "And make sure *they* know it as well."

Durant took this last comment as a dismissal; he inclined his head and turned away. *I'll be damned if I'll give the bastard a salute,* he thought, and turned away, not caring whether the Second Drone heard it or not.

H'tt had heard the comment, but ignored it as he watched Durant walk away. For just a moment there was something else, something just below the surface of his mind that the exchange had concealed . . . but he couldn't quite pick it up.

On the concourse, Durant walked slowly past the docking bays for the Adrianople squadron; some of them were closed and dark—the *Eurydice* and the *Aragon* in particular. Everywhere else, he saw small Imperial flags flying near the status board . . . upside down; a small symbol of resistance that might or might not have escaped the attention of the Second Drone and the occupying force.

Opposite the docking bay for the starship *Trebizond*, Durant walked into a public restroom. A few moments later he was joined by the ship's captain, Richard Abramowicz.

As they stood side by side, using the facilities, Durant said, without looking, "It'll have to be soon. We're expecting a VIP."

"I'm due to take us out on patrol in two watches. We'll wait for you to come aboard."

"No," Durant said. "I'm staying here."

"They'll kill you."

"Likely so. But I don't want to alarm our friends."

"But—"

"Just carry out your mission, Rich. That's an order."

Abramowicz finished his business. As the unit loudly evacuated its contents, the captain of the *Trebizond* said something impolite and highly unmilitary, followed by the words ". . . yes sir."

If Durant heard what Abramowicz had said, he showed no sign.

seLi'e'Yan

STANDING WITHIN
THE CIRCLE

PART TWO

chapter 12

The High Lord, dreaming, cried out.

Dan McReynolds and Georg Maartens jumped to their feet. A half-dozen zor were there ahead of them, attending to the now-awoken High Lord. She seemed to be shivering all over and her wings went through a hundred different positions, as if they had their own agenda. The two humans were ignored; they looked at each other nervously, wondering if they were supposed to have witnessed any of it.

They had been in the High Lord's garden for almost two hours. Sa'a had been less cryptic and more forthcoming than any zor either of them had ever met. She, in turn, had wanted to know all about Jackie; the two men had been as informative as they could, while both wondered if they'd ever see Jackie Laperriere again.

After a time there had been nothing else to say. The High Lord had bid them stay and take further refreshment while she contemplated and sought answers in dreams the waking world could not provide. They had stayed and waited patiently: And now the High Lord had suddenly awoken.

She seemed to shake loose from sleep and descended from her perch, moving quickly toward a deeper part of the garden. She exchanged a glance with Maartens, and he and McReynolds quickly followed.

"What's—?" McReynolds began, but Maartens held up a hand. The hurried procession made its way to a wide spot where huge, sunflower-like plants quivered in the artificial breeze. The High Lord spread out her arms and her wings; everyone behind her stopped moving.

From the opposite side of the clearing, T'te'e HeYen—High Chamberlain of the People—emerged, flying low to the ground. He stopped and hovered as if he had been summoned.

In the center of the clearing, the air began to distort as if it were being twisted by some unseen hand. Rays of different-colored light and a viscid darkness emerged from it. Both light and dark were too bright to look at directly.

Just as suddenly, Jackie Laperriere, holding an ornate sword in both hands, stepped out from the distortion. Almost as soon as her feet touched the flagstones in the courtyard, she stumbled and fell forward.

"Holy Christ," Dan McReynolds whispered to himself. The zor in attendance were murmuring among themselves. Dan figured their reaction was pretty much the same as his own. The colors and the blackness were already fading to invisibility as Maartens and two of the zor jumped forward to catch Jackie before she hit the ground.

Jackie let go of the sword with one hand and caught hold of Maartens' sleeve.

"Georg?" she said, her eyes wide. She looked from him to the two nearby zor, to the High Lord just beyond, to Dan McReynolds, who had taken a step toward where she half knelt. "Dan?"

"Reporting for duty," Georg answered, smiling. "Both of us."

"Permission to come aboard," Jackie said, and tried unsuccessfully to push herself to her feet. She collapsed into a seated position, not letting go of the sword with her other hand.

"This isn't *Pappenheim*," Maartens said, looking around. "Not by a long shot. Do you know where you are?"

"I have no idea."

"What happened? Where the hell have you been?" Georg Maartens asked.

" 'Happened'?" She laughed, but it was abruptly cut short as she caught sight of T'te'e, whose wings were held in a posture of sorrow.

"Eight thousand pardons," the High Chamberlain interrupted, moving toward the scene. Other zor stepped away from his path. "*se* Jackie. *hi* Sa'a," he said, addressing each of them. "I have come from the chambers of the *Gyaryu'har*. He has transcended the Outer Peace, less than a sixty-fourth of a sun ago."

"Then, that means . . ." She looked up at Georg and then at T'te'e—

then at the sword which she still gripped tightly. "I'm . . . I'm sorry. Too many things have happened in the last few days. I don't know what's real, what's a dream. It seems I've inherited a responsibility." Her eyes didn't leave the sword now. "I met . . . Qu'u."

T'te'e, the High Lord and the other zor shifted their wing-positions to postures of great respect.

"Welcome aboard," Maartens said.

After several hours' dreamless sleep, a long shower and a chance to put on some clean clothing, Jackie met the High Lord formally, along with the High Chamberlain and the High Nest's envoy to the Solar Emperor. They received her in a wide, high-ceilinged chamber not far from the High Lord's *esTle'e*. There were entrances at various heights above where they sat, and empty perches in alcoves above ground-level; but they were the only four people in the room.

The universe had changed. It wasn't clear to Jackie whether it was the universe the High Nest had expected when it sent her on her quest. The news of events at Thon's Well came as quite a shock—but even that had an analog in the sacrifice and suicide of Ge'el, Lord of e'Yen, during the Unification. *hi'i* Ke'erl wasn't quite mad after all, except in the overall scheme of things—in which every part of the pattern the High Nest had woven was completely mad. The new High Lord, Sa'a, had come to her office without the ritual of *Te'esLi'ir,* but seemed to be handling the transition reasonably well.

Now Jackie was part of it; there was no one on Zor'a or elsewhere who would challenge her right to carry the *gyaryu,* which had not been more than five meters from her person since she took it up.

"*se* Jackie," the High Chamberlain said, as she took her seat, which changed to accommodate her dimensions. "I am pleased to see you in good health." His wings reinforced the statement but showed that he was nervous about her reaction.

"Thank you," she answered. "*ha* T'te'e—"

T'te'e's wings moved slightly in embarrassment; Jackie realized it must be the prenomen that bothered him. "Excuse me—*se* T'te'e. Since we are to work together, let me reassure you that I don't hold any grudges. After all that's happened, I've got a very clear idea of who my friends and enemies are."

"If there is anything I have done to offend—"

"*se* T'te'e." She laid her hands, palms down, on the table. "Humans and zor have done an uncountable number of things to offend each other since our races first met. You and I are no exception. You handled the situation—handled my intrusion into the weave of the High Nest—remarkably well, and I'm surprised I didn't do anything to permanently offend you then.

"When I left Cicero I was full of anger. I was angry with the Imperial Navy for its narrow-mindedness, angry at the High Nest for manipulating me, angry at fate for placing me into this mess. For months I've been running through the storm, and now I'm finally under a dry roof and I have a chance to think."

His wings indicated that he hadn't quite followed her metaphor.

She hurried on: "We can't afford to concern ourselves with offense. The *gyaryu'e* have chosen me, and you and I will have to learn to work together."

"I would not consider contravening *esLi*'s will," the High Chamberlain answered. "The question was one of honor, not personal satisfaction." His wings rose to the position of Warrior's Respect to *esLi*.

"*se* T'te'e, I—" Jackie began.

The envoy cleared his throat. "*se Gyaryu'har,* if I may?" Randall Boyd said. "*se* T'te'e. I believe that both of you understand the gravity of the situation and the necessity for patience and understanding. Perhaps we can proceed with that point as given."

Jackie smiled, with a respectful nod to the envoy. "I certainly concur."

"Of course," the High Chamberlain said.

The High Lord arranged her wings in the Posture of Polite Approach. "*se* Jackie, would you fly the path of your experiences for us?"

"By all means," Jackie said. "I . . . guess I'd begin with Crossover."

"You were aboard Captain McReynolds' ship?" the envoy asked, and Jackie nodded.

"*Fair Damsel* had been contacted by *se* S'reth to transport myself and *si* Ch'k'te—" She felt a pang of regret but continued: "—to transport us beyond the border of the Empire. Dan McReynolds had claimed to have seen *Negri Sembilan,* one of the missing ships, calling there; it was the only clue we had.

"By this time *se* S'reth, as well as *si* Ch'k'te and—as far as I can tell—just about everyone else, had become convinced that I was the avatar of Qu'u. In a very real sense I followed Qu'u's path to the Plain

of Despite, particularly because I didn't know what the hell I was doing
or where I was going." This comment caused the High Chamberlain's
wings to elevate, but Jackie plowed forward. "At Crossover, with
Th'an'ya's and Ch'k'te's help, I was able to reach the *Ur'ta leHssa* and
the base of the Perilous Stair."

She felt a shiver, remembering the experience. "There, the Guardian—
who had the appearance of the captain of the *Negri Sembilan*—told me
I'd be traveling alone to the Fortress of Despite, and that taking the
sword was a one-way trip."

"Sensitives dream in constructs that make the most sense to them,"
Boyd interjected. "You were looking for *Negri Sembilan,* so the image
of its captain made the most sense for you when you reached the Perilous Stair."

"I don't think it was that simple," Jackie replied. "I met the *real*
Damien Abbas on Center. He appeared at the perfect time to provide
information and to transport me directly to where the sword was
held . . . I'm getting to that.

"When we emerged from the mental link, Ch'k'te and I began looking for some real-world analog to the base of the Perilous Stair. When I
tried to inquire about *Negri,* I was given a message to 'go to the Center.' "

"Do you recall the contents of the message?" Boyd asked, making
notes with his stylus.

"The exact words?" she asked. He nodded. Instinctively, without
thinking much about why, she placed her hand on the already familiar
hilt of the *gyaryu,* and closed her eyes.

Almost at once she felt Sergei's presence from within the sword. *Let
us help,* he said. *Try to frame the scene in your mind and we should be
able to recover the message.*

She concentrated and felt the words come to her mind. " 'You have
come to ascend the Perilous Stair to the Fortress of Despite,' " she recited. " 'You believe that you have come far, but all of your journeying
thus far is but a fraction of the task compared to what lies ahead.

" 'Go to the Center, Mighty Hero. The Icewall awaits.' "

She opened her eyes and detected surprise from the two zor. *Nice
trick,* she said to Sergei within. *Thanks.*

" 'Go to the Center,' " Boyd repeated, his expression curious.
"What does that mean?"

"In the context of the moment it was a message telling me where to go next. It was a trap: One of the vuhls—the aliens—was waiting for us in the administrative offices of the station. Crossover's shaped like a wheel." She held her hands in front of her, touching index fingers and thumbs, forming a circle. "The hub is called Center.

"We went there and fought an *esGa'uYe*. He—it—killed Ch'k'te." She folded her hands in front of her. "Ch'k'te killed it, as well. He broke his *chya* in the alien's body. The alien thought that Ch'k'te was Qu'u— seemed to know the whole legend, almost as if it thought it was manipulating the entire event for its own purposes. Naturally, since it was a legend of the People, the alien apparently assumed that a warrior of the People was the avatar of Qu'u. It was a reasonable assumption—it was just wrong.

"When it suddenly realized that *I* was supposed to be Qu'u, Ch'k'te had an opening. He was still upset about being Dominated on Cicero and—I expect—was feeling betrayed by Th'an'ya, who had transferred her *hsi* to me somehow.

"It was very easy for him to die."

"He served *esLi*," the High Chamberlain said.

"He *killed himself,* damn it. He transcended the Outer Peace. He had such guilt that he was still alive, that he found the best available opportunity to end his life—"

"You do not understand, *se* Jackie—" the High Chamberlain began, but Jackie turned to face him and his wings rose in alarm.

"No, *se* T'te'e, I *do* understand. Before the *D'sen'yen'ch'a* I did not, and before my journey to the Fortress of Despite I did not. But I do *now*.

"I must tell you, as well, that if Ch'k'te died in order to save my life, it was tragic but acceptable; but if he died because of a societal imperative that he justify his own life, then it was pointless and unacceptable. If Ch'k'te were alive today he would be worth more to this council, and more helpful and useful to our struggle than he ever would be as another quantum of *hsi* added to *esLi's* Golden Light."

"*esLi* has His own purposes," the High Lord said after a moment. "It is not our place to question whether Ch'k'te's time to hold the Outer Peace was too short."

"I concede that we cannot understand *esLi's* purposes, *hi* Sa'a. I would not think to question that: I simply mean that if what Ch'k'te lived his life by, and what he used to justify it, drove him to die needlessly, then that philosophy is *wrong*.

"Ch'k'te was Dominated by a superior Sensitive mind: an alien and hostile one against which he had insufficient defenses. He won't be the last to suffer such a fate. We can't afford to have every Sensitive who experiences Domination hurl themselves into the abyss just because of it.

"I was Dominated by an alien. Does that make *me* unworthy to carry the *gyaryu*?"

She looked around the table from face to face. She could sense their consternation; she could even feel a tinge of anger from the High Chamberlain. None of them spoke.

"A century ago the People thought that my race was the *esGa'uYal*," Jackie went on. "Now the People believe the vuhls are the *esGa'uYal*. Based on my present knowledge, I believe even *that* assumption is flawed—or even wrong. The alien invaders are certainly *esHara'y*, doing the Deceiver's work and perhaps even his bidding, but the enemy is different and more insidious and certainly more dangerous.

"After the alien at Crossover was killed, I was able to escape in his ship and take it to his next destination: a conquered world called Center."

" 'Go to the Center,' " the High Chamberlain repeated.

"Right. And it was there I encountered Damien Abbas again—the real one, not the creature who guarded the Perilous Stair in my dream. He'd been left on Center after the *Negri Sembilan* was captured, along with other officers and crew from his ship, and the ones that Tolliver took out from Cicero."

The High Lord and High Chamberlain exchanged glances. Jackie waited for one of them to say something, but neither ventured a comment.

After a moment, she continued: "Damien was able to contact me and provide me with transportation to the place where the *gyaryu* was kept. But before I was able to learn very much, his *hsi* was taken from him. His mind was rendered inert. I've seen it done before: once on Cicero and once on Crossover. The aliens killed Lieutenant John Maisel on Cicero Down, and then Ch'k'te that same way, when his *chya* was being driven into an alien's chest.

"So, without further information, I was left to confront the person guarding the *gyaryu*. Th'an'ya was . . . out of reach. All nicely arranged: no spirit-guide, no companions. I didn't fight for the sword—it was handed to me."

"*Handed* to you?" T'te'e asked. His wings formed the Posture of Polite Questioning.

"That's right. The *gyaryu* was given to me by a person—a human—who called himself Stone. He said . . . he had been advising the Great Queen, the leader of the vuhls. He told me his 'employers' had decided it was best that the *gyaryu* be placed in my hands. I asked him if they believed in *The Legend of Qu'u,* and he said they had written it."

Sa'a's wings formed the Stance of Dishonored Affront. "I would have torn his heart from his body with my talons."

"I didn't have that option."

"Did he hand you the sword?" T'te'e asked levelly.

"He didn't touch it. I took hold of it myself, and saw—"

T'te'e held up his taloned hands. "It is between you and the *gyaryu.* You obtained a satisfactory understanding of the sword and its purpose?"

" 'The Dark Understanding.' " She closed her eyes for a moment, then opened them again. "Yes. I made the decision to accept the burden of carrying it, *se* T'te'e. By the decision of the *gyaryu* I am both *Gyaryu'har* and *Qu'uYar,* the Recoverer and the Piercer of the Icewall. I have also released both Th'an'ya and Ch'k'te to *esLi*'s Golden Light."

This seemed to have an effect on both the High Lord and the High Chamberlain. They assumed calmer stances, while Boyd looked from Jackie to the High Lord and back again.

"How did you get back here to Zor'a?" he asked.

"Stone did that, too. He created some sort of pathway and told me to step onto it and it would bring me to . . . bring me *here.* He left Center by the same means. I'm not sure, but I think that I wasn't even the first person they'd helped that way."

The zor were looking at each other again.

"You have something to add here?" Jackie asked.

"Please continue, *se* Jackie," the High Lord said.

"After I left Stone, I walked the path. It was like a tunnel with nothing around it. No, it was worse than nothing—it was *anGa'e'ren.* Like jump." She thought for a moment. "It might have been jump, or something like it: I think I walked for less than an hour, and it took me a few hundred parsecs."

"So," Boyd said. "Whose side are they on?"

"I would suspect that they are on their *own* side," the High Lord answered. "The most dangerous position for an unknown foe."

"Where do we go from here?" the High Chamberlain asked, and it was not clear, either from his voice or by his wings, whether he was addressing the High Lord or Jackie.

Jackie assumed it was the High Lord being addressed, but Sa'a did not answer except to place her wings in the Posture of Polite Resignation.

"I . . . get the feeling," Jackie said at last, "that there's something you haven't told me."

"There is." The High Lord took a deep breath. "*se* Jackie, your contribution to our understanding is much appreciated—but you should know that the description you give of this tunnel is something we have already heard about."

"From who?" She knew the answer, but was waiting for someone to confirm it.

"From *se* Owen Garrett," Sa'a said, placing her wings in a position Jackie didn't recognize, but which clearly disturbed T'te'e. "He claimed to have been rescued from the *esGa'uYal* by similar colored bands of light.

"He took *Negri Sembilan* back from the enemy and returned it to Imperial space. *se* Garrett is now on his way here."

"He made it back."

"The ship reached Stanton," the High Lord added. "Imperial Intelligence is reviewing the *Negri* comps."

"Abbas told me about Garrett's escape from the vuhl ship. It was like my own experience, except they apparently *talked* to him . . .

"All right, I give: Why *is* he coming here?" she asked.

"It is a *Dsen'yen'ch'a, se* Jackie," the High Chamberlain said. "*se* Commander Garrett has demonstrated an unusual Sensitive ability—"

"Now, wait just a minute," Jackie said, frowning. "The last time the High Nest decided to conduct a *Dsen'yen'ch'a*, it was to let Shrnu'u HeGa'u loose on the World That Is. If I'm not mistaken, Owen Garrett is even less likely to know what the hell is going on than I was."

"We will not summon an *esGa'uYe* this time, *se* Jackie."

"I will stand by him during the ceremony, *se* T'te'e," Jackie said. "And I expect you to keep your word. What is the ability he has shown?"

"*anGa'riSsa,*" T'te'e answered. "The Shield of Hatred."

"That's not part of the Qu'u legend."

"No. It belongs to *seLi'e'Yan*—Standing Within the Circle. It is an earlier tradition."

" 'If you step onto it you have committed an irreversible act, one that ends with you standing within the Circle.' I was told that by the Abbas-zor at Crossover. A *shNa'es'ri,* he called it."

"A crossroads," the High Lord said.

"I'm part of that legend, too, though I'm not sure how. *si . . .* Th'an'ya told me about it. But what has Owen got to do with it?"

"The story tells of a young warrior who rouses the inhabitants of Sharia'a against the minions of *esGa'u.* If *se* Commander Garrett has developed this talent or somehow obtained it, then the Law of Similar Conjunction—"

"I believe that's how you got me into this mess in the first place," Jackie interrupted.

"—Similar Conjunction," the High Lord repeated, "suggests that he might be flying the path of Dri'i, the young warrior who taught *an-Ga'riSsa* to the warriors of Sharia'a—"

" 'Taught.' "

"That is correct."

"Owen told Abbas that the . . . colored bands had *given* him this power, and that he was supposed to teach it to someone."

"Do you know who?"

"No. That's the question everyone wants answered, *hi* Sa'a. That's what this *Dsen'yen'ch'a* has to be about."

Antares dipped low over the mountains in the distance, spreading deep-orange light through the glass of the balcony doors. Jackie sat on a low cushion in Sergei's—no, *her*—suite, the *gyaryu* placed across her lap. Somewhere in the courtyard, two zor conversed in the High-speech; there was the occasional flap of wings or scratch of talons on flag-stone, the distant hum of an aircar, the breeze passing through an eleven-tone windchime, the faint sound of *fte'e* music. Mostly, though, it was quiet and peaceful.

Jackie knew this was the destination toward which she had been guided since her own *Dsen'yen'ch'a,* perhaps since the first zor contact with the vuhls, years ago, before they knew who she was. Neither T'te'e nor the Envoy's Office truly knew how to deal with her; both had participated in the complex process that had brought this moment about. Both had gotten what they wanted, but perhaps not what they expected. Now it looked as if they were moving Owen Garrett into place, like some sort of chesspiece.

There were still some questions that neither envoy nor High Chamberlain could answer. But there was another source of information available to her. So, with the peaceful sounds of the High Nest in her ears and the sun of Antares warming her shoulders, she closed her eyes and let her hands rest on the ancient zor sword of state. Before she was able to make any meaningful progress, though, the chime at her door rang.

Reluctantly she opened her eyes. "Come."

The door slid open and Randall Boyd was standing there. "I do not mean to intrude, *se Gyaryu'har*."

"No. No problem." She stood up and rebelted the *gyaryu's* scabbard around her. "Can I offer you refreshment?"

"No, thank you." He walked into the room. "You had said the *gyaryu* was given to you by a man named Stone."

"That's right."

"After our meeting I ran an inquiry, and turned up something curious." He placed a small comp on the table beside her and gestured at it. An image appeared in the air: a wiry, spare man in an Imperial Navy captain's uniform, almost a century out of date.

Jackie's hand dropped to rest on the hilt of the *gyaryu*.

"Stone."

"Captain Thomas Stone, taken 2305. Admiral Marais' adjutant during most of the final war between the Solar Empire and the People."

Jackie made an adjustment. The picture zoomed to a headshot, showing the same tight expression, the same sardonic half-smile Jackie had seen just hours earlier while the storm raged outside the Fortress of Despite.

"That's him." She looked at the image and then dismissed it, as if she didn't want it to share the conversation. "Except that it's ninety years out of date.

"There must be more, Mr. Boyd, or you wouldn't be here."

"Oh, there is." He looked at the console, or, rather, away from *her*. "Captain Stone disappeared mysteriously and then reappeared during *si* Marais' trial at Grimaldi Base. He attempted to kill the Admiral but died in the attempt.

"If this is the same person"—he seemed to studiously avoid the word *man*—"then he is not only long-lived, but also able to return from the dead."

"He couldn't be the same person, then." She rubbed her head. "Still . . . What do you mean, he 'disappeared mysteriously'?"

"I accessed the logs of the starship *Lancaster,* the fleet flagship during Admiral Marais' campaign. While it was in jump between A'anenu and Hu'ueru, partway across the Antares Rift, Stone left the ship somehow."

"That's impossible."

"Apparently not. Chandrasekhar Wells—at that time, executive officer of *Lancaster*—presented a paper to the Science Collegium in esYen six years later, in which he laid the mathematical foundation for the energy flux that accompanied Captain Stone's departure. It was all considered completely theoretical, of course, though some of the math has been used in improving jump capabilities during the last fifty or sixty years.

"It *is* true we have no explanation for what happened aboard the *Lancaster* more than eighty-five years ago. I confess that the official logs tell very little."

Jackie didn't answer.

"Oh—there was one other interesting tidbit." He frowned for a moment, as if trying to decide upon a choice of paths. "As you know, my great-grandfather was aboard *Lancaster* as well. He later went to Zor'a to study—and became the High Nest's first envoy to the court of the Solar Emperor. He had not learned to shield; he was occasionally sharing dreams with the High Lord.

"He recounted a dream in which the Deceiver told him—or, rather, told *hi'i* Sse'e—that he would have no more prescient dreams, and that there was a power greater than either zor or human could resist. It was *esGa'u* the Deceiver with a human face." He touched the comp so that it displayed the headshot again. "*That* face."

"His mysterious 'employers.' The supposed authors of the Qu'u legend. The people who ordered him to give me the *gyaryu.*"

"I believe so. But how could they have known that you would be there to claim the sword?"

"If they *arranged* it. If they made sure that the vuhls were wrong about *who* was Qu'u. If they got me from Crossover to Center. If they sent Damien Abbas to meet me . . . No, it's even more devious than that: If they set up the conditions by which the High Nest would carry out the whole plan . . . *Damn.*" She looked away from Boyd and watched the last of the sun disappear behind the western mountains. "It's fitting, somehow: the High Nest being played, just like they played me."

"I'm not sure I understand."

"I'm sure *I* don't." She turned back to the envoy. "Thanks for providing the clue. I'll have to consider it."

Boyd had clearly expected the conversation to go differently, but he was trained well enough as a diplomat to recognize a dismissal when he heard it. "Call upon me anytime," he said, and bowed slightly as he went to the door and left the suite.

Jackie looked at Stone's image again for a moment and then dismissed it and went back to the cushion. The far horizon was aflame with the sunset behind the mountains, but she closed her eyes to it, and concentrated.

With little effort, she again found herself standing upon the black engraving of the *gyaryu* construct.

"*si* Sergei?" she asked. Sergei Torrijos emerged from the darkness and approached where she stood, sword in hand.

"I am here, *se* Jackie."

"I need some guidance."

"I admire your courage." Sergei smiled and stepped forward. "It was weeks before I dared to step into the *gyaryu* after it was first placed in my hands. How may I assist you?"

She sheathed the sword in its scabbard. "I haven't assimilated all of what's happened yet, but I'm fairly sure the enemy isn't going to give me much time for on-the-job training."

"I expect not."

"Are you . . ." She waved her hand toward the darkness beyond the image of Sergei. "All of you—are you aware how I came into possession of the sword?"

"Only to the extent you tell us."

"But you have the knowledge and experience that you had when you were alive."

"That's right."

"Tell me about Captain Stone."

Sergei looked at her curiously. "Why do you want to know about him? He died almost a century ago."

"He gave me the sword."

"*Stone?*"

"That's right—*Stone*. Scrawny fellow. He was Marais' adjutant, I understand, until—"

"Until he disappeared in jump." Sergei looked off into the darkness, as if he were trying to pick something out in the distance. "A mystery we never solved. He was a cipher, like a stage holo, something you can see but can't touch. The closer we looked, the less we saw.

"He helped the Admiral write *The Absolute Victory*. His agenda was aimed at *destroying* the People, not conquering them. Remember, *se* Jackie, we would have eradicated them if they had not changed their flight and made peace.

"When it became apparent that Admiral Marais' mission and intentions had changed, and that the Admiral had turned away from simply exterminating the People, Stone attempted to thwart the effort. He even tried to kill Marais. Twice."

"I know he attempted to kill Marais once, during the trial—"

"*Twice* during the trial," Sergei replied. "Once while it was being held on Earth, and a second time on Luna. There was an Imperial Intelligence agent that had tracked him to the site of the court-martial and prevented Stone from killing Admiral Marais."

"What happened to this agent?"

"He was—" Sergei looked away, into the distance again. "He was killed. Stone had a weapon that . . . everted the agent's body. Turned it inside out. When Stone was shot, the weapon broke into a thousand pieces."

Jackie considered the idea and shuddered. Sergei's image wavered for a moment and then became solid again. "All the loose ends were neatly tied up," he said. "Even the everting weapon. All except the explanation."

"If I may be permitted a bit of unsolicited advice," Sergei said.

Jackie smiled and nodded.

"You are most capable, *se* Jackie, both as warrior and as *Gyaryu'har*. There is no doubt you can serve admirably as the bearer of the sword.

"Your wing has now brushed against the servant of the Lord of Despite. I implore you: Do *not* underestimate Stone. He is more dangerous than anyone you may have yet faced. I don't know why he left the *Lancaster*, but he had threatened me and others in the fleet. I'm sure that if he had killed Marais with his everting weapon, he certainly would have done the same to me. If there is a pattern to the actions, I'm unaware of it."

"So . . . watch my step."

"That's essentially it, yes."

"All right, then, *si* Sergei. Tell me what you'd do if you were still *Gyaryu'har*."

"*se* Jackie, I'm no longer in that position. It's your decision. I am here merely to advise you."

"So, *advise* me, damn it. Tell me what you'd do."

Sergei sighed, and smiled. "I'd go and gather information. There must be additional data on Stone: Imperial Intelligence must have some record of the events."

"They're not likely to talk to me."

"Oh? As an official representative of the High Nest you carry considerable authority. What *is* likely is that you will learn more from what they do *not* say than by what they do."

chapter 13

The lift slowly carried Jonathan Durant and Arlen Mustafa up to the command deck of Adrianople Starbase. Durant had been summoned—it was no less than that: He was supervising the installation of a new compressor rig on the base's outer ring, and his comp had sent a signal requesting Durant's presence in his own office.

It could only mean that First Drone H'mr—who hadn't even bothered to speak to Durant when he'd come aboard, three watches earlier—had some questions he wanted answered.

In fact, it meant something more serious for Durant himself. If H'mr wanted him dead, his life had about twenty minutes left to run.

To Durant's surprise, as he stepped off the walkway that connected the outer and inner rings of the station, Arlen Mustafa had been waiting for him. Even though Arlen had been excused from duty since the surrender of the base, he was still second in command; his comp had evidently picked up the comm signal, and he'd used the station comp to find Durant.

"I'm going to—" Durant began.

"I know where you're going, Commodore. I'm going with you."

"No." Durant put his hand on Arlen's arm. "No, you don't want to do this."

"If they kill you," Arlen said quietly, "I'll be senior officer aboard. I . . . don't want to be in that position."

Without another word, he looked down at his uniform jacket. There was a very slight, almost indiscernible bulge in one pocket.

"You have no chance to do this. It's suicidal."

"We'll see."

"I could order you not to. I could confine you to quarters."

"You can stick me in a life-pod and jettison it from the station if you want to, sir. But unless you do that, I'll do what I have to do."

Durant didn't say anything, but looked at his exec, who met his gaze, more steadily than he'd been able to manage for the last several days. The alien thing—the Ór—had literally frightened him nearly to death, and he hadn't been standing up straight or meeting anyone's gaze since then.

"All right," Durant said at last. "Let's go."

Second Drone H'tt and First Drone H'mr were both waiting when Durant arrived. Mustafa was two steps behind; the two aliens exchanged glances in a remarkably human manner, though Durant wasn't sure if it was meaningful or just caricature.

"Please sit," H'tt said, gesturing to a chair. He stared at Mustafa, who, to his credit, didn't look away.

"I'd rather stand."

"As you wish. I suppose you know why you are here." H'tt looked to H'mr, who stood beside Durant's desk, his arms folded.

"Please enlighten me."

"I wish to know why you sent *Trebizond* out of Adrianople System, and what orders you provided to Abramowicz."

"I'll bet you would."

"This is dangerous ground, Commodore," H'tt said. "I suggest you tread carefully."

"Because you can kill me with a thought," Durant answered, leaning on the back of the proffered chair. "That's a powerful threat, sir, I know. The only problem is, it loses its punch if the person being threatened doesn't give a damn anymore."

"You've decided your life doesn't mean anything?"

"No, that's not it at all. I've decided that my life has been very meaningful; but the moment you summoned me up here to be disciplined by this guy"—he gestured toward H'mr—"my life was as good as over."

"What about your executive officer?" H'mr said. "Does he value *his* life?"

Mustafa went to answer but Durant raised his hand. "I'm sure he does, and I value it as well. But he's here because he's not afraid of you taking it away."

"Did you not prevent the Ór from ending that life?" H'mr said, frowning. "I do not understand. Nothing has changed."

"We've both had a chance to think."

"You are ready to die *now*," H'mr said, as if reaching a conclusion. He looked at H'tt. "Explain," he commanded.

H'tt looked from his superior to the former commander of his captured station and back.

"I lack an explanation," H'tt said.

"That is not the answer I wished to hear." H'mr stood upright and approached Durant and Mustafa. Without further comment, he slowly walked around and behind each man, as if he were examining them—measuring them somehow—for some impenetrable alien reason. When he had finished with this stroll, he came around to stand before Durant, who stood up straight, at parade rest.

Jonathan Durant was angry with the First Drone, with the situation he was in, and with the fact that neither he nor Arlen was likely to walk out of this room alive.

At least I served my emperor in the end, he thought to himself. *All you can do is kill me now.*

"Explain this to me, Commodore," H'mr said, leaning slightly forward toward Durant. "I have viewed the comp records and consulted with the Ór. Several Standard days ago, you surrendered this station and your command because the Ór was . . . using its *k'th's's* power to terminate your fellow meat-creature." He gestured past Durant to Arlen Mustafa, whose eyes flashed with anger at the last phrase. "Yet now you are insolent and willing to toss both lives away. What has changed about the situation?"

"Timing."

"Please clarify."

"I wasn't prepared to have you kill Arlen then. I wasn't prepared to spend lives then. But it's become clear to me—if that's all you've got to threaten us with, it's a pretty meaningless threat. If you kill me, you take my place. Correct?"

"Essentially so."

"And since I'm just a . . . 'meat-creature' . . . you can do that *any-way,* whether I cooperate or not—it won't keep you awake nights."

H'mr frowned at that, trying to parse the expression.

"If you want something, you should just go ahead and *take* it."

H'mr's face composed itself. Durant clenched his fists; he felt a slight pressure on his mind which began to grow. Behind him he heard a sharp intake of breath, but he willed himself not to turn around.

H'mr frowned.

"Losing your touch?" Durant asked, gritting his teeth. The pressure was significant now. Durant wanted to drop to his knees; he resisted the urge to bring his hands to his forehead. Something was happening here, but he wasn't sure what it was.

Suddenly H'mr turned away and walked behind the desk.

The probing of his mind stopped; Durant gasped for breath, grabbing the chair with both hands.

"The flight of *Trebizond* doesn't matter," H'mr said. "Of course, there are Drones aboard. When it reaches a safe haven, they will be able to pursue *useful* missions among your people."

Durant tried not to let his shoulders sag. "You're saying that you *let* it get away."

"I'm saying that it isn't worth the effort to make you tell me its destination. The jump-echo showed that it was bound for the refueling station at Brady Point. That location is already under our control."

"So what will happen to *Trebizond*?"

H'mr waved his hand. He didn't even look up at Durant. "It depends on what they do, but ultimately I expect they will be digested."

The word "digested" echoed ominously in the office; Jonathan Durant couldn't think of a single thing to say in reply.

"This interview is done," H'mr said finally.

Durant looked at H'tt, who seemed unsure of himself. The commodore felt a certain amount of perverse pleasure.

Sucks to be you, Durant thought. *I'm already dead, but you might be, too, you slimy little bastard.*

Without another word Durant turned his back and beckoned to Arlen. They left the office, feeling H'tt's stare as they turned the corner and out of sight.

•   •   •

A hundred meters away, Arlen began to ask a question, but Durant held up his hand. When they were in the lift and halfway down to the main deck of the inner ring, Durant nodded.

"What just happened?" Arlen asked.

"I don't know. I called their bluff. I'm sorry, I just couldn't stand it anymore."

"Why didn't they—"

"Kill us?"

"Right."

"I don't know that, either. If I didn't know better, I'd almost say that the First Drone wasn't *able* to do it."

"Mercy?"

"Like hell. Something . . . Something *prevented* him. Something stopped him. I know that's crazy, but it's the only explanation."

"What about *Trebizond*?"

"I have to assume he was telling the truth." The lift reached bottom and they stepped out as three station officers stepped in, saluting Durant and Mustafa before ascending. Durant waited until they were a dozen meters up and out of earshot before continuing. "Wherever he is, Rich Abramowicz is in deep trouble. But so are we."

He walked away from Mustafa, heading back to the repair site he'd left. Arlen Mustafa watched him go, new respect for his commander in his eyes, still wondering why either of them was still alive.

B efore leaving Zor'a System, Jackie received one more visitor. She was in the viewing lounge aboard the orbital station, looking out at the stars. The *Fair Damsel* was preparing to leave for Sol System; Georg had detailed the merchanter for Jackie's use—and Dan had voiced no objection.

Owen Garrett didn't have any trouble finding her; both humans and zor had been avoiding her since she'd arrived on-station. He wasn't someone she'd known well: Owen had been posted to *Duc d'Enghien* a few years into Jackie's tenure as commander at Cicero; she'd only met him in person during Emperor's Birthday celebrations at Cicero Down. (On inspection visits to *Duc* he'd been one more pilot in dress blues

standing at attention with the rest of Green Squadron.) Still, seeing him
again across the viewing lounge was a thrill.

Here's one we got back, she thought.

She assumed there was a new Green Squadron aboard Barbara
MacEwan's carrier now. The rest of the shift that had strayed too near
the alien ship was dead—they'd killed each other while Jackie watched.
The only survivor now stood across the lounge from her, offering a
salute. Physically, he looked the same, except in his eyes—they held
some reserve of anger she could almost feel.

"Commander," she said, "I understand that your new rank is well
deserved."

"Thank you, ma'am," he answered, dropping his salute. He walked
across to the viewport. "I'd rather not have had to earn it—I want to be
flying again."

"So would I." She led him to a pair of armchairs and they sat down.
"I got promoted, too, and never got into action again. But there are
other ways to help the war effort—maybe Admiral Hsien will post you
to *Negri,* if you're interested."

"Thank you," he repeated. "I'd like that—it'd be worlds better
than . . ."

"Sanctuary?"

"I don't mean to complain, but I . . . I'm not a Sensitive. I don't belong up there—they want to test my 'ability,' see what makes it tick."
He looked from her face to the sword at her belt and then back. "But I
think they're looking for something that isn't there."

"What makes you say that, Commander?"

"Ma'am." He looked at the sword again, his face frowning and in-
tense, his hands on his knees. "They want to find *other* talents. They
want me to be a Sensitive or something. I *can't.* I've tried, but I can't."

"I said the same thing."

"Commodore," he said, not looking away from the *gyaryu,* "I've
been working on it for three days. Master Byar couldn't get me past
First Talon—I just couldn't do it."

"But you can do this one thing. You can see through the vuhls'
disguise—what is that, if not a Sensitive talent?"

"Sensitive talent is . . . I don't know, like flying a fighter. Anybody
can train to fly one—to work the attitude control so he doesn't crash
into the dock; to shoot at a target without hitting the carrier instead.

But to be any good at it, you start out with some innate talent . . . No, please, let me finish," he said, as Jackie began to object. "Ma'am, I have a pilot's knack, I think. I trained to be a good one—but this ability, this thing I can do, is because the bands of light *gave* it to me. They pulled me off the bug ship, they put me on Center, they gave me this ability.

"It's a setup. I'm being *set up*, ma'am."

"We both are. We *all* are. I was pulled off Center by the same people. Things. Whatever . . . Except they talked to you, I understand."

He shuddered. "Yeah. They talked to me."

"What did they say? Can you remember their exact words?"

He closed his eyes and frowned. " 'He will provide instruction,' it said. " 'He will . . . ' I'm sorry, ma'am, I don't remember the exact words. Something like, 'He will teach the other. Their paths will cross.' "

" 'The other.' Did they mean *me*, do you think?"

"Commodore, I'd be happy to teach you, if I could figure out how. If there was a way . . ."

"If there's a way, Master Byar will find it."

"He hasn't so far."

"Three or four days is all he's had, isn't that right?"

". . . Well, yes, ma'am, but—"

"The People—the zor—are a very patient race, Commander. They take a long time to decide about things, and three days is like half an hour to them. I think you have to give it a fair chance." She held up her hand. "I know, you don't feel as if anything is happening . . . but not everybody gets the magic sword." She smiled and put her hand on the hilt of the *gyaryu*. "Of course, not everybody gets sent on the universe's biggest wild-goose chase, either."

"Are you ordering me back to Sanctuary, Commodore?"

"You're not part of my command anymore, Commander—Owen." She smiled again and seemed to relax a bit when she addressed him by his first name. "The High Nest wants to give you . . . a sort of test. Something called 'the Ordeal of Experience.' The *Dsen'yen'ch'a*. I'll be there when I come back to Zor'a; it won't happen until then. You have a right to have someone stand with you, and I've volunteered . . . if you'll have me."

"I'd be honored, but I was hoping to get back to active duty, Commodore."

"Not until after the Ordeal. That's not an order—it's a request.

Whatever this power is, I'm willing to bet that it's crucial to our chances to win this war."

Owen's shoulders sagged. "That's not quite the answer I'd hoped for, ma'am."

"I have no say in this, Owen. I realize that you want to go shoot at the enemy, but this duty should come first. I promise I'll stand by you during the Ordeal of Experience."

He considered this for several moments and then said, "Aye-aye, ma'am."

At the gate of Sanctuary, in the mountains that overlooked the valley of esYen, S'reth son of S'tlin repeated the necessary formula and held his wings in the Posture of Obeisance to the Circle of *esLi*. The eight-sided doors slid aside to admit him.

Byar HeShri, Master of Sanctuary, was not among the few People in the inner courtyard who clustered around S'reth as he began to make his way toward the House of Teachers. He arrived shortly afterward with a towel clutched in his left talons, sweating profusely.

"*se* S'reth," he said, wiping his face with the towel. "If you had told me you were coming, I would have been here to greet you."

"Younger Brother," S'reth said, stopping in his slow walk. "We all follow the path that the Lord *esLi* has laid out for us." A few of the students standing nearby could not conceal the amusement in their wings at the old zor addressing the Master as "Younger Brother." "I did not know until this sun that I would be coming here."

"Is there something I could help you with, Honored One?"

S'reth's wings showed a configuration tinged with humor, perhaps recognizing that Byar intended to match his informality with the excessive honorific. "I must use the library, *se* Byar. And I have need of your counsel."

"I am happy to help."

S'reth set his valise down on the cobblestones of the courtyard and looked around, as if seeing his surroundings for the first time.

"It is not how I remember it."

Byar HeShri stood on the window-perch, the bright-orange sun streaming past him and casting a shadow on the tiled floor of his sitting-room. S'reth had taken up a position in front of a comp display and seemed lost in thought. It was the Hour of Contemplation; Sanctuary was quiet, with only the occasional buzz of *hsth*-flies and the sighing of the soft breeze to interrupt it.

"Tell me, *se* Byar," S'reth said, looking up at last. "What do you think of *se* Jackie?"

"That is an unusual question. Perhaps it is one that should not be asked."

"Is it? What is wrong with asking it?"

"She is already the *Gyaryu'har*, you old *artha*. Perhaps it does not matter to you that this question might offend the High Nest. I choose not to offend."

"Ah. I see. I do not question her position, my old friend; I merely wondered what you thought of her."

"She seems capable," Byar answered, his wings set in a protective stance. "She has proven herself worthy."

"We know many *naZora'i*, some inside the Empire and some outside. Would you have chosen her if it were your choice? Would you have chosen one from among the exiles?"

"*esLi* chose her."

"Or *we* did," S'reth responded. "After all, it was you and I and *ha* T'te'e who opened the *shaGa'uYa* to allow Shrnu'u HeGa'u into the Ordeal."

"*se* S'reth," Byar said, placing his wings in a patient posture, "this is an old flight. It was chosen and reviewed many times. We knew that the Shroud would be pulled aside at Cicero; we knew it would involve Younger Brother *si* Ch'k'te. *si* Th'an'ya knew it; you knew it; I knew it. We have reached this point because we chose that flight more than eleven turns ago. We cast the *Ka'eLi* sticks and followed the fortune that *esLi* revealed to *hi'i* Ke'erl. Now we have a *Gyaryu'har*. It cannot be undone." He changed his wings to the Posture of Polite Annoyance. "I had believed you thought highly of *se* Jackie."

"I *do*," S'reth answered. "Very highly. But she came to the *gyaryu* through manipulation."

"A necessary pattern, as we believed at the time—"

"No, no, *se* Byar. I am not speaking of the manipulation by the High Nest, though that, too, was clearly a problem. I refer to manipulation of the High Nest itself by unknown forces, for unknown reasons."

"You have drunk too much *egeneh*. What is your point?"

"What do you know of *seLi'e'Yan*?"

Byar was clearly annoyed now; somewhere within, he knew the old teacher was trying to create a *sSurch'a*—a sudden revelation through an intuitive leap—but he wanted S'reth to get to the point and not just fly around the edges, pecking here and there.

Byar did not reply but instead held his wings in the Stance of Patient Expectation.

"I came all the way up here to examine old texts, *se* Byar. Sanctuary has the oldest extant copy of *The Legend of Qu'u*, from the loremaster Shthe'e HeChri, your most honored Nest-father—"

Byar's wings altered to a posture of respect.

"—who was, I believe, a contemporary of the great hero Qu'u. All the epics ultimately draw upon the account of *si* Shthe'e."

"When I was a student here at Sanctuary, when we were still at war with *esHu'ur*, I took a particularly keen interest in *si* Shthe'e's work. Did you know that?"

"Your monographs are still in our library, *se* S'reth," Byar said. "We require students to read them every turn." He let his wings fall into a stance of polite admiration. The scholarship of the old sage was hardly in doubt; but S'reth still had not gotten to the point of his exposition.

"Qu'u." S'reth began to idly draw patterns in the air with one of his left talons. "The great hero Qu'u is chosen, as you know, from clan e'Yen by the Servant of *esLi*. He must leave behind all he knows and journey within Zor'a to the Plain of Despite, to regain the *gyaryu*—or, rather, the sword that will become the *gyaryu*. 'Regain,' *se* Byar. A most important distinction: not 'find,' not 'create,' but to *regain*."

"That is not the traditional reading." Byar closed his eyes and recited: " 'You must travel to the Plain of Despite and find the sword that will become the *gyaryu*, the Talon of *esLi*.' And I still do not see what this has to do with *seLi'e'Yan*."

"Compare it to *si* Shthe'e's account, *se* Byar. Let me see . . ." He gestured to the comp before him and it retreated to a point he had marked earlier. " 'And the Servant said to him, "You must journey within the world to regain the lost sword that shall be transformed into the Talon of *esLi*." ' The verb form is *anSa'e*—'to regain.' And he specifically says 'lost sword.'

"We do not recognize these phrases or these words as part of *The Legend of Qu'u*. They are missing from the later recensions. This is the *basis* of the legend of Qu'u, the cornerstone of the epics, the motivation for everything we have done to prepare for the coming of the *esGa'uYal* during the last several turns . . . yet we have overlooked this crucial transformation.

"If the loremaster's original account is correct, *se* Byar, it means that Qu'u went to the Plain of Despite to *recover* the sword . . . But why? Why did *esLi*, in His wisdom, base the unification of the Nests on a talon drawn from the heart of the Deceiver?

"Why did He go to all of that trouble?"

"I would not seek to question the Lord *esLi*'s wisdom," Byar said, and began to place his wings in the Posture of Reverence to *esLi*.

More suddenly and more quickly than Byar would have expected, S'reth flew across the room and took up a position on the same perch, grasping Byar by the shoulders, preventing his wings from elevating to that position.

The old one's grasp was strong and firm; his eyes were deep and filled with emotion.

And there was something Byar—long skilled as a teacher and guide to young Sensitives—simply could not read.

Outside, the light seemed to fade, as if a cloud had passed in front of the sun. The vermillion cast of Antares seemed to retreat to a pallid yellow-gray, reinforcing the skeletal features of the old one before Byar.

"What is this, S'reth?" His surprise was so great that he could not come up with an appropriate prenomen. "What *enGa'e'li* is this?"

"It is *not*, *se* Byar—Younger Brother, Master of Sanctuary, old friend. There is nothing of *esLi*'s Golden Circle in this, not even the Lord *esLi*'s Strength of Madness. It is a terrible realization, a *saShrne'e*— pulling aside the Shroud.

"You will not question the Lord *esLi*'s wisdom, *se* Byar. But I must. I am scarcely a wingspan from flying to rejoin the Golden Light. There is something greater working here, something that spans the flight— from your honored ancestor, through the war with the *naZora'i*, up to the present.

"*Think*, my friend. Do as you teach." S'reth relaxed his grip slightly, but still held firm. "Question yourself: Who first commanded us to fight the humans?"

"The—the Lord *esLi*."

"Are you sure?"

"The High Lord received a dream. The High Lord was commanded to pursue the flight of eradicating the *naZora'i,* and it was not until *es-Hu'ur*—"

"—who was also *esTli'ir,*" S'reth interrupted, his speech suddenly coming more rapidly than Byar had ever known. "It was not until *es-Hu'ur* changed our flight and condemned us to life. I know, *se* Byar, I was there. I was *alive* then, a Sensitive here at Sanctuary. I am among the last few of the People whose wings have flown from that time to this.

"The High Lord would know the true Lord from the Deceiver, but what if *esLi* Himself were altered? What if someone—if some power—had changed *esLi* in such a way to place us on that flight? What if some *power* chose the outcome: all of it, even the outcome to the war with *es-Hu'ur?*

"What if the recovery of the *gyaryu* itself was also arranged? *se* Jackie's evidence suggests that this was done.

"We have been *manipulated,* Byar." S'reth's voice had become ragged, a whisper. His grasp was becoming weaker. "We have been placed on this flight so that *se* Jackie can stand within the Circle." The old zor took a long breath that seemed to enlarge and then contract his entire body. "This is Shr'e'a, my old friend."

"I don't see what Sharia'a has to do with—"

"*Shr'e'a,*" S'reth said. "There is so little time, old friend. The enemies . . . the enemies—"

S'reth's arms slipped to his sides and he turned from Byar to look out the window, where a storm was beginning to form in the sky. Clouds were roiling above, casting monstrous shadows on the plain below, from the foothills to the sprawling city of esYen in the distance.

"Shr'e'a," S'reth repeated, bowing his head.

Then without further comment he slipped from the perch, falling toward the floor below. Byar reached out and caught the ancient one by the waist, and fluttered down, thus burdened.

"Healer to the Master's study!" he shouted at comp, and scarcely heard an acknowledgment from it; but by the time Byar reached the floor and gently laid S'reth flat, he knew it was too late.

He placed his wings in the position of *enGa'e'esLi*—the Enfolding Protection of *esLi*—and looked upward to the window, away from the peaceful and lifeless face of his old, old friend.

chapter 14

Station One had been in a stable orbit around Earth for nearly four hundred years. Lifted into space in pieces and assembled, it had been the crowning, cooperative achievement of several governments under the auspices of the twenty-first–century United Nations. It had been repeatedly extended and improved since then; it now bore very little resemblance to the ancient structure that had been the first gateway to Sol System and, eventually, to the stars.

Now it was the transit point for civilian shuttles coming to and from the surface of mankind's original home. Jackie had not set foot on Station One since she'd been an Academy cadet on leave; the few times she had been in Sol System since—either aboard a ship or on a naval assignment—she had gone directly by shuttle to St. Louis Admiralty or to the Baikonur Spaceport, and bypassed Station One entirely.

By comparison, Dan McReynolds knew Station One well, and made friendly small talk with the traffic controller on the way in. Dan seemed to know everyone, and everyone seemed to know *Fair Damsel*. But he'd had no problem flashing the credentials of the High Nest as needed. *Fair Damsel*, accustomed to the usual delays and petty bureaucracy of a busy port, was given priority that surprised even Dan.

When *Damsel* reached anchor, Dan accompanied Jackie to the personnel airlock. She had traveled without an entourage, not wanting to make too much of the *Gyaryu'har*'s visit to the humans' homeworld;

but she had the comforting presence of the sword, and a host of advisors about whom Dan knew nothing.

"Look," he said, as the 'lock was cycling. "Are you sure you don't need someone to watch your back?"

"I'll be all right. This is an ambassadorial visit, not some kind of cloak-and-dagger."

"The last time I let you out of my sight, Jay, you damn near got yourself killed."

"I'd almost consider that patronizing if I didn't know you better. This is my own flight, Dan; it's fine. I have some people to meet on-station. I'll get cleared for *Damsel* to fly to Langley and we'll head out there. I don't expect anyone to try and kill me. Besides—" She rested her hand on the hilt of the *gyaryu*.

"Someone with a laser pistol won't give a damn how good that sword is or how good you are with it, Jay. You should have an escort. The Sultan and I—"

"—can sit in a bar on Station One and play cards for six hours. I don't need or want an escort."

The 'lock beeped, indicating that pressure had been equalized.

"You be careful, Jay. *se* Jay. You've come too far and worked too hard to mess it up now."

Jackie smiled and nodded. "I'll be back soon."

"You said that on Crossover."

Jackie considered a response and discarded it. She gave Dan's arm a squeeze and stepped into the airlock, the door closing behind her.

The reception committee was small but impressive. Two zor and two humans awaited her as she descended the slidewalk alone to the main concourse of Station One. There was a little area partitioned off with Imperial Marines standing guard; passersby seemed to be steering clear.

She recognized one of the humans at once: William Clane Alvarez, the Duke of Burlington and First Lord of the Admiralty. She hadn't expected to see him again anytime soon, and, from the look of things, he was nervous about their meeting as well. The two zor wore sashes indicating their rank within the High Nest: One, she knew, must be Mya'ar HeChra, the *esGyu'u* of the High Nest to the Solar Emperor's court. The other was unknown.

"*ha Gyaryu'har,*" one of the zor said, as she reached concourse level. Both zor placed their wings in the Posture of Polite Approach.

"*se* Mya'ar?" Jackie asked the one who had spoken, and his wings dipped in assent. "It is a pleasure to meet you." She grasped forearms with each of the zor in turn.

"You have already made the acquaintance of the First Lord, I believe," Mya'ar said, a comment that might be considered ironic or even sarcastic coming from a human; it was apparent from his wings, however, that he meant it only as a statement of fact. "Allow me to present *se* Ta'sen HeU'ur, my assistant."

Jackie inclined her head as the two zor placed their wings in postures of respect.

"Your Grace," Jackie said to Alvarez. He seemed focused on her attire—a loose-fitting crimson tunic with a light-blue sash, plain dark pants and boots, the *gyaryu* belted at her waist. She saw the same cavernous face she remembered from across the table at the board of inquiry, half a lifetime ago. "I regret that I am out of uniform to meet you."

Not that I really give a damn anymore, she added, to herself.

"I understand that you have changed professions—and uniforms," he answered, obviously ill-at-ease. "I hope . . . you realize that our understanding of things has changed since we last spoke."

"Mine as well, Your Grace."

"I can imagine." He gestured to the other human. "Admiral Sean Mbele, may I present Commodore and *Gyaryu'har* Jacqueline Laperriere"— Alvarez let a smile escape his face—"your welcoming committee.

"There'll be seventeen sideboys at Molokai, as befits your station, but I saw no reason to be ostentatious here." He glanced across the concourse, where humans with a few zor and rashk mixed in, hurried along, mostly ignoring today's reception of dignitaries.

"*Molokai,* Your Grace? I hadn't expected—"

"Both the Imperial Court and the Imperial Assembly, Commodore. But the emperor first. I am under direct orders to bring you directly to the estate."

"I'm not really prepared—"

Alvarez held up his hand. "There's a shuttle waiting for us." The small party began to walk, more or less surrounding Jackie and herding her along the concourse. "As I see it, madam," the First Lord continued, "meeting with the emperor should be no challenge after the experiences you've already had."

As they walked, Jackie noticed that a fairly large number of ill-disguised figures shadowed their movements on the concourse. *"No reason to be ostentatious,"* my ass, she thought.

"I had not known that Your Grace was well informed about my experiences—"

"Eight thousand pardons," Mya'ar cut in. "The First Lord and His Imperial Highness have been briefed by the envoy. The emperor has received a full explanation of your part in emulation of the legend, *ha Gyaryu'har*. At the moment, he has accepted the idea that the High Nest has some particular capability to combat the enemy."

Jackie didn't comment; she suspected that Mya'ar, like most of the People, associated the aliens with the servants of the Deceiver. One of her most pressing reasons for coming to Sol System was to obtain more information to support or dispel that association.

It was only a short walk to the shuttle bay, which was heavily guarded by conspicuously armed Marines. The image of walking through the orbital station at Cle'eru with Ch'k'te came to her mind unbidden, and she touched the *gyaryu*, by way of assurance. The almost reflexive movement brought a strange look from the First Lord, who must have wondered what she was doing.

The first part of the shuttle trip was uneventful, as the vessel made planetfall escorted by several space-to-ground fighters. Jackie and the First Lord's entourage sat in the stateroom, quietly discussing matters of little importance.

At last, the First Lord cleared his throat and reached inside his uniform jacket. "I have . . ." He withdrew an envelope, sealed with the personal sigil of the Solar Emperor. "If you are prepared to accept it," he said, handing her the envelope, "I have received approval to grant you a full honorable discharge from the Imperial Navy with a full pension based on two steps above current grade and station."

"Promotion to 'admiral, retired,' " Jackie answered, a bit surprised by this sudden choice of tactic. "What about the court-martial?"

"Obviously, all charges will be dropped. In fact, in view of your recent . . . services to the High Nest, His Imperial Highness is prepared to award you the Order of the White Cross."

"You were prepared to put me in irons for the rest of my life, and now you're going to retire me and give me a medal?"

"Commodore, I realize how this must seem—"

"Your Grace, I find this reversal of policy . . ." She considered several insulting conclusions to the sentence, and bit her tongue. "Your Grace: My current position and recent experience gives me a certain immunity from prosecution, even if there were still a belief that my actions at Cicero were improper.

"I'm glad to be vindicated, of course, but I suspect that you have very little control over this. What's more, my feelings don't need to be assuaged. But what about the people under my command? When we last spoke, they were being dispersed to the four corners of the Empire, and I suspect they've been dropped to the bottom of the captains' list. What are you going to do for them?"

"As it happens," Alvarez replied, his brow furrowing, "experience with the aliens rates a posting to frontline duty these days. The Admiralty does not intend to press any charges; the Cicero matter is closed."

"How pragmatic and politic of you, Your Grace."

This time it was the First Lord who appeared to be wrestling with the proper reply. "Commodore . . . Excuse me—*Gyaryu'har.*

"You obviously relish the fact that, unlike in our previous interview, you have the advantage. I am prepared to swallow my pride for the moment; I am even ready to apologize for any harm done by my own shortsightedness.

"But we have a common enemy, madam. It is not the intransigence or ignorance of humanity, nor is it the mysterious complexity of the zor. It is the *aliens* who seek to destroy the Solar Empire. If you are interested in doing your job, you must learn some pragmatism yourself. I can make things easier for you, *Gyaryu'har,* or I can make things difficult. Very difficult.

"Do I make myself clear?"

"Yes, Your Grace. Very much so."

"Will you accept your retirement as an admiral, and my reassurances about your former subordinates?"

"I'd . . . be honored." . . . *you slimy so-and-so,* she added mentally. "I'd appreciate your help."

"Yes. Well." He rose from his seat and walked to the dispenser: "Two *h'geRu,* three *g'rey'l* . . . Is that all right with everyone?"

No one objected. Five cubical containers were extruded and filled;

Alvarez handed them to the zor and humans, retaining the last one for himself.

"A toast," he said at last. "To Admiral Laperriere. To the emperor and the High Nest."

At about the same time Jackie Laperriere's shuttle was entering the atmosphere of the homeworld, Rich Abramowicz was ordering *Trebizond* to stand down.

They'd emerged from jump at Denneva System. Almost immediately, *Emperor Cleon* and *Emperor Alexander* intercepted *Trebizond*. They were two ships of the same class—and significantly more armed and dangerous than the *Byzantium*-class *Trebizond*. Abramowicz didn't know either commander—not that it mattered; they weren't talking except to give curt orders.

"You'd think *we* were the enemy," Kit Hafner said, squinting at the forward screen.

Trebizond had slowed to the point that it was essentially drifting in space, about ten thousand kilometers downrange of the jump point. *Cleon* was in her forward screen, still fully armed and ready to fire; *Alexander* was aft. Two smaller *Broadmoor*-class vessels were boosting out of Denneva System's gravity well to reach *Trebizond*, which had followed orders to heave to.

Now it was a sitting duck, with its weapons and defensive fields offline.

"We might be."

"Meaning?"

"If I were out there"—Abramowicz gestured toward *Cleon*—"I'd be damned careful before I'd let this ship get anywhere near the inner system. Who knows what might be aboard?"

"If there were bugs aboard," Hafner answered, "how'd we ever get to jump?"

"Same way we got past 'em at Brady Point: They *let* us."

There had been some fairly tense moments at the refueling station at Brady Point. Abramowicz had lied his way through an exchange with an alien (disguised as a human; perhaps one of the station's former officers), in which he'd claimed the authority of the First Drone H'mr. If the alien had decided to comm-squirt to Adrianople and hold *Trebizond* until he got a reply, the bluff would've fallen apart.

And we'd be dead, the captain of the *Trebizond* told himself. Kit Hafner was certainly bright enough to reach this conclusion on his own, once he thought about it.

Abramowicz thought about Commodore Durant, back at Adrianople. Once H'mr and the other alien leader realized that *Trebizond* had gotten away, Durant would probably be killed . . . or worse. It was hard to tell whether what had already happened to Commander Mustafa was worse: He'd been a shell of a man, jumping at shadows, ever since the base had been surrendered. But they'd found Brady Point occupied and had managed to get past mind-controlling aliens, even though Abramowicz had thought they had no chance.

After all, there was no way to go but forward.

"You think they 'let' us get *here,* too. Why?"

"Some of *them* are aboard. We're inside the Empire. Connect the dots, Kit."

"Then we have to—"

"What? Leave? Where would we go? . . . And what do you think are our chances of getting past *that?*" He gestured toward *Emperor Cleon.* The pilot's board showed the two *Broadmoors,* not yet in visual range, closing on their location. *Emperor Alexander* had its weapons armed and ready.

"Let's hope they have some way of finding the infiltrators. Anyone could be one—you, me . . ." Abramowicz smiled slightly, looking sidelong at Kit Hafner, who looked alarmed at the suggestion. "I hear that an exec on one of the ships that evacuated Cicero turned out to be an alien."

"Captain, I—"

Abramowicz held his hand up. "Belay it. Either you're an alien—and I hope to God there's a way to smoke you out—or you're not, and I have nothing to worry about. Either way, there's nothing you can do right now to convince me one way or the other. Anyway, it's *them* you'll have to convince."

He squinted at the displays next to the ship-icons. "They must have learned *something*—every few seconds they're shifting frequencies on field distributors and travelers. Maybe that gives the aliens a headache."

With no defensive fields, and weapons offline, *Trebizond* was defenseless, but remained closely guarded by four ships for two full watches—during which, as ordered, it maintained comm silence.

Abramowicz was in the gym trying to tire himself out enough to get a good watch's sleep, when his comp signaled. He stepped away from the weight-trainer and grabbed a towel.

"Captain here."

"Comm incoming, Skip," said Rhea Salmonson's voice. "Priority for you. *Duc d'Enghien* sends."

"The carrier?"

"Yes sir. Captain MacEwan."

"All right." He waved at the comp. An image resolved a few meters away, showing a carrier's flight bridge; a frowning officer appeared, looking right at and through him.

"This is Abramowicz. Sorry I'm out of uniform, Captain, but I didn't know when you'd call."

"It's all right. I'll get to the point," Barbara MacEwan said. "I've got orders for you from Admiral Hsien. I don't want to be more blunt than necessary: but you will follow these orders to the letter, or a number of the ships in this system will blow you to hell. Do you read?"

"Go ahead."

"At the beginning of next watch, you will prepare to jump outsystem to coordinates specified in a comm-squirt you will receive at that time. You will follow the specified real-space path exactly and jump at the designated time: not a millisecond before, not a millisecond after. You will be accompanied by my ship and *Emperor Cleon;* we'll emerge from jump slightly before you, and we'll be fully armed.

"Your defensive fields and weaponry will remain offline at all times."

Abramowicz wiped his face with the towel. "Where are we headed?"

"No need to tell you now, but suffice it to say, it's a place where we can check your people out."

"I don't understand."

"I didn't expect that you would. Let me put it in the simplest terms possible: If you or anyone aboard your ship is a bug—"

"A 'bug'?"

"An alien. If anyone *is* an alien, he or she is in deep trouble. Everyone else will be in the clear in short order; and for those folks it's open bar in *Duc d'Enghien*'s galley."

"How do I know *this* isn't an alien trap?"

"You have my word. You also have no choice. If you make any moves to arm, if you disobey these orders, if you divert at all, we're under orders to blow you apart so hard that you'll be nothing but background radiation."

"I see."

"Captain Abramowicz—" MacEwan bit her lip for a moment, looked off at her pilot's board and then back to him. "—I don't believe I've ever had the pleasure, but I promise you the hospitality of my ship and my mess if you're what you seem to be, with my deepest apologies. But we can't afford anything less draconic at the moment. I assure you that we *will* destroy *Trebizond* and everyone on it if you force the issue in any way. Is that clear enough?"

"Yes, Captain, it is." He tossed the towel toward the recycler. "I'll pass the word."

"See that you do. *Duc d'Enghien* out."

chapter 15

WHEN ONE OF THE PEOPLE TRANSCENDS THE OUTER PEACE
WHILE HOLDING THE INNER PEACE, THE *HSI* TRANSITS THE
PLANE OF SLEEP AS IT TRAVELS TO REUNION WITH *ESLI*'S
GOLDEN LIGHT. FOR A FEW MOMENTS THE *HSI* IS IN A STATE
BETWEEN BEING AND NOT-BEING, NOT WITHIN THE OUTER
PEACE BUT NOT BEYOND IT. IT IS THE MOMENT OF TRAN-
SCENDENCE.

—*The Am'a'an Codex*

"No," Byar said. He held his wings in as polite a posture as he could.
Saying no to the High Lord was unusual; and in the flight of the People
in the past, it might have been fatal.

But *hi* Sa'a had asked for honesty and he had felt obliged to reply.

"It is about Sharia'a," the High Lord said. "Or Shr'e'a. If we journey to the Stone of Remembrance, we can find *si* S'reth. He did not explain everything he knew."

"Clearly not, *hi* Sa'a," Byar replied. "But it does not justify the risk.
And even if it did, has *si* S'reth not earned the peace of *esLi*'s Golden
Light? Like his father before him, he served the High Nest for all of his
life."

"The service we ask is not so great."

"But it is one *more* service! . . . *hi* Sa'a, even if he were willing, we would have to locate his *hsi* on the Plane of Sleep."

Byar took a deep breath and continued: "It is most dangerous, High Lord." Byar rearranged his wings in the Posture of Polite Concern. "I know that you have read *The Am'a'an Codex* concerning the *hsi*-journey, but it has been sixty-fours of turns since someone has attempted to find the *hsi* of one of the People that has already transcended the Outer Peace. The *Codex* is not even clear on this matter—whether it is a possibility or merely a speculation. What is more, without the *Gyaryu'har* to guard—"

"The *Gyaryu'har* has gone to Sol System," the High Lord interjected. "By the time *se* Jackie returns to Zor'a, *si* S'reth's *hsi* will be beyond even the reach of the Stone of Remembrance. It must be done—and done quickly, *se* Byar. If you will not accompany me, I will do it myself—alone."

It was a dismissive comment. Sa'a appeared ready to take off. Byar was alarmed—he knew she was serious: Young and impetuous, she had already upset the Council of Eleven with her unwillingness to dip her wings into the endless, arduous rituals of the High Nest. In this time of *shNa'es'ri*, it seemed, *hi* Sa'a was what the High Nest—and, indeed, all of the People—needed.

"Eight thousand pardons, High Lord," Byar answered, bowing low in apology. "I would sooner descend to *Ur'ta leHssa* than let you travel alone to the Plane of Sleep."

"So you will accompany me."

Byar's wings moved to reflect deep regret, but he bowed his head. "I will accompany you, *hi* Sa'a. I will make the preparations."

"I am most obliged to you, *se* Byar," she answered, her wings elevating to the Stance of Affirmation.

Byar spent the next hour meditating in quiet. When he came again to the Chamber of Meditation, he found the High Lord already perched in the chamber's *esLiHeShuSa'a*, with the *hi'chya* at her belt. Her wings betrayed determination, and some apprehension to go with it. High Chamberlain T'te'e was there as well, his *chya* drawn and ready. His stance indicated that he had voiced the same objections Byar had made and had met with virtually the same answers.

Byar exchanged a wordless greeting with T'te'e and took up a position on a perch opposite the High Lord. Byar could sense the disquiet in his own *chya,* and he felt it himself.

"*ha* T'te'e, will you be guarding our *hyu* and *hsi* while we journey to the Plane of Sleep?"

"Yes," the High Chamberlain answered. "And you will guard the *hsi* of the High Lord." It was not a question or even a request.

"The High Lord will guard her own *hsi,*" Sa'a interrupted. Both of the others turned to look at her.

"High Lord, I—" T'te'e began.

"I did not ask *se* Byar to accompany me to *guard;* merely to advise. By *esLi,* I appreciate your concern, *se* T'te'e. But I ask you: Please do not burden *se* Byar in a way that *I* would not choose to burden him."

"As the High Lord wishes," T'te'e said, his voice a trifle annoyed, his wings absolutely neutral. But he caught Byar's eye and the meaning was clear: *Return without the High Lord, and prepare to transcend the Outer Peace.*

Byar considered protesting, but discarded the idea. His young High Lord was determined, and the need to understand S'reth so great that it seemed worth the risk.

"Let us begin," the High Lord said, and closed her eyes, enfolding herself in her wings and assuming a posture of obeisance to *esLi.*

Byar let his eyes close as well, willing himself to submit to the *hsi* of his High Lord, allowing his mind to drift away . . .

When he opened his eyes, all he could see was dim gray, like a vast, open *L'le* shrouded in fog; there was light but there did not seem to be a source. Half-hidden by swirling tendrils, he could make out what seemed to be broken pillars, reaching like frozen talons toward some unseeable sky.

"Come," the High Lord said, and launched herself into the air, staying close to the ground. He followed, keeping within a few wingspans of her.

The Plane of Sleep was a Sensitive's construct, a pathway beyond the World That Is; it was only their *hsi* that traveled across it, while the High Chamberlain stood with a drawn *chya* protecting their bodies in the High Lord's *esTle'e.*

The World That Is seemed far away as they flew.

Byar knew of *The Am'a'an Codex.* He had been surprised that the

High Lord knew of it as well; the last recorded attempt to travel the Plane of Sleep had been before *si* S'reth was born; indeed, before the wars with the *naZora'i*. Any Sensitive you chose to ask would say that it was too dangerous—it was a place to lose your *hsi* entirely, worse than the Valley of Lost Souls. But he could not let *hi* Sa'a go alone. It would be unthinkable; so here he was.

As they passed over it, the grim tableau remained substantially unchanged. There were more structures, all unfinished, like dream-fragments. Occasionally there were other People here, their *hsi* wandering as they dreamed. They faded unseeing into and out of the mists like ghosts, the scenery passing by around them.

The High Lord flew on with a grim determination, scarcely bothering to look back at Byar. It did not seem important which direction they flew nor how far: nothing really had a fixed location on the Plane of Sleep relative to anything else. Unlike the land of Despite, which had its rooted landmarks like the Perilous Stair and the Icewall, the Plane of Sleep was a vast, chaotic, unformed place, an ethereal shadow of reality.

After what seemed like an eighth of a sun but might, perhaps, have been a tiny fraction of that, there was a clearing below. In the center of the clearing was a circular piece of gray stone, smooth from long exposure to weather, topped by an octagonal platform.

"The Stone of Remembrance," Sa'a said, slowing to hover over it. "Or, rather, its afterecho. It is the analog to the one on E'rene'e." The actual Stone was a telesthetic artifact located on that outer world of the Core Stars of the People. It was where the *le'chya* of Nest HeU'ur was traditionally conferred on the new Lord of Nest. Few others ever came near it.

Byar assumed the Stance of Reverence to Ancestors and landed well away from the edge of the platform. Sa'a let herself settle onto the platform, her wings held in the Posture of Reverence to *esLi*—

Suddenly she was not alone on the platform. Another had abruptly appeared, his *chya* drawn and at the ready. Sa'a had not been prepared for it and quickly stepped away, reaching for her *hi'chya*.

"Who comes here?" the other asked, looking from Sa'a to Byar, whose *chya* was already in his hand. Byar did not step onto the Stone but was undecided how to help his High Lord.

"We seek the *hsi* of a wise one," she said, assuming the Stance of Reverence to Ancestors. Her *hi'chya* was out now but held at the ready. The other did not advance on her, but his wings still betrayed hostility.

"This place is sacred to *esLi*," the stranger answered. "It is under my protection and in my care. *se'e Mar de'sen*. Here I remain."

Understanding seemed to dawn on Sa'a as she heard these words. "I am honored, *si* Kanu'u," she said. "I am Sa'a, High Lord of the People. *esLiHeYar*."

"High Lord . . . ?"

Of course, Byar said to himself, a half-thought behind his High Lord in realizing the identity of the defender of the Stone. This must be *ha'i* Kanu'u HeU'ur—the Nest-lord of HeU'ur—who had spoken those words thousands of turns ago when he came to the hostile world of E'rene'e. It made sense for him to be guarding the Stone here. The actual Stone on E'rene'e marked the spot where he had originally spoken the words *se'e Mar de'sen*: the motto of Nest HeU'ur.

Sa'a recited her recent ancestry, along with some ritual phrases that Byar, who thought himself a well-versed scholar, had never heard. It was clear that Sa'a had prepared herself well for this encounter: not just *The Am'a'an Codex*, but also even more obscure texts.

Kanu'u seemed to accept this at last and lowered his *chya*.

"*Karai'i esShaLie'e*," he said: *Be welcome, Great Lord*. It was his ritual acceptance of Sa'a as High Lord of the People.

"Allow me to introduce the Master of Sanctuary," she said, nodding toward Byar. "*se* Byar HeShri."

"Be welcome, Younger Brother," Kanu'u said, choosing the Posture of Polite Approach. Byar bowed to one who had died many eights of generations before he was born, wondering to himself where in *esLi's* name this was leading.

"*hi* Sa'a," Kanu'u said. "You say that you seek the *hsi* of a wise one. Has this one gone to *esLi, or* is he merely lost in dreams?"

"He has gone to *esLi, si* Kanu'u, but only recently. It is an evil time—a time of *shNa'es'ri*—and he transcended the Outer Peace before he could communicate all of his wisdom to us."

"There is some risk," Kanu'u answered, looking from the High Lord to Byar. "Many . . . things walk the Plane of Sleep—servants of the Deceiver . . . and others."

"How could this happen? The Am'a'an Guardians—" Sa'a began, but Kanu'u made a gesture and the High Lord looked away.

"The Plane is a bigger place than it was. It is different, and different beings travel across it. That which was, may no longer be; that which is, may not continue much longer."

"*si* Kanu'u speaks wisely," a voice said.

Byar whirled to face someone who had just materialized from the shrouds of fog. The other, holding his wings in a mocking posture, rested his right hand with talons partially extended on a sword that Byar instantly recognized as an *e'chya*. His own *chya* snarled in response; he felt an urge to draw it.

"How dare you approach this place?" Byar said softly, encircling himself with his wings. "I will cut your heart from your chest for coming here, Servant of *esGa'u*."

"Brave words for a servant of the Crawler," the *esGa'uYe* responded, stepping forward another few wingspans but staying out of *chya*-range for the moment. "You have not the protection of Sanctuary about you now, Master. Were I you, I might guard my speech more carefully."

"I am not afraid of speaking the truth," Byar answered. He felt, rather than heard, the *hi'chya* of the High Lord come to guard position. He felt a chill descend from his neck to between his wings.

"State your purpose, Servant," Kanu'u said.

"As you wish," the *esGa'uYe* answered. "As a courtesy to the High Lord, who has flown so far from her safe High Nest, I seek only to provide you with information.

"The Plane of Sleep is no longer the barren province of the dull-witted servants of the Crawler. Even the *Hssa*-struck mad predecessor of *hi* Sa'a knew that: You could ask him, if you could find any remnant of his *hsi*—it certainly has not gone to the Crawler's Golden Circle." He paused, as if for dramatic effect. "After all, it is his doing: He invited Elder Brother Shrnu'u to return from his long exile and thus made it possible for us to walk here.

"As always, you foolishly do not see the end of the flight you choose. How utterly appropriate that you choose *ra* Shrnu'u for the *Dsen'yen'ch'a* rather than leave him in bitter exile beneath the Plain of Despite: It will be the new *Gyaryu'har*'s undoing. Thus have we gained access to the Plane of Sleep and many other places as well."

"We have heard enough," Byar interrupted, and stepped forward, angered by the insulting tone of the *esGa'uYe*.

"*I* am not afraid of speaking the truth," taunted the Servant of *esGa'u*. "Perhaps it is offensive to your iconoclastic ears, *le* Byar—hai!" He swept his *e'chya* upward as Byar attacked; foul-smelling sparks spilled from the contact between it and the Master's *chya*.

The Master of Sanctuary pressed his attack forward. Part of his mind told him that he had allowed himself to be goaded, to be drawn away from the Stone, but the affectionate "*le*" prenomen had offended him a step further than his rational mind could suffer.

"My *chya* will taste your foul blood, Deceiver's kin," Byar said.

"Very sharp wit, beloved Master," the Servant said, meeting a blow and stepping out from in front of another. "Practicing with your students, I see. Perhaps if my *e'chya* consumes you, I will set you up as a statue in the Valley of Lost Souls. Facing the Icewall, perhaps?"

"I do not fear *Ur'ta leHssa*," said Byar. "Tell the Deceiver he must send one *trained* with his weapon if he wishes to claim me."

"You are no Qu'u, *le* Byar."

"And you are no Shrnu'u," Byar answered.

A quick glance told him that he had come some distance away from the High Lord and *ha'i* Kanu'u, and almost out of sight of the Stone. He knew that he did not have enough of a sense of the place to find it again.

After thwarting another of the Servant's attacks, Byar took flight and reversed his direction, partially turning his back on his opponent. He flew eight wingspans closer to the Stone and then stopped without turning around.

"A coward after all," the *esGa'uYe* said. "Perhaps *ra* Shrnu'u will come and take you himself."

One, Byar thought to himself, tightening his grip upon his *chya* and willing himself not to turn.

"The *naZora'i* aliens will enjoy consuming your *hsi, le* Byar," the Servant said. While his voice sounded as distant, Byar's Sensitive talent told him that the other had come a few wingspans closer. His *chya* seemed to wish to move of its own accord.

Two, he said to himself, feeling his own *hyu* as it coursed from talon-tips to heart-chambers, skull to seat.

"They will make a brood-queen of the young High Lord," the Servant added. Now Byar could feel the *esGa'uYe*, scarcely a wingspan behind.

Three, Byar told himself.

"You are too pathetic even for the Valley of Lost Souls," the Servant said. Byar could feel his enemy's hot breath, smell the char of the *e'chya*. "I will offer you as a sacrifice to—"

Four.

Byar whirled deftly, a master of the *chya* in fluid motion. Before the surprised Servant of *esGa'u* could bring his *e'chya* up to block the blow, Byar's weapon, crowing as it shrilly proclaimed itself, swept across the *esGa'uYe*'s shoulders and neatly severed the head from the body. The wings elevated somewhat and the whole body stood for a moment before collapsing to the misty stone floor of the Plane in a crumpled heap.

The head, freed from the body, flew several meters and then rolled in a long, elongated arc to land, bloody neck down, facing Byar.

As Byar stood there, the ichor of the *esGa'uYe* dripping from the end of Byar's *chya*, the head began to speak in a chill whisper.

"Relish your little victory, Servant of the Crawler," it said. "We will claim you in the end, *le* Byar."

Then, as the three People stood and watched, the flesh decayed away from the head, leaving only a grinning skull, which in turn crumbled into dust. When Byar glanced away at where the body had lain, it, too, was gone.

There was a long silence, as none of the three seemed inclined to speak. Reverentially, but with great care, Byar flew the perimeter of the Stone of Remembrance, extending his *gyu'u* as far into the mist as he dared, but there seemed to be no more scent of *esGa'uYal*. Still, he knew better than to believe that he had truly slain anything.

He landed and placed his wings in the Configuration of Polite Expectation.

"What did the Servant mean when he said that Shrnu'u had been 'called back from exile'?" Byar asked, directing his question at both of the others. "When was he exiled?"

"Over a hundred turns ago," Kanu'u replied. "We believe that He of the Dancing Blade appeared in *naZora'e* form; he sought to deceive and then destroy *esHu'ur*. He was thwarted and the death of his physical host made it impossible for him to return from below the Plain of Despite."

Byar sheathed his *chya* and folded his arms across his chest. "Shrnu'u HeGa'u appeared in the form of a *naZora'e*?"

"That is correct," Kanu'u answered.

"And by using him in the *Dsen'yen'ch'a* for the new bearer of the *gyaryu*, we returned him to the World That Is," said Byar.

"I believe this to be so."

"*hi* Sa'a," Byar responded, turning to face the High Lord, "I believe it is time for us to summon *si* S'reth. It appears that he has one other matter to answer for."

"That decision was not his alone to make: The High Lord and Chamberlain T'te'e also concurred," said Sa'a. "I will not hold a warrior who has transcended the Outer Peace responsible for all of the ills that beset us at this time."

"*hi* Sa'a—"

"Enough, *se* Byar." She arranged her wings in the Stance of Rightful Assertion. "We will not speak further of this."

Byar nodded and inclined his head. Sa'a moved to the center of the Stone, while *ha'i* Kanu'u, *chya* still drawn and in his hands, took up a position at the rim. Byar drew his weapon as well, and turned outward, ready for any intrusion.

He felt the Stone begin to thrum, and sensed the High Lord casting her *gyu'u* far into the soupy gray ocean that extended away from the Stone.

Karai'i esShaLie'e, Byar heard in his mind after several moments. *S'reth, I am. Why do you summon me from the Light?*

"We must understand your vision," Sa'a said, her voice seeming small and subdued. "There are things we must know."

Ask someone else, S'reth's mental voice responded. *I desire my rest, to feel the Light upon my wings, and I still have far to fly.*

"We will not trouble you long, *si* S'reth. A few questions only."

The Light calls me, but to the High Lord I still answer.

Byar felt a brief surge of joy at seeing one of the People emerge from the mist in front of him. It was S'reth, but not the one he had known for most of his life: Instead of the old and tired S'reth, he saw a warrior of the People in the prime of his health, wings and talons still intact, face full and smooth.

"*se* Byar," S'reth said. "I should have expected you to be a participant in this foolishness."

Same old S'reth, Byar told himself. "Elder Brother, it is a pleasure and honor to speak with you once more."

S'reth inclined his head, his wings indicating pleasure as well. "*hi* Sa'a. *si* Kanu'u."

"*si* S'reth," the High Lord said, giving a wing-position of honor and deference. "*se* Byar informed me that before your—before you began your flight to *esLi*—you experienced *sSurch'a* regarding the legend of *seLi'e'Yan.*"

"You have summoned me to inform you about this."

"Yes," Byar said. "What can you tell us?"

"I . . . can only answer questions that you ask," S'reth replied. "And only a few: My *hsi* journeys far from the Light to speak with you and *esLi* cannot protect me for long from the predators of this Plane."

"I understand." Byar glanced over his shoulder at the others, who stood waiting. "*si* S'reth, you told me that the account of Loremaster Shthe'e described the *gyaryu* as a 'lost sword' and that Qu'u went to the Land of Despite to regain it. You wished me to reach the same *sSurch'a* regarding this crucial difference, but I did not. Why is it important?"

"As *si* Shthe'e originally wrote the tale," S'reth answered, "Qu'u went to the Plain of Despite to *regain* the sword to unite the clans. It had been lost somehow and the Servant of *esLi* sent the warrior to recover the 'lost sword' for hi A'alu.

"If that was indeed so, then the *gyaryu came from* the Plain of Despite: Whether given freely or wrested away, it was at some point a tool of Despite. Older versions of the legend acknowledge this in a way that the accepted ones do not.

"According to *se* Jackie's account of her quest, the person who placed the *gyaryu* in her hands informed her that his employers had originally written the legend, and thus both the quest of Qu'u and the quest of *se* Jackie were manipulations by these beings. And if that were so . . . it would have been the plan of the *esGa'uYal* all along to have us give up the sword, sacrifice *si* Sergei, and cause *se* Jackie to emerge.

"If *se* Jackie had known the original legend, she would have known all along that she would recover the sword in the way she did because the *esGa'uYal* willed it so."

"But what about *seLi'e'Yan, si* S'reth? How does Standing Within the Circle apply to this situation?"

"Ah." S'reth's image shimmered, as if the sun had emerged from behind a cloud for a moment. "Consider this, Younger Brother. The *esGa'uYal* set the People against the humans several eights of turns ago; the *esGa'uYal* brought about *esHu'ur.* They did not wish for us to cooperate. Yet by the merest *accident* we gained understanding of each other.

"Now they have provided us with a new *Gyaryu'har* and an understanding that by her efforts, and with her protection, the High Nest can withstand the onslaught of the *esHara'y,* the insectoid aliens. But to do that, we must perform *seLi'e'Yan:* We must Stand Within the Circle while everything beyond is laid waste. The very spirit of *esLi* was touched by the Deceiver to move us in this direction, and we—you—may have no other choice.

"Just as in the city of Sharia'a—once named Shr'e'a—we possess the power to withstand the attack of the *esHara'y*. But, *just* as in Sharia'a, we must watch as that which we do not defend is destroyed."

"But you specifically said that it was *Shr'e'a, not* Sharia'a, that we should examine."

"Indeed," S'reth said, his wings moving to a position Byar did not recognize. "The legend of *seLi'e'Yan* was changed as well. If you look before the time of Unification, you will find there are things present that have been forgotten—and things absent that have since been added."

S'reth shimmered again, and became more translucent. "I do not have much more time, my good friend. You risk much, causing me to tarry even this long."

Byar arranged his wings in the Stance of Honored Approach. "Tell me one thing more, *si* S'reth. When we summoned Shrnu'u HeGa'u into the *D'sen'yen'ch'a* for *se* Jackie, did we indeed bring him out of exile?"

"Yes." S'reth's wings arranged in a posture of sadness. "He had been trapped beneath the Plain of Despite since the turn in which *esHu'ur* condemned us to life."

Byar looked away toward the High Lord, who stood still, as if unable to respond.

"I must go, my friend. Remember me, and do *esLi*'s will." S'reth began to fade away, his transparent image acquiring a golden shimmer as Byar placed his wings in the Posture of Reverence to *esLi*.

"It is time to return now," Byar said to the High Lord.

The best compromise for evening dress was a bit of a step backward. The empress had offered the help of the court's own dressmaker for a gown; but Jackie had concluded that any such garment would make it impossible to wear the *gyaryu*, which she wasn't about to part from. In the end she decided on a fairly traditional admiral's uniform, with a badge bearing the *hRni'i* insignia of the High Nest attached to the crimson sash of her office. With the sword belted at her waist she actually cut a rather dashing figure; she had only the briefest of regrets that the uniform, like the rank, was to be retired before she went back to the High Nest.

Despite protests to the contrary, Dan had claimed the privilege of escorting her to the event. He arrived just as the sun was beginning to dip toward the ocean. Within a half-hour he had been fitted out by the Imperial tailor and he disappeared to get changed.

He found her in a spacious gallery, removing a minute speck of dust from one trouser-leg. She'd never seen him in civilian formals, but it wasn't much different on him than full-dress uniform—handsome but essentially misplaced. Still, he carried himself with confidence as always, and out of the corner of her eye she caught him looking at her from a distance, with an expression she couldn't quite read.

"Looking for someone?" she asked.

"I . . . think I found her," he said at last, taking her hand in his. "Never thought I'd say it again, but that uniform looks damn good on you."

"Thanks. I think."

"Compliment intended," he said, looking away and up at one of the grim portraits on the wall. The subject of the depiction scowled back, looking down from some centuries ago; perhaps he was disapproving, or perhaps indifferent.

In the distance the waves crashed on the rocks below and the deep-orange sun spread across the horizon.

"That's Anderson, isn't it?" he said, pointing at the picture.

"I didn't buy the guidebook."

"They say he had ice-water in his veins. Ten years after Emperor Willem took the throne and founded the Empire. Anderson fought a seventeen-hour battle at Aldebaran without ever leaving the pilot's seat."

"Single-minded."

"And he must've had a hell of a bladder," Dan said, and suddenly they both found themselves laughing. He gave her hand a little squeeze; just for a moment a familiar look came into his eyes, one she hadn't seen in a dozen years. She felt her barriers going up within, the natural defenses that told her to watch out for approaching danger.

"We'd better get in there," she said, pulling her hand away, but he didn't seem inclined to let go.

"Wait a sec, Jay," he said, cradling her hand in both of his. He looked at his shoes and then back at her. "I have to tell you something, before I lose my nerve."

"Dan—"

"It's not quite what you think. Jay, we parted under a cloud many years ago. We both understood and *didn't* understand why it happened.

I—It seems to me that we've done all we can to turn our backs, but not very successfully.

"S'reth offered me a chance to help you out because he knew that we'd been friends many years ago. I took a tough line with you when you came aboard—"

"I didn't ask for any favors."

"I wasn't *offering* any. I meant what I said when you came aboard my ship at Cle'eru, and if things had gone differently . . . I was willing to take a very nice sum of money to cart you over the line and through every free port I knew, whether we found anything or not.

"But then you disappeared. You went on-station at Crossover and disappeared. One of *my* crew—Ch'k'te—was found dead in the admin center, along with a . . . a something. It was then that I realized what I must've sounded like."

"You sounded like the captain of a ship."

"Jay, for Christ's sake, leave the 'Iron Maiden' stuff to Anderson and the rest," he snapped back, nodding toward the portrait but not letting go of her hand. "I cut you loose years ago and I let you go weeks ago.

"The night we jumped from Crossover to Tamarind, Pyotr came into my cabin and told me how glad he was to be rid of the responsibility for escorting you. I practically decked him. Then I locked my door and got really drunk. *Really* drunk." He smiled, the boyish, crooked grin she remembered. He let go of her hand, running one of his through his hair. "I called myself all kinds of fool and promised myself that I wasn't going to let you go again."

"Dan, you can't be serious—"

"Hear me out. I don't expect a romance after all this time; I'd *welcome* it, but I can't expect it. You—You're—I don't know, you're in a different league now; it's not the same. I'm not looking to sleep with you. Particularly."

He smiled again and seemed to tense, perhaps expecting her to punch him again, as she'd done at Cle'eru. "I've talked it over with the Sultan and the other officers. I made a formal application to Captain Maartens, who agreed to endorse the idea. We all see the way the wind is blowing: We'd—I'd—be pleased if you'd allow me to put *Fair Damsel* at your disposal. We're not crucial to the war effort, but you . . . might need some folks to cover your ass sometime."

"You want to be my—What? My entourage? My traveling band? Dan, I appreciate the offer, but I don't think so."

"Would it make you feel better if I told you it wasn't particularly selfless? That I had some ulterior motive?"

"Like what?" This time it was Jackie who tensed, wondering if she *was* going to have to punch him again.

"Like *that*." He pointed to the *gyaryu*. "All of my sources say there isn't a place in the Solar Empire that's safe from the enemy, except within shouting distance of that sword of yours.

"I figure that if it's riding around aboard my ship, we should be as safe as anyone, anywhere."

"Are you crazy?" She let her hand rest on the hilt, almost without considering it. "The last time I was aboard, Sh—" She lowered her voice, almost as if unwilling to continue speaking the name out loud. "—Shrnu'u HeGa'u got aboard and tried to kill me. He opened the hangar-bay doors in jump. Remember?"

"I remember. But you didn't have *that* with you then."

"My predecessor had *this* with him when the vuhls took Cicero. It didn't seem to help."

"S'reth said that he went to Cicero *intending* to lose it. I assume you'll put up a fight."

"You're damned right."

"Then we want to be there with you. Look, a couple of weeks before you, uh, returned from your quest, I was with Maartens' squadron at Corcyra. I was at Thon's Well and saw the size of those alien ships. Nowhere is safe now, Jay. *Nowhere*." He looked down at his shoes. "I don't know why I'm trying to explain this to you."

"We should go in now," Jackie said, extending her arm to Dan. He took it but seemed unable to look at her.

"I'd like you to consider my offer before just rejecting it," he said. "Think about it, Jay. No strings attached."

"And if I still say no?"

"Well, then . . . I guess we take our chances out there"—he waved his free hand in the general direction of Waikiki—"with everybody else."

"All right," she said, and tried to smile, but felt weary at the effort. "I'll consider it. Time to make our entrance, don't you think?"

He smiled back. "Admiral, it would be my pleasure."

The entrance of the fleet's newest flag officer created something of a stir. She was pried away from Dan almost as soon as she entered

the huge reception hall, built onto the rim of Diamond Head and overlooking the sparkling Pacific Ocean. There were many names and faces
to remember; unsolicited, scraps of information seemed to come forth
from the *gyaryu,* advising her when someone particularly important
drifted into view.

She found herself thinking about the idea of tackling this sort of reception in a powered chair, like *si* Sergei: She realized that while it removed the possibility of a quick escape from an undesired conversation,
it did tend to keep people out of one's personal space. The press was
enormous, so much so that it took almost Herculean effort to reach the
buffet table on the other side of the hall where she could take a moment
to compose herself while ordering a drink.

se *Jackie,* she heard in her mind as she stood waiting. It was Sergei's
voice from within the *gyaryu. Be on your guard.*

For what?

esHara'y. *Some of the persons in this room are servants of the Deceiver.*

Well, isn't that terrific, she thought, and began to look around the
room, trying to locate Dan. The hairs on the back of her neck rose as
she scanned around as if someone were standing directly behind her.
She whirled, hand near her sword—

"Commodore—excuse me, *Admiral*—so *good* to see you again!"

Instead of whatever she'd expected, she found herself face-to-face
with a short, mousy-looking man of middle age, dressed in an outfit
that would have looked fashionable—and appropriate—on someone
twenty years his junior.

"Mr. Sharpe," she said, as noncommittally as she could manage.

"Hansie—*please,* madam." As she was handed her drink, Hansie
Sharpe took hold of her off-elbow and managed to steer her gently but
expertly through the flow of reception traffic toward a small alcove.

It was rather like a shuttle pilot making his way through a familiar
asteroid-belt: The little man knew just which turns to make and which
directions to avoid. *Like K'ke'en,* she thought to herself, remembering
the crippled zor at Cle'eru.

At last he let go and took hold of her hand and pumped it vigor-
ously. "You look marvelous, dear lady," he said, his little eyes sparkling.
"I am *so* sorry we could not spend more time together when we first
met—a host's duties are *endless.*" He smiled ferally, spreading his hands
wide in a self-deprecating gesture.

"I quite understand, Mr. Sh—Hansie." She corrected herself at the last moment. "What brings you here?"

"Well. When one receives an invitation from one's emperor, one can hardly *refuse*. A *dreadful* bore, these diplomatic soirées, but you'll get used to it."

"I imagine so . . . What I meant was, what brings you to Sol System?"

"Business mixed with pleasure. Actually," he said, leaning in and speaking sotto voce, "I am hoping to plead my case with the emperor. I had to leave so much behind."

" 'Behind'?"

"On Cle'eru. Abandoned. Imagine that: One of the jewels in the Imperial Crown, a world where humans and zor lived in harmony, evacuated and left defenseless. I scarcely was able to get away myself."

"And here you are." *"Lived in harmony"*? she thought to herself. *As if you believe that!*

"And here I am. Hawaii is gorgeous, but there's a waiting line years long to get any kind of permanent accommodations, except on the big island, and that's so *far* from the center of things."

"Pity," she said.

"Of course, the rules are all different for the *military*. I suppose you would be staying at Schofield? I hear that flag officers' billets are simply *gorgeous*."

"No . . . Actually, I'm staying here at Diamond Head." At this, Hansie's eyebrows rose. "As a guest of the emperor." They rose further, though Jackie would not have believed that possible. "Besides, this"— she pointed to the new boards on her shoulders—"is my retirement uniform. I'm leaving the Navy."

Hansie Sharpe's shoulders seemed to droop. Jackie suddenly realized why the little man had sought her out: He was looking for someone to help him out with a good word to the emperor. An admiral might have the emperor's ear.

"Leaving?" he said. "I would think that your career . . . would be just beginning to take off."

"Oh, it is. Just not the way I had intended."

"I'm not sure I understand you, madam," he said, and his glance darted from her to somewhere else in the room and then back.

She pointed to a patch on the arm of her uniform jacket. "I'm an official representative of the High Nest now, Hansie."

"The High Nest?" He seemed genuinely concerned, perhaps even ill-at-ease. "With the *Envoy's Office?*"

"Not exactly."

"Rather a step *down* for you, is it not, Admiral?"

"Because it means working with the zor, you mean," she answered, a trifle annoyed even though she knew Hansie's opinions of them.

"Well . . . I mean, it's hard to imagine that someone of your talents could find enough to do—"

"There's a hell of a lot more to do working for the High Nest than drinking *g'rey'l* and eating canapés at some damn reception," she snapped. Hansie seemed to take a cringing step back as she said it. As occasionally happens in a crowded roomful of conversation, there seemed to be a sudden, powerful lull in the noise level.

She sipped at her drink, trying to decide how she'd extricate her boot from deep within her esophagus where she'd just planted it.

"Allow me to give you a piece of *friendly advice,* Admiral," Hansie Sharpe said, tight-lipped, when the sound level in the room had risen somewhat. "In my experience, everything of any consequence to the health, wealth and welfare of the Solar Empire and its *subject* races—including the zor—is decided either here or on the other side of this planet, at the Imperial Assembly in Genève. The vaunted *autonomy* of the *zor*"—he pronounced the word as if it had a foul taste—"is a clever fiction invented eighty years ago to prevent them from starting another war. It was to save face, nothing more.

"In my opinion, the single greatest service ever performed by a zor High Lord was to commit suicide and take three enemy ships with him. Nothing else they do, or say—even if you could understand it when they said it—contributes materially to the war effort. And when *we* win this war, as *we* undoubtedly shall, the emperor will have something to say about noncooperative 'allies.' Then we will see what becomes of their 'autonomy.' "

She opened her mouth to provide an angry retort. Hansie hurried on, forestalling her: "This is wartime, Admiral Laperriere. Fortunes are made—and lost"—he placed his hand on his breast and gave a little bow—"in this climate. If you wish to throw away a seemingly promising career to work with lukewarm allies who do not even have the honor to support their protectors and patrons, I can only pity you. If you choose to continue your military career, I can only applaud you. In any case, I will not bother you anymore." He gave another bow and backed away into the maelstrom of formalwear and dress uniforms and was presently lost to her sight.

Almost as soon as she lost track of Hansie, Dan McReynolds surfaced nearby. She must have looked upset because he looked concerned.

"What's the problem, Jay? I saw you talking to that little parasite; what did he want?"

"He wanted to educate me, I guess." She straightened her uniform jacket a bit at waist and cuffs. "He believes that the zor are holding back, that we're going to brush this invasion aside and then take away the autonomy of the High Nest."

"I'm not surprised. I've had my ears open: Nobody seems to think of this war as anything but a scheme by the military to keep its funding up. It's surreal, Jay."

"They don't know what's going on out there. If they did, what could they do about it?"

"Panic."

"Damn straight, Dan. How could any of these people, except the emperor perhaps, face down the idea that in a few months, or years, everything could be gone?"

"Fiddling while Rome burns."

"It's worse than that. It reminds me of *Ur'ta leHssa,* the Valley of Lost Souls. Especially in the outermost parts, the Lost Ones move about, continuing to do what they have always done, unable even to lift their heads to see the Fortress of Despite above them. The ones in the Center know their fate—they can see the Icewall, but can't bring themselves to pierce it, so they become like statues with nowhere to turn but within. But on the edge, they don't even know that they're trapped."

"I'm not sure I understand the comparison, but I assume you know what you're talking about."

"Yeah." She set her drink on a side-table. "Georg Maartens said he'd detach you to be my shuttle service, huh?"

"I can show you a private message he prepared in case you asked."

"There may not be a safe place even with the sword," she said. "I can't guarantee anything."

"Nobody asked for a guarantee, Jay."

"All right," she said after a moment. "Tell your partners that I accept their offer. Let's get the formalities over with down here, and then I'm expected out at Langley."

chapter 16

Trebizond made six jumps with its escorts, starting at Denneva and ending in the zor Core Stars. Rich Abramowicz had no idea where they were headed; Barbara MacEwan, his only contact with the ships guarding his own, wasn't about to provide that information.

The first jump transit was from Denneva to Schumann, a heavily populated system fifty-odd parsecs from Sol System. It had a large shipyard well away from what was now a war zone.

Schumann had three Earthlike worlds circling a K2 orange star, each slightly different, all beautiful. It was a prime shore-leave destination for Navy crews headed for R&R.

Trebizond had eight hours in Schumann System—time to skim the gas giant, refuel and line up for the next jump. All information was delivered in a brief, precise comm-squirt from *Duc d'Enghien,* and was executed forty-five minutes later, down to the millisecond.

The second jump transit took the ships from Schumann to Kiu Ho, Mu Herculis, a G5 star less than ten parsecs from the homeworld. It was almost at the limit of *Trebizond*'s jump range to travel so far in a single transit—more than sixty parsecs—but the ship emerged on the exact tick of the ship's chrono. Kiu Ho had extensive naval facilities even though it was far into the Inner Sphere; it had been settled by one of Old Earth's larger countries well before the War of Accession and had retained its military base through the constant efforts of its representatives in the Imperial Assembly.

Jumping to Kiu Ho made Abramowicz wonder whether they were ultimately headed for Sol System itself. He hadn't attended the Naval Academy there; he'd been promoted up from OCS outside the Inner Sphere. Like most Imperial citizens, he'd been born and raised elsewhere—Sol System was a place on a stellar map, written about in history books, not a place to which people actually *went*.

At Kiu Ho they weren't even permitted to fly to the gas giant: Their scoops were kept stowed, and an unmanned oiler came alongside to provide them with enough fuel to make their next jump. Abramowicz's hopes for a tour of the home system were quickly dismissed as he received orders for the next jump.

From Kiu Ho they jumped to Harrison System, on the other side of the Inner Sphere. Harrison was another world that had been settled before the War of Accession. It was a system with two large industrial worlds and wasn't much of a place to visit; they didn't stay more than a few hours—just long enough to refuel and line up the next jump. Once again, there were oilers out at the edge of the system.

By this time they clearly were expected at each destination. Aboard *Trebizond,* nerves were frayed and tempers were short, particularly with the unspoken message the escorts sent.

Someone's an alien. And somehow, somewhere, there was somebody who could tell the difference.

They next arrived at Escorial, a full-member world in the Solar Empire, sixty-one parsecs away from Harrison. A century ago it had been at the Solward edge of what had been called the New Territories: systems captured from the zor during the wars of the late 2200s. By this time, there were betting pools in the wardroom and in every mess aboard the ship, for where they were headed and when they'd get there.

At Escorial the two *Emperor Ian*-class ships and two *Broadmoors* were detached and replaced by four zor naval vessels, so that only they and *Duc d'Enghien* remained as escorts for *Trebizond.* By the time they emerged at A'anenu, at the edge of the Antares Rift, it was obvious where they were headed: the zor Core Stars, only twenty-five parsecs across the Rift.

What awaited them there was anyone's guess.

The Langley complex covered a vast area of Callisto, etched silver and black, lit by the eerie swirling light of Jupiter hanging in the sky. Imperial Intelligence was a vast, largely unseen labyrinthine bureaucracy that the Navy knew well but didn't trust much. Jackie's gut feelings were still based on her original career experience; reaching the center of the hidden machine might have made her uneasy, except that the last few months had taken much of the fear away . . . but not the wariness.

She stood on the bridge of *Fair Damsel* and felt, more than heard, the soft hum from the *gyaryu* as she watched Langley resolve itself on the ship's forward screen. She didn't know the true origin of the name, but in the Navy, "Langley" meant "spooks": warrant officers with no apparent duties; Sensitives with no military discipline; mysterious packages and sealed orders. When she had taken command at Cicero there'd been an intel guy stationed there, but a few months afterward he'd received transfer orders to another posting, as there was nothing going on at that end of the Empire.

Jackie smiled inwardly. *It's always good to know that the spooks are fallible.* She remembered what *se* Sergei had told her within the *gyaryu* before she'd left Zor'a: *"What* is *likely, is that you will learn more from what they do* not *say than by what they do."* They couldn't all share the bigotry and tunnel vision of a Hansie Sharpe, but she was still probably better informed than they were.

Don't give anything away, she thought to herself. What was the famous expression? *"Better to be silent and be taken for a fool, than to open one's mouth and remove all doubt."* She'd only gotten this far by being underestimated.

A small four-person shuttle transported her from *Fair Damsel* to the surface. It was driven by an unsmiling and uncommunicative MP who acted like he was under 3-V surveillance during the entire trip. After a few fruitless minutes of trying to initiate pleasantries, Jackie sat back and convinced herself to relax, becoming a passive observer for a short time. The *gyaryu* lay across her lap in its tooled scabbard, and even without communicating with the inhabitants she could feel the *hsi* within it like a living, palpable thing.

When she emerged from the shuttle airlock, a rashk was waiting for her. In her long career in the Navy, she'd met very few of the heavyset, bucolic reptiles; they mostly stuck to their three homeworlds in Vega System. The ones that left were usually merchants and traders. They didn't join the military services, and even Jackie's exoculture and exobiology courses at the Academy hadn't dealt with them very much. But here she was, and here he—she—it?—was, in front of her, standing nearly two meters high. It was an upright-walking blue-green lizard with six limbs, and a broad tail that curved up at the end; a wide, horny head with a three-nostril snout; three elongated, bleary eyes and a wide, toothy mouth that showed a perpetual grin. The rashk was wearing something that looked like a tent-sized purple silk bathrobe, with the Imperial Intelligence emblem over the breast; no doubt it satisfied some color sense of the being, but to Jackie it clashed horribly.

"*Gyaryu'har* Jackie Laperriere, are you," the rashk's voder rumbled. The device, perched over where a human's sternum would be, allowed the rashk to form human sounds which would normally be beyond its vocal range.

"Honored," she said.

"M'm'e'e Sha'kan," it replied, pointing to itself and bending at about the level of the bathrobe's sash. Its tail curled up behind. "For you a guide M'm'e'e has come to be, questions to answer and ask. Welcome here at Langley you must be made to feel, to M'm'e'e the director has said, and this dictum follow M'm'e'e shall!" The rashk clapped its hands, making a loud, moist sound. "Sorrows for the predecessor to you; with him, M'm'e'e have had many talkings. To the Three he has gone, yes?"

"He has . . . transcended the Outer Peace," Jackie replied. "You knew *si* Sergei?"

"Much known was he to M'm'e'e Sha'kan!" the rashk answered at once—so emphatically that it seemed like the response to an accusation. "We were friends of greatness, indeed, as shall you be to M'm'e'e when we have come better into each other's knowledge. Ha ha ha." This last exclamation, which the voder rendered the best it could, sounded like three sharp coughs, but seemed to be laughter.

This is a test, she thought to herself, and the *gyaryu* seemed to murmur assent. "M'm'e'e Sha'kan," she said, "I am pleased to make your acquaintance. I have come some distance in hopes of asking some questions that you might be able to answer."

"Answer questions shall M'm'e'e!" the rashk said.

He, the *gyaryu* offered on its own: the first question she'd wanted to ask in the first quiet moment.

"But first, refreshment for the guest provide must M'm'e'e. Come this way, ha ha ha," he said, clapping his hands and sweeping down the accessway, leaving Jackie no choice but to follow.

O nce the initial surprise had worn off and she'd accustomed herself to his speech patterns, Jackie actually found M'm'e'e quite charming. He was young for a rashk away from home: The rashk were a long-lived race, and "young" made him almost twice her age. He had "emerged from the Three"—hatched, she supposed—a few years before Marais' death, when the relationship between the People and the Solar Empire had only recently changed. As the scion of a rashk diplomatic clan, he had been drawn to apply to the Intelligence Academy and was one of the first of his race to serve in the Agency. While the Agency itself was hide-bound and peculiar, as an institution it apparently was a good judge of talent; after twenty-seven Standard years in the Intelligence Service, M'm'e'e had achieved his current position of Third Deputy Director. He seemed particularly proud of this "happy circumstance," as he put it: "the most auspicious of omens."

He had known Sergei for nearly twenty years, though they had mostly met on neutral ground at court at Oahu, that fertile breeding-ground of diplomatic intrigue. Somehow, a three-hundred-kilo lizard in a purple bathrobe didn't seem like the sort of person capable of engaging in "intrigue"; but the universe had already done a good job of convincing Jackie how strange it could be.

After a considerable amount of forced reminiscences and small talk, M'm'e'e suddenly charged toward relevance with the speed and determination of a Cicero snow-ox.

"Here come you, information for the High Nest to get," he said abruptly, slapping his two upper left hands on the table. She had been about to set her drink down, but thought better of it. "And talk is all M'm'e'e do can!"

Too bad you didn't reach that conclusion half an hour ago, she thought to herself. She smiled, though, knowing that she'd enjoyed hearing him talk about himself almost as much as he had enjoyed doing it.

"Information to get you must have, questions to ask, questions to ask," he said. "By the Three, time wasting it is, though this phrase to M'm'e'e means little: Perhaps *Gyaryu'har* Jackie Laperriere explain to M'm'e'e it can. What like to know you would?"

She reached into an inner pocket of her tunic and drew out a comp. M'm'e'e pointed to a pad in the table with his two left hands and she placed it there. The image of Thomas Stone formed in the air about a decimeter above the table.

"I want to know as much as I can about this man."

The rashk's nose wrinkled and one eyebrow drooped in an expression that, on a human, might have been quizzical. He leaned back in his chair and folded his hands across his chest—once, then twice, in sequence—and said, "You have data references with you brought?"

"It's all in the comp."

M'm'e'e casually extended one right hand to the table and tapped it near the pad. Controls appeared, configured in a splayed shape and pattern she didn't recognize.

Built for a rashk, she realized after a moment. A service record appeared below the picture, rotating until they could both read it.

"From the war era," M'm'e'e said. "Old news, this is. Undoubtedly back to the Three this individual has gone."

"Don't bet on it."

"Clarification?" the rashk replied, the other eyebrow drooping. "Why in this old service record interested are you?"

"I believe that there's more information on him here at Langley. I want to see it."

"Not the source of service records are we," M'm'e'e began. "Countless persons have there been, and not enough storage could we possess to, tabs upon whom keep, as you say might."

"Look him up."

"Happy to oblige is M'm'e'e," he answered. "But dubious is M'm'e'e also." He began to key in a request. A reddish patch glowed in midair below and to the left of the service record. "Intriguing," he said at last, and leaned forward, resting his huge head on his two pairs of hands.

"What does it mean?"

"Death of an agent, symbol represents," he said, nodding toward the red patch. "More to this there is," he added, and continued to key. A series of images flashed by: a holo of a pistol; a figure shaped like a human mummy; an arcology complex seen from afar; a 3-D graph of some sort—

"Wait!" Jackie said. The graph, which had been undulating back and forth, became still. M'm'e'e looked up at her. "I can't absorb it that fast," she added.

"Apologies must M'm'e'e tender!" he said, and gestured to split the 3-V image into several pieces. The series she had seen appeared in sequence, along with a few images she'd missed.

When it all had been displayed, she leaned forward. "Is this all attached to Stone's record?"

"Indeed is it. More to this than the nose could first sniff is there, ha ha ha," he said. "Official investigation, but closed was it by Imperial edict.

"Usually accessible is it not," he continued. "Well-informed you are," he added.

"What's it all about?"

"Slowly, slowly," M'm'e'e said, leaning back and folding his hands again. "Information with price comes."

"Price?"

"Give and take, take and give. *Price.* Exchange of information there must be, *se Gyaryu'har.* Even to *se Gyaryu'har,* free comes nothing."

"I'm not sure I understand."

"Dissembling does *se* Jackie Laperriere, *Gyaryu'har;* more than she says is she knowing. To understand that knowing, M'm'e'e wants to know also."

"Information for information."

"Give and take, take and give. Record—" He gestured toward the series of images. "No record found would be, unless Stone particularly queried was. Knew you to ask, database answer provides. How knew you to ask, clever *se Gyaryu'har*? Sword question gave, answer to get?"

She tried to read the rashk's expression and took a moment to send out a quick call for help to the sword that hung by her side. *What does he want?*

Information. Sergei's voice came into her mind, clear and calm. *M'm'e'e is a trader, like most of his race. He won't tell you what he knows until you tell him what you know. Remember,* se *Jackie—what they do* not *say is perhaps more important: This matter is obviously significant.*

"You say there was a death involved. An agent," Jackie said to M'm'e'e. "That doesn't seem like a good-enough reason for an Imperial edict. There's more to this than *you're* saying, isn't there?"

"Give and take, clever *se Gyaryu'har*. Take and give."

"All right." She leaned forward, folding her hands on the table. "The service record shows Stone died in 2307 after having gone missing during the last war. What would you say if I told you that I spoke to him less than three weeks ago?"

"Dreaming of the zor People, this is?"

"No." *I'm not so sure,* she thought, but kept that comment to herself. "No, this was real life. I met Captain Stone in person. He arranged my return to Zor'a from hundreds of parsecs distant, by means that are almost too unbelievable to describe."

"Imagination of M'm'e'e is great, ha ha ha. Continue."

"Do you know where Crossover is?"

"Six days' jump from Cicero is Crossover. Pirate port."

"That's right." *What, did everyone know about Crossover but the Imperial Navy?* "I was at least three or four days' jump farther out than that. I *walked* home. Through jump. Stone created—or summoned—a sort of rainbow bridge. I stepped onto it and I wound up in the High Lord's *esTle'e* on Zor'a."

"Also in report of pilot Garrett was," M'm'e'e said. "Debriefing Admiral Hsien received, of this colored bridge also. Same means must be, yes?"

Well, all right, she thought to herself. "Yes, I believe that it's the same phenomenon. It got him off the alien ship that captured him at Cicero."

M'm'e'e didn't say anything for several moments, as if he were trying to gauge the truth of her statement.

"Your sudden reappearance, explanation it provide would. *Gyaryu* also returned after unfortunate incident at A'alu Spaceport not long before; clarifies does it." It was clear to Jackie he was fitting pieces together. "Stipulation is, that you with Stone character on far world met, there obtained sword you, interestingly, with the death of long-talk friend *se* Sergei coincident, not long after suicide of not-so-insane High Lord Ke'erl HeYen.

"Fulfillment of Qu'u legend, Perilous Stair climbed, Icewall pierced, all complete—even appointment of female High Lord all pattern of greater dream fits, yes? Ha ha ha. M'm'e'e to understand begins."

That was quick, she thought. "You know about all of that?"

"Of that, zor no secret have made. Old rashk proverb is: 'People smell what their nostrils told to smell have been.' Stipulation: Zor to humans mysterious greatly are, though many years since war have gone. But pattern of behavior long centuries built has been; zor the wingspeech but speak cannot help, quoting of zor epics in official releases do. When Jupiter ion-storm erupts, comm into noise falls, people the noise ignore. After time, zor speech like ion-storm becomes; regular occurrence in mysterious references to speak, people the noise ignore.

"Zor wings have the story given away, yet few to noise have listened. *M'm'e'e* listened. *M'm'e'e* heard. You the sword from Plain of Despite have brought; you the sword from Deceiver have wrested. You the *Gyaryu'har* have become—something else also, M'm'e'e suspects. Take and give. Many thinkings M'm'e'e must perform." He leaned his head back, and his eyes drooped shut.

"M'm'e'e?"

The rashk appeared to have gone to sleep.

"M'm'e'e," she repeated, a bit louder.

One eyelid slowly lifted. "Eh?"

"The record."

He reached out a hand and tapped his control pad with a finger. A regular human control pad extruded in front of Jackie. "Many thinkings," he repeated, and his eye closed again.

While soft, vaguely moist snoring sounds began to erupt from the rashk, and his four arms began to move gently in a slow, almost hypnotic pattern, Jackie began to navigate through the data presented. It was clear that M'm'e'e had placed strict boundaries on the information, but within its scope she could take it in and analyze it any way she pleased.

It was a remarkable story. A highly placed agent had been aboard the fleet flagship—*Lancaster, si* Sergei's ship—up until the time the fleet took A'anenu, the huge naval base where the envoy's great-grandfather had happened upon the *esLiHeShuSa'a,* the shrine to *esLi.* The agent had been discovered—or perhaps feared discovery—and had sent no further reports after the taking of the base.

Though there was no firsthand report of the incident from the agent—he had left *Lancaster* to remain behind with the ships guarding A'anenu—it was clear that Stone, then serving as the Admiral's adjutant, had literally disappeared from *Lancaster* while it was in jump. This fit with the information she'd been given back on Zor'a.

Stone had left nothing behind; in fact, an official log report from *Lancaster* indicated that Stone's cabin had been completely empty—with a millimeter of deck, wall and ceiling removed as well.

Some weeks later, when Marais had returned to Sol System, he was shot at by a 'copter signed out under Stone's name. Stone had then appeared a second time, at the old Grimaldi base on Luna, and had attacked Marais again—this time very nearly killing him, but for the intervention of an agent who was killed by the peculiar eversion weapon. There was even 3-V footage of the event.

> COMMANDER LYNNE RUSS (trial counsel for Admiral Marais): Admiral, the witness is answering the question. The perception that the accused won the war is an evaluation of the military accomplishment of the accused. It is therefore valid.
>
> REAR ADMIRAL THEODORE MCMASTERS (Tribunal President): Objection overruled. Defense may proceed.
>
> COMMANDER SIR JAMES ARONOFF (Judge Advocate): I beg to remind the Admiral that this decision will permit the witness to engage in rhetoric which might influence the cause of the accused but which is in no way evidence.
>
> MCMASTERS: Does the trial counsel wish to lodge a formal protest?
>
> *(Lights extinguished and sound of life support stops. After a moment, dim emergency lights appear. Tribunal in shadow; defense table and some of the wall is lit. Marais is now standing.)*
>
> MCMASTERS: What the hell is happening?
>
> *(A bright, multicolored light begins to form in the lit area: a rainbow spilling out of nowhere.)*
>
> CAPTAIN THOMAS STONE: Perhaps I can answer that, Admiral.

"Freeze," Jackie said. The clip stopped moving.

She set it to reverse slowly and watched the form of Thomas Stone step backward into nothingness, a cornucopian swirl of color accompanying him.

"An interesting phenomenon is that," M'm'e'e said, eyes open now.

"The energy phenomenon similar to that recorded upon the *Lancaster* is, favorably also with the recorded pattern of our agent at Hilton Head arcology compares it does."

The image hung in midair, frozen, a droplet of time from most of a century ago.

"This is how you to Zor'a returned, my thinkings to M'm'e'e say," the rashk said. "Also how Garrett from alien ship escaped. Walking from some other place did Stone come."

"Proceed," Jackie said to the image, without directly answering M'm'e'e; but it was probably true.

(Stone holds a pistol of unknown design, pointed at Marais' chest.)
MARAIS: All right, Stone. Answer.
(Stone looks around. No other figure moves while he does so.)
STONE: I am here, my dear Admiral, to kill you.
MCMASTERS: Now, wait just a damn minute—
(McMasters stands, but freezes when Stone turns the pistol toward him.)
STONE: This weapon has a most unusual effect. I will be happy
    to demonstrate its effects if you'd like.
MARAIS: That won't be necessary. I assume you intend to explain
    yourself, at last.
STONE: Of course. The problem, Admiral Marais, is that you
    have failed to play your part as originally intended. You had the
    greatest opportunity ever afforded a human: the opportunity to
    utterly and completely destroy a rival species and demonstrate
    the superiority of your own. Yet at the last moment you refused
    to deliver the coup de grâce.
       That is a fatal weakness, Admiral. It is one that has plagued
    humanity throughout its history. Humanity is too violent to
    be civilized and too civilized to be ruthless. It will be your
    downfall in the end.
       But since you failed to do what was necessary, it is obvious
    that you cannot be allowed to live. If humanity will not destroy
    the zor, then surely the zor will have to destroy humanity. The
    destruction of their precious Dark Wing should assure that.
MARAIS: But there was no need—
STONE: Of course there was need, you fool. What do you think
    this was all about?

MCMASTERS: Tell me. What *is* this all about?

STONE: This is a conflict between races. My employers determined that it was best that humanity defeat the zor, whose fanatic predilections made their evolutionary chances significantly less than their more adaptable human opponents. With my help, Admiral Marais wrote a book that described the single available solution to the quandary into which humanity had placed itself: the destruction of the zor by fighting them on the same terms as they fought humanity. The rest you know: Marais carried the plan forward up to the critical stage, at which point he allowed the mystical nonsense that passes for zor religion to get in the way of carrying out his historical mission— to eradicate the zor.

MARAIS: "Mystical"—

STONE (to McMasters): Your precious Admiral had even begun to believe that he was the Destroyer their myths had foretold. This ridiculous messianic complex stayed his hand when he should have slain. Humanity has proven itself incapable of dominance.

MARAIS: By showing mercy?

STONE: When did you show mercy before? At Sr'chne'e? At A'anenu? Even the pathetic creature that you saved on A'anenu naval base, the zor Rrith, did not want your precious mercy.

"A hit, as you humans say would," M'm'e'e said. "A palpable hit."

"Shhh," Jackie said, listening intently.

STONE: . . . Humanity and zor cannot live side by side. It has been foreseen.

MARAIS: What else has been foreseen? How else have humans and zor been used as pawns in your game?

STONE: Regrettably, you will never know. *(Pause.)* Good-bye, Admiral Marais.

"Freeze," M'm'e'e said suddenly. The scene froze with the figures all beginning to move: Marais diving for the floor, Stone changing the point of aim from Marais to an emerging figure moving from the shadows.

"Our agent, that is," M'm'e'e added quietly. "Observe. Stone by him killed is, but he attacked as well is."

(A beam of multicolored light lances out from Stone's pistol and engulfs the new figure. Stone falls to the deck, his right arm and a good part of his right side vaporized. The new figure twists in the energies around his frame, a gurgling scream escaping his lips and then ending suddenly. The pistol crashes to the deck, shattering into many pieces and erupting into light.)

"The everting weapon," Jackie said as the clip ended. "Stone's pistol."

"On this clip and the remains of the crashing did the Intelligence Service a reconstruction perform, but from it no great amount of learning could we obtain. Stone a human was, and autopsies performed were."

"What happened to your agent?"

"Everted, he was." M'm'e'e touched a key, and the mummy-image reappeared, growing and coming forward. It was vaguely human-shaped, like a man twisting in the wind, but made of some sort of papier-mâché—

Bone, she realized. *The outside of the body is bone, and the stringy gristle must be what's inside—and around the head must be the brain, turned inside out—*

"Everted," M'm'e'e repeated. "Killed Stone did he, but caught in the beam of the alien weapon was he, everted, within out came and outside within went. Another example." He keyed another image, and a 3-V of an empty room appeared. It had a missing wall that opened out to empty sky. On the floor was a larger body with the same characteristics.

"Another agent, it was. Energy patterns Stone to pointed. Twice this Stone, with the everting weapon, men killed has. Twice, agents of the Imperial Intelligence Service. You say, him you met, far beyond Empire world. Enemy of Agency is he, *dangerous* is he. No everting did he try?"

"On me?"

"On *you.* Attacked, were you? Qu'u legend, many times hero agent of Deceiver fights must. He of Dancing Blade—Shrnu'u HeGa'u named is—point man for *esGa'u.* According to legend, with Dancing Blade person Qu'u before gate of Fortress a duel fight must.

"So, fought him, did you? This Stone, Shrnu'u HeGa'u is he?"

"No."

She wasn't sure why she was so quick to dismiss this connection;

she thought about the *Dsen'yen'ch'a* at Adrianople Starbase, the challenge at the tower against Shrnu'u HeGa'u.

He of the Dancing Blade, his *e'chya* in his hand, scorn in his voice as he destroyed her *hsi*-images . . .

Stone, sitting in the drawing-room on Center while the storm raged outside, sardonic and reserved . . .

Stone on the video, turning his everting weapon on the nameless intelligence agent . . .

The horrible image of human figures turned inside out, mummified by their own innards. The rainbow bridge through jump. The pseudopods of *anGa'e'ren* reaching for her from the open clamshell doors aboard the *Fair Damsel* as it hurtled through the darkness.

She looked away from the image.

"*se* Jackie Laperriere, *Gyaryu'har,* not well is feeling? To drink something else, perhaps? Help needed, is?"

Jackie didn't answer. "*. . . I've got other employers,*" Stone had said to her. "*They've been watching this affair play itself out, Commodore, and it is their consensus opinion that it is best for their interests that the* gyaryu *be placed in your hands.*"

"*My employers determined it was best that humanity defeat the* zor . . ." the Stone on the video had said.

Stone.

Shrnu'u HeGa'u.

"No," she repeated.

Stone had referred to his "employers"; he even credited them with writing the Qu'u legend. If he *were* merely a functionary, no more than a representative . . . If he *was* Shrnu'u HeGa'u, it would be frightening. But if he wasn't, then who *was* he?

I will not submit to this panic, she told herself sternly. *All of it—the casual reference to the "employers," the attack of* anGa'e'ren, *the terror weapon that everted human bodies—was intended to frighten me.*

Can't think through fear. Pull yourself together, damn it.

"*se Gyaryu'har?*" M'm'e'e asked, and there was obvious concern in his voice. He shifted back and forth in his chair.

"I'm sorry, M'm'e'e. I was . . ." She forced herself to relax and smile a bit. "I was having a thinking."

"Many thinkings necessary will be, before end of problem reached is. Healthfulness is, or not?"

"I'm fine. I—I'm fine." *Qu'u is destroyed by the Deceiver, but* esLi *saves him and brings him back to the World That Is. I listen to Shrnu'u HeGa'u—Stone—who sends me through* anGa'e'ren *back to Zor'a. Am I still following the damned legend or not? . . . What's happening?*

"What did Stone do to me? What is his part?"

"M'm'e'e not so sure is. Many travelings, too many thinkings. Resting in quiet needed might be for *se Gyaryu'har* Jackie Laperriere, or not?"

"No . . . thank you." She mentally shrugged off the fear and concentrated again on the frozen image. "Is there anything else related to this investigation?"

"Telemetric evidence is," he answered, working the console in front of him. The ghastly everted corpse disappeared and was replaced by a diagram of Sol System with a long orange curve drawn across it. "Just before scene on screen happening was, something near number six jump point appeared. Unusual energy distribution. Recorded on *Lancaster* same, evidence found on Earth same, pattern of Restucci distribution available is." A 3-D graph of fluctuating energy appeared, hovering next to the diagram. "Record from starship *Charlemagne* is. Short video clip, see it will you?"

"Certainly."

M'm'e'e issued several more instructions. Diagram and graph disappeared and were replaced by a 3-V depiction of space. A multicolored *something* flashed across and the video clip ended. M'm'e'e caused it to appear again, frozen at the start of the clip.

"Zoom twenty-seven," he said, and the *something* became a bright band of light, just coming into view from starboard. "Zoom two–forty-three," he said. "Apologies are, computer to being addressed in base-ten accustomed is."

"No problem," she answered, as the *something* became a broad, colored ribbon, consisting of six parallel bands: red, yellow, green, blue, orange and violet. The telemetry data displayed on the bottom of the screen made it out to be sixty to seventy meters wide and, at the moment of depiction, almost two hundred kilometers long.

It was clearly the same sort of path she'd walked through jump to reach Zor'a.

"Less than nine seconds in visual range of *Charlemagne* was it. Also, Ganymede Observatory and Jodrell Bank recorded it did. Endpoint of phenomenon, Grimaldi Base was. After happened Stone appearance, disappeared."

"His transport. He was brought in by—his 'employers'—on that."

"Correct assumption is, M'm'e'e believe would. Stipulation: Phenomenon close to your conveyance is. Conclusion: Same Stone is, human appearance for convenience was. Why choose same guise? M'm'e'e asks."

"He must've known we'd put this all together," Jackie agreed. "Unless . . ." She thought for a moment.

M'm'e'e's arms folded and unfolded several times. "In Standard speech is, 'unless' followed by predicate conclusion is. What 'Unless,' *se Gyaryu'har*?"

"Wouldn't you agree, M'm'e'e, that Stone, both back then"—she gestured toward the midair images—"and now, made a particular effort to try and show how much everyone was being manipulated? I mean, think about this for a moment. He said that his employers intended for Marais to die. *Why didn't they kill him, then?* Certainly beings capable of creating footpaths through jump could've found a way to vaporize Grimaldi Base and kill Admiral Marais.

"He said that his employers *wrote* the Qu'u legend. If you believe him, they arranged for the zor to leave the sword unprotected, for the vuhls to capture it and for me to emerge from nowhere and capture it back . . . and then got me home again. Why did they go to all the *trouble*?

"It's inconsistent and it's confusing. Whoever or whatever Stone was—is—working for, they're clearly technologically advanced, but a long way from omnipotent. Unless they wanted *this* outcome all along."

"M'm'e'e would want to know, 'this outcome' is, *se Gyaryu'har* to which refers."

"I don't know." She folded her hands in front of her. Almost mimicking her gesture, M'm'e'e did the same, with both pairs of hands. "Answering that question might be the most important thing that either of us could ever do."

chapter 17

The *r'r's'kn* lay like a ragged tear across the outer reaches of the solar system. It was inexplicable, almost indescribable: an area of space twelve-twelves of *chn*klii* wide and tall, connecting this solar system with another one an unimaginable distance away.

This system, with its two blue stars and no habitable planets, was almost useless in and of itself; in fact, one of the stars flared dangerously and unpredictably on a regular basis, several twelves of *vx*tori* apart— limbs of its chronosphere stretched across the system, disrupting comm traffic and making jumps dangerous. It might have been one of these flares that had created the *r'r's'kn* in the first place, disturbing space-time in some way that First Hive didn't understand.

First Hive understands what's important, First Drone H'mr thought to himself, as he and Second Drone H'tt stood in the command center of the station that commanded the *r'r's'kn*. Beyond the rip in space was another solar system, a place that would be an enormous distance from where he watched . . . but for this remarkable thing in front of him.

For H'mr, H'tt and others sent from First Hive, it was the way back home—and through it was possible the connection with the Ór, the advisor to the Great Queen. Invisible but easily tasted by anyone with enough *k'th's's,* there was a cable of power that led through the *r'r's'kn* all the way to where the Ór lay deep in First Hive, by the side of the Great Queen.

"I brought you here to show you something," H'mr said, gesturing with his mandibles. "The meat-creatures think that they have the ability to resist our *k'th's's*. G'en's partisans think so, too."

"That is why she has failed? Why she will . . ."

"That's right." H'tt could see the fierce joy glistening on H'mr's carapace. "S'le was *her* admiral, after all. Since he lost his hive-ships to the *k'th's's*-mad lord of the winged meat-creatures, it will only a be body-length or two further for G'en to die as well."

"What of her *N'nr* Deathguard? They are scattered throughout the fleet. They are aboard every ship and at every base. They serve Great Queen G'en and won't abandon her."

"Oh, you think so?" H'mr exuded amusement. "There are other Deathguard as well. With R'se and R'ta dead, and G'si a prisoner of the egg-sucking zor, *N'nr* lacks leaders. Given the choice between serving a doomed Great Queen as *N'nr*, or following *another* Great Queen as *P'cn*, you can imagine what they'll decide."

"'*P'cn*'?"

The tentacles beside H'mr's mandibles wriggled. "That's right—*P'cn* Deathguard. They are everywhere. *We* are everywhere. It is time for the *N'nr* to choose . . . along with everyone else."

H'tt heard the words, but also heard the threat they held. H'mr's *k'th's's* was superior to his own, and seemed to be ready to digest H'tt if he said the wrong thing—or the right thing in the wrong way.

"What did you bring me here to see?"

H'mr turned again to look out through the panoramic viewscreen that showed the rip in space. He gestured, and a portion of the screen rippled and magnified.

The First Drone said nothing, but both he and H'tt could feel the beginnings of *k'th's's* from within the *r'r's'kn*. As they watched, a hive-ship appeared in the rip. It navigated through and out into the system that held the station where the two Drones now stood.

Once the ship was clear of the *r'r's'kn* and moving toward the station, another one began to appear; it followed the same flight path. Shortly, a third hive-ship emerged from the rip.

"They replace the ships lost at—" H'tt began, but H'mr gestured him to silence.

Several smaller ships filled the rip and emerged on the other side. Once they were clear, one, and then another, and then another hive-ship made its way through the *r'r's'kn*.

"*Five* ships," H'mr said, turning again to face H'tt. "We understand the meat-creatures have gathered their fleet at another system." He named the coordinates. "They have correctly determined that if we capture this system, we will have short-range access to their large naval base with our *s'kn'a'a* vessels."

"Can they not do what they did before—destroy their own ships to destroy ours?"

"They will not. This time, the commander of *this* fleet will not give them the chance."

"They still have the woman meat-creature with the sword."

"You mean the Har—" H'tt began, but never finished the sentence.

H'mr rounded on H'tt. "Do not repeat that *u'shn'n* to me," he said angrily. "The Har—" He lowered his voice. " 'The Harbinger' is no more than a tale to frighten children. To associate it with this meat-creature is obscene. What's more, *one* meat-creature with *one* talisman can kill *one* Drone at a time, but she lacks the *k'th's's* to do more." He gestured at the formation of five hive-ships and outriders navigating toward the station. "She could do nothing against *this,* even if she were . . . the Harbinger."

"I see."

"I hope you do. When this fleet is finished with its work, the *P'cn* Deathguard will deal with the next problem . . . with Great Queen G'en herself."

news of S'reth's passing came to Jackie when *Fair Damsel* berthed at Dieron Station Four. The station was not as old as Sol System's Station One, but it was still old by human standards: It had been placed in one of the Lagrangian points of the huge asteroid belt in Dieron System when its sun, Epsilon Indi, less than four parsecs from Sol, had been colonized by sleeper ships in the late twenty-first century.

Jackie realized it had been more than seven years since she had been home; there might not be another opportunity. After leaving Langley she had left a message for Mya'ar to send to the High Nest: She was going to Dieron for a few days and then would return to Zor'a to take her place. Mya'ar's response had been polite and diplomatic—what else?— but his wings had spoken understanding and perhaps even sympathy.

Home. It was a strange concept after all these years in His Majesty's Service, in space and on far worlds. Spoken aloud or considered pragmatically, it seemed to be a neutral word, bereft of context and connotation; but her subconscious wrestled with it as she slept, throwing images and memories onto the shore of her waking mind like debris from the deepest part of the sea.

The present was there waiting for her when she stepped onto the deck of the station: a Signal Corps captain approaching, uniform cap tucked under his arm. Jackie was flanked by Dan McReynolds and Sultan Sabah, scarcely ten meters from the cargo hatch; but she knew immediately that the uniformed officer was out of place on the deck of a civilian orbital port, and looked and felt it. She knew the captain was looking for her.

"*ha Gyaryu'har?*" the captain asked, stepping toward her.

Jackie noticed the High Nest emblem on his shoulder-patch.

"I have a message for you."

"Let's have it."

The captain handed her a comp. She took it and touched the blinking indicator with the stylus.

```
ha Gyaryu'har:

It is my duty to convey to you the news that our
sage friend, S'reth son of S'tlin, has transcended
the Outer Peace. He provided an important sSurch'a
prior to embracing the Golden Light of esLi, which
profoundly affects the flight the High Nest must
undertake.

The High Lord sends her respects and asks eight
thousand pardons for requesting that you complete
your Nest-business as soon as is feasible, and re-
turn to esYen for consultations.

If circumstances permit, please examine the epic
seLi'e'Yan as a guide.

                              esLiHeYar,
                              Byar HeShri
```

Jackie handed back the comp and stylus. A chill ran through her as if a sudden cold breeze had passed along the station causeway.

"Is there a response, ma'am?" the officer asked.

"What?" She looked at Dan who looked concerned, and then back at the officer. "No—no response. Send my respects to *se* Byar and acknowledge my receipt of the message."

The officer nodded, saluted and turned on his heel. He made his way across the deck as quickly as possible.

"Hell of a hurry," the Sultan said. "What's—" He saw the look on Jackie's face and fell silent as if he regretted having started the sentence.

"S'reth's dead," she said to Dan. "Byar HeShri told me, essentially, to hurry up and get the hell home."

"What're you going to do?" Dan asked. "Do you want to bug out?"

"I waited years to get here," she answered. "I'm going to go for a walk in the woods on North Continent. I'm going to go see my dad and get some advice."

"Mind if we come along?"

"Frankly, yes. Will that keep you from coming along?"

Dan grinned. "I expect not."

"Then let's get going."

ꓶhe shu੮੮le trip to Stanleytown Spaceport was uneventful. Jackie was still unaccustomed to traveling civilian, but transporting the *gyaryu* through customs was eased by her diplomatic credentials: While the officials didn't seem to be bothered by someone representing the High Nest, it was clear they didn't want to delve into it. Once in the terminal, the three made their way to an aircar rental booth; but before Jackie could get started on the transaction, she heard her name being called.

"None of that," the voice said, and Jackie turned to see a familiar figure making her way across the terminal toward her. A few meters from the booth they embraced, while Dan and the Sultan nervously stood by.

Jackie brought the other woman to where the two men stood. "Dan, Sultan, this is my cousin Kristen. Kris, this is Dan McReynolds and his ship's chief steward, Drew Sabah."

"So this is the *famous* Dan McReynolds," Kristen said, looking him up and down. Kristen shared some of Jackie's facial features but was at least half a dozen years older, and had none of her cousin's military bearing. She looked relaxed and weathered, a strange counterpoint to the pale skin common among spacefarers.

However, she did have Jackie's piercing gaze. Dan felt it boring into him; he felt like he was being examined from head to toe.

"Enough of *that*," Jackie said after a moment. "All right, Kris, out with it. How did you know I was coming?"

"We're expecting a cargo for the farm," she said. "I was looking at incoming traffic on comp this morning, and I saw the *famous* Captain McReynolds' ship inbound to Station Four with an indication that he was carrying a zor diplomatic passenger. All on the flight plan. I guessed it might be you."

"She's your cousin, all right," Dan said.

"What's *that* supposed to mean?" Kristen asked.

"I think it's a compliment," Jackie interjected, smiling.

Kristen snorted but let her face relax into a smile. "You're here to see Uncle Don, I'd guess. He's over on First Landing Hill at your mother's grave. I can take you—you all—there, or we can go up to the farm and meet him when he gets back."

"Do you think he'd rather be alone?"

"Well, *I* don't go with him," she said, as they began to walk toward the parking garage. "He still gets up there every other sixday or so, usually when he's here in town to take care of something else." They stepped into sunlight on a long concourse over a main thoroughfare, and Kristen looked off toward the mountains. "Of course, it's always, 'Just since I'm in town, I may stop by,' but we both know he makes up errands so he can visit often."

"They were married twenty years, Kris."

"Your mother's been *gone* fifteen years, Jackie. It's just a plastic plaque in the ground. Leave the dead to the dead."

"You never could tell Dad that," Jackie answered, as they stepped into the cool shade of the aircar park.

"Even if I could, it wouldn't change anything. Ah, well. *La vie continue,* and all that."

Jackie felt a bit guilty leaving Dan and the Sultan at the mercy of her cousin; but she'd already decided to walk up First Landing Hill alone to the cemetery. In the last few months she'd left enough people like Ch'k'te and John Maisel behind, unburied and scarcely mourned, that the idea of a final resting place now seemed comforting somehow.

It was certainly a comfort to her dad. Don Laperriere sat on a bench a few meters from the plastic rectangle that marked her mother's grave. He seemed lost in thought, as if he were considering something her mom had just said; he had always been like that, willing to give any comment, even an offhand one, the dignity of consideration.

He didn't seem surprised to see her.

"Come over and sit down," he said, smiling. She did so, and he took her hand in his two weathered ones. "Kris told me she thought you might be coming in."

Far off in the trees, two dippers, scavenger birds native to Dieron, engaged in a quick and friendly argument and then took off in a flurry of bluish green wings.

"I suppose everyone on the *planet* knows. So much for surprise entrances."

"You've been away a long time."

"I've been busy, Dad." She pulled her hand from between his and laid it on top. "I'm sorry."

"Your last comm said you were being transferred to the zor naval service."

"A lot has happened since then. I'm not even sure where to start."

Don Laperriere leaned back against the bench, stretching his arms out. "We've got plenty of time," he said, nodding toward the grave. "Best start at the beginning, Jacqueline."

"I've got two problems, Dad. First, I don't think that I *have* plenty of time; and second, I'm not sure there's a beginning to the story. I feel like I came on the scene in the middle of the play and I've been trying to get context ever since."

"So you thought you'd ask your old man to explain it to you."

"Not exactly . . . Well, I don't really know why. I guess I just wanted to see you and the farm again. Things have gotten too complicated. Maybe there's some perspective I can gain from being here."

"So, begin in the middle instead. What's with this sword?" He pointed to her side.

"It's the *gyaryu*. The zor sword of state. It's mine now."

"Yours? Didn't it belong to that old man, the one who went into exile with Marais? What's his name—?"

"Sergei Torrijos. He died about ten days ago, just before I got back with the sword. It had been taken . . ."

A little at a time, she found herself telling the whole story to her father—not so much in sequence but in layers, beginning with recent events and peeling back like an onion or a *rRi*-fruit to reveal the structure upon which future events had been laid. He remained mostly silent, listening intently, occasionally interrupting with a question or making an observation.

It took almost an hour. At several points Jackie heard her voice almost breaking and she was unable to continue for a moment. Each time, her dad waited out the pause with an understanding smile, as if to tell her what he'd said at the beginning: that there was plenty of time.

"That's quite a story," he said, when she'd run out of narrative. He leaned forward, elbows on knees, and picked up a stray bit of grass from the lawn under the bench and toyed with it idly. "Imagine that: My daughter, an admiral, and—what? The High Lord's Champion or something.

"It sounds like we're in a hell of a lot of trouble."

"The enemy is more dangerous than any civilian realizes—except maybe the emperor. I think the Admiralty has gotten the message, though. From what I hear about Thon's Well, they're convinced."

"It sounds like we're in a hell of a lot of trouble," Don Laperriere repeated; except this time it was obvious that he wasn't referring to the Solar Empire, but rather to a place closer to home. "Dieron's been a full member of the Empire since day one, so there's never been much unrest; we're too close to Sol System and to Tau Ceti System to have a naval base. We're wide-open to this invasion, Jacqueline. No getting around it."

"You might be safer elsewhere."

"Oh?" He looked from her to the grave and back. "Where did you have in mind?"

"Zor'a."

"The zor homeworld."

"Yes."

Jackie's father looked at her with his mouth turned up very slightly in a smile, as if he were mildly amused by such a suggestion.

"I don't really think that's an option," he said at last. "This is where I belong."

"You just said—"

"That Dieron is in terrible danger. I know. But it isn't as if I should be picking up and leaving, not at this stage, anyway." He looked at the grave again. "I belong here, with Grace"—he nodded toward the ground—"and Kristen on the farm. Why, I've only been offworld once in my life, to see you graduate from the Academy and get your commission.

"What would I be on Zor'a? A tourist? The zor are fine people, I don't have any quarrel with 'em. Down on South Continent there's an agricomplex run by some zor folk, trying to crossbreed some of their native plants with Dieron's own strains; we visited there six months ago to help them with one of their projects. But afterward we came *home*. If I read you right, *everywhere* is in terrible danger, Jacqueline. Dieron, Zor'a, Sol System itself, probably.

"I wish for all the world that you could just leave it all and come home to the farm, but even if your duty didn't call you away, you'd never be able to stay put. But you won't be running back here to Dieron if we're attacked, will you?

"If you're the . . . what?—zor champion, or something?—I'd guess that Dieron would be a little bit lower on your priority list than any of a hundred other worlds." He stood up and stepped carefully onto the grass around the grave marker, knelt on one knee and arranged the few flowers laid before it in the deep green grass, then stood upright again.

"Let's walk a bit," he said, and took his daughter by the hand. The feel of it and the look in her father's eyes were comforting.

They walked farther up the hill, to the silvery memorial to the first settlers of Dieron. It was a representation of the cold-sleep ship that crash-landed more than two centuries ago, with statues of the Dieron Six standing beside it. The survivors of that original ship—six of two hundred—had eked out a meager existence until two sister ships arrived a few months later, and those six brave men and women had given the colony its name: Sharon *Demeter*, Shoei *Ikegai*, John *Erickson*, Eric *Rashid*, David *Okome* and Micaela *Natal*—names every Dieron schoolchild committed to memory. Their faces were forever frozen in the metal statuary at the top of First Landing Hill, a memorial to the founding of the colony.

Don Laperriere let go of Jackie's hand and stood there, arms folded, looking at the memorial, an unknowable thought in his mind to match the unreadable expression on his face.

"Dad, I—"

He didn't look away, but said, "They almost didn't make it through the first winter, you know. They didn't realize that they'd settled in red-bear country. This colony was put together against very long odds.

Hell, it was long odds for people even to make it to the stars. Five hundred years ago, Epsilon Indi was a dot of light in an Earth telescope." He looked skyward, light and shadow on his face. "Now it's the suns."

"I don't think this is necessary, Dad. Or particularly fair."

"Jacqueline." Her father looked at her again, sadness in his eyes. "Jackie. Dear Jackie. I'm quite sure that at one time in your life you felt the way I do about Dieron, about *home*. I'm not sure that you feel that way anymore. I'm not sure that you can. —No, let me finish." He held up his hands when she began to protest. "The universe is a very big place and my part in it is very small. Dieron is very small, too. But it's all I ever had, all I ever wanted.

"If your information and your fears are true, the Solar Empire may not have very long. That would be a tragedy. Many worlds aren't even self-sufficient, and the end of the Empire would ruin them. But the real tragedy will happen one world at a time. If Dieron is attacked, it can't hardly defend itself. Even if it isn't destroyed by these aliens, it's for damn sure that this world will never be the same.

"Everything we've ever worked for, everything they've ever worked for"—he gestured to the six statues, grouped near the abstract representation of the crashed sleep-ship—"won't amount to anything. That won't be on any Navy report and won't make the emperor's daily briefing. The zor High Lord won't hear anything about it, either."

He took his daughter in his arms and hugged her close to his chest. "I'm sorry, Jackie. I can't help but hurt you to tell you this, because I can't ask you to do anything about it. The universe is too big and Dieron is too small."

He held her out at arm's length again. "Well, Admiral. Are you ready for some home-cooked food?"

The farm wasn't much different from how she remembered it. Dan and the Sultan, spacers for most of their lives and city-dwellers before that, had expected something a bit more low-tech and rural. Much to Jackie's amusement, they were surprised enough at the modern conveniences to receive a good tongue-lashing from Kristen.

Don Laperriere's spread was several thousand acres on North Continent, in some of the most fertile soil on the planet. Parts of it were worked by tenants, and part by robots; it was all managed from a control center that was at least as complex as the bridge of a starship.

Weather control, fertilization, irrigation and planting were all managed hour by hour, day by day, mostly by Jackie's father and cousin. They both had agronomy degrees. More important, they both had that special feel for the land that any farmer has to have. They were a long way from being hayseeds and truly loved their work.

The meal was prepared and eaten with a deliberate emphasis on hospitality and courtesy. Neither Jackie nor her father brought up the weighty subjects of interstellar war, the High Nest or invading aliens; every time it crept into the conversation from other directions, one of their hosts carefully shunted it aside.

Afterward, Jackie and Kristen went for a walk while Don Laperriere served mugs of his own home-brewed beer to Dan and the Sultan on the back porch of the farmhouse. The sun had gone down and two moons were finding their way above the distant hills.

"Good stuff," the Sultan said, after taking a long drink of the beer. Then he stood up, muttered something about taking a walk, gave Dan a sly grin, and strode quickly off the porch, leaving Dan alone with Jackie's father.

That son of a bitch, Dan thought, holding his mug with both hands.

"So," Don Laperriere said.

"So."

"Merchanter now, I hear."

"Yes, sir." *What am I so nervous about?* he asked himself. "*Fair Damsel,* best ship in space."

"Better than serving aboard a warship, I guess. Especially in wartime."

"Damn straight," Dan answered, smiling, looking at Jackie's father's face done up in silvery moonlight and deep shadow. The other was just looking at him, or through him.

"Dan, if you think—"

"Mr. Laperriere, if I—"

They stopped at the same time after both trying to speak at once. Don Laperriere took a long drink from his mug, and when Dan didn't go on, he let his face soften into a smile. "Your pal likes to have you squirm," he observed.

"Drew Sabah is a sadistic bastard sometimes," Dan agreed. "But he's also one of my best friends in the world. He thought . . . I don't know. I don't know what to expect, either."

"You mean, from the father of the girl you left behind? You made the choice, son. You were both adults at the time. I'm not going to work you over for that, not after all this time."

"It seems like Kristen wouldn't mind doing it."

"Kris sees the world in black and white, good and evil, right and wrong. Nothing in between. You plant it deeper or you pull it up by the roots. Jackie used to think of things that way, too, I remember."

"Yes, she did," Dan agreed, sipping his beer. "When I first met her, and even when I left to take my own command. 'Clean break,' she said. 'No hard feelings.' Fair winds, fare thee well—all that." He smiled. " 'Course, the next time we met, she punched me in the mouth."

"She *didn't*."

"Damn straight," Dan said again, and mimicked a right hook sailing up into his jaw, his face turning aside at the blow. "Knocked me on my ass. That woman can *hit*." They laughed together for a few moments.

"I know. I taught her how. I guess the Academy taught her even more, though."

"The Academy taught her a lot of things," Dan said, looking away at the smaller moon, low in the sky. "In the last six months she's had to unlearn most of them. The emperor was ready to string her up by her epaulets at one point, but she turned into a deputy of the High Nest and they backed off. It's as if she's been cut adrift from everything that she ever believed."

"It wouldn't be the first time," Don answered, setting down his by-now mostly empty mug on the porch beside his chair. "Twenty years ago, when she first began to consider a military career, she made it *very* clear to us that Dieron was too damned small for her." He gestured vaguely toward the moons. "She wanted us to move away from here, to go to the homeworld.

" 'This *is* my homeworld,' I told her. 'No, Dad, I mean Earth,' she said. 'Humanity's homeworld.' Well, we argued: I'd never been there, but you study it in school: the wars, the ecological disasters, the whole thing. 'Look,' I said. 'Dieron has centuries of history and we've mostly done it right: not much overcrowding, biosphere management, stable environment, no wars. What's Earth got that Dieron doesn't? What's wrong with Dieron?'

" 'It isn't *enough*,' she told me. Dieron wasn't enough for her—at *sixteen!* This place wasn't enough, her mother and I weren't enough, *you* weren't enough. I suspect that the Service wasn't enough, either. I don't know if she's still looking for something, but I hope she has time to find it."

So where do you go from here?" Kristen half sat and half leaned on a rock ledge overlooking a stream. Umbrella-trees partially obscured the view of the moons rising in the night sky.

"Back to Zor'a," Jackie answered. "The High Lord—well, actually, one of her advisors—sent me a letter that I got just before I came down planetside, asking me to hurry back."

" 'Her'?"

"esShaLie'e," Jackie said, and the zor word sounded out of place to her even as she said it. " 'High Lord' is a bad translation; it doesn't denote either gender, and it happens that the current High Lord is female. hi Sa'a is the daughter of the previous High Lord, Ke'erl."

"Hmm." Kristen crossed and uncrossed her arms, as if she was a bit uncomfortable with the idea. "How well do you speak, uh, zor?"

"The Highspeech? Well, I'm fairly fluent, though without wings I can't communicate certain things."

"Learned it at the Academy, I suppose."

"Six months ago I could barely get the tones and glottals in the right place. Ch'k'te—" She felt a chill run through her. "My exec on Cicero taught me some of the language, but recent experiences gave me fluency."

" 'Recent experiences' . . ."

"It's . . . hard to explain." Jackie sat on a small boulder, hands in her lap, feeling the *gyaryu* pressing against her hip. It was quiet here in the woods: no sounds of life-support systems, no electronics at all—just animals going about their business and the wind rustling in the leaves.

"I'm not sure I understand."

"I'm not sure I do, either. Lots of things seem to have changed—"

"Present company included," Kristen observed. "I don't think I've seen your dad look so worried for years: What did you tell him, that the world's coming to an end?"

Jackie looked away, toward the nearby stream, unable to answer.

"Listen, cousin. You get to fly through here like a celebrity. I have to *live* here. What in hell is going on?"

"The world's coming to an end."

"Very funny—"

"I'm not joking, Kris." Jackie couldn't keep the pain from her expression. "We're at war with a powerful enemy, capable of destroying us, defeating us, even taking our place. Things will happen so fast that there will be no time to react, let alone counteract them."

Kristen didn't seem convinced. "This is all a long way from Dieron."

"Not really. What's about to happen will touch everywhere. Even Dieron. And I'm all but powerless to stop it."

A storm rolled off the Livingston Mountains late that night, thunder in a bass rumble and lightning bright enough to scour the fields with flashes of near-daylight. The planetside sounds might have been what brought Jackie close to consciousness, but it was a soft voice calling her name that finally woke her up.

She sat up in the bed in the guest bedroom on the ground floor and looked out the window. Out on the front lawn, twenty meters from the farmhouse, she could see a human figure illuminated by the distant flashes of lightning.

"Jackie," the voice said again, and she felt a chill, recognizing the voice.

"Mother?" Her stomach jumped. As she used to do when she wanted to leave quietly, she got out of bed, walked to the window and swung her legs out. She was wearing nothing but a long T-shirt, a concession to modesty that she'd have skipped if she'd not been in her father's house. The only thought that passed through her head as she dropped the half-meter to the grass was, *What the hell, it's a dream.*

"Jackie," the voice repeated, and the figure beckoned to her.

She hadn't dreamed about her mother for years. Grace Laperriere had died of a heart condition a few years after Jackie had received her commission. Grace had always been fragile, like a fine porcelain doll her father had collected; her advice and her wisdom had been gentle and well measured as well. Her death, which took everyone in their small family by surprise, had been hard to handle. The impact of Grace's absence from the house, once they'd buried her on First Landing Hill, was out of all proportion to her quiet, soft-spoken nature.

"Mom," Jackie said, a chill from the night air running through her.

"Jackie, you should put something on your feet; you'll catch cold."

Grace Laperriere walked a few steps toward her daughter. She was just as Jackie remembered her, small and fine-featured. "You're looking well."

"Th-thanks. What brings you—"

"I was worried about you, dear." Grace turned aside with her hands folded in front of her and seemed to dig at something with the toe of one shoe. "You seem to have changed a lot recently."

"Lots of things have changed, Mom. I—I didn't realize you were watching."

"I watch," she said. Lightning played across the distant peaks, illuminating the scene in weird, yellow-white light. "Mostly I watch your dad, but I watch you, too."

Jackie took a step or two closer. Her mind was racing, trying to establish perspective: *Is this a dream, really?* The ground felt damp and cold underfoot; the air was sharp and tangy.

She didn't answer, and her mother went on: "I think you've gone too far afield, dear. You were always a wanderer and you've been away a long time."

"My career kept me away."

"It always did," her mother answered, and then there was a peal of thunder almost coinciding. Her mother's gaze fixed on her. "Even when you were needed. Even when I died," she said.

A chill breeze rippled the grass on the lawn. Grace Laperriere's expression, framed in sadness, bathed in shadow, was clear from ten meters away.

"What are you saying?" Jackie felt her hands clench into fists, but she couldn't look away.

"It's time for you to come home," Grace said, extending her arms. A tear seemed to be forming in one eye.

Jackie couldn't look away, and somewhere in the corner of her mind she realized that she couldn't. The mountains, the lightning, even the umbrella-trees that lined the yard, were becoming hard to see because of the attention she was fixing on the figure of her approaching mother, now a few meters away. Almost involuntarily, feeling the wet grass under her bare feet, Jackie began to step toward the figure that was smiling now, teeth bared—

Suddenly another peal of thunder reverberated across the sky. Without conscious effort on her part, Jackie's hands came close together and the *gyaryu* seemed to materialize in them. Around her, eleven misty images snapped into existence: She recognized Sergei, Marais and

Kale'e—the last zor to bear the *gyaryu*. From that hint she determined that the other zor-images around her must be other bearers of the sword from previous eras.

Her mother's image began to melt and change, like a snake shedding its skin: The arms came together and were now holding a sword that hissed and snarled, making Jackie's flesh crawl. The shoulders grew wings and the face changed from her mother's, to take on the form of another—one that she knew well.

She quickly retreated several steps, scarcely able to look away, while the *hsi*-images around her retreated in like fashion. But instead of attacking, the zor lowered his *e'chya* slightly, his wings expressing an emotion of deep irony, while the rest of his stance suggested that he was not at all concerned.

"Shrnu'u HeGa'u," she said softly. "I should have known."

"*ge* Qu'u," he answered.

She didn't recognize the prenomen but the *gyaryu* did, and found it insulting: the sword snarled at the zor's remark.

"We have fought each other in many ages and worn many guises. It *astounds* me, Crawler-servant, that you are so easily deceived this time."

"There isn't anything you won't stoop to, is there?" Jackie answered. "I didn't know who you were the last time, but I damn well know now."

"Spare me the bravado," he said, whirling rapidly and lashing out at a *hsi*-image, which he struck in the chest; it burst and vanished and she felt a sharp pain between her breasts. "You know *nothing*, for the Crawler adores fools and despises those who think for themselves."

The comments were intended to anger her. She felt angry; but it was a cold and serious anger, giving her a feeling of near-calm. She concentrated and felt the strength of the *gyaryu* course through her. Almost at once, without effort, the *hsi*-images of Sergei, Marais and the eight remaining zor seemed to gain solidity. They no longer mimicked her movements but began to move on their own, spreading out to take up positions along a wide front, all well out of the reach of the *e'chya*. Another *hsi*-image faded into existence: another zor she didn't know.

Shrnu'u HeGa'u backed away, sensing that the battleground had suddenly and abruptly changed beneath him. "My Master has changed the rules of the game, Mighty Hero," he said, his voice and wings conveying, ever so slightly, less confidence. "I have been watching you closely."

"Too close for me," she said, moving forward, the *gyaryu* held out in front of her. The previous bearers of the sword began to advance as well, of their own volition. For each step they took forward, Shrnu'u HeGa'u took a step back.

"The rules have *changed*," he repeated. "The battleground of the mind is not enough. The Plane of Sleep has been breached, and your own side has breached it."

"I don't believe that," she replied, wondering to herself what the hell it all meant.

"Go to the Stone and ask," he said, continuing to retreat. Lightning continued to illuminate the scene. "Your wisest ones will not know what is truth, what illusion." A breeze ruffled through his wings. "The Inner Peace is broken and it comes about because of fools who thought themselves wise. Go and *ask* them," he said, over the thunder that cascaded through the air. The storm was close enough to feel now, descending across the plain, rain beginning to sheet down.

"You've been on *Fair Damsel* all the time," she said suddenly. "From the time I came aboard at Cle'eru. Watching. Ch'k'te said so. *You* opened the doors. *You* confronted me at Crossover—in the Center—and Ch'k'te killed you—"

"A vessel only," Shrnu'u HeGa'u said over the rising wind. He began to rise into the air, his wings fighting against the storm and the strong gravity. "You cannot kill me, mighty Qu'u. And I cannot kill you. If my Master traps you in *Ur'ta leHssa*, you can suffer worse than death; but death is beyond us both."

"Then what are you trying to do?" she shouted. "Why are you here? Why do you come to me in a dream, when—"

" 'Dream'?" The zor howled something unintelligible. "Do you believe this to be a *dream*?"

He raised his wings in a gesture that was untranslatable, but somehow seemed almost obscene—

And again the entire scene was suddenly illuminated by a bolt of lightning close by—close enough to make the hairs rise along her arms and neck. It seemed to strike the hovering figure of Shrnu'u HeGa'u amidships—

There was a sharp *crack*, a report like the firing of a rifle—

She felt something, someone, grasping her left arm and turning her around. She pulled loose and stepped back, bringing the *gyaryu* to guard . . . and found herself facing her father, standing there in nothing but his shorts, a frightened look on his face. Kristen was running across the yard, an ablative fire-extinguisher in her hand, to an umbrella-tree that was on fire. Dan and the Sultan, similarly undressed, had just come out onto the front porch.

Is this—? she asked the sword.

The esGa'uYe *is gone,* Sergei's voice told her.

Fifteen minutes later, the five of them stood wrapped in towels in the farmhouse kitchen, mugs of hot tea in their hands. Kristen was muttering something about "damn fools" and military officers and their common heritage, but Don Laperriere had not lost his worried expression.

"I didn't see anyone else there," he repeated. "You were shouting something about dreams and then the lightning hit the big umbrella-tree near the vegetable garden."

"I thought I *was* dreaming." Jackie had retrieved the scabbard from her room and again wore the *gyaryu* at her belt. "I don't know how I got the sword into my hands—I didn't take it with me when I went out to—"

She stopped suddenly and looked away, anger and sadness fighting for control of her expression.

"What?" Don asked. He sat down in a big wooden armchair at the corner of the room. "What did you go out for?"

"It was Mom," she said. Sadness won, and she couldn't keep the tears from her eyes. "Mom called out to me and I . . . thought it was a dream . . . so I went out to talk to her. She said— She said—"

Her father covered his face with his hands.

"But it wasn't her. It was—an old enemy, taking her form. He—*it*—tried to take control of me." She crossed her arms in front of her, and stopped trying to wipe the tears away. Anger came into her voice at full strength. "It was Shrnu'u HeGa'u again, Dan; the one that opened the hangar doors. Someone aboard your ship is a—vessel—for my enemy. 'You cannot kill me . . . ' he said. 'And I cannot kill you.' "

"That's why you had the sword out," Don said, looking up. His eyes were red. "You were fighting this . . . dream-thing."

"In the middle of the night," Kristen said. "In a lightning storm. Could've gotten yourself killed."

"I don't choose the goddamn time and place," Jackie shot back. "You don't understand."

Kristen grabbed her by the elbow and led her into the dining-room. Jackie could see the fury in her cousin's voice.

"You're damned right I don't," Kristen answered, whispering. "This is *insanity*. We have a nice quiet life here, cousin. We did when your mother was alive; we do now. We farm our land, we watch the seasons change. No magic swords, no dream aliens, no craziness in the middle of the night.

"It *had* to be your mother, didn't it? The one thing that would destroy his peace of mind, get your dad thinking about the past. You had to bring up—"

"You think I made this up? You think I'm *trying* to upset him? What exactly are you accusing me of, Kristen?"

"I—I don't know." Kristen walked away from her and stood by the mantelpiece, looking out a front window at the rain that continued to fall. "Look, I don't need to be told how big the universe is, or that I don't understand it. You've told me that everything's in danger of coming apart, but I don't know what to do about that: All I know, really, is this world, this farm, this little family.

"Your father treats your mother's memory as a precious little triptych to put on his dresser. First, *Here's* when we got married. *Here's* Grace and Jackie going to the lake. Then here we are at the Academy graduation.

"And, finally, off on its own, *here's* where Grace Laperriere sleeps now, at peace at last.' They must've fought, laughed, cried, made love—all of that—but he thinks of her as a collection of memories and precious moments: a life's travelogue with no ugly edges, no hints of the unfairness of it all.

"That's all he's got left, Jackie. You went off to space and now you're back and you've changed. That thing at your belt, that damn sword, makes you something different—something that drives you into the yard in the middle of a storm shouting about dreams. Sorry to say it, cousin, but I don't think you can stay here. Whatever happens, when you leave I have to pick up the pieces and try to put them back together, even if some big old monster is going to come along and plow me under."

"Are you throwing me out of my own house?"

"Since when is this your house anymore? You're a stranger here and you may always be. God willing we aren't all destroyed by what you say is coming, maybe it'll be your house again someday. But not now."

"Dad wouldn't ever say this to me."

"That's right." Kristen turned to face her again. "You're absolutely right. And that's why *I'm* saying it to you. Catch the shuttle, cousin. Go back to Zor'a. Write, visit when it's all over, but go do what you have to do. Come back when you're done."

"If there's something to come back to."

"If there's something to come back to," Kristen agreed, and then stepped forward and hugged her cousin. "We both love you very much, Jackie. Don't think too badly of me for telling you to go, but you must realize that I'm right."

In her cabin aboard *Fair Damsel,* jumping for Zor'a, the darkness of *anGa'e'ren* was only a few meters away.

Jackie had a long argument with herself, and she reached the conclusion that her cousin had been right. It was a lesson learned at great expense, but one she knew would stay with her, like it or not.

chapter 18

First Talon. THE INITIAL SUBJECT OF SENSITIVE STUDY IN
THE SANCTUARY CURRICULUM. IN IT, THE STUDENT MAKES
THE FIRST IDENTIFICATION OF THE *HSI*, OR LIFE-ENERGY,
THAT DWELLS WITHIN EACH PERSON, AND THE *GYU'U*, OR
TALON OF THE MIND, WHICH CAN MANIPULATE IT.

—Dr. Ariana Sontag,
Dictionary of Zor Sociology,
New Chicago University Press, 2314

As they traveled out to the station near the jump point, Owen Garrett
attempted, unsuccessfully, to concentrate on First Talon. Even with his
eyes closed he could sense and hear Byar HeShri nearby.

"Stop watching me, damn it," he said under his breath.

"I am not watching you."

"You're *always* watching me, Master Byar." Owen didn't open his
eyes; he was still trying to trace the glyph of First Talon in his mind.
"When we reach *Trebizond* you'll be watching."

"It is why I have accompanied you."

"So that you can see Dri'i in action. Is that it?" Owen gave up and
opened his eyes to see the Master of Sanctuary looking away from him,
out a viewport of the shuttle, at E'rene'e System.

Probably just looked away, Owen thought to himself.

"This is a talent that the People have not witnessed in many eights of turns, *se* Owen. I am understandably curious."

"There's no guarantee that it's *anGa'riSsa.* It could be something else, something more dangerous."

"Can you sense the presence of *esGa'uYal*?"

"You know that I can," Owen answered.

"I know that you have *told* me so and that you have discovered two of the creatures within the High Nest. I know that the experiences you had with *Negri Sembilan* and on the world Center are best explained by the talent you describe."

"This is a hell of a time to be doubting this talent, Master Byar."

"I do not doubt it—I am merely telling you what I *know.* I believe that you possess this talent, and sincerely pray to the Lord *esLi* that I am correct."

If you had any hairs, you'd be splitting them, Owen thought to himself.

"I'm so encouraged," he said aloud.

"Your sarcasm is noted, *se* Owen."

Their shuttle landed on the hangar deck of the *Trebizond.* It was a *Byzantium*-class starship, two generations out-of-date; not the sort of thing you'd see in plane-of-battle nowadays, but serviceable for IGS work. It was shorter in the beam than *Negri Sembilan* but almost as broad, with a comparable jump range.

"We're expected, I see," Owen said to Byar, as they stepped onto the outside lift and descended to the deck. All the officers and crew of *Trebizond* were on hand, waiting for their arrival.

Eleven zor warriors followed them down, each holding a pistol in one hand, the other one resting lightly on a scabbarded *chya.* Whatever the High Nest thought of Owen's ability, there was no sense in taking any chances.

Owen had read the report forwarded from *Duc d'Enghien,* which had come all the way back to the zor Core stars escorting it. According to *Trebizond*'s captain, Adrianople had been taken by a pair of bug hive-ships. Commodore Durant, an officer Owen had heard of but never met in person, had chosen to surrender the base. About two weeks ago, the commodore had gotten word that a bug VIP was on the way, and had ordered *Trebizond* to take its chances.

They'd made it through a bug-controlled refueling station and turned up at Denneva. From what intel had indicated, the captain was under no illusions: There were bugs aboard his ship—that's how they'd gotten through the intermediate stop.

That's why Owen was here, after all. The assumption—which might or might not be correct—was that the bugs didn't know what he could do. For his part, Owen had his doubts: The bugs must have realized that he was aboard *Negri* when they'd got it away from Center System, and he'd been told he was being watched.

"*Dangerous,*" the bug had told him. "*Ór . . . ordered you to be . . . watched. You were immune to the* k'th's's."

It was better for him to assume that the bugs knew about him and his power.

"You must be Commander Garrett," the man wearing captain's bars said, saluting. "I'm Richard Abramowicz, captain of *Trebizond.*"

Owen saluted in return. The captain was showing unusual deference, given that he was the superior officer; he seemed uncomfortable, but that might be simply because this was an uncomfortable situation.

"I'm Garrett, sir," Owen answered. "May I present Byar HeShri, Master of Sanctuary, my . . . teacher."

Abramowicz stepped forward and grasped forearms with the zor, whose wings elevated slightly. Clearly the captain understood a bit about zor custom.

"I'd like to present my crew," Abramowicz said, dropping his arms to his sides and turning to face Owen once again. "I'm . . . not sure what . . ."

"It'd be my pleasure to meet them," Owen answered. "*All* of them."

Abramowicz had no reply, but gestured to the line of officers. "My exec, Commander Kit Hafner."

"Commander," Kit said to Owen, also saluting.

Owen didn't reply, but tried to look studious. He nodded and thought about Damien Abbas, the captain of *Negri*—how he'd been taken off the bridge of his own ship and left behind on Center, and then killed arbitrarily by the folks that gave Commodore Laperriere the sword.

It was enough to stir up his resentment at being used as a pawn, and to make him feel the anger that made his talent work. Behind, Owen heard the rustle of zor wings. He knew that, without Sensitive shields, some of his emotions radiated and could be felt by those with talent.

He half listened as Abramowicz introduced each officer in turn; but somewhere in the back of his mind he heard another voice. At first it was just noise, but after a few moments he could hear his name being spoken.

Garrett, it said. *I know you can hear me, Garrett.*

He tried not to betray to Byar or anyone else that he'd heard anything. He was halfway down the first row now, hardly even comprehending the words Abramowicz was speaking.

Who is this? Owen asked mentally.

I am among the crew of this u'shn'ni *ship.*

Owen didn't understand the word but got the meaning—and it wasn't complimentary.

I'll find you, Garrett answered. *When I find you, you're dead.*

It is your choice, Garrett, the voice answered. *But there is another avenue open to you.*

There were four more officers left in the line; then Abramowicz would begin on the middies and warrants.

You want to make some kind of deal? Owen frowned. Abramowicz noticed and reached a hand toward him, concerned; the procession stopped where it was. Things seemed to have become remote and soft-edged, like a dream.

Byar's wings rearranged themselves again. The zor escorts moved forward quickly, their pistols at the ready.

I would like to make you an offer—I would like to help you develop your k'th's's *power.*

"So you can digest it," Owen said out loud. The entire scene suddenly snapped into focus.

He looked around the hangar deck, alarmed. There was a buzz in the ranks until the exec shouted them back to attention.

Byar came alongside.

You can be more powerful than this winged meat-creature as well, Garrett. He cannot be what you will become.

Owen looked across the ranks of officers and, behind them, the crew of *Trebizond.* They stood at attention, but he could see worry in their faces. Abramowicz looked worried, too: He didn't know what to make of this encounter.

And what will that be? Owen asked, still searching for the source of the voice.

There's a new day coming, Garrett, the voice continued, not answering his question. *Our Great Queen has sadly miscalculated, and has only a few more vx*tori to live. Her successor . . . could use a person of your talents.*

You mean a "meat-creature," don't you? he answered. Owen began to walk down the row of officers, looking into the blur of faces—officers in the front rank, crew in the back—one after another, trying to locate the elusive impostor.

Your talent sets you apart from the meat-creatures, the voice answered. *You can resist the k'th's's of a powerful Drone: There is much that First Hive could learn from you.*

It is also obvious that the winged ones seek to manipulate you, to make you a part of their foolish mysticism.

We can free you from all of that, Garrett.

The exchange was only heightening his anger, making his senses more acute.

Still, the alien voice had a point: The zor *were* manipulating him; they wanted to fit him into a legend, just as they'd forced Commodore Laperriere into one.

No, Owen said at last, as much to himself as in reply to the alien. *I won't replace one set of puppet-strings with another.*

He stepped between Hafner and the helm officer—he thought he remembered her name as Salmonson. They stepped aside as he moved into the second rank to stand before an engineer's mate in dress whites.

"Nice try," Owen said.

"You're a small-minded fool," the bug disguised as a crewman said. "The *P'cn* Deathguard would've found a place for you, and I came all this way to make the offer to you."

"Don't worry," Owen answered. "You'll have a chance to answer some questions."

"I don't think so."

The crewman smiled unpleasantly, baring his teeth. A distant look came into his eyes for a split-second before he collapsed to the deck. A few moments later his form began to change and elongate, tearing the fabric of the uniform in several places.

Crewmen and officers stepped back from the lifeless alien form. Owen could feel the revulsion hanging in the air, but felt distant from it.

The words *"small-minded fool"* echoed in his mind, and he wondered just for a moment if he'd made the right decision.

ea, perhaps, Director likes would?"
M'm'e'e Sha'kan turned away from the table and walked to the dispenser. Extending his upper left arm he entered a request, and an oily, bluish purple liquid oozed from the tap into a cup that dropped into place. He carried it back to the table gently and lovingly in his lower hands.

The director shook his head as if to say, *If that's tea, I'll pass.*

M'm'e'e settled himself onto a seat and took a sip from his drink. "Mmm-hm," he ventured after a moment.

"Tell me about the new *Gyaryu'har*."

"Tell?" M'm'e'e repeated. "What to tell is, I the Director little enlightenment provide can. The interview taped and monitored was, surely, and from it conclusion drawn will have been?"

"I prefer personal opinions. As you know."

"M'm'e'e knows," he agreed, and sipped again, extending a finger to wipe a drop of the beverage from his upper lip. "Understanding from my thinkings Director desires."

The director nodded.

"Clever she is. This must you consider: Though weeks only since her return passed have, already informed is she about things that during her absence transpired have. Also, about many things did she also know seem to, things from former *Gyaryu'har* Sergei Torrijos, old friend, have come must.

"Yet she the former *Gyaryu'har* not since Cicero seen has, then in a coma was he; or not? Need to know must we, what at Adrianople Starbase in zor ceremony transpired. Stipulation: Some intelligence from comatose *se* Torrijos to new *Gyaryu'har* came, before she to zor service seconded was.

"Else how could she so well informed be? Surprising that she even rules of engagement knew, the way to obtain information much less knew, so soon to current status elevated.

"M'm'e'e of his own abilities more confident was, before this interview place took."

"There is another possibility."

"Intrigued, is M'm'e'e," the rashk answered, clapping each pair of hands and then performing some sort of complex weave with them. "Please—Director will M'm'e'e enlighten!"

"Prior to the seizure of the Cicero naval base by the enemy, Torrijos consulted with Laperriere at least once in private. We assume that the two were strangers, and that she was brought into the High Nest's plan subsequent to the attack."

"Target of plan she was, all along; Director that must know. M'm'e'e knows, by the Three!"

"Yes, yes, of course. But she was supposed to be unaware of it until much later." The director sat back in his chair, which conformed to his new position. "What if something passed between them when they first met? All of Laperriere's testimony—all of what happened before her disappearance, in fact—is out of harmony with her previous career. She was even tested for Sensitive talent. The test revealed nothing that would recommend her to be the next *Gyaryu'har*."

"Director then suggests . . ."

"Consider this, my friend," the director said, leaning forward again. "Let's assume that the new *Gyaryu'har* of the High Nest was the target of their plans from the very beginning; that Torrijos went to Cicero with the specific intent of passing his title to her.

"For simplicity's sake, let's also assume that she was unaware of this until Torrijos arrived. Then something happened between them—*on Cicero*—and by the time she returned to Adrianople, she was already acting as his successor."

"Contradicts that conjecture, does the evidence: Inside sources say the High Nest to participate in ceremony on Adrianople her ardently desired to prevent. High Chamberlain of the High Nest indeed opposed to her was."

"A ruse."

"Of High Chamberlain, part of ruse was this?"

The director thought a moment, disentangling M'm'e'e's sentence structure. "Not just by the High Chamberlain. This ruse was perpetrated by Laperriere herself. She was part of this plot at least that long ago."

"*Legend of Qu'u*, what of?"

"Oh, *that* again."

"That again, yes," M'm'e'e said. "Director, surely, on the part of zor, the profound reliance upon myth rejects, does not?"

"M'm'e'e Sha'kan," the director answered. "I am prepared to accept a great deal in service of my Empire and in the proper execution of my duty to the Agency. But I do not see how a legend eight thousand years old bears upon the situation."

"Signs and portents, Director, portents and signs. Fits well, so it does."

"M'm'e'e—"

"Director!" M'm'e'e Sha'kan rose from his seat in a single heaving motion, his substantial bulk towering above his human companion. Rashk expressions did not change very much; they always appeared to be smiling broadly, but the director knew the other was animated with something far from amusement. "Director, from the Three do we come, return to it shall we. Always, say our people, 'if floor wet is, walls leaking are': Not from official sources news must hear we, disaster on the way is.

"Knows well M'm'e'e, bias against zor in the Agency is, mistrust always, suspicion constant is. Read wings, then, Director! Zor seen *have*, know *do*. Considered have you, the walls truly leaking are?"

"And if they are?"

M'm'e'e sat down again, cupping all four hands around his drink. He gazed down into it for a long time before answering.

"Director," he said quietly. "While we here discuss what knew *Gyaryu'har*, when she it knew, walls leaking *are*. Signs and portents, Director. Matters it little, then, how *Gyaryu'har* herself in plot involved: Holds sword *now* does she. She an ally be can, or rival, or enemy. Better an ally, thinks M'm'e'e."

"All right," the director said. "What do you propose?"

M'm'e'e thought for several moments and then described a course of action. Despite the tortured grammar and syntax, it was immediately clear to the director that this was the ultimate destination of their discussion; that his alien companion had thought long and hard about how to present it and had awaited the exact question he had just been asked.

Jackie stood at the parapet and looked across the valley she had only seen once before, and that was in a *Dsen'yen'ch'a*: In the distance, etched against the landscape, she could see esYen, the capital city of the People.

"Quite a view," she said to Byar HeShri, who stood behind her. She

did not turn to face him, but ran her hand across the smooth stone of
the wall-top, causing motes of grit and sand to drift over the edge,
falling hundreds of meters to the valley floor below.

A few seconds' flight for someone with wings, she thought; and a
portion of her memory dredged up the cruel barbs of Shrnu'u HeGa'u,
referring to her wingless state.

She pushed the thoughts away, suppressing anger and the pang of
embarrassment that seemed to reverberate between her mind and the
ornate sword that hung at her belt.

Byar HeShri stood respectfully.

"What happened to *se—si—*S'reth?"

"*si* S'reth transcended the Outer Peace, *se* Jackie," Byar answered,
and then approached, half walking and half flying.

"Yes, I know. That's why I'm here, along with half the Empire." She
turned to face him. "But why now? I had questions for him."

"So did we all," Byar said, his wings forming the Stance of Regret-
ful Disappointment.

"Was there— I mean, did anyone cause—?"

"*si* S'reth was very old." Now it was Byar's turn to look away. "*Very*
old. When the *naZora'i*—humans . . . eight thousand pardons, *se* Jackie—
were the enemy of the People, *si* S'reth was emerging from here." Byar
placed his claws on the edge of the parapet. "His youth belonged to an
era when our species were on opposite sides of the great *sSurch'a*. He
watched things change; he saw . . ." The Master of Sanctuary let the sentence drift off the edge of the lookout and vanish into the clear morning,
as if he could not encompass its meaning with some simple phrase or turn
of wing.

Jackie sensed something left unsaid. "*se* Byar, you called me back
from a great distance and asked me *here*, particularly, for a reason. I can
accept that *si* S'reth's death has occurred since he was very old; and I can
even wish him the ultimate joy of union with the Lord *esLi*. You're not
surprised—and you know how *I* felt about him.

"But what does this have to do with Sharia'a and *seLi'e'Yan*? What
do you know now that you didn't know before?"

"You are very perceptive, *se* Jackie. I would expect no less of the
Gyaryu'har . . . yet I am still surprised that you can sense this."

"Out with it, Master Byar."

"The High Lord decided that it was necessary to go to the Plane of
Sleep." As briefly and succinctly as he could, Byar summarized the

experience at the Stone of Remembrance and the fight with the Servant of the Deceiver.

" 'Go to the Stone and ask,' " she said. "Shrnu'u HeGa'u said it to me. Now I understand what he meant."

As Byar spoke of his conversation with S'reth on the Plane of Sleep, his eyes narrowed and his wings arranged themselves in a posture of extreme deference to *esLi*. Jackie found herself unable to hold his gaze and looked away again, across the valley.

"I would hardly consider an *esGa'uYe* a reliable source of information," she said when he had finished, but already knew what he would say in reply.

"I consider *si* S'reth credible, *se* Jackie. He told us that the servant was speaking the truth."

"And that's the last word on it. Because you needed to test me, or because you wanted a *sSurch'a* to prove that I was the genuine *Gyaryu'har*, you summoned—" She lowered her voice. "You summoned Shrnu'u HeGa'u from long imprisonment and nearly let him kill me."

"You must see the need—"

"It *had* to be Shrnu'u HeGa'u. Not any of the others, not a lesser spirit, but the damned *e'Gyaryu'har*." At the word, Byar visibly flinched; Jackie wasn't sure that the title was correct, but the meaning was clear. "The Deceiver's top wing-brother, the chief general, the anti-hero. Qu'u's ancient enemy."

"I will not deny that he is all of those things, *se* Jackie, and more, and worse. Yes, it had to be *that* one—because we sought Qu'u. The Law of Similiar Conjunction—"

Jackie held up her hands. "All right. I give. Who made the decision? Who *chose* the flight, *se* Byar?"

Byar seemed to take a long time to answer.

"*si* S'reth did," he said. "We all agreed on the need for a servant to be summoned to the *Dsen'yen'ch'a*, but *si* S'reth insisted it be *that* one, for *that* reason. We could not have foreseen—perhaps even *hi'i* Ke'erl could not have foreseen—what the consequences of this summoning might have been."

"No one in the High Nest, perhaps."

Byar did not reply but his wings seemed to inquire, as if there were a question he wished to put, but somehow could not verbalize.

"Permit me to explain," Jackie said. "From the beginning of the

High Nest's involvement with the aliens, you—we—have assumed that the relationship evolved along lines foretold by *The Legend of Qu'u*. Everything done, every move made by the High Nest was based on the idea that a new Qu'u would emerge to combat the servants of the Deceiver.

"To have a Shrnu'u for Qu'u to fight, the legend demanded that he be summoned forth: That is why *si* S'reth probably insisted he be chosen. What's more, by summoning Shrnu'u into the Ordeal, you made it possible for him to assume material form in the World That Is.

"Shrnu'u HeGa'u, my ancient enemy, the one who has sought to destroy me at every turn, was present—it seems—to deliver the *gyaryu* into my hands at Center and to arrange my departure. Shrnu'u HeGa'u, Servant of the Deceiver, the ancient enemy of the Lord *esLi* and thereby the High Nest, has completed the fulfillment of *The Legend of Qu'u*.

"If I am here, it is *him* you have to thank."

A breeze ruffled through Byar HeShri's wings and stirred the edge of Jackie's cloak.

"*se* Jackie," Byar said carefully, "if you are correct, then I must wonder . . . If *si* S'reth knew that we had to follow an earlier legend in which the sword is *recovered* from the Plain of Despite, then why did he not tell anyone until it was nearly too late to understand? If our High Lord had been a wingspan less daring, or less discerning, we might never have known. Why did he not reveal this?"

"Because in the end, S'reth was a teacher. He needed us to discover through *sSurch'a* what we were to do. Perhaps he even foresaw his own death, his own absence from the councils of the High Nest at the time we needed him most. Now," she finished, placing a hand on the hilt of the *gyaryu*, "we have to fly this path alone."

Byar did not reply but instead gazed out across the valley, looking away from Jackie.

"There's still something I'm not sure I understand," Jackie continued at last. "Why is Shrnu'u HeGa'u trying to kill me?"

The Master of Sanctuary did not turn around. Another breeze resettled his wings, as if the wind were trying to choose his wing-position. "Shrnu'u HeGa'u is a servant of the Deceiver and you are a servant of *esLi*. Why should he *not* seek to destroy you?"

"I understand that. Then, I have a different question: Why did he give me the sword? Why didn't he just kill me when he could, at Center? What was the point?"

"Despite does not have a 'point,' *se* Jackie. There *is* no point. Shrnu'u HeGa'u seeks to destroy you because that is his nature."

"Unacceptable. Stone could have killed me on Center—yet he gave me the sword instead. If this, too, is S'reth's doing, then I can only assume that he caused this entire drama to play itself out because there *was* a point. We must figure out just what *sSurch'a* he wished us to have. There must be some part of the legend we overlooked."

Byar turned to face her. "Or perhaps there is some clue in the antecedent legends, the ones on which *seLi'e'Yan* is based. Our Elder Brother assumed that we should pay heed to an earlier redaction of the Qu'u legend. Perhaps there are other clues."

"Such as?"

"We will not know, *se* Jackie," he replied patiently, "until we look."

The number of people who turned out for S'reth's memorial was larger than Jackie would have expected. S'reth was the oldest zor she had ever met or even seen; he had emerged from Sanctuary during Marais' war with the zor, most of a century ago, and had served as Speaker for the Young Ones in the Council of Eleven for a number of years. He had even served as a plenipotentiary ambassador to the otran for almost a decade.

In short, he knew *everyone*.

Still, there were more and more, and different, people than she'd expected. As *Gyaryu'har*, Jackie had an excellent vantage point in the Hall of the People: a perch modified for humans (a flatter area, accessible by a narrow stairway), just a few meters below where the High Lord normally observed.

As she stood, trying to remain impassive at the throng, Jackie picked out the portly figure of Rear Admiral César Hsien entering the Hall with his staff. The admiral looked uncomfortable, to say the least: Despite his studied dignity he seemed unable to keep himself from gazing upward at the huge domed ceiling of the Hall, ninety meters above his head, and at the hundreds of perches and other accessways filled with zor, some of whom were gazing back at him.

She didn't know whether he saw her from ground level, and she couldn't imagine why he might be here: The Navy was full of admirals, active and retired, and César Hsien had never shown any particular love for the People; the Admiralty could hardly have chosen a more insulting

way to pay its last respects to an honored servant of the High Nest. A
quick inquiry of the *gyaryu* provided no further insight into the reason
for his presence.

She thought about asking the High Lord, but a glance upward indicated that Sa'a was occupied with three Lords of Nest, whose wing-
positions did not seem to brook interruption.

It was clearly time for a bit of personal reconnaissance.

Bᵧ ᴛʰᴇ time Jackie reached ground level—a longer journey without
wings—Hsien had made his way over to a wide, semicircular table
containing remembrances left by visitors: Mostly comps and books, but
there were also small arrangements of living plants, as well as plaques
and statues and memorabilia of all kinds. Hsien had been left alone by
his adjutants for the moment. There were only a few zor standing near
the table as Hsien approached, stopped for a moment as if in thought,
and then placed a small holocube on a vacant spot. He said something
quietly to himself, looking again toward the apex of the tall chamber;
then he turned away.

Only then did he catch Jackie's glance. She was waiting with her
arms crossed, at the edge of the throng milling (and flying) near the
table of memories. His two staff officers had already begun to approach, as if to form up around him, but he waved them off and advanced to where Jackie stood waiting for him.

"Admiral," he said to her. "*se Gyaryu'har*. I hope I pronounced that
correctly."

"Admiral," she answered. "I'm . . . surprised."

"I should say the same. But I believe that I understand your surprise; perhaps an explanation is in order." He turned back to the table,
nodding for her to follow.

He picked up the cube from the place he had left it and pressed a
stud on the top. A scene formed in the air above it: a rolling plain with
mountains in the distance, silhouetted against a deep-blue sky. In the
foreground, horses grazed in the brush.

"Alberta," he said. "North America, on Terra. Where I grew up. I
wanted to share it with *se—si—*S'reth's family and friends."

Jackie didn't answer, still not sure where Admiral Hsien was going
with this. He pressed the stud again and the scene disappeared. He put
the cube carefully back on the table.

"*si* S'reth saved that place for me," Hsien said, looking directly at Jackie, as if to challenge her. "That's the place I come from. Open plains. Big sky. When the—the *vuhls*..." He was almost unable to speak the word, though not from distaste; there was something else. "When my command reached Adrianople, we found that they had already taken it. They... invaded my mind. The idea of such emptiness and wide-open space frightened them. Because I was a part of them, it frightened *me* as well.

"To think that something I've known since I was old enough to walk would frighten me..." He let the sentence trail away. "*si* S'reth and the other Sensitives arrived at Adrianople in time to save me from being consumed or destroyed or irrevocably changed. No—that's not quite true: By bringing me back from that experience, by saving my life that way, it *did* change me. That's why I'm here, to answer your question."

"I didn't—"

"You don't have to be polite on my account, Admiral. Madam. *se Gyaryu'har*. Even if I had a personal axe to grind with you, which I do not, you are out of my jurisdiction. *Far* out of my jurisdiction. Not that it kept one of my subordinates from telling me off in your defense."

"Telling you off?"

"A ship captain under my command defended your actions and character, leaving no room for uncertainty. 'If it pleases the admiral,' indeed."

She could hardly keep from smiling. "Barbara MacEwan," Jackie said.

Now it was Hsien's turn to be amused. "That's right. Captain MacEwan stood up to this old bastard to defend someone whose career was in doubt." They began to walk across the hall to an area set up for refreshments. "I'm not sure, but I think I like her."

"She's the best."

"Do you think so?" He stopped walking for a moment, and Jackie also stopped, to face him. "I pulled rank and used medical leave to come here for this; to say thanks and... farewell. As soon as this is over, my flag is going to Josephson System with a task force to use against the aliens; we'll staff each ship with additional Sensitives. I'd like to include Captain MacEwan and *Duc d'Enghien*. What do you think?"

Certain death, she thought to herself. *What possible chance*—

"I'm sure she'd be honored," Jackie said. "Surprised, if she was as . . . forthright . . . as you suggest. But honored." *It's what the Navy is there for,* she told herself. *But without the* gyaryu *to defend them, they're powerless against the vuhls.*

Unless she took the *gyaryu* there with them.

"What are your orders, sir?"

"I wouldn't really discuss them here. We're deploying to Josephson System shortly." He gestured to the crowd. "Perhaps after the ceremony we might confer." He straightened up as if he had suddenly concluded that he had no more to say to her. "Now, if you will excuse me," he added, offering a polite salute and turning away toward his staff, who were waiting at a respectful distance.

The Large meditation chamber at Sanctuary was crowded when she arrived; there was obvious tension hanging in the air. Most of the perches were occupied, three and four stories up; every rated Sensitive and senior student at Sanctuary had turned out for the *Dsen'yen'ch'a.* Owen Garrett was sitting on a cushion in a loosely belted robe, a *chya* across his lap, his eyes closed. A teacher Jackie didn't know was standing next to him. Something was making Owen tense, almost angry; he seemed to be working hard at contemplating serenity. A large *esLi* disk hung in the alcove behind him, gently backlit orange.

As she approached, his eyes opened and focused on her. He had a determined look on his face, as if the Ordeal were something he knew he needed to get through. Still, he seemed to be glad to see her; *that* was something, at least.

The last time Jackie had attended a *Dsen'yen'ch'a* it had been her own—though she hadn't known it at the time. There had been only a few in attendance at Adrianople Starbase: the High Chamberlain T'te'e HeYen, herself and Ch'k'te . . . along with the one that had been invited to participate. She wondered to herself if he'd turn up here as well. Now Ch'k'te was gone, Th'an'ya was gone, and so was Adrianople Starbase. T'te'e was offworld somewhere; the Ordeal was under the direction of Byar HeShri.

She had every confidence in Byar's skill. Still, she wasn't sure what to expect—and it was certain that Owen didn't know, either. Unlike her own Ordeal, though, the subject had a true and trusty friend upon whom he could rely.

Byar fluttered down from somewhere to land next to Owen; he gently grasped one of Owen's forearms. The teacher nodded to the Master and departed for another perch. Jackie bowed to the Master of Sanctuary, who grasped forearms with her. He did not speak, but kept a gentle hold on her right arm and led her to a cushion beside Owen, gesturing briefly toward the *gyaryu*. She sat and placed the scabbarded sword across her lap, hilt to the right, her hands resting lightly upon it.

Byar stood between Jackie and Owen and placed a hand on each of their shoulders.

"We are assembled in this place of quiet," he began, "to examine a Sensitive skill which has appeared among the People."

It was a ritual phrase, but she saw Owen's shoulder tense under Byar's grasp. She caught his eye; he was angry, but trying not to show it. "It is rare," Byar continued, "that a new Sensitive phenomenon occurs; and it is long established by law and by custom that the appearance of such a skill requires the examination of the *hyu* and the *hsi* of the bearer. This serves both as a guide to the Flight of the People and as an assurance that the bearer's Inner Peace is maintained.

"What is unusual about this circumstance is that this talent seems not to be new to the People, but instead is one that has lain hidden for many turns. It is *anGa'riSsa*: the Shield of Hatred. As this talent may not be well known to many among the People, I beg eight thousand pardons for a few moments to speak of it." His wings moved to the Posture of Polite Approach.

"In the time of the Warring States, before the end of the War of Unification, the Lord of Despite strove against the servants of *esLi*. Chief among the generals of *esGa'u* was Shrnu'u HeGa'u—He of the Dancing Blade—who led the Army of Sunset. This army swept from the shore of the Western Ocean to the foothills of the Spine of Shar'tu, and laid all to waste before them. At the Plain of Ca'ra'man, through a cruel deception, Shrnu'u HeGa'u and his minions destroyed the Legion of *esLi*; and those who still held the Inner Peace were forced to flee where the Eight Winds drove them.

"At last, the Army of Sunset arrived at Sharia'a, the City of Warriors."

Jackie watched Owen's shoulders tense again.

"The sorceries of the Army of Sunset were potent, and the defenders of the city slowly gave way to despair and depression," Byar went on. "As it happened, however, *esLi* still smiled upon the city: A young warrior named Dri'i, who had been at the shattering of the Legion, was within the walls of Sharia'a. The *hsi* of Dri'i was strong; as the warriors of the city gradually succumbed to the *e'gyu'u* of the servants of *esGa'u*, he was moved to anger.

"He went from place to place in the city, from warrior to warrior, communicating this anger to the defenders of Sharia'a. Gradually they were moved to resist that with which the *esGa'u Yal* attacked them. And while the Army of Sunset laid waste outside the walls, the warriors stood firm until the agents of *esGa'u* withdrew their siege and sought easier targets. Thus was the power of the servants of *esLi* preserved until it was time for them to emerge in the service of the Golden Circle once more.

"We believe that this talent has emerged in this young warrior." Byar looked down at Owen, who nodded, tight-lipped, trying to maintain composure. "This is the subject of this Ordeal."

Byar placed his wings in posture of deference to *esLi,* all over the chamber, beside and above them, wings moved in response.

"*esLi* commands that the journey begin. *esLi* commands that the Ordeal commence."

Through the chamber, Jackie could hear the word *esLiHeYar* being spoken, a sound as gentle as a breeze. She closed her eyes, feeling the tendrils of Byar's consciousness extend toward her.

A gong sounded in the distance.

"I raise my head toward the orb of the Sun and survey the land of my clan-fathers. I scan the horizon and watch for the legions of *esGa'u*. Though the searing heat burn away my skin—"

Gong.

"Though it singe my wings until, blackened, they drop away—"

Gong.

"Though the madness-of-daylight comes upon me, I shall not swerve from my duty."

Gong.

The room was absolutely quiet, as if there were not a living soul in it. Jackie opened her eyes, not knowing what to think; she expected to see the meditation chamber, or perhaps some representation of Sharia'a . . .

Instead she found herself looking at a holo display, focusing on six aerospace fighters. In the near distance she could see a vuhl hive-ship.

She was back aboard *Duc d'Enghien* at Cicero.

Even before Owen opened his eyes, he felt something familiar under his hands—not the hilt and scabbard of a *chya*, but the controls of an aerospace fighter. He almost didn't want to look but he did, and saw what he'd half expected to see: the cockpit of Green Five, in the absolute comm-quiet that had come just before he was pulled into the ship directly ahead of him.

"No," he said to himself. "This can't be happening again."

Somewhere beyond where he sat, trying to make the controls respond, he was at Sanctuary; this was a test, some sort of zor mental construct. It was an exact reenactment of something that had already happened—

No, he thought. *Not* exact. *There's something I can do now that I couldn't when this happened.*

He felt his anger beginning to rise. Over the last few weeks he'd made an effort to throttle it, to harness the power the teachers at Sanctuary said he possessed: First Talon, Second Talon, focusing on the Inner Peace.

The hell with that.

He let go. He let go of all of it: all of the resentment, all of the disgust, everything that reminded him of his fellow Green pilots' deaths. He gripped the controls with such emotion that pain coursed through his wrists and forearms . . .

And suddenly the controls responded under his hands. The hive-ship loomed so large that it filled the entire forward screen, but there was still plenty of room to turn. He heeled the little craft to starboard on a steep pitch and after a moment he was facing open space. Off in the distance his navcomp picked up *Duc d'Enghien*.

"All right," he said, to no one at all. "All right!"

Teach, he thought to himself.

"If I've got attitude controls, maybe I've got comm," he said aloud. "Green Five to Green Leader. Gary, respond."

The Green comm channel was still quiet, but he could just make out the backfeed from *Duc*'s flight bridge. If he could reach Green Wing Commander—

Save them *first,* he thought. Maybe he'd wind up failing and flying his bird back to the carrier alone, but he had to try. "Gary, this is Owen. I don't know if you can hear me or not. If you can't answer but you can still hear, listen to me. Listen to my voice.

"They're going to kill you, Gary. They're making you see things that aren't there, and they're going to kill you just like they killed Admiral Tolliver and the crew on the ships that went out with him. You have to fight it—You have to . . . you have to *hate* them. You have to hate them with everything you've got."

You have to feel what I'm feeling right now, he thought, pitching the fighter over. Green One—Gary Cox's plane—and Green Four—Anne Khalid's—were in visual range. They were on an intercept course with each other.

"Green Five to all Greens, copy my comm: *Fight* this thing. Focus on your hatred." He listened to his voice; he sounded like some sort of damn Sensitive himself. "Listen to me—*you can do this.* This is the *enemy.*"

Silence. Owen was closing on Schoenfeld and Khalid now; navcomp had picked up Aaron Schoenfeld, aft and a bit to port, closing on his tail.

"For God's sake, someone respond!"

They can't do it, he thought. *They're going to die, and they're going to take me with them. One shot from Gary's guns, and I'm—*

"Green Five," his comm said. "This is Green Six. I copy, Five." It was Aaron Schoenfeld's voice—it sounded strained, like he had something heavy on his chest. It was a voice from the grave, and it electrified Owen.

"I've got your flank, Owen," Schoenfeld added. "What's— What's going on?"

"No time to explain. Break off: I've got to get through to Gary and Anne and Devra."

"Break off?"

"No," came another voice. It was Gary Cox, the wing leader. "I read also, Green Five."

"I copy." It was Anne Khalid's voice. She was beginning to change course. "Coming around again, Green Leader."

Owen's navcomp showed another fighter coming alongside, to starboard. "Green Two copies also, Green Leader," said Devra Sidra.

"Form up," Gary said. "We're going in."

"Are you crazy, Gary?" Owen said. "We can get away—get back to base before they take us over again."

"They're not going to."

"This makes no sense, Green Leader."

"Are you disobeying orders, Five?"

Six ships against a hive-ship three kilometers long? Owen thought angrily. *We're going to be plasma.*

But this *wasn't* real—in reality they'd all killed each other, and he'd been pulled inside the hive-ship and interrogated . . . and given *an-Ga'riSsa.*

"No sir, Green Leader," Owen said.

"Form up in config Gamma," Gary said. "Fire at will."

The six fighters approached the hive-ship, weapons blazing.

Jackie Looked around. The bridge—or something made to resemble it—was deserted except for her and Byar HeShri. He stood by the pilot's chair, where Barbara MacEwan had sat watching as they raced away from the doomed fighter wing. Jackie stood beside the huge pilot's board where she and Ray Santos had also stood, fists clenched, watching the little fighters kill each other—all except one.

No Ray Santos; no Barbara MacEwan.

"I thought we were going to see Sharia'a," Jackie said to Byar, without turning. "I don't want to see *this* again."

"It may not turn out the same way, *se* Jackie."

"Oh?" She was furious, and spared a moment to look over her shoulder at him. "Who'd you invite to the party *this* time?"

"*I* invited no one," he answered. His wings moved to the Stance of Restrained Affront. "The *esGa'uYal* are free to walk the Plane of Sleep on their own."

"Meaning?"

"There is at least one present here, *se* Jackie. Can you not feel it?"

"Is it . . ." *Shrnu'u HeGa'u,* she was going to say; but she had become accustomed to the feel of Qu'u's ancient enemy. This was different: vaguely, disturbingly familiar, in a way that was annoyingly elusive.

"Something is happening," Byar said, gesturing toward the pilot's board. It was: As she watched, Green Five—Owen's fighter—began to turn aside from the vuhl hive-ship. For several moments the other fighters continued to move toward each other as they'd done in real life; then they, too, began to move away.

"They're going to escape," Jackie said.

"I do not think that is their intent," Byar answered. "Look."

Owen fired his weapons at the hive-ship, which seemed unshielded and unable to defend itself. Meter by meter, millisecond by millisecond, he expected a gun turret to train on him and destroy his fighter; but it wasn't happening. What *was* happening, was that the Green Squadron's concentrated fire was literally slicing off parts of the enormous vuhl vessel.

Owen hadn't faced bug ships in battle . . . *Well,* he thought, *except that one time at Cicero—but that hardly counts as a "battle."*

Could their hive-ships actually come apart that way? He'd read what he could about the battles at Adrianople and Thon's Well; no one had gotten close enough to attack them in detail.

Gary Cox's fighter continued to lead the Green Squadron a few dozen meters above the surface of the hive-ship, firing at the surface. Owen would have expected to break off at any time—they should be running out of energy to power their weapons by now—but the telltales in front of him showed one hundred percent across the board. It was as if the ship was a passive target, waiting for them to destroy it.

There was a wrongness about the entire scene—as if Owen's five dead colleagues flying again wasn't wrong enough . . . But this wasn't a fight, it was a slaughter. As pieces of the hive-ship were sliced away, he could see insect bodies tumbling into space as the compartments depressurized. It was a hideous way to die.

What they deserve, he thought to himself. *It doesn't matter: This is what was supposed to happen.*

He wanted to call *Duc d'Enghien,* to call Commodore Laperriere and tell her the bugs could be defeated—that there was a way to fight them. They *could* be killed.

Every one of them can be killed. Every one.

What the hell is happening, *se* Byar?" Jackie said. The six fighters had done considerable damage to the hive-ship they were attacking: it had been laid open like an animal carcass, with a huge gouge amidships. "Why are they doing this? Why doesn't the vuhl ship fight back?

"I don't understand this *Dsen'yen'ch'a* at all." She put her hand on the *gyaryu*. "Is this something to make Owen Garrett feel better? It's a *dream*. It never happened. Gary Cox and his wingmates killed each other because they couldn't resist Domination. Owen couldn't, either, but he was pulled into the ship instead of being killed."

She looked away from the board to Byar, who stood a few meters away. The rest of the *Duc*'s bridge had become ethereal, almost invisible, as if it were a 3-V mockup. Behind Byar there was nothing but a sort of misty glow.

"I have no explanation," Byar said. "If the aliens do not fight back, it is because they cannot. This is a *sSurch'a:* It is intended to tell us something about *se* Commander Garrett's talent."

"This is symbolic . . . of what?"

"We will have to ask Commander Garrett when the Ordeal is complete. Something changed. Presumably," Byar added, walking toward Jackie, "he used his ability to fight the Domination of the aliens—and the outcome is different."

Byar's face was suddenly brightly lit, and both of them looked back at the pilot's board. The vuhl ship had suffered a major explosion where the gouge had been, showing empty space beyond . . . and something else.

"What's *that*?"

Byar's wings moved to the Cloak of Guard. "The stars are wrong, *se* Jackie."

"Magnify two hundred," she said to the air. The pilot's-board view changed, closing in on the vuhl ship; as they watched, the two parts of the ship—the aft and fore sections—fell apart in an additional explosion, tumbling out of view. A ragged, irregular patch of stars that didn't belong there, stretched across a patch of space hundreds of kilometers wide.

"It looks like a hole. A tear in space. I've . . . never seen anything like it."

I've never seen anything like it," Owen said into comm. "It's like a gateway to another place."

"Damn straight," Gary Cox answered. "Form up, Green Squadron. Let's see what we have."

"Maybe we should comm *Duc* before we go in, Green Leader," Owen said. "If we—"

"*Form up!*" Gary interrupted. "This is the gate, Green Five. This is the destination."

"What?"

"The destination," Gary repeated. "This is where we've been going all along."

Six aerospace fighters dove for the distortion, where different stars shone.

his isn't right, *se* Byar. Sound the gong. Stop the Ordeal."

"I beg to differ, *se* Jackie. We must follow this through to its conclusion." He gently grasped the forearm of her off-arm; she had the *gyaryu* in her hand, not remembering having drawn it.

"This is out of control."

"Yes." Byar's wings moved to a posture of reverence to *esLi*. "Eight thousand pardons, *se* Jackie. But it always was."

uddenly, as the fighter craft reached the rough boundary between Cicero space and the other side of the rip, reality seemed to shatter. An intolerable brightness blinded Owen in his aerospace fighter, and Jackie and Byar on the bridge of *Duc d'Enghien*.

When they could see again, they were standing all together, dusty ground beneath their feet. An orange sun shone from a blistering-hot sky.

Jackie looked up and saw towers above, glowing a pale yellowish white at their tops.

"What—?" Jackie began, but Byar held up a taloned hand.

"Ah," he said. "This is where I expected we would be, at the start."

"Sharia'a?"

Byar moved his wings to Standing Within the Circle. "Correct, *se* Jackie. Now we will see—"

"See what?" Owen said, looking around him. "See me play Dri'i?" Owen stepped to his left, directly into the path of a zor warrior . . . who stepped *through* him. "Not likely, Master Byar. Looks like your little setup isn't going to work out as you planned it. They don't even know I'm here."

It was true for all three of them. They were *in* the scene, but not a part of it: The armed zor warriors who moved from place to place neither saw nor heard them.

"How do we know this is Sharia'a?" Owen asked. "It could be anywhere, any time."

"The towers," Byar replied, gesturing. "The warriors of Sharia'a decorated the towers of their city with the bones of their enemies."

A horn sounded somewhere. The gates of the city swung wide open and eleven zor entered, flying a meter or so above the ground. One carried a green banner bearing the glyph of Outer Peace.

Jackie looked at the lead figure. He was a warrior of the People, but there was something subtly wrong with him she couldn't quite figure out. The *gyaryu* confirmed what she already suspected: This was a servant of *esGa'u*, and a high-ranking one, at that. It wasn't Shrnu'u HeGa'u, though; of that she was sure.

"Why is an *esGa'uYe* within the walls of Sharia'a?" she asked Byar. "This isn't part of the legend."

"Nor is this," Byar said, looking across the wide courtyard before the gate.

A group of four warriors bore a small wooden palanquin which held a sword-rest. The sword-rest in turn held a blade that was unmistakably the *gyaryu*. They stopped a few meters away and bowed to the servants of *esGa'u*.

"No," Jackie said. "This has to stop. The Ordeal must end before—"

The scene began to fade as the three of them watched. Dust swirled to obscure their view of the *esGa'uYal,* and of the warriors of Sharia'a who were preparing to present the Talon of State to them.

A gong sounded somewhere: once, twice . . . three times, four times.

Jackie opened her eyes and found herself in the meditation chamber again. She had the cold sweats and Owen looked pretty much the same. Byar's back was slumped, and his touch on their shoulders was heavy, as if he might have fallen otherwise.

"What does it mean?" Owen managed to say. He looked at Jackie; his earlier anger had been replaced by fear.

"I . . . I don't know."

"They were all there." He closed his eyes tightly, formed his hands into fists. "Gary, Aaron, Devra, Anne, Steve . . . I heard them again. They didn't die."

"Yes they did. It was a—" Jackie began, then stopped. She wasn't sure exactly what in the hell it was. A dream? An alternate reality?

Two alternate realities, actually: First, the battle at Cicero; except it had turned out differently—presumably because Owen had the power of *anGa'riSsa.* And second, the confrontation between servants of *es-Ga'u* and *esLi* at Sharia'a—except the defenders were preparing to give up the *gyaryu* to the *esGa'uYal.*

Most of the observers of the *Dsen'yen'ch'a* had flown off, either on their own or due to some signal from Byar. He took brief flight, making a slow circle around the perimeter of the room, and then settled back in front of the two humans.

"I beg your indulgence," he said. "*se* Owen, *se* Jackie, I think we should retire and contemplate this Ordeal so that we can decide how to proceed."

"Proceed?" Owen said, opening his eyes. "I know damn well how to proceed. Admiral Hsien is leaving Zor'a System in two Standard days, and I'm leaving with him. I've had enough of study and Ordeal and Sensitive tests.

"I'm sorry, ma'am," he said to Jackie. "Unless I'm ordered not to, by someone in the chain of command, I'm going back to active duty." He looked toward the *esLi* disk, then back at Jackie. "There are still enemies out there, and I'm going to help kill them."

chapter 19

FOLIO 182: SCROLL 9, LEAVES 14–20

(14) . . . WHEN THE BROTHERS HAD TIRED OF THE
ENTERTAINMENTS OF THE CITIES OF THE COAST,
THEY CARRIED THEIR FLIGHT INLAND TO THE CITIES
ALONG THE SPINE OF SHAR'TU, THE GREATEST OF
WHICH WAS SHR'E'A. IN THOSE DAYS SHR'E'A WAS A
CITY OF WARRIORS, AND WAS RENOWNED FAR AND
WIDE THROUGHOUT THE LANDS OF THE WORLD.

[*esGa'u's* Shield]

SHARNU HAD HEARD A TALE OF THE FAMED SWORD OF
SHR'E'A, A GREAT WEAPON SAID TO HAVE BEEN FORGED
IN THE MORNING OF THE WORLD, AND WHOSE
WIELDER WOULD RECEIVE WISDOM FROM ALL
OF THE MIGHTY WARRIORS WHO HAD HELD IT BEFORE;
THEN . . . HE DECIDED THAT, SINCE HE WAS THE
GREATEST WARRIOR [OF THE PRESENT] DAY, THAT HE
AND HIS BROTHER HESYA SHOULD JOURNEY TO
SHR'E'A TO OBTAIN THE SWORD . . .

[Sword of Shr'e'a]

[*gyu'u'aryu{?}*]

[Challenge of the Deceiver]

. . . AND THAT, IF THE WARRIORS OF SHR'E'A WOULD
NOT YIELD THE SWORD UP, SHARNU AND HESYA WOULD
EACH [WORK] ACCORDING TO HIS TALENTS TO BRING
ABOUT THE FALL OF SHR'E'A AND THUS SECURE THE
SWORD.

{unknown wing}

. . . FOR, WHILE THE [UNTRANSLATABLE WORD] OF {unknown wing}
THE INHABITANTS OF SHR'E'A MIGHT [NOURISH?] THE
BROTHERS' [UNTRANSLATABLE WORD], THIS MIGHTY
SWORD IN THEIR TALONS WOULD BE SWEETER STILL.

(15) . . . FLEW OVER THE BROWN LANDS RAVAGED [Ravaging of *esHu'ur*]
BY THE RECENT WARS UNTIL THE SPINE OF SHAR'TU
WAS IN SIGHT. THE GREAT CITY HAD ELEVEN TURRETS
SHEATHED IN BONE, SAID TO BE TAKEN FROM
THE SKELETONS OF THOSE WARRIORS THAT HAD BEEN
DEFEATED BY THE SHR'E'A'I OVER THE CENTURIES. [Warrior at Rest]

(16) [UNTRANSLATABLE]

(17) [DAMAGED] . . . THE EMERGENCE OF THE ARMY OF
SUNSET ON THE PLAINS OF SHR'E'A . . . AND
[UNTRANSLATABLE] DID PLACE [UNTRANSLATABLE] ON
THE LAND . . .

THE [IMAGE?] PLEASED SHARNU GREATLY, AND [Strength of Madness]
ALSO IT BROUGHT [UNTRANSLATABLE PHRASE] TO
HESYA, AND EVEN SHARNU WAS [DISTURBED?] AT
THE WING-POSITION OF HIS BROTHER AS THEY
DISCUSSED THE MATTER . . .

(18) . . . SHARNU'S SORCERIES OF DESPAIR HAD [*Ur'ta leHssa*]
SETTLED ON SHR'E'A, AND THOSE WHO COULD STILL
GO ABOUT, SHOWED LITTLE WILL OR EMOTION AS
THEY PERFORMED THEIR DAILY TASKS. MANY OF THE
RESIDENTS SIMPLY REMAINED IN THEIR HOMES, OR
SOMETIMES IN THE STREET WHEREVER THEY FELL, EYES
TURNED, UNSEEING, TOWARD THE SKY.

BUT STILL THE WARRIORS OF SHR'E'A DID [Defiance of the Warrior]
NOT OPEN THE GATES TO SHARNU AND HIS ARMY OF
[UNTRANSLATABLE WORD] THAT SURROUNDED THE
CITY. SHARNU'S RAGE KNEW NO BOUNDS, AND HE
SUMMONED HESYA TO HIM TO SPEAK OF THIS.

(19) "BROTHER," HE SAID TO HESYA, "THESE [Patience of Despite]
SHR'E'A'I HAVE A STRONG WILL, BUT THEY CANNOT
RESIST FOREVER; STILL, I AM WEARY OF THIS SIEGE,
AND WILL NOT WAIT UNTIL THEY YIELD. IF THE
STRONG ARE CONSUMED BY THE [UNTRANSLATABLE {unknown wing}
WORD] OF OUR ARMY, ONLY THE WEAK WILL REMAIN
TO SERVE US WHEN WE TAKE THE CITY. WE MUST LEARN

WHENCE THEY DRAW THEIR STRENGTH, AND
TAKE IT AWAY."   {unknown wing}

THE TALENT OF HESYA SERVED THE SAME   [Challenge of the Deceiver]
MASTER AS THE TALENT OF SHARNU, BUT IN A
DIFFERENT WAY; INSTEAD OF [UNTRANSLATABLE
WORD], HE WAS GIVEN TO FAIR SPEECH AND
DIPLOMACY, AND UNDER THE GREEN BANNER OF
TRUCE HE ENTERED SHR'E'A WITH TEN OTHER
WARRIORS OF [UNTRANSLATABLE], WHOM HE HAD
PICKED FOR THIS PURPOSE.

HE SPOKE POLITELY TO THE WARLORD AND PRAISED   {unknown wing}
THE FINE CITY. INDEED, HE SAID, THE PEOPLE WHO
SERVED WITH THE [UNTRANSLATABLE WORD] ARMY OF
SUNSET OUTSIDE HAD NO DESIRE TO DESTROY SHR'E'A,
BUT RATHER TO LEARN FROM ITS STRENGTH; AND IF
THEY HAD THE USE OF THE KNOWLEDGE PROVIDED BY
THE LEGENDARY SWORD, THEY COULD OVERCOME THE
[UNTRANSLATABLE WORD] ARMY, AND THAT MUCH
HONOR WOULD BE GAINED . . .

(20) . . . ON THE FOURTH SUN WAS SUSPICIOUS
STILL: BUT AT LAST HE GAVE IN, AND CAUSED THE   [Sorrow of Deception]
SWORD TO BE BROUGHT FORTH AND ESCORTED
OUT OF THE CITY IN THE COMPANY OF HESYA . . .

. . . IN FULL VIEW OF THE CITY, THE   [*idju'a'ru*{?}]
[UNTRANSLATABLE WORD] FELL UPON THE ESCORT,
AND WHEN THE BATTLE WAS OVER, NEITHER THE
SWORD NOR HESYA WAS TO BE SEEN . . .

. . . WHEN THE WARRIORS OF SHR'E'A SAW THE SWORD [*Ur'ta LeHssa*]
OF THEIR CITY IN THE TALONS OF SHARNU THEY
REALIZED THEIR DOOM, AND OPENED THE GATES TO
THE INVADER, AND THE BLOOD OF THE DISHONORED
FLOWED THROUGH THE GUTTERS FOR MANY SUNS . . .

The clouds near the horizon made the light that passed through the windows a dirty-orange color. Jackie carefully placed the folio back on the high reading-desk, removing the talon-gloves from the holes in the pageturner. With no talons of her own, it was a necessary substitute, permitting her to manipulate the controls and read the manuscript. She pulled the gloves from one hand and then the other, setting them on the desk beside the ancient manuscript, and took up the stylus for her comp.

That's what we saw in Owen's Ordeal, she thought. *We saw the servants of* esGa'u *coming into Shr'e'a under the truce banner.*

Sharnu = Shrnu'u, she wrote on the pad. That seemed fairly clear. Shr'e'a would be Sharia'a—the Spine of Shar'tu was still called that, and corresponded to the descriptions in the folio. And the Sword of Shr'e'a had to be the *gyaryu.* She had seen it during Owen's *Dsen'yen'ch'a*— and now she knew what happened next.

"Hesya," she said softly, aloud, to no one in particular. *He* was the *esGa'uYe* who had come into Shr'e'a, the one she recognized as a servant of *esGa'u.*

Who the hell was Hesya?

And what in the world had happened to the legend in the intervening time? In the classical literature of the People, *seLi'e'Yan* didn't mention a great "Sword"; the warriors were forced to witness atrocity outside their walls. A young warrior, Dri'i, had roused them to anger and then they stood fast, for hatred of Despite. The army of *esGa'u* was commanded by Shrnu'u HeGa'u, and in the classical story he had no brother. On top of all that, the outcome of *seLi'e'Yan* was completely different: Sharia'a withstood Shrnu'u's attack. They *won.*

The version of the legend in front of her was completely different. There was no young warrior to rouse the anger of the warriors of the city: And they had held—and then *given away*—the Sword of Shr'e'a.

> *. . . a great weapon said to have been forged in the Morning of the World, and whose wielder would receive wisdom from all of the mighty warriors who had held it before . . .*

It was the *gyaryu.* It *had* to be.

Jackie ran her hands through her hair, looking around the scriptorium. From across the room she saw Byar HeShri flying toward her. Stopping short enough to offer a brief, respectful wing-configuration to her, he settled on a perch opposite the stool that had been provided.

"You have finished your reading," Byar said, gesturing toward the scroll.

"For the third time." She rubbed a reddish spot on her left hand where the talon-glove had pinched a bit. It was the only way for a human to read the older zor folios, which were rolled and unrolled by touch-sensitive controls accessible by inserting talons into a device attached to the reading-frame. "The missing passages and the unfamiliar words and wing-positions are a problem, but the story is clear. But, it's not the same outcome as in *seLi'e'Yan* we know—not at all."

Byar glanced at the scroll and then back to Jackie. His wings indicated curiosity. "But it *is* the same as what we witnessed during the Ordeal. The *gyaryu* appears, and *si* Dri'i does not. The Law of Similar Conjunction suggests that the new ability of *se* Owen represents the difference between the two disparate versions of the legend."

"So, Owen gets the *anGa'riSsa* talent and . . . the legend changes?"

"Essentially, yes."

"Except that the legend is even more different: Sure, Dri'i is missing; but the Army of Sunset itself is different. As for the Sword—it's handed over to the *esGa'uYal*. There's more to it than just adding in an angry warrior."

"Granted. There is more to this than a simple change." Byar's wings moved to a position that conveyed concern. "I am interested in knowing how you came to consult this particular passage."

"I found a reference to it in *The Shthe'e Codex:* the *hiShthe'eYaTur.*"

" 'The Flight Over Mountains,' " Byar said. "What *si* S'reth once called 'The Flight to Nowhere.' S'reth had great regard for Loremaster Shthe'e HeChri, but he dismissed the *Codex* as a pile of *artha*-droppings, disorganized and contradictory."

"Well, it's certainly disorganized." Jackie touched a display control on the desk and a small holo appeared in the air between them. She adjusted the view and the holo melted to show a single page, heavily annotated with her own reference markers. "I found this entry using a fuzzy-logic search, starting where I think *si* S'reth may have left off." She jabbed a spot with her finger. "There are half a dozen obscure references having to do with earlier redactions of 'Standing Within the Circle,' dating back to the pre-Unification period. That would be well over eight thousand Standard years ago, older than any written human record still extant.

"It's clear that *si* S'reth would've made it to this point eventually, but I don't know what he would have found. If he'd been at the *Dsen'yen'ch'a* . . . Damn. There's no point in even thinking about that."

"No indeed," Byar said. He held his wings in a position of reverence to *esLi*. "May I suggest that you fly the path? Review what we know."

The expression "fly the path" chafed a bit, but Jackie ignored it; she knew what Byar had meant. "All right, let's assume that the *esGa'uYal*— our enemies, the folks that gave me the sword and are now seemingly trying to kill me to get it back—have some relationship with these two brothers, Sharnu and Hesya. We know that Sharnu is now called Shrnu'u HeGa'u. Who's *Hesya* in the current incarnation? The accepted version of *seLi'e'Yan* doesn't mention him . . . and *does* mention Dri'i, the young warrior who teaches the warriors the Shield of Hatred.

"The Law of Similar Conjunction would make Owen out to be the avatar of Dri'i, just as I'm supposed to be the avatar of Qu'u.

"From what I read, Shrnu'u is only the most prominent *esGa'uYe*. He has the Despite version of the *gyaryu*." Byar signaled his assent. "But there must be others in his host, other villains, demons, whatever."

"I believe that there is a complete list in the *Hyne'e TaLssa*," said Byar. "The author apparently went quite mad while compiling it, but there are several sixty-fours of *esGa'uYal* listed." He leaned forward slightly and touched the display control and then issued a verbal command. Another holo replaced Jackie's annotated one. "This book is post-Unification and is not often consulted, but it may provide us with an answer."

Jackie took the stylus and drew a link between her comp and the displayed holo and then scrawled the name *Hesya* in the Highspeech. "Search," she said.

The holo blurred for a moment and then focused in on a section of the page.

"*Four matches at probability five-eighths or higher. First match,*" a soft zor-voice said. "*Hesagu HeGa'u. Soldier of Despite. Mentioned three times in* seLi'e'Yan; *Servant of* esGa'u; *slain during the siege of Sharia'a.*"

Jackie looked at Byar, whose wings remained impassive. "Proceed," she said to the air.

"*Second match: Hes Hsu. Demon of the Air. From the* Ga'anth, *mythological treatise.*" The holo mentioned a date only a few centuries old. "*Based on the traditions of Nest HeSa'an. The research done for the* Ga'anth *used several eights of references to passages and compilations in* Hyne'e TaLssa. *Do you wish a summary of these references?*"

"No. Proceed."

"*Third match: HeHsye. Splinter nest from Nest HeChri.*" Byar's left wing elevated a centimeter at the mention of his nest. "*All of its members were captured and sent to* Ur'ta leHssa *according to Loremaster Ka'ash.*"

Jackie turned to Byar. "Mean anything to you?"

Byar nodded. "Ka'ash was widely read when *Hyne'e TaLssa* was first published. But his work is now largely discredited."

Jackie shrugged. "Proceed," she said to the holo.

"Fourth Match: Hesya HeGa'u. The One Who Weaves. Deceived the Legion of Golden Light during the War of Despite. He then betrayed his cousin Shrnu'u before the siege of Sharia'a. Mentioned in seLi'e'Yan *four times."*

Jackie leaned forward to examine the indicated passage. "Hesya HeGa'u . . . appeared among the Legion of *esLi* as a warrior-sage, but betrayed them at the Battle of Tha'era by providing a copy of their battle-plan to Shrnu'u HeGa'u—"

"Tha'era was the battle that destroyed the Legion," Byar said. "It led ultimately to the siege of Sharia'a in *seLi'e'Yan*. Of course." His wings moved to a posture of affirmation.

"Wait . . . Apparently this Hesya also betrayed Shrnu'u by leading him to believe that the inhabitants of Sharia'a could be defeated by an extended siege rather than a direct assault, when an attack might have taken the city. Let's see— When he was discovered to have acted against *esGa'u*, he was imprisoned in *Ur'ta leHssa*, but he escaped by . . ."

She let the sentence trail off and looked out the window at the setting sun. Byar leaned over and glanced at the page.

"He pierced the Icewall," Byar said. "Then *esLi* imprisoned him on the Plane of Sleep."

Jackie had a moment of recognition, remembering her mind-link with Ch'k'te on Cicero—and her words to the High Chamberlain just before her own *Dsen'yen'ch'a*.

Now it was Byar's turn to look away. "The Plane of Sleep," he repeated, almost as if to himself.

"Didn't you just—?"

"Of course," Byar said, making a gesture in the air with one talon, seemingly tracing something. "Of course: the Servant of *esGa'u* who attacked me on the Plane of Sleep. '*Relish your little victory . . .*' it said to me. '*We will claim you in the end . . .*'

"Clearly another servant of *esGa'u* was freed by our actions. *At least* one other. This one may be even *more* dangerous, as he can appear to be a friend, yet he has betrayed both sides in the past."

"'Betrayed both—'" *Stone*, she thought. *Hesya. He's not Shrnu'u at all: He's Hesya, "the One Who Weaves."*

She looked down at the *gyaryu* hanging at her belt: Stone's gift, returning it to her from the Plain of Despite . . . from Center.

"Master Byar," she said, gripping the edge of the desk with her hands, "are you aware of the . . . inhabitants of the *gyaryu*?"

"This is not a subject I should discuss, *se* Jackie—"

"I need your advice, damn it," she interrupted, as his wings rose in a posture of deference and then dropped again. "There's a little bit of the *hsi* of each of the previous holders of the *gyaryu—in* the sword. I can talk to them, ask their advice.

"I have assumed that the oldest *hsi* in the sword belongs to Qu'u himself. But if every person who held the sword left some *hsi* behind, then Hesya is in the sword as well.

"Stone must be in the sword also," she said, perhaps to herself. "The person who would not explain to me why he was there, why he was letting me take the sword . . . Some part of his *hsi* is in here." She touched her hand to the hilt.

"Stone . . . or Hesya HeGa'u," she finished. Outside, the light seemed to fade, as if a cloud had passed in front of the sun.

Byar shivered, remembering another conversation not too long ago.

"And, perhaps, other *esGa'uYal*." She pulled her hand away from the hilt as if afraid it would burn her.

"*se* Jackie." Byar's wings moved to the Posture of Polite Approach. "I . . . do not know the inner secrets of the *gyaryu*, but it seems to me that if it contains the *hsi* of your predecessors . . . this represents a con-siderable force in the service of *esLi*." His wings altered to a position of reverence. "It would be difficult for a servant of *esGa'u*, no matter how strong, to overcome it."

If esLi *has not been corrupted as well,* she thought to herself. "There's only one way to find out, though: to ask Qu'u himself."

The idea of seeing Stone again troubled her. If her assumption was correct, that Hesya was indeed Stone, it would mean that she would be encountering the same mysterious figure in three completely differ-ent contexts—on Center, in a vid almost a century old, and potentially within the *gyaryu*—within just a few weeks.

There was clearly no way backward. There was also no way to go forward without knowing what might be within the *gyaryu*. The imme-diate future depended on her confidence in the sword; she could not function as *Gyaryu'har* if everything that now defined her life turned out to be some sort of deception. Again.

Not that it would be anything new, she thought.

All during the aircar ride from Sanctuary to esYen, Jackie thought about it, letting the debate go back and forth in her mind. Byar accompanied her and concentrated on his own meditations, leaving her alone. It seemed to suit the moment. She tried to keep her thoughts away from the *gyaryu* itself, preferring to keep the sword's inhabitants out of it—in case there were hostiles among them.

By the time they reached the city she had an idea what to do. When they reached the High Lord's garden, she had decided.

The High Chamberlain was conferring with the High Lord when they approached the part of the *esTle'e hi* Sa'a had set aside to receive her ministers. It was not the same place the High Lord's father had chosen for the purpose. It was, however, the first place Jackie had ever seen in the High Nest, when she had stepped out of *anGa'e'ren* a few weeks earlier, near the center of that particular clearing.

T'te'e looked upset. The position of his wings and the tension of his claws indicated that someone—or something—had angered him. As Jackie and Byar approached, he seemed to shrug the emotion away, arranging himself in a more restrained and formal posture.

"*se Gyaryu'har*," he said to her. "Master Byar." His wings were arranged politely.

Byar silently offered a stance of respect to the High Lord and the High Chamberlain.

"*se* T'te'e." Jackie inclined her head.

hi Sa'a gestured to a stepped bench for Jackie, and a slightly lower perch for Byar.

"I take it that your studies were fruitful," the High Lord said.

"I think I know what we should do," Jackie said. "If I'm interrupting—"

"No," Sa'a said. "We were discussing a matter that would interest you, but perhaps we should hear your news first."

"It's rather complicated."

T'te'e's wings rose a bit, perhaps indicating that contradicting a suggestion of a High Lord wasn't quite polite; but again Sa'a defused the situation.

"Very well," she said, her wings conveying some slight amusement. "*se* T'te'e brings us word of a peculiar request from the government of our friend the Solar Emperor." She looked at the High Chamberlain. "*se* T'te'e is not particularly pleased."

"They want the *gyaryu*," he growled, his wings moving to an angry position. "They want you to bring it to them," he said to Jackie.

"They *what?*" Jackie's hand strayed near the hilt for a moment, then she carefully put her hands in her lap.

The High Lord gestured. T'te'e touched a comp on a lectern beside him. A holo appeared in midair. It showed a figure in a neatly tailored suit; a certified logo of the Solar Empire hovered above his left shoulder.

"From His Imperial Majesty Dieter Xavier Willem, Solar Emperor, greetings to the honorable Sa'a HeYen, High Lord of the People, and best wishes for your continued health.

"It has come to the attention of the Imperial Government that our good friend High Lord Sa'a has obtained the return of the sword known as the gyaryu, *a powerful* chya, *and that it has now been settled upon an Imperial subject, one Jacqueline Laperriere, Admiral IN Retired. The Solar Monarch shares in the High Nest's great joy at this happy turn of events coming at a time when both races are in imminent peril.*

"As a result of counsel from trusted advisors, the Solar Emperor suggests that this sword may provide significant assistance to human Sensitives, whose skills are largely inferior to those of our friends among the People. Taking the current holder of the sword as an example, it seems apparent to us that association with the sword confers significant improvement even to those who previously demonstrated little or no Sensitive talent.

"That being the case, it is the opinion of the Government and the Emperor that it would be of greatest benefit if Sensitives—particularly those to be assigned to frontline naval vessels—should have an opportunity to enjoy the benefit of this gyaryu.

"The Government and the Emperor sincerely hope that the High Lord and the High Nest concur in this view, and will aid us in using this sword to help train our Sensitives and prepare them for duty against our common enemy.

"As Admiral Laperriere is an Imperial subject, who has taken both a citizen's and a soldier's oath of loyalty to her Emperor, we are certain that she will obey the request of her Government and the command of her Emperor to report to the Sensitive training facility at New Chicago as soon as possible to commence this process.

"His Imperial Majesty Dieter Xavier Willem wishes to reiterate his friendship and affection for the High Lord, and his pleasure in continuing his Imperial protection for the People."

The holo winked out.

"An interesting proposition," the High Lord said.

Jackie saw T'te'e's talons clench, sitting on his perch.

"Our *Gyaryu'har* is an Imperial citizen and former member of the Navy and is therefore expected to take one of our most important artifacts and place it in the hands of—"

"—*artha,*" the High Chamberlain interjected, and then glanced at Jackie. "Eight thousand pardons," he added, with little sincerity.

"—humans," the High Lord corrected. "*naZora'i.* But I do not understand why they have reached this conclusion. Can you enlighten us, *se* Jackie? Which of the emperor's . . . advisors provided this insight?"

"I'm not sure." She frowned, thinking, repressing the reflex to ask the *gyaryu* for help. "I didn't meet with any human Sensitives while . . . oh.

"M'm'e'e Sha'kan. I discussed the sword with him at Langley, the Imperial Intelligence HQ."

"That is a rashk name," T'te'e said. Zor traditionally did not think much of the rashk, and considered them cowardly and duplicitous. "What did you tell him about the sword?"

"Nothing that would lead him to the conclusion that it could be used to benefit Sensitives . . . We primarily discussed Stone. M'm'e'e had some interesting data, which corroborates other information we had here at the High Nest.

"He knows the legend of Qu'u, I'll give him that; he doesn't seem to discount the beliefs of the People as readily as most humans do. Perhaps M'm'e'e thinks that studying the sword could somehow . . ."

"*. . . the People . . . outside had no desire to destroy Shr'e'a, but rather to learn from its strength . . .*"

The phrase from the old recension of *seLi'e'Yan* jumped into her head unbidden. "No, wait—it's a trap. They . . . *si* S'reth feared something like this." She described the passage, in which Hesya lured Shr'e'a's warriors to allow their sword to be taken outside the walls.

Sa'a nodded, as if she were familiar with the tale.

"*se* Jackie," Byar said, "High Lord. Do you think this rashk knows of this version of the legend? Furthermore, do you think he seeks to follow it? For if so, then *he* . . . might well *be* Hesya, returned from *Ur'ta leHssa.*"

"The *esGa'uYe* told us that many of his brothers walk the Plane of Sleep now. It is possible that Hesya is among them." Sa'a's statement seemed matter-of-fact.

Jackie wasn't sure when it had become so easy to talk about beings of legend as if they were going to arrive on the next shuttle.

"We can't let him have the sword," Jackie said at last. "If *we* represent the Shr'e'a'i, it would be disastrous to trust him with it."

"Even if we do not," T'te'e interjected, "it would be unthinkable."

"There is an additional problem," said Jackie.

"Your studies," Sa'a said. "Please enlighten us."

"I believe that the *gyaryu* is indeed the Sword of Shr'e'a, as described in the original legend of *seLi'e'Yan*."

Sa'a inclined her head, as if this was not news to her, but T'te'e seemed to have set aside his anger and was listening intently.

"If that is so, then it was held by others—likely, numerous others—before it was recovered by Qu'u from the Plain of Despite."

"Some of them must have been *esGa'uYal*. And since each person who carries the sword leaves *hsi* behind, there might well be some sort of—taint? I am afraid that the *gyaryu* may not be trustworthy."

"Is there any way to find out for certain?"

Jackie looked directly at the High Lord, whose wings conveyed no insight into her thoughts on the subject.

"Yes," Jackie answered at last. "We can inquire directly."

I⅁ ⱳas clear that the High Lord was in no mood to be gainsaid. Jackie saw something pass between Sa'a and Byar: It was no more than a glance and a rapid cascade of wing-gestures. *se* T'te'e had said his piece and now he was standing at guard, his *chya* at the ready. His wings were again held in an angry, defiant stance.

"When *hi* Sa'a chose to fly the perilous path into the Plane of Sleep," he said to Jackie, "I stood guard while *se* Byar accompanied our High Lord there. *se* Byar knew without being told, but you are . . . new to the High Nest. "I do not seek to touch your honor, but I promise by my own, that nothing will protect you if you return without her *hsi*."

Jackie looked from T'te'e to Byar, whose posture was almost as defiant as the High Chamberlain's. She could offer no promises, make no guarantees about the High Lord's safety.

She nodded. "Very well," Jackie said. "I understand."

"I am ready," Sa'a said. She took up a position on a perch behind a high-backed chair; Jackie sat on the chair, which conformed to her back.

With the *gyaryu* in her lap and her hands upon the scabbard, Jackie closed her eyes and imagined the black plain, covered with *hRni'i* . . .

Afew moments or hours later—there was no way to tell—she opened her eyes again to find herself sitting on the plain. The High Lord stood behind her, her eyes still closed, her wings wrapped around her like a cloak.

"*hi* Sa'a," Jackie said, getting to her feet.

The High Lord opened her eyes and she could not help but gasp. "The *gyaryu*," she said. "We are within the *gyaryu*."

Jackie did not answer, but brought the sword to a one-handed guard. She gestured toward the distant light and the two began to approach.

Sa'a could not maintain her usual composure, but conveyed expressions of surprise and wonder with every step. She saw Sergei and Admiral Marais first. As more and more inhabitants of the *gyaryu* approached, it was apparent to Jackie that the High Lord knew a great many of them.

"No High Lord has ever seen this," Sa'a said quietly, her wings forming a position of reverence to *esLi*. "I hope that I have not touched your honor by insisting on accompanying you."

Jackie stopped her progress toward the lit entrance to the garden, now plainly visible. "*hi* Sa'a." She turned to face the High Lord, who had gotten a step or two ahead of her. "You have not touched my honor: rather, you honor *me* by accompanying me.

"I may have faced the *esGa'uYal* and walked through *anGa'e'ren*, but this place still scares me. Every time I visit here—and it's not too often—I worry that there might be something I don't know, don't understand." She gestured into the darkness above them. "As for this visit, I can't even imagine what might be before us."

Sa'a seemed to relax just a bit; though, at the reference to the dark, she let her hand come to rest on the *hi'chya* she wore.

"What is before us now?" She pointed to the entrance to the garden.

They stepped through the entrance. A warrior of the People walked toward them, his wings held in a position of pride.

"*si* Qu'u," Jackie said. She gestured to Sa'a. "This is the High Lord of the People, *hi* Sa'a."

Qu'u bowed to the High Lord. "Be welcome, great Lord," he said. "You are not the *Gyaryu'har*, yet for you to come here must indicate some great peril to the People."

"I would not endanger my Inner Peace otherwise," she answered. "I am greatly honored to meet the great hero of the People."

"I thank the High Lord for her kindness."

Before either could insert yet another profession of honor or gratitude, Jackie said, "Great Qu'u. High Lord. We are here to learn an important truth."

"I await your question," Qu'u said.

"We have studied the many versions of the legend that surrounds your deeds," Jackie said. "In the story, there is an indication that the *gyaryu*, the sword on which we now stand, was recovered from the Plain of Despite."

"That is true."

"Wait. Before you answer, let me clarify," Jackie interjected. "In the story common in our time, it is not the sword that is recovered, but rather that which will be *reforged* into the sword. In other words, the *gyaryu* is not . . . well, it's not the *gyaryu* until it is returned to the World That Is.

"Yet an earlier version claims the opposite: that the *gyaryu* itself is recovered. There is evidence to support that the sword was held at one time by Despite, when it was taken in a ruse by a pair of brothers—"

"Sharnu and Hesya," Qu'u said.

Jackie and Sa'a exchanged a glance.

"It was decided," Qu'u began, "that the *gyaryu* could not be seen to be tainted by Despite. The Lord *esLi*"—his wings moved to a posture of respect—"had chosen me to go to the lands of the Deceiver to recover the sword. The two brothers—He of the Dancing Blade, and the One Who Weaves—took it from Shr'e'a, as the legend tells."

"The old legend."

"—Yes. The *old* legend. The High Lord A'alu knew that if there were any doubt about the *gyaryu*, the Nests could not be united. Therefore, she caused the legends to be changed."

"What about Dri'i? Why was he added to the story?"

"It was a logical part of the revised legend, *se Gyaryu'har*. A warrior of the People using a known talent to stand within the Circle."

"Then the Shield of Hatred was known in your time."

"Yes, *se Gyaryu'har*. It was much practiced in the time of the Warring States. It was a way for warriors of the People to understand how warriors of Sharia'a could have resisted the Army of Sunset."

"So Shr'e'a did fall."

"There is no account of that event, *se Gyaryu'har*. It is not the tale the Sharia'a'i tell."

"Yet it fell."

"It fell," Qu'u said at last. His wings dropped to a position of sorrow. "The warriors of Shr'e'a let their Sword be taken through the gate and . . . when it was taken away, they surrendered.

"This is not the story that *hi'i* A'alu wished as the guide for the Flight of the People."

Jackie looked away from Qu'u and at the High Lord, who stood impassively, waiting for her to continue. Sa'a seemed to have expected this admission from Qu'u.

"I have one more question, *si* Qu'u," said Jackie. "If this is indeed the Sword of Shr'e'a, and if every person who holds the *gyaryu* leaves *hsi* behind, then when Hesya took the Sword from Shr'e'a, he must have held it. He must be *here*."

"He is." Qu'u turned away and beckoned for them to follow. Jackie and Sa'a were only a step behind as they made their way through the garden.

Jackie had never been to the other side of Qu'u's post within the *gyaryu*. In fact, she had only come to the garden once, when she had first held the sword. The garden was roughly circular, with an entrance on either side; one led onto the black plain from which they had come. She didn't know where the other one led.

As Qu'u approached, all she could see was darkness, as if there were *another* black plain beyond. Standing before the entrance, Qu'u turned to face them once again.

"Those who held the sword before I recovered it from the Plain of Despite are beyond this point," he said. "They cannot emerge from here and cannot communicate with the holder of the *gyaryu*."

"You guard the entrance," Sa'a said matter-of-factly.

"It would be sensible," Qu'u answered. "I would willingly defend the *gyaryu* against those beyond"—he shrugged toward the darkness— "but that is given to a power far greater than myself."

"Meaning—?"

"The Lord *esLi* defends us.

"Neither *ra* Hesya, nor any other Servant of Despite, can reach beyond the barrier of Light."

He stepped aside and Jackie leaned forward to glance into the darkness . . . and beyond, cascading through the black *anGa'e'ren*, was a luminous band of light divided into six colors, ranging from a deep violet to a bright crimson.

chapter 20

THE ART OF WAR TEACHES US TO RELY NOT ON THE LIKELI-
HOOD OF THE ENEMY'S NOT COMING, BUT ON OUR OWN
READINESS TO RECEIVE HIM; NOT ON THE CHANCE OF HIS
NOT ATTACKING, BUT RATHER ON THE FACT THAT WE HAVE
MADE OUR POSITION UNASSAILABLE.

—Sun Tzu,
The Art of War, VIII:11

Josephson System was fifteen parsecs closer to the captured naval base
of Adrianople than the heavily defended base at Denneva. From
Josephson it was an easy jump to a dozen well-populated Class One
worlds within the Empire, Denneva among them. From Adrianople
these worlds were mostly inaccessible.

It made sense for the enemy to try for Josephson; it made sense for
the Imperial Navy to defend it. Accordingly, Admiral Hsien had deployed the most experienced elements of the Imperial fleet there, while
Admiral Stark's flag moved to Denneva to defend the base.

Against the luminous backdrop of the Milky Way and the distant
double-suns of Josephson System, the gig moved quickly toward its

destination: a berth in the shuttle bay of the fleet carrier *Duc d'Enghien*. The carrier was equipped—and plenty big enough—for *Fair Damsel* to dock directly, but Dan McReynolds had decided that he'd prefer to stay in his own mooring with the other merchanters attached to His Majesty's Fleet.

The *Duc* had accordingly sent the gig out to fetch its single passenger. Jackie had again decided to forgo an entourage, despite Dan's protests (which didn't seem terribly sincere, in any case); there would be enough of that when she reached *Duc* anyway.

She could have attended this briefing by holo, but it provided an opportunity for Jackie to see Barbara MacEwan in person—something she hadn't done since the retreat from Cicero. They'd made their ways from the zor Core to Josephson by separate routes.

As the little vessel approached its mothership, Jackie was impressed—as always—with the dimensions of the fleet carrier. It measured nearly a kilometer in length, and almost half that in beam width, with appendages making it wider still. With no need to be aerodynamic it most resembled a sort of ungainly octopus with an elongated, flattened cylinder constituting its main bulk, and arms stretching out in six directions to hold the launch and landing-clusters for its fighter craft.

Between the arms, the carrier had huge, almost translucent networks of thin fiber cables—*Duc*'s sensor net, linked directly to the huge 3-V display on the carrier's flight bridge. At the angle from which Jackie's gig approached, two of the nets seemed to be on fire, with the reflected sunlight caught and multiplied by the cables, making the carrier appear to be an enormous, ungainly phoenix. The filters on the gig's forward screen fought to stay polarized against the glare.

The short trip complete, the gig set down in a perfect landing on the main hangar deck. While she waited for the airlock to pressurize, Jackie could see that Barbara MacEwan had turned out pipers, officers in full dress and seventeen sideboys, as befit her rank.

I'm going to hate this, she thought. *And Barbara is loving it.*

It did seem as if Barbara MacEwan, captain of the *Duc d'Enghien*, could hardly restrain her amusement as the band struck up a frightening bagpipe approximation of a zor state anthem as Jackie descended to the deck. Barbara and her senior officers delivered perfect salutes, which Jackie returned.

"Permission to come aboard, Captain," Jackie said.

"Permission granted, Admiral." Unable now to restrain her smile, Barbara took Jackie's proffered hand in both of hers. "I know," she added quietly, "that there's *another* title now, but I wanted the chance to call you 'Admiral.' Glad to see you in person, ma'am."

"Glad to be here. Admiral Hsien is aboard, I assume."

"He came over from *Gibraltar* a few hours ago." Barbara looked down the row of officers, still at attention. "Only *fifteen* sideboys for old Hsien," she added, with another grin. "You outrank him."

"You're enjoying this," Jackie said between her teeth, as they turned to inspect the waiting crew.

"Damn right," Barbara answered in the same, low-pitched voice. "Admiral, permit me to introduce my officers. My exec, Commander Ray Santos." She indicated the officer to her immediate left, whom Jackie knew well. They exchanged salutes and a handshake.

"Commander Van Micic, my new wing-coordinator." Jackie took the hand of a tall, thin man, obviously a Service veteran; his hair was thin and light on top, and his face had gone craggy. "Karen Schaumburg made captain and was posted to *Montgomery* after Thon's Well," Barbara added, explaining the change in command.

"Honored," Van Micic said to Jackie. "I've heard much about you, Admiral, and have looked forward to meeting you."

"Thank you," Jackie replied. "—I suppose." She looked at Barbara, whose face remained impassive, with a sort of *Who, me?* expression.

"My wing-commanders." Barbara introduced six junior officers, including two of the People. They arranged their wings in the Posture of Polite Approach and each took a rapid glance at the *gyaryu* as they offered textbook salutes. Jackie made a polite greeting in the High-speech, which caused Barbara to raise an eyebrow.

Jackie could see Owen Garrett in the formation among the staff for *Duc*'s Green Squadron; they made eye contact for a moment and then Garrett looked away. Barbara didn't introduce him.

The captain of *Duc d'Enghien* took Jackie through half a dozen more introductions and then dismissed the honor guard, the bagpipers and the junior officers. In the company of Ray Santos and Van Micic, the *Gyaryu'har* and *Duc*'s captain made their way to the lift.

"All right," Jackie said, when they were on their way to the bridge. "Tell me what you said to Admiral Hsien."

"What do you mean?"

"Out with it, Thane." Jackie noticed a faint smile from the two other officers and a wince from Barbara when she used the nickname. "He told me himself that some officer"—Jackie smiled, remembering the exchange with Admiral Hsien—"told him off. I assumed that it was you, and told him so. He confirmed."

"Oh, *that.*"

"That."

"He had just finished blaming you for doing what you did at Cicero—not trying to fight the enemy. He wanted to know how we should fight them at Adrianople, which, by the way, had already been taken by the time he was asking me this question—"

"—Anyway . . ." Jackie interrupted.

"*Anyway,* he tried to disparage your choice of tactic and I told him that if it hadn't been for you, we'd all be dead. Or worse." She and Ray exchanged a glance. "I was polite."

" 'If the admiral pleases.' He particularly liked that," said Jackie.

"I *told* you I was polite," Barbara repeated. The two other officers chuckled and Barbara turned her head to glare at them, reducing the chuckles to throat-clearing noises.

Before the captain of *Duc d'Enghien* could snap out a reply, the lift doors parted.

"Captain on the bridge," said the Officer of the Watch, standing at his station.

"At ease," Barbara said, walking across the flight bridge. "Don," she said to the comm officer, "please offer Admiral Hsien my compliments and ask him to meet us in my briefing-room at his convenience."

Admiral Hsien arrived a few minutes after Jackie, which left her a brief chance to evaluate the situation. While Barbara MacEwan worked at a comp preparing for the coming briefing, Jackie exchanged pleasantries with two others: a human Sensitive named Howe, and one of the zor wing-commanders, Gyes'ru HeKa'an. Gyes'ru—a polite, young warrior of the People obviously in awe of the *Gyaryu'har* (or the sword itself; she couldn't tell which)—had Sensitive talent as well, and had been included in this meeting so that the fighter wings could be briefed.

As for Howe—Jackie forgot his first name as soon as he had muttered it—there seemed to be little respect between him and Jackie, from the moment they met. The human Sensitive was a civilian, quite ill-at-ease in a military setting, though he had apparently been aboard *Duc d'Enghien* for a few months already; he was unwilling to meet anyone's eye and would not even touch Jackie's outstretched hand. His thoughts were well shielded but with the *gyaryu* close by, Jackie could almost feel his disdain: though whether it was for her, for the zor, or for the military in general, she couldn't tell. She looked at Gyes'ru HeKa'an for some indication and he placed his wings in a posture usually reserved for when an adult must be patient with a child.

Without wings, Jackie could not offer a comment of her own, so she merely nodded.

When the admiral arrived, everyone came to attention. Jackie realized, as she offered a salute, that it wasn't necessary for her to do so anymore, but decided it didn't matter. Hsien indicated with a gesture that everyone should sit, and he took his place at the head of the table.

"Thank you for coming so promptly, *se Gyaryu'har*," he said to Jackie. "Captain MacEwan, please patch in the other commanders."

Barbara nodded and touched the comp. The far wall dimmed and became a holo-image of a large conference table; there were a few dozen people sitting there, mostly human, but with two or three zor among them. Jackie recognized several commanders, including Sheng Di of *Sheng Long* (one privilege of coming from a shipbuilding family, she thought: *your name gets into everything*); Erich Anderson of *Emperor Ian*, the ship of class, descendant of the famous Admiral Anderson; and Sean Van Meter, Hsien's senior commodore. Each was sitting in a ready-room similar to the one aboard *Duc*. Hsien held out his hand in an *As you were* gesture, as a few of the younger officers made to stand and offer a salute.

"Captains," Hsien began. "Permit me to introduce the *Gyaryu'har* of the High Nest to those who do not know her: Ms. Jacqueline Laperriere, Imperial Navy Admiral, Retired." He smiled slightly, more wistful than amused. "With permission from the High Nest, she will be traveling with this fleet for the time being.

"We have received orders from the Admiralty to ascertain and, if possible, counter the enemy's next move. As you can see from the display—"

Barbara pressed another key; a 3-V stellar map appeared at their end of the table. From the expressions of the holo-images, the other captains were examining the same map on their own ships.

"—the enemy has made several incursions into Imperial space during the past four Standard months, beginning with the first contact at Cicero in October of last year.

"Intelligence reports detail the outcomes of these attacks: When there have been survivors . . ." He let his voice trail off for a moment and then continued: "When there have been survivors," he repeated, "they have reported devastating Sensitive attacks. In only one case have the enemy vessels been completely destroyed: at Thon's Well, approximately one Standard month ago, when the High Nest's fleet flagship *Nest He Yen* was also destroyed."

The zor present placed their wings in a posture of reverence to *esLi*. A few of the human officers noticed, though they likely didn't understand it. Admiral Hsien may have suspected the meaning of the gesture, however, and he paused for a moment before continuing.

"We cannot afford to lose battles in the ways we have done, and we cannot afford to *win* battles the way we did at Thon's Well. First Lord Alvarez wants another solution. We believe that the enemy will strike here at Josephson System, with the intention of using it as a jumping-off point for further invasion of the Solar Empire. If it were taken, Denneva would be vulnerable to attack from short-range jump. We have therefore deployed here, and will remain until intel indicates that the enemy has changed focus . . . or until it attacks here. We have no way of being sure, but comp projections and . . . other indications—"

Such as the High Lord's dreams, Jackie thought to herself.

"—assign a high probability to the likelihood of a battle here in Josephson System in the near future. There is no way to know for sure.

"What we do know, however, is *this:* At Adrianople, the combined effort of zor and human Sensitives was able to interfere with the enemy's ability to control minds—sufficiently well for my command to escape. We also know from the battle at Thon's Well that modulating the harmonics of starship defensive fields affects them.

"Accordingly, each of you has had an additional Sensitive assigned to your crew along with an engineer to work on your field projection equipment. I expect that these individuals have been accommodated within each reporting structure in conformance to my orders.

"If we can rely on some protection from the most dangerous aspects of this enemy strength—and I allow that this is a big 'if'—then we can concentrate on tactical solutions.

"Captain Vorwoerd," he concluded, "I believe you have prepared a study for us to examine."

One of the holo-images stood and began to speak. The star map was replaced by a depiction of one of the vuhl hive-ships: huge and irregularly shaped, with numerous glyphs indicating identified weapons systems.

se Jackie, she heard in her mind, from the *gyaryu.* It was Sergei's voice. It must have startled her because Captain Vorwoerd hesitated, and Barbara looked at her, surprised. Jackie shrugged. Vorwoerd's report continued.

You don't usually start conversations, she said silently.

We only respond to external stimuli. Someone attempted to probe the gyaryu.

Human or alien? She was suddenly alert, her hand near the hilt of the sword. Even knowing that there might be *esGa'uYal* hidden in the *gyaryu,* she had to rely on Sergei and the others to protect her from them.

Human.

She looked around the table. The Sensitive, Howe, was studiously looking away and listening to the briefing, but she could feel the slightest bit of tension from him.

Are you in danger? Is he—

He is an amateur, Sergei answered. *He may sense power from the* gyaryu *but has no idea what it really is.*

Suggestions?

Show him.

How?

Allow me, said Sergei's voice. She thought a moment and nodded slightly. She felt something from the *gyaryu,* like a sort of soft, nearly inaudible humming. She heard a faint rustle from Gyes'ru's wings—he'd felt it, too.

She watched Howe's eyes drift closed. It went unnoticed, or at least unremarked upon. A corner of his mouth twitched once, twice.

Then his eyes flew wide-open. His nostrils flared. He seemed to look long and hard at his hands, which had clenched tightly before him: When he opened them, it was obvious his nails had dug deeply into his palms, enough to draw blood. He turned his gaze at Jackie, fixing her with a look of . . . fear? anger?

Barbara MacEwan, sitting to Howe's right, turned away from the holo, alarmed, ready to say something—

"Mr. Howe," Admiral Hsien said, holding up a hand to stop

the briefing. None of the remote attendees had seen anything.

The Sensitive didn't answer and didn't look away from Jackie.

"*Mr. Howe*," Hsien repeated, with far more asperity this time. "Is something wrong?"

Is Howe an esGa'uYe? Jackie asked the *gyaryu*.

Certainly not.

"Mr. Howe!" Admiral Hsien said yet again, almost shouting. At last, the Sensitive looked away from Jackie to rest his glance on the admiral.

"Sir."

"Is something wrong?"

"No sir," he said, carefully folding his hands in front of him. "No, Admiral. Nothing is wrong." He looked back at Jackie, and then away as she met his glance evenly.

"Continue, Captain Vorwoerd," the admiral said, annoyance in his voice.

What did you do? Jackie asked the *gyaryu*.

Simply showed him what he would be fighting. He was unconvinced that the enemy was worthy of his attention. He understands now, though he may bear some ill-will toward you. Our apologies, se Jackie.

I can handle it, she answered.

At the end of the briefing, the human Sensitive appeared to be interested in making his escape as quickly as possible but was cornered by Admiral Hsien. Jackie would have liked to speak to him directly, but she was intercepted by a staff officer who had entered the ready-room.

"Admiral Laperriere?" the officer asked, though it must have been obvious. "I'm Laura Ibarra. Lieutenant-Commander Ibarra, *Duc*'s intelligence officer."

"How can I help you, Commander?"

"I . . . received a directive from Langley, ma'am. I understand that you have been assigned to the fleet to assist the training of our Sensitives." She cast a disparaging glance toward Howe, who was not having a comfortable time of it with Admiral Hsien.

" 'Training'?"

"Why, yes. I admit that I do not know the particulars, merely that it has something to do with . . ." She gestured casually toward the *gyaryu*. "You might be able to provide our special attachés with skills they will need."

"I am not a teacher," Jackie said carefully. "And the *gyaryu* is not a teaching tool. It is—"

"It is a device capable of imparting Sensitive skill to someone who never had it before," Ibarra interrupted. "It also imparts extensive knowledge to anyone who holds it, so I understand. Surely," she added, lowering her voice, "as a loyal subject of the Solar Emperor—"

"So *that's* what this is about. Yes, Commander, now I understand where this is going.

"Please present my compliments to Director M'm'e'e Sha'kan, and tell him I'll have no part of this. The *gyaryu* belongs to the High Nest, and remains in its scabbard on my belt. Tell him—" She stepped past the intelligence officer, who took a few steps backward. "Tell him that Hesya won't get hold of the Sword of Shr'e'a again."

"I don't understand," Ibarra said, to Jackie's retreating back.

"I'm sure M'm'e'e Sha'kan will."

Ships continued to arrive at Josephson System. On the bridge of the *Fair Damsel,* the holo display showed them maneuvering toward space-moorings; Jackie sat in one of the engineering stations and watched the colored icons dance.

She was unsettled. It didn't take a Sensitive to notice, and it had become even more pronounced after she returned from the briefing aboard *Duc d'Enghien.* Most of *Damsel's* crew seemed to be giving her a wide berth. Naturally, this didn't apply to its captain.

"Pretty nice," Dan said, gesturing toward the display as he came onto the bridge. "Georg Maartens got this installed for us. State-of-the-art deep-radar, just like on the ships of the line.

"Too bad they couldn't give us some firepower to go with it." He dropped into the pilot's chair. "On the other hand," he added, leaning his chin on his palm and his elbow on the arm of the chair, "if we had lots of gunnery, they'd put us on the damn front line."

Jackie didn't answer. Pyotr Ngo, working on an opened command panel on the other side of the bridge, scowled across at Dan, and then returned his attention to his work.

"What's up, Jay? You haven't said ten words since you came back from the carrier."

"I don't know. Something's happening but I can't quite figure out what it is. I think we're in the middle of another legend . . . but I don't like how this one comes out, either. What's more, I'm not alone this time: Garrett's wrapped up in this, as well—he's being used just like I am."

She leaned back in the chair and rubbed her forehead. "I'm also not completely sure I trust this," she added, touching the hilt of the *gyaryu*.

"Don't *trust* it? Isn't it Excalibur or something? How can you *not* trust it?"

"It's hard to explain. All along, I feel like I've been pushed from one event to another. There's no control at all: I want to take a stand, make a decision, do *something* that wasn't ordained by some damn legend written eight thousand years ago.

"But it's not working out that way. I got led all the way to Center; it cost me one of my best friends. I took on this job"—she patted the hilt of the *gyaryu*—"and now I learn that the same group that manipulated the war between zor and humans eighty-five years ago is manipulating this war as well. They may have even screwed with the sword itself.

"What the hell do they want? What's this all about? Where am I being led, and the rest of you, the rest of *them*"—she gestured toward the holo—"along with me?"

"You want an answer to that?"

"No. I don't know what I want." She stood up and walked off the bridge, and Dan watched her go, letting the pilot's chair slowly turn, following his gaze.

"You know—" Pyotr began, but Dan held up his hand.

"Yeah. I know," Dan said.

Laura Ibarra leaned back in her chair and rubbed her eyes with the heels of her hands. The chair responded to the pressure, gently reclining and adjusting to her new position.

"Enable AI one-seven," she said to the air. A holo blurred into view on the desk before her, twelve centimeters high: a grayish green lizard with four arms, dressed in a bright-fuchsia bathrobe.

"Ready for input," it said.

"All right. Let's start again." Laura sat forward, shaking her head slightly as if to clear it. "Analyze audio clip six-four-seven, starting with time mark two-zero-zero."

There was a slight pause. *"Do you wish to hear the clip?"* Laura had modified the artificial intelligence almost immediately after she'd installed it, forcing Standard speech patterns over the standard rashk ones; it was hard enough to deal with her superior's verbal skills in person—she wasn't going to put up with it in software.

For a few seconds' delay, it was worth it.

"Proceed."

" ' . . . —*scabbard on my belt. Tell him— Tell him that Hesya won't get hold of the Sword of Shr'e'a again.*' "

" '*I don't understand.*' " Laura's own voice.

" '*I'm sure M'm'e'e Sha'kan will*' "—softer now, and footsteps as Laperriere walked away.

" '*Commander, a w*—' " The voice of that annoying Sensitive, Howe. Laura cut it off with a word to the computer.

"Analyze content and meaning. Again," she added wearily.

"*Use cached analysis?*" asked the holo, its arm movements mimicking M'm'c'c Sha'kan's.

"Will the new results be any different?"

Another pause. "*According to existing configuration, the following parameters are considered: Transmissions; none received since last analysis. Database queries one-six, one-seven, one-eight complete: One-six yielded one result; one-seven and one-eight yielded no results. Other queries incomplete.*

"*Use cached analysis?*" the AI repeated.

"Display results of successful query," Laura said.

A holo appeared above and to the left of the little rashk-image. It showed four lines of zor-script, with the margin symbols indicating wing-positions.

The annotations had been provided by Imperial Intelligence; subtle shades of meaning were sufficient for a zor reader. A translation of the text in Standard appeared below it.

ACROSS THE SPINE OF SHAR'TU
I WILL HUNT-YOU   [Warrior at Guard]
BEYOND THE CLOUD-CAPPED PEAKS OF GAM'E'YAN   [Honor to *esLi*]
I WILL HUNT YOU

YOU SHALL NOT HIDE FROM ME   [Guarded Approach]
AMONG THE BONE-SHEATHED TOWERS OF SHR'E'A
OR WITHIN ITS BLOOD-SOAKED RUINS

                                            [Talon of Warding
                                            against *esGa'u*]

BETRAYED LONG AGO.

"Cheery. 'Bone-sheathed towers.' 'Blood-soaked ruins.'"

"*Contradiction, unless sarcasm was intended,*" the AI interjected. Rashk AIs—like rashk—had only a vestigial sense of humor.

"This is the only reference to Shr'e'a in the database?"

"*Correct. However, there are numerous references to a close-match name: 'Sharia'a,' the name of a prominent fortress city on the zor home-world.*"

"Probability that they are the same?"

A brief pause. "*Ninety-four percent. This fragment appears in simi-lar form, with different meaning, in a later recension. This version con-tains the form 'Sharia'a.' An etymological analysis reinforces the similarity.*"

"Display the later version."

YOU SHALL NOT HIDE FROM ME   [Guarded Approach]
IN THE SHADOW OF THE BONE-SHEATHED TOWERS
OF MIGHTY SHARIA'A
VICTORIOUS LONG AGO.   [Honor to *esLi*]

"The meaning is *completely different*. Are these from the same story?" Laura asked.

"*The probability is ninety-one percent that the two fragments are different versions of the same work.*"

"Someone *rewrote* an epic poem and completely changed its mean-ing? When?"

The holo displayed dates for the two poem fragments. Converted from zor reckoning and year measurement, they were roughly twenty Standard years apart. Both dates were thousands of years ago.

"Correlate these dates with zor historical events."

"*. . . Six Standard years following the date of the first fragment is the accepted date of the Treaty of A'sakan, establishing e'Yen as the High Nest HeYen. Eight years foll—*"

"Stop. The first text is pre-Unification and the second is post-Unification?"

"*Correct.*"

"Search for evidence of similar reworking of zor epics around this time, with particular reference to the name Sharia'a."

"*Time to complete, estimated at twenty-three seconds.*" The AI's arms moved rhythmically as the seconds ticked off, and Laura consid-ered the possible consequences.

At last the hands stopped moving and the AI spoke. *"There is no evidence in the database of revision of other legends prior to zor Unification. The accepted version of seLi'e'Yan is believed to be based on an actual event that took place during the wars of Unification."*

"Summarize."

"The fortress of Sharia'a was renowned for its warriors. During a particular period, the sorcerer Shrnu'u HeGa'u, a traditional enemy of the zor hero Qu'u"—references appeared above the AI image, listing informational pointers on the Qu'u legend, on which Laura had already been briefed—*"attempted to lure the defenders of Sharia'a outside of their impregnable walls, and worked 'magics' on them to destroy their morale. After they were roused to anger by a young warrior named Dri'i, the warriors of Sharia'a stood against Shrnu'u HeGa'u. They had to—as the epic puts it—'Stand Within the Circle' while the lands beyond their walls were laid waste. Ultimately, the warriors of Sharia'a were able to emerge and help the forces of Light at a crucial point in the war, helping assure its victory."*

Laura stood up and took a turn around the cabin, thinking about what this might mean.

"What is the significance of this epic to the zor culture? Is it held in as high esteem as the Qu'u legend?"

"Insufficient data to determine relative esteem," the AI replied, waving its lower, and then upper, arms in some pattern that no doubt meant something to a rashk. *"seLi'e'Yan is, however, cited as a pattern for warrior behavior. Dri'i is often cited as a model for a guard against rashness in the face of provocation. seLi'e'Yan is a standard part of the zor literary canon."*

"But there is evidence that the story on which it is based had a completely different outcome—and someone changed it."

"Correct."

She bit her thumb, thinking. "Play back audio clip six-four-seven, beginning at time mark . . . two-zero-six, and ending four seconds later."

" ' . . . my belt. Tell him— Tell him that Hesya won't get hold of the Sword of Shr'e'a again,' " came Jackie Laperriere's voice, followed by a single footstep. Then the clip cut off.

"Shr'e'a," Laura said to herself. "Not Sharia'a. Definitely *Shr'e'a*. And we can only find one reference to it; and nothing at all about Hesya, whoever he—or she—is . . . Proceed with analysis of content and meaning."

"Use cached analysis?" the AI repeated.

"No. Recompute based on query results."

"Supposition," said the AI, moving its arms in an undulating pattern—upper arms, then lower, then upper again. *"Admiral Laperriere believes that an enemy—identity unknown to the Agency but known to her—seeks to gain possession of her sword. The term 'Sword of Shr'e'a' is in excess of ninety-percent likelihood to allude to the* gyaryu.

"Further, it is likely that the enemy is either associated with the Imperial fleet, the Agency, or the Solar Empire itself. This predicate is determined from verbal tone and visual clues including defensiveness and anger, and corresponds with Admiral Laperriere's refusal to cooperate with requests for assistance with Sensitive training."

"She thinks that the Agency, or someone within it, is this 'Hesya.' Probably M'm'e'e Sha'kan."

"Likelihood eighty-three percent."

Laura dropped into her chair, letting that sink in: Laperriere considered M'm'e'e—or perhaps the Agency—the enemy?

There was an enemy, all right. It was *out there,* crashing into Imperial space: It had kilometers-long ships and could manipulate minds. The enemy was the one that Laperriere herself had found, somehow, when they'd tried to take Cicero.

Something had happened to Laperriere, even since she'd visited M'm'e'e Sha'kan at Langley. M'm'e'e believed—correctly—that Jackie was following a path set out in a zor epic, but this path had evidently moved beyond *The Legend of Qu'u.* She'd been briefed on Qu'u, but was out to sea on this one.

Perhaps M'm'e'e could sort this out.

"Save analysis," Laura said. "End program."

"I'm sure M'm'e'e Sha'kan will," Laperriere had said, when Laura had told her she didn't understand.

If the *Gyaryu'har* of the zor High Nest thought of her own race as the enemy, M'm'e'e had better damn well know what it was about.

chapter 21

T'te'e HeYen flew at top speed in response to the mental shout that had awoken him from a sound sleep. He heeded neither the branches that tore at his wings nor the courtiers and officials that crossed his path or could not get out of it.

He arrived breathless with a claw near his *chya* in the High Lord's garden. Sa'a stood with her eyes wide, the *hi'chya* held out in front of her. She seemed to have just mastered herself, as her own claws were slowly and gradually relaxing their grip on the sword.

She turned to face T'te'e as he settled into the Posture of Polite Approach.

"No doubt I have awoken every Sensitive in the High Nest. Even the ones on other worlds," the High Lord said, after a moment. "Eight thousand pardons to you," she added, inclining her wings slightly; she was disturbed, but her wings held the slightest bit of amusement.

"There is some . . . unease," he replied.

"I can well imagine. I assume you felt it as well."

"I feel the coming of the *esGa'uYal*. Perhaps not as clearly as you do, *hi* Sa'a."

"You should thank the Lord *esLi* that you did not." She sheathed the *hi'chya* and walked slowly to a table. With great care she poured a small goblet of *h'geRu* and turned slightly with a gesture, inviting

T'te'e to join her. "The enemy is coming to where the fleet is located: I could sense it, like a great black wave striking a shore.

"But that is only part of it," Sa'a continued, sipping the blue liquid. "I felt Shrnu'u HeGa'u as well."

"He is with the enemy fleet?"

"That alone would be cause for concern, but would not . . . would not frighten me as my dreaming did. Shrnu'u HeGa'u is already among our own forces and has been there for some time. He is very close to his ancient enemy . . . to the *Qu'u Yar*."

"To *se* Jackie?" T'te'e asked. "She must know this, from the *gyaryu*, unless—"

"Unless the *gyaryu* can no longer be trusted," Sa'a said, finishing the thought.

T'te'e walked to the table and took up the other glass of liquor. The idea chilled him, but he kept his wings impassive, waiting for the High Lord to continue.

"*si* Qu'u"—she raised her wings in homage to *esLi*—"told us that the servants of Despite who had held the *gyaryu*, were not able to interfere. There was a ribbon of colored light that he attributed to *esLi*."

"*se* Jackie walked from the Fortress of Despite to this garden on such a ribbon when she recovered the *gyaryu*, and *se* Owen used a similar path to escape from the aliens' ship. The *Gyaryu'har* does not attribute this path to *esLi*, but rather . . ."

The High Chamberlain seemed unwilling to finish the thought. Instead, he placed his wings in a posture of reverence to *esLi* and continued: "Mighty Qu'u within the sword is no more than a *hsi*-projection—he cannot know what has happened to the sword since he transcended the Outer Peace."

"We have permitted this, *se* T'te'e." Sa'a tasted her *h'geRu*, looking at him across the goblet. "We have permitted *se* Jackie to fly this path, to enter this trap. The High Nest even summoned *si* Qu'u's ancient enemy back to the World That Is."

"We chose this flight many turns ago, High Lord. We chose it long before *se* Jackie herself was chosen by *esLi* to fight this battle."

"If she is not on guard, Shrnu'u HeGa'u can destroy her. And there are other enemies that will distract her."

"*se* Jackie is always on guard, *hi* Sa'a." He placed his wings in a posture of respect. "She will be aware that Shrnu'u HeGa'u is near—and I pray to *esLi* that she will be ready for him."

•   •   •

The vessels jumping into Josephson System registered on dozens of deep-radar sensors at once. Five hive-ships, each nearly three kilometers long, and dozens of outriders and lesser vessels, had materialized near the edge of the solar volume and were moving at more than a quarter of light-speed into the gravity well. The assembled fleet that opposed it had in excess of thirty ships of the line, along with two fleet carriers—many of them veterans of the recent actions at Thon's Well and Adrianople, along with a few survivors of Cicero.

Admiral Hsien had arranged his elements into three squadrons. The first was a strong force on the Orionward side of the system, where any enemy was expected to appear; this group included eight frontline vessels and a screening force of four lesser ships (including *Pappenheim*) with the squadron flag aboard the starship *Sheng Long*, less than two years out of the New China yards.

The second, stationed near the system's gas giant, was approximately the same size, and was supported by the fleet carrier *Xian Chuan*. The squadron flag sailed with the starship *Emperor Ian*, commanded by Commodore Erich Anderson. *Fair Damsel* and other screening elements were attached to this force, as well as Admiral Hsien's flagship, *Gibraltar*.

The third was placed in the fourth orbital to defend an attack against the inhabited planet. Hsien's senior commodore, Sean Van Meter, commanded a somewhat smaller force, from the bridge of *Canberra*, a ship that had seen every major battle of the war other than Cicero.

As soon as the aliens materialized at the jump point, Hsien ordered his first squadron to intercept it. Ship-comms called all Sensitives to their ships' bridges and brought defensive-field modulations online.

Though she could not know it, the image that came to Jackie as the ships hurtled into real-space was much the same as the one that had roared into the High Lord's dreams: a black wave crashing into a shore. In her mind's eye, though, the wave was high enough to overtake First Landing Hill and envelop the monument to Dieron's founders.

Beyond it, she could see the solitary figure of her father, hands by his sides, standing stock-still—

The bustle of activity on *Fair Damsel*'s bridge brought her back to reality. Ray Li was intently working at the navigation station as the little merchant ship got under way.

She heard her name being called—seemingly from a long way away.

The *gyaryu* was out of the scabbard and in her hands. It was emitting a faint hum and it caught the phosphor light from overhead like a sliver of fire along its edge.

"Jay," Dan repeated, the pilot's chair turned around to face her. "Jay . . . Are you all right?"

"They're coming," she said absently.

"No shit," Ray Li said, without turning around. It would've been funny if the situation weren't so frightening.

"We've received a general scramble," Dan said, still facing her. "The field modulation is in operation. Are you—Is it—?"

"I'm okay. They're out there, trying to—It's working, for now. What's happening?"

Dan's face betrayed some relief. "*Sheng Long* and the forward squadron is headed on intercept. We're supposed to make for the gas giant and keep you close to the fight but out of the line of fire . . ."

"What are we supposed to do now?"

" 'Do'?"

"Yes, *do*. Unless you tell me otherwise, I'm following orders. You have any other plans?"

"No. No—let's go with whatever the admiral wants to do. I—I'm not sure as I have any better ideas."

"Glad to hear it," Raymond Li said, still not looking toward her.

"Shut up," Dan said to Ray. "All right, Jay, it's your play." He turned the chair back around to face the forward screen. The starfield slowly swung by, with the distant gas-giant a reddish blob half-lit by the system's primary.

She placed her hand on the hilt of the *gyaryu*, watching the planet gradually grow forward.

Sergei? She asked, sending her mind toward the *gyaryu*—

•   •   •

Suddenly, the scene changed.

She was standing in a flagstoned courtyard. Around her were several eights of warriors of the People, armed with *chya'i* and bone re-curve bows. Others were scattered around the courtyard, perching or lying down, some gazing open-eyed and senseless toward the sky. The aura of despair was palpable and almost impossible to shrug aside.

The *gyaryu* was in her hands in this vision as well. *This is an illusion,* she thought. *I am on the bridge of* Fair Damsel. But the scene didn't change.

She looked up. An orange sun bloomed through dark, blood-red clouds, and was reflected off the pale, yellowish towers above. Beyond the walls, she could feel something terribly wrong that twisted her insides.

"Sharia'a," she said, to no one in particular.

Two zor were operating the great gate mechanism. The double-width gates began to swing open, heightening the feeling in the pit of Jackie's stomach.

"No," she said, again mostly to herself. "*Shr'e'a.*"

The zor around her were all tense as well, looking from her to the gate and back. *They must see me as one of the People,* she told herself; this was millenia before the first contact with humans. *Of course,* she thought: She was back at Shr'e'a, just as in Owen's *Dsen'yen'ch'a.* The towers were pale and yellow because they were tiled with the bones of warriors defeated by the Shr'e'a'i.

This is Shr'e'a, and I have its Sword. What was more, since it was Shr'e'a and not Sharia'a, Dri'i wasn't here. Owen—if he *was* supposed to be Dri'i—wasn't here, either. He was aboard *Duc d'Enghien,* but wasn't part of this . . . whatever it was.

She wanted to run forward and close the gates but found herself rooted to the spot. Several warriors came to stand beside her as she waited, chilled despite the hot wind that blew from beyond the gate.

"I am here," a younger warrior said to her, and she abruptly recognized him: Gyes'ru HeKa'an, the wing-commander from *Duc d'Enghien.*

"You know where 'here' is," she answered, not looking away from the gate.

"Sharia'a," he replied. "But something is terribly wrong. They never opened the gates."

"Something is wrong with the *tale*," Jackie said. "This is *Shr'e'a*, and they are about to make a grave mistake."

Gyes'ru looked at the *gyaryu* in her hands. "This is not the World That Is. We are closing with the ships of the *esGa'uYal*, and already they batter at our *gyu'u*, seeking to draw us into the Valley."

"Stand with me," she said, which was neither answer nor confirmation. Gyes'ru formed his wings in a posture of affirmation and turned, *chya* at the ready, facing the gates.

They had swung wide open. Eleven People were coming onto the flagstones, flying a meter or so above the ground. One of them bore a bright-green banner inscribed with the glyph of Outer Peace, indicating a parley; this one remained hovering while the others landed, taking up positions around and behind their leader, who held his wings in a stance of respect. It was the scene she'd seen during Owen Garrett's Ordeal, except that it continued.

No gong would sound to end it—and she had no idea who was controlling the scene.

"Honored One," the banner-bearer said to her. "I am Hesya HeGa'u, and I have the honor to represent the Army of Sunset."

Eights of *chya'i* and bows were at the ready. Hesya did not seem to be fazed a bit by the number of hostile People around him; indeed, his wings betrayed a bit of amusement at the warriors who seemed poised to attack and whose wings displayed their hostility as he spoke the words.

He looked around the courtyard, his gaze seemingly caught on each helpless zor scattered on the ground. *These are the weak ones*, she heard in her mind: *I am not here for them.*

I am only here for you, he added, as his eyes came to rest on Jackie and the sword she held out before her.

As in the *Dsen'yen'ch'a* half a lifetime ago, Jackie felt the same engagement, as if this were a duel between the *esGa'uYe* and herself. She felt the presence of many others nearby: the ones she knew—Sergei, Admiral Marais, Kale'e—and the sixty-fours of ones she didn't. They were all here—ready for whatever came next.

"Intruder!"

Commodore Sheng Di, commander of the *Sheng Long*, spun the pilot's chair to face away from the board. A zor warrior stood on his bridge, a meter-long gleaming black sword in its hand.

Directly after his gunnery chief had spoken the word, two Marines had stepped forward, their pistols trained on the new arrival; it did not move a centimeter in response, but gazed directly at Sheng. He didn't recognize the zor—there were few enough under his command that he truthfully couldn't tell them apart other than the obvious things like major wing-markings; but he knew the sword.

"Wait," he said, one hand raised. "Hold your fire. That's the *gyaryu*. But if *he* has it, then . . . what's happened to Admiral Laperriere?"

His exec, Daniel Hamadjiou, walked slowly around the arc at the back of the bridge toward the zor who stood with its winged back to him. Sheng didn't look at Hamadjiou; zor had lightning-quick reflexes, and he wasn't about to draw attention to the exec.

Hamadjiou took a step closer, then another, until he was in arm's reach of the zor. Then, very slowly, he reached his hand toward the zor's wings.

And passed right through.

"It's a projection," Sheng said, stating the obvious.

The zor's wings elevated just a bit, the right hand of *Sheng Long*'s exec weirdly among them. The zor inclined his head toward Sheng, his gaze and the position of his sword never wavering.

T he Leader of the *esGa'uYal* handed his banner to another.

"This conflict is needless," Hesya said. "Shr'e'a is a great and noble city, the home and teacher of mighty warriors. We do not wish to destroy you; we wish to learn from you."

There was some murmuring among the assembled warriors, but Jackie did not take her eyes off of Hesya. "Learn from *us*?" she asked, knowing what the answer would be.

"From you, and from the Sword of Shr'e'a." Hesya looked at the *gyaryu* then, and Jackie felt it snarling in response.

"We have nothing to teach servants of the Deceiver," Jackie answered. "You will not have the Sword. I have already told you that. Perhaps I did not make myself clear."

"We wish only to learn from the Sword," Hesya said. "It would only be—"

"You shall not have it," she interrupted, advancing on Hesya. Two of his companions interposed themselves and then shied away, unable to bear the proximity to the snarling, glowing sword. She felt the *hsi* of the *gyaryu* flowing through her, and from the edges of her vision she could see *hsi*-images of her predecessors forming.

"Now, now." Hesya's handsome zor-features began to melt and change. Jackie stopped, a meter away, watching as the zor-head changed and became . . .

"Stone."

Whacⁿ?" Dan asked without turning completely around. "Jay, what the hell—"

The comm line was erupting in a welter of incoming messages. Dan held up one finger to Pyotr Ngo, sitting at the comm station. After a few moments the queuing software filtered out all messages but one. An image of Admiral Hsien appeared above and to the left of the pilot's chair.

"McReynolds, what the hell is going on there?"

"I'm not sure, sir. Everyone's calling us at once, wanting to talk to Jay—to Admiral Laperriere. She just said the word 'stone,' but hasn't moved from that spot for five or six minutes." He jerked his thumb over his shoulder.

"There's a—an image—on my bridge," Hsien said, his face a mask of barely controlled calm. "A man, with a sword in his hand. *Her* sword. There's apparently one of these on the bridge of every ship in the fleet.

"It's Marais, McReynolds. Admiral-by-God-*Marais* is standing on my deck, holding the *gyaryu*."

Sheng Di tried his best to look calm as his squadron closed with the hive-ships. Other than a single nod to him, the projection had ignored everything going on around it. Comm from the other ships in his squadron—and, seemingly, every vessel in Josephson System— confirmed that each ship had a similar guest.

His Sensitives reported that interference from . . . outside . . . had diminished immediately. Whatever it was, seemed to be working. If it let him fight a battle without worrying about things beyond his control, then Sheng Di was happy to have it—and the projection of a zor warrior—on his bridge.

His plane-of-battle was in order. *Sheng Long* and its sister ships, *Sheng Feng*, *Sheng Biao* and *Sheng Jian*, occupied the center position;

they had the greatest ability to concentrate fire on the enemy. On his port wing and slightly ahead of the other vessels, he had deployed the two zor vessels *HaDre'e* and *HaSa'an;* in the original battle-plan they had been most likely to resist mental attacks from vuhl Sensitives. The starboard flank consisted of *Turenne* and the brand-new *Brittany,* a sixth-generation starship of the Normandy-class commissioned only eight months ago at Mothallah. There were support ships behind, but Sheng didn't want them to be exposed—that would only mean that his first-raters hadn't done well against the enemy. There were also no carriers, which meant no fighters; based on the briefing about the battle at Cicero, there was no way to protect them, at least not against hive-ships.

The plan was simple. Concentrate as much as possible on the hive-ships, preferably just one or two: If the vuhl objective was to take Josephson System, they would want to get through Sheng's force and deep in the gravity well rather than just destroy ships. It was Sheng's job to make sure they didn't get there—or at least that they would pay a heavy price—and then to fall back while the second squadron advanced. He would be engaged for longer than the reinforcements, since his velocity relative to the incoming ships was low. By comparison, the other squadron would have to boost out of the gravity well to intercept, so they'd have less of a chance to concentrate fire on the enemy.

Don't claim to be surprised," Hesya/Stone was saying. "Though I must congratulate you: Your knowledge of the legends has certainly improved since we last met.

"But you *can't* change this outcome. You know the true story now: Shr'e'a conveys the Sword to Hesya and is then destroyed by despair when it's taken away in sight of their walls. It *has* to be given up, or it won't be there for Qu'u to recover."

"What about Dri'i?" Jackie asked.

"*Admiral.*" Hesya/Stone smirked. "You already know the answer to *that* question. Dri'i is a fiction; he doesn't even exist." He gestured to the courtyard before the gate, at the eights of warriors perched or lying about, unable to move, already trapped in *Ur'ta leHssa.* "This is Shr'e'a—these Crawler-servants have no Dri'i to rescue them.

"This is beyond your control, *se Gyaryu'har.*" He said it with a characteristically human sneer, and crossed his arms in an un-zorlike fashion. "Admit it," he added. "You don't know what you're doing."

"You're counting on that," Jackie said, moving a few centimeters closer to Hesya/Stone. Her sword didn't falter, but her feet felt like lead. She could hardly see anyone nearby, though she could sense the presence of Gyes'ru a meter or two away.

Suddenly, two of Hesya/Stone's companions vanished, leaving behind only a faint afterimage. He did not turn to look, but his right eyebrow lifted a few millimeters. His smile never wavered.

Brittany hadn't had a veteran commander, all the new hardware in the world wouldn't have saved it. Fortunately, Micaela Clemente had been hunting pirates in lesser ships for most of twenty years; she knew how to fight and knew how to withdraw.

"I've got about one-tenth manuever capability," Clemente said.

Sheng was dividing his attention between the pilot's board and the small holo of Mic Clemente's bridge hanging in the air a few meters away. Behind her, he could see her front viewscreen, tinged with bright orange—*Brittany*'s defensive fields were working overtime to disperse the energy that the vuhl hive-ships had poured into it. Half of Sheng's units were already disabled and he'd only managed to destroy a few outriders and one of the hive-ships facing him.

"Use it," Sheng answered. "I'll send *Pappenheim* and *Tamil Nadu* up to provide covering fire."

"I'm getting under way now. But they'd better stay clear."

"You worry about *Brittany,* Mic," Sheng said. "I'll worry about the small fry. Get out of there as ordered."

"I'm still at thirty-percent weapons—"

"Belay that. We'll cover your exit." He looked at the board; his namesake ships—the Shengs, built at his uncle's New China shipyard, were holding their own so far, but he'd already lost *HaSa'an* and been forced to order *HaDre'e* to withdraw. *Turenne*'s fields were already in the yellow, but she hadn't taken any serious damage yet.

" 'Comm to *Pappenheim* and *Tamil Nadu.* Cover retreat of *Brittany* from main battle area. *Sheng Long* sends.' "

A few moments later, Sheng watched as the two fifth-generation ships began to advance into the space being vacated by the heavily damaged *Brittany.*

Damn, Sheng thought to himself. *We're not going to be able to hold this much longer.*

"Comm, get Admiral Hsien."

"Aye-aye," the comm officer said.

Sheng leaned back in his chair after taking a sidelong glance at the zor warrior standing at the back of his bridge. "All right, folks," he said. "Let's see if we can take out one more of them before we back away."

It may be beyond my control," Jackie said, after what seemed to be hours, "but I think it's beyond your control as well.

"You didn't want the zor and humans to become allies: Marais was to succeed or fail, but not reach understanding. You didn't want your— clients?—to be discovered infiltrating Cicero. You didn't want me to figure out how to use *this*." She turned the *gyaryu* over in her hands. "Now you're trying to lock me into the legend of Hesya and Sharnu.

"*It's not going to work,* Stone. I understand now: You have technology on your side, you can mess with my mind, you can interfere with perception of reality—but we have to make our own decisions, don't we? You can't take the sword from me—I have to *give* it to you.

"I'm not going to, damn it. *I'm not going to do it.*"

Two more of the companions disappeared—one directly behind Hesya/Stone, and one to his left.

"Two more gone. What does that mean? Are you losing your power?"

"It doesn't matter in the end," Hesya/Stone replied. "It just doesn't matter in the end. Sooner or later, the Warlord of Shr'e'a gives over the Sword and starts the cycle.

"History is an unavoidable, unstoppable force."

He looked around at his companions as if he'd come in the gates with six instead of ten, and as if it didn't matter that four of them had disappeared. Some of the People facing the *esGa'uYal* had vanished as well—it was as if there was no one here of importance other than Jackie and Stone.

The ancient enemy, she thought to herself. Or *was* it?

"But you've got to wait, to see how it comes out," Jackie answered. "Just like I do."

As the second hive-ship shattered and then exploded, the retreating ships of Commodore Sheng's squadron sheared off, trying to avoid debris. *Turenne, HaDre'e* and *Brittany* were already well away.

Sheng Biao, the aftmost of the four sixth-generation ships left, had sustained the most damage; its fields were already radiating into the white as the four remaining hive-ships hurtled into the gravity well after them.

But there were other reinforcements. The second squadron had come partway out from its station, led by the carriers *Duc d'Enghien* and *Xian Chuan;* the sixth-generation starships *Emperor Ian, Mandela* and *Nasser;* Admiral Hsien's flagship *Gibraltar;* and a number of smaller ships. As the damaged components retreated, the fresh reinforcements advanced directly into the plane-of-battle.

Given the relative speeds, though, there wouldn't be much time to engage—just some passing shots. Still, those passing shots would have giga-ergs of energy in them, and the carrier fighters were already preparing for pursuit.

Admiral César Hsien sat in the pilot's seat of *Gibraltar,* trying not to look over his shoulder at the image of the long-dead Admiral Marais. He could hear the cheering on the systemwide comm as the alien ship broke into four, then eleven, then several dozen pieces, weirdly illuminated by the explosion that followed.

"We haven't won a damn thing yet," he said to the *Gibraltar* bridge crew, letting loose the scowl that had traveled with him during his ascent to flag rank. The crew became quiet and focused on its work.

Admiral Marais, the *gyaryu* held before him, betrayed a small smile.

No, Admiral. She hasn't said anything else. Her eyes are following something—but it isn't anything on my bridge."

"And when the ships blew up—"

"She reacted. She stepped forward a few centimeters. But nothing other than that."

"Have you tried to talk to her?"

"She's not answering, Admiral. And I wouldn't try to . . . interrupt. She's the reason that you have Admiral Marais standing on your bridge, and for all I know, she's the only thing keeping those aliens from—"

"You may be right." Hsien's face looked haunted for a few moments, then it slid back under the professional "officer" mask. "Carry on, Captain McReynolds," he said, and disconnected.

• • •

"Actually," Stone said, his smiling face never wavering, "I should compliment you on having accomplished this much. My employers—and my clients—had not anticipated this outcome."

"So much for infallibility."

"I never claimed that. Though I can see how you might infer that, from previous statements." He looked away, as if taking note of the absences in his ranks for the first time. "My employers don't know the outcome, as you say, but they don't view it that way: They perceive this entire little drama as a set of probabilities. What happens depends on purely random factors."

"Such as Owen Garrett."

Stone smiled again but did not answer.

"Are your employers *betting* on the outcome?"

" 'Betting'?" Stone chuckled a bit. "Nothing so crass. In fact, they don't truly *care* about one or another outcome. They merely want to watch it play out."

"Your *clients* won't want to hear that. What do they think of all of this?"

"Them?" Stone's zor-claws stretched out in a gesture. "They think they're invincible. After all," he added, the wry smile returning, "we told them that they were."

On the pilot's board of *Canberra*, Commodore Sean Van Meter watched the vuhl ships spread across a wide plane. Three capital ships remained from Sheng Di's command—four had been damaged and one destroyed during the fighting so far. As for the squadron traveling with Admiral Hsien's flag, only *Nasser* had been forced to withdraw from the battle zone.

"Comm from the flag, Skip," the comm officer said. Van Meter nodded and turned the pilot's chair to the side. Admiral Hsien's image appeared in the air.

"Reporting, sir."

"Get under way, Sean." Hsien was sitting in the pilot's seat of *Gibraltar*. "We're going to be pursuing these bastards soon enough, so I'll want someone in front of them."

"Aye-aye, Admiral. We estimate intercept at"—Van Meter glanced at his helmsman, a zor warrior, who held up an open hand with four claws extended—"forty minutes."

"That should be about right. Leave two of the *Broadmoors* behind, but get the rest of your squadron in the way of the bogeys."

"I'll be there, sir."

Barbara MacEwan had six flights of fighters launched and was trying to pay attention to them on *Duc d'Enghien*'s huge pilot's board.

"Blue Squadron's getting a little ragged, Van," she said. "Get them lined up *here*." She gestured toward a group of smaller craft trailing the three remaining hive-ships.

"Aye-aye," Van Micic said. "Blue Squadron Flight Controller, this is Excom," he said, and began issuing course changes.

Barbara's eyes strained toward the back of the bridge, where the image of a zor warrior, sword extended, stood next to Alan Howe, *Duc*'s assigned Sensitive. The zor was motionless, except for his eyes, which met hers when she glanced at him; the human was straining hard—his hands clenched on the railing and his eyes tightly shut.

Alan and the zor warrior, along with the defensive-field mods, were what was standing between *Duc* and the enemy mental powers that had destroyed her original Green Squadron at Cicero. Now, her new Greens were being managed by Owen Garrett as Flight Controller, who was too valuable to send out there.

In the meanwhile *Duc* had a battle to fight, and every erg of firepower at Barbara's disposal was being used against the hive-ships and their outriders as they advanced on the second squadron's position.

On *Fair Damsel*, the command crew were all on the bridge, clustered around the pilot's board watching the battle. Dan, Ray, Drew Sabah and Pyotr watched the vuhl forces creeping down into the gravity well while Jackie stood immobile, the *gyaryu* held out in front of her, eyes staring at something they couldn't see.

"They didn't expect *this*," Pyotr said. "They're getting bogged down."

"They didn't expect that she"—Dan nodded toward Jackie—"could protect the whole fleet."

"Is that what's happening?" Ray asked.

"What do you mean?"

"I mean," Li said, looking away from the board, "we don't know what's going on in *there*." He pointed at Jackie. "That's the real battle, whatever she's doing."

"Tell that to Admiral Hsien."

"If he thinks otherwise, he's kidding himself."

"Okay," Dan said. "Tell that to every commander out there." A transponder code near one of the enemy hive-ships vanished. "The ones that survive will tell you they're fighting a pretty damn serious battle." Dan put his hands on his hips. "If the enemy destroys enough ships . . ."

"They've already taken out seven—no, *eight* front-liners," Pyotr Ngo said. "Both of the zor sixes, along with two *Shengs, Turenne, Brittany*—"

"Isn't that one of the new ones?"

"Got it in one," Pyotr said. "They got out but lost most of their maneuver, from the look of it. Your old pal Maartens covered their retreat."

"Where's *Pappenheim*?"

"There." Pyotr pointed to a spot in among the three remaining *Sheng*-class sixth-generation ships, closely trailing the enemy's advance. "Not exactly out of the line of fire, but he's not leading the charge, either."

"Smart man."

Two pinpricks of light winked out among the crowd of vuhl small craft—two fighter craft exploding as enemy fire destroyed them. Then, suddenly, one of the vuhl hive-ships vanished from the display.

Two more companions vanished: Now there were five remaining, including Hesya/Stone himself. Jackie could see that the zor who stood around her with weapons at the ready had been reduced in numbers as well.

It reminded her eerily of her own *Dsen'yen'ch'a* at Adrianople Starbase, when she had taken her first steps down the road to the spot she was in now. There was only one difference: This wasn't Sharnu—it was Hesya. And this time he had friends as well . . . but fewer and fewer of them.

"You're running out of allies."

Hesya/Stone's wings moved to a posture of amusement. He took a step toward Jackie, who raised the *gyaryu* to defend herself.

"Really, madam. I realize it's a reflex, but don't think you can threaten me with *that*." Still, he didn't advance any farther.

"I'll stick with my reflexes, thank you. I'll keep it right where it is. What's happening in the battle?"

"Does it matter?" Stone asked.

"It matters to *me*."

"Well, then. Not to put too fine a point on it, my invincible clients are *losing*. But things are just starting to get interesting."

"Deploy to port," Hsien said, indicating a position on his own pilot's board.

Sean Van Meter nodded. "We're about ten minutes downrange, Admiral. I've got enough throw-weight to launch some missiles at the nearest hive-ship, but I'd intended to get *Mauritius'* fighters off the deck."

"Get the fighters out there. I—"

"Excuse me, Admiral," said Dame Alexandra Quinn, *Gibraltar's* commander. "I think we've got a situation." She pointed to the icon for *Mandela*.

"You've got your orders, Sean. Hsien out." The admiral squinted at the info for *Mandela,* which was changing rapidly. " 'Flag to *Mandela*. Chris, your shields are in the white. Back off.' "

Sean paused and looked across at comm, which was trying to send the message. The comm officer shook her head.

"Damn. 'Flag to *Emperor Ian*. Erich, redirect fire to *Mandela's* targets. *Ian,* acknowledge.' "

"I read you, sir," came Erich Anderson's voice from comm. There was no visual. "I'm trying to raise *Mandela,* but can't reach her. I won't want to approach too close in case she blows."

"Understood, but try to draw fire anyway."

"Will do."

"Anything from *Mandela*?" Hsien asked. If its defensive fields were radiating all the way into the white, it meant they were almost overloaded. If it could maneuver itself out of the plane-of-battle, it could disperse them; but to do so in the face of enemy weapons would be to expose the hull of the ship to direct fire.

"Nothing, sir," the comm officer said.

"It may have lost maneuver," Quinn added. "*Ian* will have to get clear."

As she spoke these words, the mass-radar icon for *Emperor Ian* veered off, making a close approach to one of the enemy ships that had targeted *Mandela*. Almost at once, *Mandela's* icon disappeared. On the forward screen of the *Gibraltar*, a bright spot appeared, expanded, and was gone, leaving only an afterecho and the metallic reflections of debris spinning outward from the site.

The fighters from *Duc d'Enghien* and *Xian Chuan* were in it now, with those of the fifth-generation small carrier *Mauritius* (which could only fly four wings instead of the six available to her larger sisters) en route. Unlike capital ships, fighters were intended for attacks on specific targets, usually particular weapons-emplacements or to overload one section of an opposing ship's field.

It didn't pay for a fighter to stay anywhere for very long. Ships of the line could withstand incoming fire: Their defensive fields could absorb energy, distribute it evenly and disperse it through radiation. Fighters had no such protection; their objective was to be *elsewhere* when the torpedo or beam showed up. Fighter craft were—on the space combat scale, at least—very small and maneuverable, hard to hit and hard to track.

On each flight deck of *Duc*, a flight controller watched the vid pickups on each of his or her fighter pilots' visual arrays. Green Squadron flight deck was under Owen Garrett, who—truth be told— would rather have been out flying a fighter against the bugs than supervising, no matter how damn valuable his talent was. His squadron, which still had six craft deployed, had been making its hits count against one of the hive-ships while avoiding the smaller craft that swarmed around it.

For Owen, watching six holos was probably as close as he was going to get to the action; the dull feeling in the pit of his stomach got worse every time the target hive-ship grew large in one of those six views. It reminded him of another hive-ship, another battle and another part of his life.

No one seemed to be of special interest to the bugs, though. No one was being made to believe that his mates were his enemies; no one was being pulled inside.

The bugs, evidently, had a lot more on their minds.

The ᴄᴀᴘɪᴛᴀʟ ships from Van Meter's squadron formed up near *Sheng Long* and its two sister ships, with the fighters from *Mauritius* joining the fray. On the pilot's board of *Gibraltar*, Admiral Hsien watched as they finished off one more hive-ship in a huge catastrophic explosion.

Two more of Hesya's escorts vanished, leaving only two: one to either side of Hesya—the one to his left still holding the banner.

"It appears as if your clients are running out of time," Jackie said. "Don't you have any magic tricks to save them? No ribbons of rainbow light for the vuhls to escape on?"

"Spare me your droll comments," Hesya/Stone said. "This is the last time our . . . clients will underestimate you."

"They don't think of us as 'meat-creatures' anymore, then?"

"Oh, don't be deceived into thinking *that*. They still believe themselves to be superior. That isn't likely to change. What they believe, is that no race with inferior *k'th's's* powers can compete with them. The Ór told them—*we* told them"—Stone's smile returned, as sardonic as ever—"that as long as it lived, they'd not be defeated."

"Thon's Well and Josephson makes it two in a row."

"*Defeated*, dear lady. Losing hive-ships is no small matter, but they're far from defeated.

"In fact," he continued, "when you lose a few battles, there's only one thing you can do: make changes at the top."

"Meaning—?"

"Meaning that when word gets back to . . . the powers that be, there'll be some changes made."

A single alien ship remained, doling out unimaginable firepower. The destruction of the other ship had taken a number of defenders with it—McReynolds' sensor equipment could hardly keep track.

Five alien ships would have been enough to vaporize the entire fleet, as had been done at Adrianople, and was almost done at Thon's Well . . . Except that without the ability to seize the minds of Imperial commanders, the ungainly hive-ships could not outmaneuver their smaller opponents. Fighter craft were able to execute wave-attacks, with *Duc d'Enghien* moving closer to provide some broadsides of its own.

Ｉ STILL have a few questions for you, Stone," Jackie said, not moving her blade from where it was pointed at Hesya/Stone's chest. "There are some things I don't understand."

"I'm always willing to answer questions," he said, the sardonic grin remaining on his face. "I don't know if you'll want the answers, though."

"I'll be the judge of that. You've been lurking in the background during this whole affair—probably ever since Cicero. Even before."

"Before," he agreed.

"But all this time it's been *Sharnu* who's been attacking me. Sharnu—Shrnu'u HeGa'u—came from the underworld to fight me in the *Dsen'yen'ch'a*. He attacked me aboard *Fair Damsel*. He attacked me on Dieron. For all I know, it was Shrnu'u HeGa'u who killed Damien Abbas on Center. If you're so damned powerful, why didn't he succeed? What were those things—just tests?"

"If you like."

"I *don't*. I don't like what you're doing to Owen Garrett, either. He doesn't know what his part is, any more than I do . . . but he hasn't met you, Stone. He doesn't know about Hesya.

"Byar HeShri told me that Despite doesn't *have* a point, and that Shrnu'u HeGa'u attacked me because Qu'u is his ancient enemy. But why change now? Why are you here *now*? Because I've figured out the connection with the Shr'e'a legend, you've wrapped yourself in it to try and deceive me. But why not just try to beat me over the head again? Where *is* Shrnu'u HeGa'u?"

"Where he's been all along," Stone answered. "Right behind you."

Ｈｅ is very near . . . he is near—" Sa'a's wings ran through a dozen positions in rapid sequence. Her *hi'chya,* which had been lowered to her side, was raised again, extended before her, her talons clutching it tightly. T'te'e glanced around the garden; the *alHyu* and other servants were keeping their distance, but their wings betrayed concern and not embarrassment: Many of them had seen the same sort of behavior in the previous High Lord, but this seemed to smack of true prescience and not madness.

"What of the *esGa'uYal*?" T'te'e asked.

"The *esHara'y* are nearly all destroyed," Sa'a answered, not looking at him. "Four talons are broken but a fifth remains. But the real danger is not at the end of the *chya*-arm—it is near the heart."

"Can anything be done?"

"*esLi*," Sa'a almost whispered. "*esLi*'s protective wing."

T'te'e extended his own wings in a posture of reverence to *esLi*, but even as he and most of the attendants completed the gesture, Sa'a swung in a graceful circle with the *hi'chya*, her wings cascading like a waterfall—

Jackie turned away from Hesya/Stone—knowing it could be a trap, knowing how dangerous it might be, but fearing the attack of Shrnu'u HeGa'u as well—and suddenly, as she did so, a fierce gust of wind coming from the bone-sheathed towers above her made her stagger and fall:

—She was on one knee, the cargo hold of *Fair Damsel* suffused with bright, actinic light. Her *chya* was held before her and she faced the sixty-four–limbed darkness of *anGa'e'ren*. She could remember it all now: the taunting voice of Shrnu'u HeGa'u, the sinuous twisting of the dark pseudopods. Somewhere above the hold floor, her ancient enemy stood at the deck controls; a quick glance over her shoulder revealed his identity, free of any glare or obscurement—

—Thunder rolled off the Livingston Mountains and lightning cracked overhead. Her *hsi*-images seemed to be out of reach, impossibly far away. Half kneeling, half crouching on the rain-soaked ground, she watched as her mother's image began to melt and change like a snake shedding its skin: The arms came together and were now holding a sword that hissed and snarled, making Jackie's flesh crawl. But as her mother's image disappeared, the face that replaced it was not that of Shrnu'u HeGa'u . . . or, rather, it was as if she was seeing him for the first time: It was the face of someone very familiar—

• • •

Suddenly there was a brilliant flash of lightning, seemingly right outside the cabin of the aircar. The light was bright enough to blind her for a moment; but not before she caught a glimpse of some sort of rainbow, like a series of colored bands, scoring through the cabin. When her vision had cleared, the *gyaryu* was in her hands, pointing downward at Damien Abbas, who looked up at her with frightened, sightless eyes.

"This is the same," his voice said, his lips moving like an automaton's. "But it is different."

The eyes then focused. "I have you now, Crawler-servant." There was something in his hand: not a blade, but a cutting-laser, and the face was suddenly not that of Damien Abbas, but rather—

Thrown to the deck as if by some unseen hand, Jackie mostly avoided the cutting-laser's beam. Instead of catching her amidships, it clipped her in the shoulder and chest. The pain nearly blinded her and the smell of burned flesh made her want to retch.

Everything was happening at once and seemingly in slow motion. She saw Dan whirl around in the pilot's chair; Drew Sabah, the Sultan, holding the laser in his hands and getting ready to fire it again; Pyotr Ngo diving for the deck under the comm console; Ray Li grabbing for the extinguisher to put out the fire from the panel behind Jackie where the shot had struck.

Hesya, and Shr'e'a, had disappeared. Shrnu'u HeGa'u—Drew Sabah—had brought the pistol around to fire on Pyotr, who was reaching for a weapon strapped under his console.

Help me, she thought—shouted—at the *gyaryu*. *Help me.*

There is a way. You already know it.

My hsi *is weak. My* hsi-*images are far away.* The pain from her arm and shoulder were narrowing her vision. *I haven't the power.*

Summon them, the *gyaryu* replied. *Use esLiDur'ar.*

Drew Sabah stood like a statue, unmoving. Time had stopped: Dan was half out of his seat; the flame from the fire was in midcrackle; Pyotr had reached his pistol, had it in his hand, and was bringing it to bear on the image of his old friend.

She called out for them: Sergei, Marais and the others.

• • •

On more than three dozen ships scattered around Josephson System, the projected images vanished.

Howe cried out in pain and slumped to one knee as the mental onslaught reached him nearly unimpeded for the first time. Barbara MacEwan felt it as well, a chorus of voices speaking unintelligible phrases. She wanted to cry out but could not; wanted to turn around, but could not.

Van Micic's gray-haired head was bent over the tactical display, but he was able to turn aside enough to give Barbara a look of complete horror.

No, she thought. *No. We are too damn close to winning this . . . No!*

From reserves of anger she didn't know she had, she fought against the invading minds that called out to her to change the course of the *Duc d'Enghien,* which was closing with the only remaining alien ship. The carrier had been approaching to deliver a close-in broadside in support of its fighter wings, but she'd intended for it to make a course change after it reached firing range. Without ordering the change, the *Duc* would ram right into the flank of the alien vessel.

But if she let herself speak, she knew that it would not be her voice that would give the orders.

On the Green Squadron flight deck, Owen Garrett looked away from the pilot's board that tracked the Green fighters. Things had gone silent on the main bridge.

He felt the same sense of quiet he had first experienced in the Shield on Center, sitting opposite Damien Abbas. The flight deck came into sharp focus: Every sound, every indicator glyph on every display, every curve of every face assaulted him. He stood up from his post and turned around, looking in all directions.

But from the bridge—from Commander Micic and Captain MacEwan—he heard nothing in his headset.

"Commander?" Erin Simon, his second, had turned away from her station.

"Something's happening," Owen answered. He made a gesture toward the wing-commander's station and dashed off the flight bridge toward the lift leading down the long arm from Green to the main hull of *Duc*.

It took several long, agonizing minutes for Owen to descend to *Duc*'s main hull and dash up through "officer country" to the bridge. He had his pistol in his hand, and no one seemed interested in getting in his way; a half-dozen Marines in the gangway followed him, their weapons drawn as well.

Barbara MacEwan heard voices in her head. They asked, demanded, *commanded* her to turn the *Duc*, now bearing down on the alien ship. But something inside her kept her from doing so.

Another, one of the voices said. *This one must die. Another will give the command.*

There is no time, said another. The voice's timbre had not changed, but it seemed to be a different personality, another alien.

Kill it.

Command it.

The alien ship occupied the entire forward screen of *Duc d'Enghien*. Barbara gripped the arms of the pilot's chair and thought, *I am going to die, but by God I'm going to take these bastards with me.*

Kill—

Command—

The door to the bridge slid aside and Owen burst in. He knew Captain MacEwan: Interrupting the proceedings during battle would have earned a sharp rebuke at the very least. Instead, she didn't even turn around.

No one was moving at all. Alan Howe, the ship's Sensitive, had collapsed facedown on the deck, one arm stretched out. Owen looked across the bridge until his glance reached Helm Station.

The helmsman turned to face him, the huge bulk of the alien ship had grown to fill the screen behind.

"You have already lost," the man said, a smile crossing his face.

"We'll see," Owen said, and shot him.

Jackie felt the pain recede as the *hsi*-images merged with her, and energy like liquid fire flowed from the *gyaryu* up her sword-arm into her wounded body.

Things snapped into real time all of a sudden. Sabah—or whatever had replaced him—was pinned behind a console a few feet away, exchanging fire with Pyotr Ngo. Dan was trying to make his way over to Jackie, while Ray Li worked to put out the fire behind her.

The *gyaryu* was light in her sword-hand, like a natural extension of her arm. The pain was still there, but distant, concealed, as if it had been shut inside a box.

Knowing she had only one chance, she thrust upward with all of her strength, driving the *gyaryu* deep into Drew Sabah's exposed back. The point of the blade caught the overhead light as it emerged from the front of his body—

"You—have—presumed too much," Shrnu'u HeGa'u said, leaping to the top of the parapet at Sanctuary. "You have chosen to fight the Crawler's battles."

He raised his wings in an obscene posture, his face twisting in pain. "*esGa'u'Canya'e'e!*" he shouted—*esGa'u will pluck out your heart with his talons*—and hurled himself backward and fell, screaming, over the side of the parapet. Several seconds later, there was a terrible crunching sound, of bones breaking against rock—

A rainbow path cascaded across the deck of the *Fair Damsel,* casting weird shadows on the crew. Jackie's skin crawled and the *gyaryu* snarled as it passed near, even as she felt the sword slice through sinew and bone. For a moment, everything was obscured by harsh, polychromatic light, and then it was gone: and so was the body of Drew Sabah. Jackie fell forward to hands and knees, one hand still clutching the *gyaryu.*

In her head, Barbara MacEwan heard a horrible scream, syllables that could not be reproduced by a human voice. The grip on her mind was suddenly broken.

"Come about!" she managed, but the helmsman was slumped in his seat and changing shape—twisting and stretching the uniform he wore as he slipped to the deck.

Her limbs were impossibly heavy, and the hull of the alien vessel so close, that the two ships' defensive fields were discharging against each other. Barbara threw herself forward, shouldering the alien body out of the way, and played her hands across helm control, bringing *Duc d'Enghien* to an abrupt course change.

It was almost too late. Fleet carriers were not made for tight maneuvering and there was hardly enough room for it; the intersecting energy fields had reached bright orange on both ships and it was impossible to shed energy *and* maintain them.

Under the stress of the turn, the two starboard arms of the carrier were torn away and sent cascading toward the hull of the enemy. The forward arm creaked and buckled, but still hung at an odd angle, while the port and aft arms and sensor were torn from their moorings. Red signals showed on every damage-control panel; there were a dozen hull-breaches imminent or already happening along the length of the *Duc.*

With the sole alternative the hypersaturation of her ship's fields, Barbara took the only course she could think of—one that every battle instinct contradicted: She dispersed the fields, leaving what was left of the ship's hull open to the destructive fire of enemy weapons. With whatever momentum remained, the mauled, defenseless carrier began to pull away from its collision course.

The alien vessel was unprepared for the multigiga-erg discharge from the *Duc*'s defensive fields, and seemed incapable of firing its weapons. Crippled for some reason Barbara didn't yet understand, the carrier maintained its forward course, hurricanes of energy tearing at its hull, until it was suddenly, blindingly, overwhelmed by it.

At the edge of Josephson System, another new sun was born.

In the High Lord's garden on Zor'a, Sa'a HeYen lowered her *hi'chya* and placed her wings in a posture of homage to *esLi.*

chapter 22

You wanted to know, the voice said in Jackie's head. It had a tone that suggested it had been saying it for a while.

She wasn't sure whether she was awake or asleep. *Asleep,* she guessed, since there was no pain in her shoulder. Somewhere in the waking world above, ships were probably still firing on each other, but there was no evidence of it in whatever state she was now in.

You wanted to know.

"I'll bite," she said. "*What* do I want to know?"

What this was about. What effect your actions have had.

"Fine. Enlighten me."

Open your eyes.

She did.

She was in a room. More properly, it was a sort of hollowed-out cavern, brightly lit with actinic blue light. It was close, or seemed so, with curved ceilings and walls—certainly not a human or zor habitation—and it was bare of recognizable decoration, though swirls and abstract patterns on the walls changed color at regular intervals.

A seam appeared on the wall opposite. An insectoid creature pushed into the room, followed by another, close behind. Jackie felt for her sword and didn't find it; she realized that she must be merely an observer here—*a fly on the wall,* she thought to herself.

There weren't too many people who had ever seen the alien enemy in the flesh. Fewer still had heard the clacks and chitters of the vuhl native tongue; but this was the first chance she'd had to get a good look at them alive.

Their dull-black insectoid bodies stood on four strong legs, which were jointed in the middle like human knees. Past the midsection, the aliens' bodies rose upright, with two more limbs that ended in many-fingered hands. Their heads were shaped like rounded cones, topped by short eyestalks that seemed in constant motion; their faces were largely occupied by a fanged mouth that ended in vicious-looking mandibles. Tentacles protruded from either side of the jaw, waving like streamers.

You wanted to know, the voice said again. *Now listen, and watch.*

The native tongue suddenly collapsed into recognizable speech. "... five hives completely obliterated. The Drones could not even rescue the lesser-Queens," one of the aliens said. Its tentacles waved in a circle; those on the being's underside waved as if in a strong current, first one way and then another.

"What of the meat-creatures? They are not mind-strong," the second one said. "They have been no more than food for the *k'th's's* before. Could they not be controlled?"

"They were protected this time."

"They *cannot* protect themselves," the second answered dismissively. It seemed to rear up somewhat, as if bearing down on its companion. "There is nothing of resistance in them, even the strongest. The Ór promised—"

"The Ór, the Ór. Always it returns to that, does it not?"

"And why *should* it *not*? The Ór promised us conquest of every race we encountered—to breed, to kill, to feed to our *k'th's's* if we pleased. For twelve-twelves of cycles this has been true. Why should it suddenly change?"

The other alien was silent, as if it had no answer to this question.

"Yours are the fears of a weak hatchling," the second alien continued. "Every breeze and color-change makes you mind-clouded and abdomen-clenched. Had we not shared the red stripe and silver octagon of the Ninth Sept of E'esh, you would be a meal for my *k'th's's*, and a poor one at that. It was some trick of the enemy—"

"No."

A third alien had joined them. This one was larger than the other two. Instead of being dull-black, it was shiny, with an overhue of gold. As soon as the other two heard it speak, they bent their bodies forward, splaying their tentacles and dipping their mandibled jaws toward the floor. They spoke some indefinable series of syllables, chant-fashion.

When the chanting was over, the third alien gave some sort of gesture with its head and then exuded some clear substance like sweat from its body and rubbed its mouth-tentacles across it. It then extended these damp members to the others, who each caressed one, letting the liquid slide onto their shells.

"There is fear in First Hive," the third alien said, after this ceremony was complete. "The Great Queen might deny this, of course, but many know it to be true."

"Of course," the other two said in unison.

"There are only two possibilities. One is that the Destroyer has come." This word seemed to echo ominously, as if it were being spoken down a long tunnel. All three aliens seemed to alter their postures, lowering their bodies toward the gently curving floor.

"But if it *were* the Destroyer, we would know—for the Ór would be dead. The Destroyer cannot come to First Hive—or to any Hive—as long as the Ór lives."

"But the battle—" one of the others began.

The golden-hued one did not seem to notice the interruption, as it continued: "As long as the Ór lives," it repeated. The tentacles were completely dry now, the clear ooze having leaked completely off them onto the bodies of the other two.

It touched the others' bodies gently, caressingly, in a gesture that seemed almost human. "The only other answer—the only logical one—is that the Harbinger has appeared."

The aliens seemed again to lower their bodies, though not as far or as forcefully as the first time.

"The Harbinger . . . the Harbinger is real?" the first alien said. "I had always thought—that it was a story for hatchlings. A story to frighten them."

"That is what G'en thought. But G'en was wrong. The Harbinger has come."

The two lesser aliens seemed to rear up then, their tentacles and body-parts waving madly.

"Great Queen G'en . . ." one of them said—Jackie wasn't sure which—and the greater alien snapped its tentacles back abruptly, leaving brownish welts on the others' bodies.

"No," it said suddenly, harshly. "G'en. The *P'cn* Deathguard occupy the *k*rdn'a'a*. Great Queen K'da sits upon the Seat of Majesty now." It gestured to a nearby wall, which dissolved into color and light and then focused into a 3-V scene: another alien, even more impressive, with golden thorax and abdomen, surrounded by a press of other aliens. It moved and thrashed, its body pierced by a spike several centimeters wide thrust through its midsection and extending into the air; the other aliens seemed to whirl and dance around it, occasionally nipping or pricking the obviously dying body—and smearing the liquid that emerged onto their own carapaces.

"Great Queen no more," the greater alien said.

Quite a display," said a familiar voice. "Wouldn't you say?"
Stone walked out of the darkness. Jackie's hand was near her sword-hilt—she seemed to be embodied again—and she could see the whorls and patterns of the *gyaryu* beneath her boots. The aliens and their brightly-lit chamber were gone.

"Hideous," she managed to answer.

"Oh, it gets better." He smiled. "You see, when the impaling does its job—when all of her internal organs fail, as they ultimately must—they eat her. I understand that the eyes and the egg-sacs are the most delectable, and the most sought-after."

"This is all because of the battle. I guess we won."

"Well, that's the proximate cause, anyway. But there's more to it than just that: You see, this whole war hasn't gone the way they expected, not at all. Cicero—Center—Thon's Well—and now this. Not to mention a few incidental things along the way. They didn't anticipate losing a single ship, particularly the five your fleet have just destroyed. Now K'da is the Great Queen, and *her* Deathguard—the *P'cn*—have replaced the *N'nr*. There's merry havoc all across their fleet, all across their empire, right now.

"But as for winning the war, I guess they'll have to learn to live with disappointment. Except for poor G'en."

"What about—K'da? Has anything changed?"

"No, certainly not." Stone made a dismissive gesture. "She's just as screwed as the Great Queen she conspired to have impaled. Except, of course, she *believes* in the old tale of the Harbinger."

"Enlighten me on *that*."

"Well, to understand the Harbinger, you have to understand the Ór."

"I'm all ears. What's the Ór?" Jackie asked.

"Now, now, Admiral. *Qu'uYar*. We can't be giving the whole story away, can we? Then no one will act according to the proper motivations.

"The Ór is a sort of advisor who has helped First Hive to the dominant position, as long as the Destroyer doesn't turn up. The Harbinger is just a precursor."

"With the Destroyer yet to come, I suppose."

"A palpable hit, madam."

"Look, I'm tired of all this shit." She moved toward him, the sword in her hand, but a rainbow of light crossed her path, blinding her suddenly—

Whoa, hold on!" Firm but gentle hands grasped her shoulders and arms and eased her back to a prone position. Jackie opened her eyes and saw Dr. Arthur Callison, *Pappenheim*'s medical officer, standing above her. She let herself go limp, and he let go.

"Sorry," she said. "Dreaming." One hand reached down and felt the sword-belt: The *gyaryu* was still in its scabbard, solid and reassuring.

"McReynolds told us not to try and take that away from you," Callison said. "But for the sake of my other patients, I'd appreciate it if you wouldn't draw it here."

"No problem." She moved her hand toward her head and felt the pain in her shoulder.

Back in the real world, she thought.

Callison picked up her other hand, holding her wrist to check her pulse. He drew in the air with his off-hand, which had a transmitter-thimble on the little finger; it left a heartbeat-pattern and a set of numbers softly glowing in its wake. "Pulse is elevated, but the BP is normal. Give that shoulder some more rest, but the wound is fairly well healed.

"Damn, Admiral, you're going to put me out of business with those zor healing techniques." He placed her hand on her chest and patted it reassuringly—regardless of the century, proper bedside manners hadn't changed.

"*esLiDur'ar,*" Jackie said. "It can be taught, but I don't think I can teach it." She gently touched the bandaged shoulder; it felt more like a bad bruise than a shot from a laser. "How long since—"

"Twenty-two hours. The last enemy ship was destroyed a few minutes after McReynolds reported that you'd been shot." Dr. Callison raised his hand as she began to frame another question. "Look, you should get some more rest. In fact, I'd suggest that you go back to sleep *now*. There isn't anyone in Josephson System who needs you right now; Admiral Hsien has taken the frontline ships and jumped for Adrianople."

"Adrianople? They'll—" She sat up, felt a shooting pain in her shoulder, and slumped back down again. A wave of dizziness swept across her field of vision.

"Hold on, there," Callison said again. "You're in no position to sit up yet . . . Yes—Adrianople. Hsien took what had survived the battle and jumped out of here—he assumed there'd be no better time to take Adrianople back."

"He won't have . . . protection from—" She reached down, again to touch the *gyaryu* in its scabbard. "I can't . . ." she began again, but never quite completed the sentence.

Later, after some amount of dreamless sleep, she felt a hand holding one of hers. She opened her eyes to see the hand and the rest of the body attached to it: Dan McReynolds, doing a bad job of hiding his anxiety and worry.

Pyotr Ngo stood at the foot of the bed, looking out-of-place and uncomfortable.

"Dan," Jackie said.

"Jay."

"Pyotr," she said.

"Good to see you," Pyotr said gruffly. "Glad to see you're all right."

"You both look like hell."

"You're not exactly Miss Solar Empire yourself. Tactful, as always," Dan answered. He let go of her hand. He reached into his pocket and produced a comp. He flipped it onto Jackie's bed. She picked it up and inched up a bit in bed to look at it.

For a split-second, a reflection from the overhead lighting ran along the top edge of the viewer, a rainbow of light. Resisting the impulse to drop it, she touched the surface with her thumb. A 3-V display hovered in the air above the viewer: a solar system, the display slowly changing as the planets orbited the sun. A numeric display showed IGS and astrographic information.

"What's this?"

"I don't know. Thought you might. Our navcomp was programmed with this destination after—"

"After you killed *it*," Pyotr interrupted. "Whatever the hell *it* was that replaced the Sultan."

"Pyotr, I—" Jackie began, and wasn't sure what to say.

"Look, before this goes any further, I have something I have to say."

Jackie tensed, expecting the worst.

"For a few months," Pyotr said, grasping the bottom railing of the bed with both hands, "I've done nothing but get in your way. I've objected, I've bitched, I've suggested that we drop you off and get the hell out of town. And I watched you kill one of my best friends.

"—No, wait," he said, as Jackie and Dan both started to object. "No, that last one is wrong. I watched you kill *something* that *might have been* one of my best friends or might have taken his place. Whatever it was, it almost killed *you* a couple of times while you were a member of our crew. Now we know who it was . . .

"I—Hell, I'm no good at this. Look, the Sultan's gone. He's been gone a long time—long before yesterday. So I'm going to do something I don't do often: God knows I don't like to do it—I'm going to tell you I was wrong and that I owe you an apology.

"Whoever you are, *whatever* you are, you're all right by me. Dan is right: In this whole crappy business, there may not be a safer place than right next to you. Even though that doesn't seem to be *that* safe." He came around to the head of the bed and extended a hand. "If the chance comes, I'd like to buy you a drink."

It seemed an odd way to end the speech, but Jackie realized it was a sincere gesture. She took his hand in both of hers, feeling a sharp twinge in her shoulder.

She ignored it. "You're on," she said. "In fact, I want to get absolutely plastered with both of you. If the chance comes."

She let his hand go. Satisfied, his expression went back to its usual semi-scowl, but he favored her with a wink.

"Thank God that's over," Dan said. "He's been talking about that for hours. Ever since—"

"Yeah . . . Ever since I killed 'it.' How long has it been?"

"A day and a half. This is the first time that we've been let on board to talk to you. Most of the fleet—"

"Adrianople. Arthur Callison told me. Dan, that's suicide."

"Admiral Hsien didn't think so. He left us behind—most of the small ships, including *Damsel* and *Pappenheim*, thank God. His command is going to take its best shot: The admiral thinks that this battle knocked the vuhls back on their, er, back legs."

"I hope he's right." She shifted position and found it painful. She arranged herself the best she could. "I know we destroyed all five hive-ships. How were the casualties on our side?"

"We lost several ships, and what's left isn't in the greatest shape. *Xian Chuan* lost its flight deck, and *Duc d'Enghien*—"

"Lost?" An image of Barbara MacEwan flashed across her mind.

"No, but it's pretty badly mauled. It took out the last bogey on its own, though I wouldn't think her captain will be writing the battle up in a manual of tactics."

"I can't wait to hear about this."

"You will. Meanwhile, I want to know the significance of *that*." He gestured toward the 3-V of the solar system, still slowly orbiting half a meter above Jackie's lap.

"I don't know." She looked carefully at the display: an F8 star, white bordering on green; six planets, including two gas giants and a single habitable planet with two small companion moons. From its coordinates it was somewhere near the home system of the otran, the warlike, feline species that had not achieved interstellar travel when it was first contacted.

The system was unremarkable, except that she'd seen a rainbow flash when she picked up the comp. This was some sort of hint from Stone, but it could also be a trap.

"Could," my ass, she thought. *Of course it's a trap. But he's trying to tell me something.*

She checked the absolute magnitude of the star: about 2.5—it was bright, clearly visible from Earth.

Or Zor'a, for that matter.

She tapped the comp. "Is this static or smart?"

"Smart. Maartens cleared it to connect to *Pappenheim* main comp."

"Good." She touched the comp: "Display the location of this star in the Terran sky."

The system display was replaced by a pattern of line-bordered constellations. The star blinked at a point in the southeast corner of Sagittarius, the Archer.

"Mean anything to you?"

"Nothing definitive," Dan answered. "Try Dieron."

"That's an idea." She touched the comp again: "Display the location of this star in the Dieron sky."

The display changed to show more familiar constellations to Jackie, who had looked up at them since she was too young to remember. The star was almost dead center in the cluster of stars the Dieroni called the Lost Ones, commemorating the many colonists who had died during the cold-sleep trip to Epsilon Indi, Dieron's double-suns.

"A hunter and the Lost Ones. All right." She took a deep breath. "Display the location of this star in the Zor'a sky," she said to the comp.

This time, the constellations were completely unfamiliar, but the annotations appeared.

"It's just outside of Qu'u," she said. "It's in the companion—in Hyos." She looked up at Dan: pain, or perhaps anger, in her eyes. ". . . A hunter; the Lost Ones; Hyos. It can't be."

"*What* can't be?"

"Hyos. If I'm Qu'u, then Hyos is the companion. My companion. But that was . . ."

"Ch'k'te," Dan said, understanding.

"Yes. Ch'k'te. But he's dead, Dan—I watched an alien turn his aura off on Crossover Station a few months ago. I gave his and Th'an'ya's *hsi* back to *esLi* when I got this." She touched the sword that lay next to her.

"So—"

"So, I don't know. I have no idea. It's some damn solar system, and Stone wants me to go there, and it has something to do with Hyos. With . . . with Ch'k'te."

"So we'll be going there," Pyotr said. It was a question, but sounded more like a statement of fact.

"I'd guess," Dan answered. "Jay?"

"I don't think I can ignore this. Whatever it is."

"Told you," Pyotr said to Dan, scowling. "But I guess it makes sense."

"No it doesn't," Dan said. "Nothing about this makes any sense, but I don't think we should be surprised." He reached over and picked up the comp. "Take your time and get your rest, Jay. I have a feeling things are only going to get hotter around here."

Laura Ibarra's report, and news of the battle at Josephson, arrived at Langley only hours apart. M'm'e'e Sha'kan, Third Deputy Director, was pondering the meaning of the first, when a comprehensive account of the second was downloaded into his office comp.

Intrigued and as excited as he was, he forced himself to take his time with the analysis. It was almost a Standard day later when he finally permitted comp access to the director of Imperial Intelligence. As requested, he holoed himself into the director's office while remaining at his own desk, flimsy printouts of intel reports scattered in front of him.

"Director will the report from field agent Ibarra read have," he said, with little preamble. He could not keep the fatigue out of his voice; he hadn't had sleep or immersion since the first reports had arrived.

"I can't say I like it much," the director answered. "What do you make of it?"

"Full thinkings not yet complete are," M'm'e'e answered, letting his arms wave, though not energetically. "With results battle evidence of power of Admiral Laperriere showing, we in danger are, if she us an enemy considers."

"Surely that's a bit of an overreaction by Commander Ibarra."

"Director . . . Director, named specifically was I."

"Laperriere also suggested that you'd understand.—Do you?"

"Full thinkings not complete are," M'm'e'e repeated. "No. M'm'e'e not completely understanding is: Conjecture, Laperriere me believes, source of request for gyaryu is, thinking you, Director?"

"Lucky guess. Or insightful."

"Insightful. Assertion, whatever skill required is, sword to employ, learned it well has she. Underestimate her again, shall M'm'e'e not, for powerful, powerful now she is."

"Powerful enough to—"

"To do what, M'm'e'e say cannot. But in the sea, small one does not wait to measure large one's teeth, to know that dangerous he is. Item: MacEwan's report—image of zor holding sword, aliens from mind control kept. This, interplanetary distance from Laperriere was, while battle raging was." His four arms hung nearly limp at his sides, making him devoid of expression even if the director could have understood it. "By the Three, Laperriere powerful is."

"Laperriere? Or that damn sword?"

"Director—" M'm'e'e's hands folded across his bulky chest, two pairs, one above the other. "—*Gyaryu'har* Torrijos knew we well. Do this, he could not. Even if he as sacrifice to Cicero was sent, why necessary was this, then, if he this do could?

"Indeed, Director, image of Torrijos aboard starship *Emperor Ian* seen was. Image of Admiral Marais, *Gyaryu'har* also, aboard fleet flagship seen was. Conjecture, probably likely, under control of Laperriere these images were.

"Totally different order of dangerous, is this. Sword powerful is, but in Laperriere's hands, even more."

"I will have to advise His Imperial Majesty in a few Standard hours. Must I tell him that the best weapon we have against the aliens is someone who considers the Solar Empire the enemy?"

"Not Empire, certainly," M'm'e'e said. "Scheming of Agency dislikes Admiral Laperriere. Presented at court was she: Majesty will not easily believe, she an enemy of Empire has become. But more to this must there be."

"So . . . you plan to do *what*?"

"M'm'e'e must have many thinkings," he answered. "And, with Director's permission, research must M'm'e'e do—on Shr'e'a, and other things."

"I thought Ibarra said that there was no information on this legend, except for some poem fragment."

"In *Imperial records,*" M'm'e'e answered. "Obviously, closer to the source M'm'e'e looking must be. Time it is, for M'm'e'e to Zor'a to go."

Jackie stood at the door to *Pappenheim*'s observation deck. Alan Howe sat alone, gazing into the deep darkness, filled with unfamiliar star patterns. He had been left behind along with many of the crew of the crippled carrier, *Duc d'Enghien*. Barbara MacEwan had been assigned to command another vessel in the assault on Adrianople.

Jackie didn't want to disturb him; she also loved to look at the stars, regardless of their configuration. In any case, she'd recently seen things darker than star-filled space—and perhaps that was true also of the Sensitive across the deck from her.

He seemed finally to notice she was there. He turned a bland face to take her in, though there was the slightest hint of panic in his eyes. He did not rise, or speak, as if this might be some chance encounter—but she knew he knew better. She crossed to the place he was sitting and took a seat next to him: on his left, so that her body was between him and the *gyaryu*. A Sensitive's talents wouldn't be affected by so little physical distance, but she didn't want to throw it in his face.

"How are you feeling?" she asked, eventually, not looking at him.

"Admiral, I'm sorry, but I—"

"Wait." She turned to face him. "I don't think that our first actual conversation should start with some sort of apology. Unless it comes from me." She extended her hand. "Jackie Laperriere—Admiral, Retired."

"Alan Howe." He took her hand carefully, and quickly let go of it. "Specialist—Third Class, I think." He ran a hand through his hair. "I don't think about ranks much."

"Good thing I don't want a salute."

"Yeah." He smiled faintly, as if it pained him to do so. "I was trying to tell you, a minute ago, that I didn't mean anything a few days ago— I was just curious about . . . about *that*." He gestured vaguely toward her sword-belt.

"You could've asked . . . Of course, I probably wouldn't have answered. Even if I knew the answer.

"Barbara's report says that you hung in pretty well out there," Jackie continued.

"I passed out. They didn't even take me along to Adrianople."

"Still, you didn't let them get you." She tapped her temple. "They can. That's their power—Domination. They didn't expect to have any trouble with us, and we've given them more than they bargained for."

"How do you know that?"

"I was told. Do you want more details?"

"Not if you're going to—"

"No. I'm not 'going to.' I have—Well, there are enemies. Not the aliens that we just fought, but other enemies. They've been manipulating things from behind the scenes for at least a century, and likely, even longer. One of them tried to take the sword away from me during the battle and almost distracted me long enough for another one to kill me."

"That's when the image disappeared. When we lost our protection."

"Yes. I'm sorry. If I'd known—"

"No apology necessary," he interrupted. "Not to me, anyway." He looked out at the stars again, and was silent for a long time. "Can I tell you something in confidence, Admiral?"

"Only if you stop calling me 'Admiral.' "

"Jackie." He smiled; again, only for a moment. "I'm rated a T4 Sensitive, which is pretty good by human standards—good enough to get you on a 3-V talk show, write a column for a tabloidcast, or make a little extra money as a spy."

Jackie felt her stomach jump at this last word.

"But I'm out of my league here. I can't handle something like this."

"Meaning—?"

"I think it's time I went home."

"Disability? Sorry, Alan, I can't accept that. We're in it up to our asses here, and you're in it with us. We can't spare you."

"But I can't—"

"Can't *what?* What makes you think *I* can? Four months ago I was a base commander at the edge of the Solar Empire, with no pretensions to heroism. Three months ago, I was being court-martialed for running away from a fight. And, two months ago, I watched my best friend kill—and be killed by—an alien, right in front of my eyes.

"Three days ago I did something I didn't know I could do, and nearly got the entire fleet killed—or worse."

"And saved a lot of lives."

"And saved a lot of lives. But think about what *you* did."

"Pass out?"

"You survived a battle with the vuhls. Come *on*, T4 Sensitive! What you learned will help you survive the next time. Lives are depending on it. My old friend Barbara MacEwan is depending on it. You don't want *her* angry at you, do you?"

Howe smiled again, and it seemed to stay for a few seconds longer. "No. No, I guess I don't."

"Good. Now that we've got that out of the way, let me ask you some questions about what happened aboard *Duc*—*before* you passed out."

chapter 23

LET YOUR PLANS BE DARK AND IMPENETRABLE AS NIGHT,
AND WHEN YOU MOVE, FALL LIKE A THUNDERBOLT.

—Sun Tzu,
The Art of War, VII:19

When the jump-echoes began to register, Jonathan Durant was walking along the main concourse, largely unoccupied since the vuhls had taken over Adrianople System. His comp signaled at once; H'mr was summoning him to the starbase's flight deck.

"Locate Commander Mustafa," he said to his comp. A holo appeared above it, showing Mustafa to be in Engineering Section a few bulkheads farther along on the station's rim.

Durant thought about it for a moment, then walked to the side of the deck and opened a maintenance panel. He removed his ID badge and placed it and his comp on a small shelf, then closed the panel and walked briskly away in search of his exec.

Ships continued to emerge from jump transition, appearing on *Gibraltar*'s pilot's board. Admiral Hsien was watching the board intently as his ships assumed their formations; the battle-plan had been put together in just a few hours, with two basic contingencies:

If Adrianople System was too hard to take, he'd ordered ships to jump on their own for a default location—likely Brady Point, the unpopulated system used for refueling.

If Hsien thought it was possible, though, then his command would proceed to take Adrianople.

There wasn't really any middle ground.

Hsien was focusing on the enemy deployment. None of the bogeys in the system had the mass-signature of a hive-ship: there were IDs for Imperial and merchant ships along with some unidentified small craft—but no hive-ships.

"Comm to all ships," Hsien said. "Condition green. Proceed as planned. Flag sends."

Descending into the gravity well: *Sheng Long, Sheng Feng* and *Sheng Jian; Gibraltar* and *Nasser;* the carriers *Xian Chuan* and *Mauritius; Canberra, Pride of esCha'ar* and *Pride of esNa'u, Emperor Ian, Emperor Alexander, Empress Louise* and *Empress Patrice.* The fourteen capital ships had crew and staff from a dozen more ships damaged at Josephson. On several bridges a cheer rang out when Hsien's comm arrived: They *wanted* this one.

Find him." H'mr said. He squinted at the pilot's board, which recorded the incoming ships with the usual meat-creature inefficiency. The First Drone had all he could do to keep human form.

H'tt could feel the anger that he made no effort to conceal. He gestured at a comp console. "His comp shows him to be in Section Twelve on the outer ring, but continues to ignore signals."

"Send T'tl and two meat-creatures. Bring Durant here—I'm sure he will be most *insightful* on the tactics of this invading fleet."

H'tt gave the order. H'mr turned away from the display and stood straight, closing his eyes, to communicate with the Ór.

"They outnumber us, but will not expect their own kind to attack them," H'mr said after a moment. He opened his eyes and smiled in a way that usually disturbed the humans on the station.

•   •   •

Barbara MacEwan paced the bridge of *Mauritius*. She would have preferred the familiar surroundings of *Duc*—her ship—but it was scarcely able to fly after the maneuver she'd put it through at the end of the Josephson battle.

It could've been worse, she thought. *Not much worse, but we all could've died instead.*

"They're deploying from the station." Owen Garrett was sitting in the helmsman's seat. "Six smaller ships, with several bug ships following them."

"Are they pursuing?"

"It looks that way. But I don't trust the bastards."

"You're not in charge of deciding that, mister," Barbara said. "Admiral Hsien is. He gets the nice uniform, he decides the tactics."

"What are your orders, ma'am?"

"Keep your course."

Arlen." Durant beckoned to his second, who was bent over a piece of equipment that was being repaired. Arlen Mustafa pointed to some part, nodded to the tech, and picked up his jacket and walked toward Durant.

"What can I do for you, sir?"

"Comp," he said, holding out his hand to Mustafa. Mustafa looked curious for a moment and then pulled the comp out of his pocket. Durant unhooked Mustafa's ID and took both pieces of equipment over to a high shelf in the repair bay and left them there.

"Sir?"

"Come on. We've got something that has to be done."

"You don't mind if I ask *what?*" Mustafa asked as they walked back toward the main concourse.

"We're under attack," Durant said. "Someone's come to rescue us— maybe Rich Abramowicz got them to come."

"How many ships?"

"I'm not sure. I left my comp behind."

"Because . . ."

"Because if I don't have it on me, the bugs will have to find me the old-fashioned way. Same with you."

"They'll want you to advise them on tactics," Mustafa said. "Okay, what do you plan to do when they find you?"

"Simple." He was walking at speed now; Durant wasn't sure how much time he had before one or another of the bugs on the starbase came looking for him. "We're not going to help them. In fact, we're going to make sure they *can't* force us to help them."

Just before they entered the concourse Durant turned right, following a section of corridor toward a small extension dock. As soon as they went that way, Mustafa knew where they were heading.

"This is where the First Drone's ship is docked."

"That's right," Durant said. "This is what he will want to use to get his sorry ass out of Adrianople System." He stopped walking and turned to Mustafa, anger in his eyes. "We're not going to let him."

"He can control minds," Mustafa said. "In case you forgot."

"I hadn't." Two-thirds of the way down the access corridor, Durant stopped walking and pulled open a panel. "That's why we're going to take out some insurance."

Durant began to operate a control pad.

"You're going to jettison the dock?"

"Not at once. This is our insurance—if he decides that he's interested in compelling either of us, then we'll blow it into space."

"And us with it."

"There *is* that." Durant looked away from his work for a moment. "But honestly, Arlen—I've been prepared for that for a while. Haven't you?"

N**one of** the ships accelerating toward Hsien's fleet could match it in firepower or missile throw-weight. He deployed the three *Sheng*-class ships on the port side of his plane-of-battle, with the two *Pride*-class zor vessels along with them. The four *Emperor Ian*–class ships were to starboard. *Gibraltar, Nasser, Canberra* and the two carriers formed a wedge in the middle.

No hive-ships rose to meet them. This wasn't about killing ships, of course: It was about recapturing a significant naval base, a victory that didn't involve the destruction of a flagship or the sort of agony they'd just gone through at Josephson.

There was something missing here—Hsien felt it in his bones. It simply wasn't possible that the enemy had thrown everything they had at his fleet at Josephson and left nothing behind here.

It felt like a trap.

"Captain," he said to Dame Alexandra Quinn, the captain of *Gibraltar*. "Stay the course. But don't fire at any human ships."

"Sir." She frowned at him. "What if they fire on *us*?"

"Ignore it. That's what your defensive fields are for. I don't want to kill anyone we don't have to. They . . . may not be acting of their own volition."

Dame Alexandra knew exactly what he meant.

"Very good, Admiral."

H'tt stood in the doorway of the commander's office. It took several seconds for the First Drone to look up at him, though it was obvious to both Drones that he was aware of H'tt's presence.

"You have something to report?" H'mr said at last.

"They have not returned fire," H'tt said. "They seem to be headed for this base."

"I see. Have you found the commodore or his second?"

"T'tl has not found either of them, on the main concourse or the inner ring. He's still looking."

"So why are you bothering me?"

"You haven't thought this out, have you?" H'tt stepped into the office and leaned forward on the front side of the desk. H'mr sat back, putting a few extra centimeters between himself and the Second Drone.

"I'm not sure what you mean."

"You realize that these ships have come from the direction of the *ch'n'n* target. How did they defeat five *ch'n'n* ships with five hive-Queens aboard? Without enough *k'th's's* power—"

"Well, clearly they *have* enough *k'th's's* power," H'mr spit out. "They must have the Harbinger."

"But you said—"

"Things *change*, Second Drone," H'mr interrupted. "Things change."

"You would turn your back on Great Queen G'en?"

H'mr rose to his feet. This time H'tt stepped back, unsure.

"Things change at First Hive as well. Someone new has her *gr*xto'o* planted on the Seat of Majesty—Great Queen K'da. We will find a new configuration when we return to First Hive: *P'cn* Deathguard instead of *N'nr* Deathguard."

"You—you're going to abandon this system?"

"I'm not going to stay here and die . . . or worse," he added. "And I'm not going to leave the *or⁂xan'u* to be captured by the meat-creatures, either."

H'tt didn't have a response, but he looked quickly from H'mr to the door and back again, as if gauging the distance.

H'mr, however, was H'tt's superior in rank, experience and reflexes. To achieve the status of First Drone—to whom Deathguard warriors and lesser-Queens answered—required intelligence and *k'th's's* power. H'tt had considerable *k'th's's* power of his own, but hadn't fought his way through as many intrigues at First Hive.

And no amount of *k'th's's* power could combat the play of energy from H'mr's concealed pistol. H'tt writhed in an agony that H'mr could feel—but the First Drone didn't show a shred of emotion as he watched his second cross the boundary from dying to dead.

"Weakling," he said, stepping over the body transformed back to its original shape. "Begin destruct sequence," he ordered, walking out of the office.

As Adrianople Starbase grew in the forward screen, Gyes'ru HeKa'an collapsed to the deck on *Mauritius'* bridge. Seconds before his *hsi* was overwhelmed, he felt a frightening surge of power in his mind: a mental attack stronger than any he had felt during the attack on Josephson.

There was something more frightening about it, though; it had the feel of the Lord of Despite—like an arc of power, an *e'gyu'u* that threw him aside.

Owen Garrett caught Gyes'ru as he fell. In his head, Owen could hear buzzing. He assumed that something much more powerful had hit Gyes'ru—hard enough to knock him out.

Barbara MacEwan was kneeling at Gyes'ru's side within a moment. "Medic!" she shouted.

"Skip," Van Micic said, from near the pilot's station. "We're recording a large explosion near the hub of Adrianople Starbase."

Barbara stood up as a medic took her place next to the zor Sensitive. "Did someone drop a missile on it?"

"Not as far as I can tell," Micic answered.

"Then what the hell—?"

"I don't know, ma'am," Micic said. "It didn't take the whole station down. If I were to guess, I'd say someone just blew something up."

"Comm from the flag, ma'am," the comm officer said. "Query on the status of our Sensitives."

"If *I* were to guess," Barbara said, hands on her hips, "I'd guess someone just blew something up that projected Sensitive power."

H'mr arrived at the extension dock and came face-to-face with Jonathan Durant and Arlen Mustafa. Durant stood next to a wall, leaning casually against it. He appeared unarmed, but showed no sign of fear.

"I would suggest that you step aside," H'mr said.

"Make me." Durant smiled, but didn't move away from the wall.

"Commodore." H'mr smiled slightly. "There is no need for this. I intend to leave this place."

"You seem to forget that we're enemies," Durant said. "You and your lackey— Where is he, by the way?"

H'mr didn't answer for a few seconds, looking away from Durant. Suddenly a huge shudder ran through the station. Alarms began to ring.

"He won't be joining us," H'mr said, turning back to Durant and Mustafa. "Step aside, Commodore . . . unless you'd like to come along."

"The only place we'll go together is straight to hell," Durant said. He lifted his hand slightly, revealing a mechanism connected to electronics partially exposed by an open panel. "This is a dead man's switch. I'm not sure you're familiar with the term."

"Enlighten me."

"This is the electronic coupling for the extension dock. If the proper signal is sent, the joint blows apart. Explosive decompression—fun for *you*, for Arlen . . . and for me. This beauty—" He gestured to where his hand lay. "This is the dead man's switch. If I let go, it goes off.

"If you kill me, I let go.

"If you try to use your Sensitive power on me, I let go."

"And if I try to take over your pitiful second-in-command—"

"I let go." Durant didn't look aside; both of them knew the First Drone was trying to get a rise out of the humans.

"I don't understand," H'mr said, after a moment. "Your ships are approaching this station; your rescue is at hand. Why do you wish to die? . . . Why do you wish for *all of us* to die?"

"You don't get it," Durant said. "You really don't. You vicious alien bastard—you're my *enemy*. You killed people under my command; you destroyed ships; you've apparently killed your own second without any remorse. Why the hell *shouldn't* I want you dead?"

H'mr shrugged his shoulders and turned away. Then he turned to face Durant and extended his *k'th's's* as fiercely and powerfully as he could manage, trying to seize control of the minds of the two pitiful meat-creatures in front of him.

Durant's hand began to move as pain coursed through his head. Suddenly, a sharp brightness made him close his eyes tightly. He heard Arlen cry out, but he held his position, keeping his hand on the switch.

Slowly Durant opened his eyes to see the vuhl body sprawled on the deck before him. A few dozen meters down the concourse he saw an Imperial Marine trooper with a pistol still aimed at where H'mr had stood.

Carefully, he reached up with his other hand to disable the switch. He heard Arlen slowly exhale behind him.

"I didn't want to die today anyway," Durant said at last, lowering his hands to his sides.

*P*appenheim *was* crowded with wounded, but Jackie was able to find a quiet place—Georg Maartens' cabin—to spend a few hours in meditation. The captain of the *Pappenheim* offered to vacate, to walk around his ship while she communed; but she wanted to have someone keep an eye on her, and asked that he stay.

Maartens had learned to do his office work even in far more chaotic circumstances and settled at his workdesk to catch up on battle reports while Jackie sat in a comfortable armchair with the *gyaryu* in her lap and closed her eyes.

When she opened them, she was standing on the black surface of the sword.

"Sergei," she said into the dark, "I need to talk to you."

Her predecessor as *Gyaryu'har* appeared from nearby and walked into her sight range.

"I need to know what happened. I need to understand," she told him.

"I'm glad to help," he answered. "What do you want to know?"

"I tried to contact you before the battle started. Instead, I wound up in Shr'e'a. *Not* Sharia'a: *Shr'e'a*, the original name, in the original version of the story.

"Stone tried to get me to give him the sword, and when I wouldn't do it, Shrnu'u HeGa'u tried to kill me. In the meanwhile, you—and a number of others in here—were projected into the World That Is."

"And we returned to aid you in healing when you were attacked."

"Right. While you were out there"—she gestured, as if "out there" were a direction from within the sword—"the vuhls, the *esHara'y*, couldn't get through. When you came back, the ships you were all protecting were defenseless."

"Not precisely."

"You mean the field modulations and the Sensitives. But they—"

"No, I mean other than that. They were not defenseless: They could Resist." She could almost hear the capitalization in Sergei's voice. "They have begun to learn."

"Not from me."

"No, not directly from you. But from what you have told us about *your* experiences before obtaining the *gyaryu,* it is clear that you have begun to learn, as well.

"Let me clarify: When was the first time you faced an attempt to Dominate you?"

"Directly?" Jackie answered. "That was aboard the Cicero orbital station. Noyes."

"How did you defeat him? You had no guide, no sword, no Sensitive talent. *si* Ch'k'te was under the control of the alien at the time, so he couldn't help you. I was apparently unavailable."

"I don't remember. I came onto the bridge, and Ch'k'te was facing away—and he turned around, tried to reach me—"

As fear crept up in her mind, she felt a rising tide of hatred, directed unilaterally toward whatever sentience was controlling her exec and her friend.

She remembered now. At that moment she had been angry, filled with emotion against the Noyes-creature.

"I was angry. Terribly angry. I hated that thing—the thing that killed Ch'k'te later, on Crossover. But I hated it later, in the garden, when it—"

"You were more unprepared the second time, I think. But later, when it had you captive, you escaped. How?"

"I was angry again. I'd seen Maisel killed, I'd lost my command. I hated the thing that had me . . . had me—"

The *gyaryu* mental construct seemed to waver. Sergei waited, unmoving, as she mastered herself somehow.

"Are you suggesting that the power of hatred and anger is the way to fight these aliens—and that it *doesn't* come from the *esGa'uYal?*"

Jackie asked, when she'd composed herself. "That we've had it all along:
the idea that hatred can be a basis for Resistance? Then . . . Then why
did they go to all the trouble to arrange Owen's escape if he's not the
key?" Jackie thought for a moment. "Barbara MacEwan had no *hsi-*
image or Sensitive to protect her. Somehow she kept from being Dominated . . . by being *angry*."

"Anger is powerful." Sergei smiled. "Especially coming from a
MacEwan."

"You knew Barbara?"

"No, I was thinking of her great-grandmother."

"But . . . that's not a viable tactic for space battles. Or battles anywhere else, for that matter. Soldiers that become 'mad dogs' on the bat-
tlefield, wind up as *dead* mad dogs. We can't give up reason, at least not
all the time: I'd never lead an army that fought that way."

Sergei didn't answer.

"But the Destroyer might," she said at last. "The Harbinger—
whoever he or she is—couldn't, but the Destroyer might."

"Even if that is true," Sergei asked, "would you wish to follow such
a leader?"

For that question, Jackie had no answer.

"It's still my ship," Barbara MacEwan said, leaning on the rail that
surrounded the aft end of *Fair Damsel*'s bridge. It had been two days
since *Mauritius, Canberra* and Admiral Hsien's flagship *Gibraltar* had
returned with news of the victory at Adrianople; Barbara had come
aboard the merchanter to pay a courtesy call to the *Gyaryu'har*.

The crippled, half-wrecked *Duc d'Enghien* took up more than half
of *Damsel*'s forward screen. It looked like hell: The gossamer sensor-
nets were torn or completely gone; three arms were missing and one
hung at an odd angle. Tiny lights that looked like fireflies against the
hull showed where repair crews were working.

"We lost . . . three wing hangars: Red, Orange and Green."

"Green Squadron? Owen Garrett's squadron?" Jackie asked.

"Yeah." Barbara looked out at the *Duc* again. "The command
staff were mostly killed, along with the off-duty flyers. The fighter pilots that were deployed survived, of course . . . but Owen would've
been killed if he hadn't gotten up to the bridge."

"It might never fight again," Jackie said.

"You underestimate my crew." Barbara didn't look away from the sight. "Ray has them putting in work round-the-clock. If we get any kind of breather—and you seem to think we might—we'll get her ship-shape and running again. *Mauritius* fought well enough at Adrianople, but I'd rather have my own ship back."

"It's a wonder any part of it is running at all."

Barbara straightened up. "What's *that* supposed to mean?" she asked, half scowling at Jackie but not really meaning it. "You're not criticizing my piloting skill, are you, Admiral?"

Dan snorted, but quickly turned in the pilot's chair, busying himself with something else.

"No. Wouldn't dream of it," Jackie answered, smiling.

"How'd the old man take it when you told him you were leaving?"

"He wasn't happy. But he allowed as to how he had no jurisdiction over me and that I should do what I thought best."

"And with the, uh, Great Queen dead, it might actually take a little time for the enemy to regroup. Especially now that we've taken back Adrianople," Barbara said.

"For now."

"They'd better plan to bring their best game if they want it again. But hopefully they'll be busy for a little while, fighting among themselves."

"I hope that's true," Jackie answered.

"So what *do* you expect to find, where you're going? Aren't you worried that it might be a trap?"

"Of course. I have no idea what I'll find, but I can't afford to ignore it. When I took up the sword"—Jackie touched the hilt, instinctively, with her hand—"Stone helped me escape by walking a rainbow path through jump. If I'd stopped to argue about it, I might not be here to quibble about this.

"He seems to try to trick me and then tries to help me, in turn. I can't read his motivation or figure out his objectives: All I can do is move from spot to spot, trying to make the best decision and not to second-guess myself. Right now, I think this is the correct course."

"Sounds good to me."

"Barbara, I know you have to get back aboard *Duc*, but there's one more thing I want to know."

"What's that?"

"When the aliens tried to Dominate you, when you were closing with their ship, you were able to resist somehow. I've read the official report but I need to hear it from you directly: What happened during those few minutes?"

"Right. Well." Barbara looked away, as if unwilling to meet Jackie's gaze. "When Alan Howe collapsed, I could—feel them—trying to control me. They wanted me to give the order to turn *Duc:* They must've known that we were on direct intercept, and whatever else they did, they didn't want us to collide.

"I knew, though, that if I said anything it'd be what *they* wanted, not what *I* wanted. So I kept quiet."

"You were angry," Jackie said.

"You're *damn right* I was angry."

Jackie could see it in Barbara's face as she looked out at her heavily damaged carrier.

"I thought, 'It's over, I'm going to die. But I'm going to take them along with me.'"

"Could they hear that?" Jackie asked.

"I'd guess so. Then Owen Garrett came onto the bridge and shot the—the thing that had taken the place of my watch helmsman. They'd been arguing what to do, then they went away entirely. They even stopped firing weapons."

"That's when I stabbed Shrnu'u HeGa'u. It must've disrupted the hell out of their Sensitives."

"All I knew was that I could move again," Barbara said. "So I moved and did an emergency maneuver."

Jackie didn't comment but looked away, gripping the rail.

"A credit for your thoughts," Barbara said.

"About what they're worth, too. Look, I don't expect to be too long on this errand. I'll be back and maybe we can put our heads together to see what we've learned."

"All right. Fair winds, and all that." Barbara sketched a salute, then extended a hand. Jackie turned and gripped it with both of hers, feeling grounded in reality.

"Watch yourself, Thane," she told Barbara.

"You too, Hero," MacEwan said, and walked off the bridge, on her way to her gig.

chapter 24

Mya'ar HeChra generally slept soundly and well. He had long since accustomed himself to the crashing of waves on the shore beneath the sprawling diplomatic enclosure of the People on the western shore of Oahu. But tonight something had awoken him. He could not recapture the rhythms of his own Inner Peace to return to sleep.

His *gyu'u* and his inner perception could just about pinpoint the time but could not find the reason. It troubled him in a disturbing, elusive way, which bothers all Sensitives: something marked but somehow not recognized.

He donned a robe and made his way to the lanai, silently cursing the wretched gravity here on Terra. Their single moon was half in shadow and the stars were exceptionally clear and bright; even the lights of the sprawling seaborne food-gathering platforms did little to interfere with the view.

What had woken him up, a sixteenth of a sun ago? It left him ill-at-ease, like the sentinel who looks aside for a moment and feels sure that something has slipped past his guard. He was sure it was something of the Deceiver: not the sharp tang of an insectoid alien, though there were a few on Oahu even now. (Though the emperor, *esLi* be praised, was protected from those—they were spies, nothing more.) No, he was sure that it was a servant of *esGa'u*. Newly arrived, he guessed. Perhaps it was He of the Dancing Blade himself, though Mya'ar thought it unlikely—that One reserved his plottings these days for *se* Jackie.

He took a few more moments to consider and then called for his *al-Hyu*. An aircar would have him at Diamond Head in another sixteenth of a sun. There would be no more sleep tonight.

In an elegantly furnished apartment sixty floors above the beautiful natural lagoon at Hanauma Bay, just east of the Imperial enclosure at Diamond Head, someone else was also suffering a sleepless night. But here there was no philosophical musing, no Sensitive's inner reason bringing about the insomnia; it was a matter of mundane concern.

A bit less at ease with himself, a bit less sober than he customarily wished, Hansie Sharpe sat in a plush wing chair. He was alone, and decidedly miserable. It had been a difficult last few weeks here, though his hosts—the impossibly wealthy and punctiliously polite Natan and Aliya Abu Bakr—had continued to insist that he could stay for as long as he wished. They were off-planet at the moment, in mourning for their nephew who had been lost at the First Battle of Adrianople.

Their generosity had gone from being a godsend, to a relief . . . to, finally, more and more of a burden. At court Hansie had tried every avenue and utilized every favor he had left, but it was increasingly obvious to him that he had no more chance for Imperial favor than any of the dozens of others who had managed to get here after the war swept them away from their own private comforts.

"You are a parasite," he told himself. The slightly disheveled reflection looked back at him from the glass doors that gave out onto the Hawaiian night. "That's all you are. A bloody parasite."

There: He'd said it. Far away from Cle'eru, he was bereft of his many creature comforts—no leverage, no money to speak of, no more strings to pull and no more credit to cash in. In other words, no future.

Beyond the glass doors, the Pacific Ocean stretched off into infinity. It was a hundred and eighty meters down from here: straight down, with the low-friction surface of the Lunalio Gevway at the bottom of the building.

He'd never thought about suicide before; when his voice had been one that people listened to, he'd dismissed it as the act of a weakling or someone with limited creativity, unable to see obvious choices.

He'd also never felt so helpless before, so lacking in direction. Suddenly the prospect of leaving this all behind seemed incredibly appealing.

Something interrupted his reverie. There was a flash of light, like a phosphor surging and then going out. He stood up abruptly and turned, and to his surprise, saw someone in the apartment standing at his . . . his hosts' . . . sideboard, pouring himself a drink.

"Who the hell are you?" Hansie wanted to know.

"Someone who's a bit thirsty." The man—a slightly-built, almost cadaverous-looking man of middle stature, his hair cut in military fashion—turned to face him. "Can I pour you one, Hansie?"

"Do I . . . know you?"

"I'll take that as a yes." The stranger poured another tumblerful of liquor and walked across the apartment and handed to him. "I'm a friend," he said, adding, "I'd guess I got here just in time."

"Meaning—?"

The stranger again walked across the room, until he reached the glass doors. He seemed to spend a moment contemplating the moon-flecked waves of the ocean far below. "Really, Hansie, a swan dive into the gevway would be *such* a mess."

Hansie almost dropped his glass. He steadied himself and took a sip instead.

"There's no reason for that, though. This is your lucky day." The stranger took a long drink and then casually set his glass on the mantel-piece above the decorative fireplace. He reached into the pocket of his blazer and withdrew a small box, perhaps five by ten centimeters, and set it on an end table next to Hansie's armchair.

Hansie looked from the stranger to the box and back again.

"Go on," the other said. "Open it."

Hansie set down his glass and picked up the little box and slid it open as if he were handling some kind of poisonous snake. (Of course, he'd never done anything of the sort in his life.)

Inside, he found two small ampoules and an epidermal syringe. One ampoule held a pale drop of—something?—in a clear solution, with a female symbol—a circle with a cross below—on the cap. The other held only the clear solution and had a male symbol—a circle with an arrow extending outward—atop it.

It wasn't too hard to figure out what the stranger had in mind.

"Why me?"

"Why not?"

"Who's . . . ?" Hansie tapped the cap of the female ampoule with one perfectly manicured finger.

"Does it matter?"

"Why the hell *wouldn't* it? Of *course* it matters . . . You want some of my genetic material. I can only assume you're planning to—"

"That's right," the stranger interrupted. "And you're going to help me do it. Frankly, no: The identity of the other parent shouldn't matter to you."

"Why might I be willing to do such a thing?"

The stranger named a monetary figure. "All you have to do is to use the syringe and then take this little box to a birthing-lab and deposit it. No need to worry about expense. No need to worry about the off-spring, either—unless you care. I know you don't have any heirs of your own body; perhaps you'd like a son after all this time."

"Or a daughter," Hansie said.

"A *son*," the stranger said. His face, which had held a smile just short of a smirk throughout the entire conversation, suddenly became cold as stone.

"As generous as your offer might be, I'm . . . not accustomed to selling myself in this way. I *do* have a few standards left."

"I see." The stranger walked back to the mantelpiece and took an-other sip from his drink. "Well, there are always alternatives.

"Sumeria," he said suddenly, and the glass doors slid silently apart in response to the voice activation code. The faint breezes of the night, and the scent of flowers, wafted into the room.

Hansie's stomach jolted. The keyword had been spoken in a flawless imitation of his own voice. Only Natan and Aliya and himself were keyed to have access—and perhaps still Amir, their dead nephew as well.

"Go ahead," the stranger said quietly. "This is only a small errand. The rewards are great. But if you'd rather contemplate the alternatives—" He walked quickly over to Hansie, took the box out of his hands, and shut it.

It took only a moment for Hansie to grab the box back from the stranger. "No. No, wait. It isn't like that. It's just—"

"It's just *what?*"

"It's . . . not about the money."

"I see." The stranger folded his arms across his chest. "What's it about, then?"

"I've . . . been trying to get an Imperial appointment. A diplomatic posting. A government position. God knows, I'm not particular at this point. I don't suppose—"

The other let a smile creep back onto his face. "Oh, is *that* all." He reached into an inner pocket. "You want this." He handed Hansie a folded piece of Imperial stationery.

Hansie could see the seal through the stationery, but he calmly made himself take it and unfold it. It was an Imperial order, an assignment for a minor governorship. It was dated for early next week.

In fancy embossed letters the appointment read: SIR JOHANNES XAVIER SHARPE.

He almost dropped it. His hands were shaking as he set it carefully on the table and took up his glass.

"Mohenjo Daro," the stranger said, in Hansie's voice. The glass doors closed again and it was quiet.

"And all I have to do . . ."

"A little bit of your genetic material. Deliver the box to Shikoku Labs in the Olympia Island Arcology near SeaTac. Half a day, round-trip. And if it doesn't touch your *honor* too much, you can have the money, as well. No difference to me or my employers."

"I'll have to consider it."

"Five minutes. I'll wait."

In the end, it didn't take that long for Hansie to make up his mind.

With astrographic data in hand, Pyotr calculated a least-energy single jump to the system that had been left in *Fair Damsel*'s navcomp. There was no need to take any extra risks; his flight plan placed the ship a billion kilometers from the center of the gravity well, outside the seventh orbital.

As they emerged from jump, Dan immediately engaged the ship's defensive fields. He had gunnery slaved to the pilot's board, and was ready to acquire any target that might be waiting for him. Jackie had the *gyaryu* ready and in hand, but wasn't sure what to expect.

There was nothing. Neither enemy vessels nor attacks by *esGa'uYal* were forthcoming.

"All right," Dan said, after a few moments. "This is nice." He glanced aside to Jackie, who was looking directly at the pilot's board. "Why don't you put it away now?"

"Seven planets," Jackie said, not answering him. "One habitable." She lowered the sword but didn't put it in its scabbard. "I'd guess we should go there."

"I always knew you had a talent the Imperial Grand Survey could use," Pyotr said. "Habitable planet. You think we should go there, huh? Dan?"

"All ahead one-third, and shut up," Dan said.

"One-third." Pyotr frowned, but his heart wasn't in the argument.

It took six hours to move into the gravity well, during which the crew of *Fair Damsel* had a chance to thoroughly chart the system. There were some peculiarities that the IGS records hadn't shown: For example, like most "young" star systems—Main Sequence stars with planets capable of bearing life—the system had a large Oort cloud a few light-days from the primary. Close observation showed that the cloud was active and unstable, with a higher-than-expected number of comets following long, interplanetary orbits.

One comet was no more than a hundred million kilometers from the place they emerged—no real danger, but close enough to affect the Muir limit of the calculated jump point. The survey, almost certainly conducted by an unmanned probe, had taken no note of it.

When they were most of the way into the gravity well, Dan and Jackie came back onto the bridge. Dan found a seat at the engineering station, leaving Sonja Torrijos in the pilot's chair.

Pyotr Ngo and Ray Li were standing over the pilot's board, running some sort of simulation. A graphic hung in midair, showing some object describing a long arc through and out of the system.

"Comet," Jackie said, coming down to stand beside Ray and Pyotr and noting the data annotations hanging in midair.

"Got it in one, Admiral," Pyotr said. "That's the one that we noticed when we jumped insystem. Look at this." He touched the board at the nav station and the simulation moved. The object moved to a position well beyond the last orbital, light-minutes beyond the jump point. As they watched, it moved along the projected track.

Suddenly Pyotr said, "Pause simulation." The object stopped, display icons popping up next to it. "Magnify one hundred."

The object resolved to a comet-image, and the band of light expanded to show a small arc. The rest of the system faded out of view.

A few centimeters from the position of the comet-image was a hazy red cube, marking the approximate volume of the jump point.

"It wasn't that close when we came in."

"No, not when we got here," Ray Li said. "But it *was* that close—only a few hundred kilometers from the optimal center of the jump point—at this point in its trajectory. That was sometime in January 2386, about eleven years ago. We ran this sim back two hundred years, and this is the only time it was this close. Other than this approach, it never synched by more than fifteen thousand klicks."

"Was it pulled here somehow?" Dan asked.

"I don't think so," Ray answered, "unless it was pulled *back* afterward. But the one time it coincided with the jump point, it reduced the Muir limit by two-thirds."

"And anyone emerging from jump—"

"You mean, if the jump field didn't evert them or blow their ship apart?" Pyotr scowled. "I can't imagine. Hull breaches, system failures. Maybe even a misjump, throwing them to some other system or even into deep space. Not too much empirical evidence for this sort of thing."

"Looks like you've got enough material to write a paper."

"Yeah. Great. But there's more. End simulation," Pyotr said, gesturing at the pilot's board. A planetary display sprang into view.

"This is planet five, the orbital just beyond the habitable world. Pretty barren piece of rock, too dense to have any kind of livable gravity. Not much atmosphere.

"Now, take a look at this. We noticed this first, which got us looking at the comet." He touched the board. "Change view to center on longitude sixty west."

The planet rotated slowly to show a deep, irregular scar several kilometers long, stretched across the pockmarked and pitted face of the barren rock. It was as if someone had drawn a glyph on its face.

"Magnification two hundred."

Closer up, it looked more like a burn scar—a plasma torpedo-track slicing across the surface of the planet, forming a long, gouged canyon.

"Magnification eight hundred."

Even closer, at about the limit of *Fair Damsel*'s equipment, it was obvious what they were looking at.

"That's a ship, or what's left of it," Jackie said. "Let me guess. There's a trajectory from the jump point to the planet."

"It was at perigee when the comet made close approach. There's a reasonably straight line from the jump point to the planetary surface, right about at *this* area of the surface." He pointed to the other end of the track. "I made some assumptions about the ship's incoming vector; there are only a handful of values that fit the equation.

"I'll bet you that drink I owe you, Admiral, that the ship spread across that landscape, jumped from the direction of the zor Core Stars about eleven years ago."

"Could anyone have survived?"

"Not aboard *that*." Pyotr jerked his thumb at the image. "But in a life-pod, maybe . . . But only if they reached planet four."

"Lost Ones," Jackie said. "There are no FTL comms in a life-pod. If they were badly damaged when they jumped in, there might have been no way to comm in an emergency. Once they were in a pod it would've been out of the question."

"This happened eleven years ago," Dan said. "There aren't likely to be any survivors."

"This chain of speculation leads nowhere," Ray said. "Except maybe to planet four."

Jackie put her hand on the hilt of the *gyaryu*. "Stone sent us here for a reason: *Something* is here for us to find."

Iᴅ ᴏᴎꞀᴠ took a few orbits around the habitable planet for *Fair Damsel* to locate the settlement. It was on a continent that spanned the equator, in a hilly range near the shore of a large inland lagoon. The gravity was just over half a Standard g. A meteorological survey showed a very moderate weather pattern.

"It's a paradise," Dan said, looking over the data. "If there are zor here, it's temperate enough to make them comfortable. The gravity lets them fly. From the scan, it looks like they've done pretty well for themselves."

"Except for one thing," Jackie said, after a moment. "They've been here for eleven years, isolated and out of touch with the People. But here's what doesn't fit: The ship must have been badly damaged when they came out of jump and they may have had to make an emergency landing. But they should've been rescued by now."

"If this *wasn't* their original destination," Pyotr said, "it would've been like finding a drop of water in an ocean. There must be thousands of systems in the IGS database—it would've taken *years* to find them."

"Well," Dan said, "I guess it's about time we found out."

• • •

*F*air *Damsel*'s little shuttle set down on the planet's surface forty kilometers from the settlement. They'd made no attempt at concealment, wanting to be well clear of inhabited areas in lieu of a proper landing-field. Jackie and Dan took airbikes from the cargo hold and set off toward the cliff, enjoying the feel of the warm sun and fresh air.

Dan had wanted to take Ray Li or Pyotr with them, but Jackie advised against it. "They won't be shooting at us," she pointed out.

"What about your enemy? Sharnu?"

"I think this is Hesya's play, if anything. And I don't think he'd have dragged us out here to be killed."

"It would have to be more public?"

"That's about right."

As they came within sight of the settlement, they could see four zor rising to a low altitude and coming to meet them. As they landed the bikes, the zor landed before them and arranged their wings.

"The Stance of Honor Before *esLi*," Jackie said quietly. "They sense the sword."

"*ha Gyaryu'har*," the leader said to Jackie in the Highspeech. "*si* Sergei has joined with *esLi*." It was more of a statement than a question.

"A few eights of suns past," she answered. "I am Jacqueline Laperriere . . . his chosen successor."

"By High Lord Ke'erl?"

"By High Lord Sa'a," she corrected. "*hi'i* Ke'erl has also joined *esLi*."

The wing-positions of the zor lowered to denote sorrow. "I am Elar HeU'ur," the lead zor said. "I am the commander of what remains of the crew of *HaChren*, an exploratory vessel. We were badly damaged when we emerged from jump—"

"The comet," Jackie said. "We saw the wreckage on planet five."

Elar's wings rose a bit, to indicate surprise. "The Eight Winds blew us here, *ha Gyaryu'har*."

"I recognize that tone," Dan said. "Cursing his luck, is he?"

Jackie and Elar turned to face him. She'd half forgotten he was here, and realized he must have been standing there next to the bikes, watching them walk back and forth.

"*se* Elar," she said in Standard, "may I present Captain Dan McReynolds of *Fair Damsel*."

"We saw your landing," Elar said to Dan in Standard, not missing a beat. "Welcome to *alTle'e*—the Garden of the Servants. It is the name we have given to this beautiful planet.

"My fellow crewmembers: my Cousin, Mres HeU'ur, biologist; Dra'sen HeChra, exoculturalist; and Arash HeA'ar, engineer. We are among the few that survived the destruction. We have been here for eleven Standard years."

"I would like to meet the rest of your *L'le*," Jackie said.

"It would honor me to introduce you."

Jackie and Dan rode the bikes slowly toward the zor settlement, the zor flying slowly alongside.

"Tell me," Jackie said to Elar. "Why were you not rescued?"

"I have asked myself that many times, *ha Gyaryu'har*. I have concluded that they simply could not find us. We had been conducting planetary surveys in this area of space and had completed seven such analyses; we had been sending our reports by FTL-squirt to the regional naval base at New Basra, but evidently our flight plan never reached them."

"And when you came out of jump, you were at close proximity to a comet near the jump point."

"Our misfortune. Our vessel was critically damaged and partially depressurized. Half of the crew and passengers were blown into space in a matter of moments."

Dan winced at the description.

"We were able to rig two life-pods to escape before the fifth planet's gravity captured *HaChren*. We managed to land here and use materials from the pods to build shelters. We have a comp and a solar array to power it, but nowhere near enough to power an FTL-squirt. Perhaps in our children's time."

"*Children?*" Dan asked. "You have children?"

"Of course." Elar's wing-position altered slightly to indicate amusement, which Jackie noticed. "Several have been born since we arrived. Unfortunately, our lack of contact with the People has . . . affected them."

Each of the other zor altered wing-position at that statement. It seemed to show either tolerance or sympathy; Jackie couldn't quite tell which.

The settlement was more primitive than any *L'le* on a zor world, but they had done a good job of using the materials at hand.

As they approached, the rest of the inhabitants turned out to see them. They were of various ages and bore the emblems of a variety of Nests, along with a colorful badge Jackie didn't recognize. The adult zor all wore *chya'i*.

Something else attracted her attention: A juvenile female zor stood near the front of the assembly, and also wore a *chya* that somehow seemed familiar to Jackie. As she dismounted her bike, the crowd seemed to part for her. The young female zor showed no deference in her own wing-posture; instead, it conveyed anger—something deep-seated and raw.

This *is why I'm here*, Jackie thought to herself.

"You are the *Gyaryu'har*," the zor said to her in the Highspeech. "They told me that the *Gyaryu'har* was an old *naZora'e*."

Most of the wings nearby rose in alarm or offense. Even Dan understood something was wrong.

"She just pissed on your leg," he said.

"Not exactly," Jackie answered in Standard, without looking at him. "Things change," she continued, speaking to the juvenile in the Highspeech. "He died a few eights of suns ago. I did not realize that the High Nest had to consult with *you* before the transition."

"*You* pissed on *her* leg," Dan said now. Jackie ignored him.

"You mock me," the zor responded.

"You chose a flight over rocky peaks. You wear a *chya*, so you speak for yourself. Do you wish to challenge me?"

"No." Her wings approached a position of conciliation. "I ask eight thousand pardons. I recognize your authority. *esLiHeYar*."

The other zor nearby seemed to relax a bit.

"May I address you by name?" asked Jackie.

"I am Ch'en'ya."

"Jackie Laperriere," Jackie said, placing a hand on her own chest. "From Dieron."

"I am from *here*." Ch'en'ya's wings retreated to show amusement. She gestured at the other zor. "They are waiting to see how I next give offense."

Jackie looked at the other zor; they did seem to be waiting for something to happen.

"*se* Elar," Jackie addressed the leader. "With your permission, perhaps *se* Ch'en'ya could show me your *L'le*." *And get this encounter off-stage,* she thought.

Elar inclined his head. The assembly began to disperse. Dan looked
at her.

Jackie shrugged and said, "Maybe they can show you their work-
shops or something."

C hʼenʼya seemed bewildered for a moment. Then she moved
her wings to the Posture of Deference to *esLi* and began to walk toward the edge of the cliff. Jackie walked alongside her.

"This is a beautiful world," she said to Ch'en'ya.

"It is the only one I have known," Ch'en'ya answered. "I have been
condemned to life here from the time I was born, *ha Gyaryu'har.*"

"Why do you say that you are 'condemned to life'?"

Ch'en'ya stopped short and turned to face her, anger in her wings.
"*Why?* I am a Sensitive in emergence, *ha Gyaryu'har*, the most skilled
one on this planet. I am too untrained to reach any others and I have no
access to Sanctuary: Indeed, there is truly no one to teach me. But I *can*
read the shadow of *esGa'u*'s wing. It is why the ship was stranded here."

"*esGa'u*'s wing," Jackie repeated. A chill breeze suddenly seemed to
cut across the bluff. "Do you truly believe that the Lord of Despite
placed you here? Do you think he has taken a particular interest in *you*?"

"Yes. For longer than my life. He twisted my mother's mind. He
caused her to give her *hsi* away to my father, so that when she gave birth
to me here in *Ur'ta leHssa*, there was not enough *hsi* left for her to survive the experience. And if I ever meet my father—" She placed her
hand on the hilt of her *chya*.

" 'Gave away'—?" Jackie began, and then stopped.

It hit her so hard that she nearly stumbled.

"I *know*. I know who you are," she said now. *And why I'm here,*
she thought to herself.

Ch'en'ya did not answer; instead she looked out across the bluff,
away from Jackie.

"Your mother was *si* Th'an'ya. Your father was *si* Ch'k'te. *This* is
where she went, where she knew she would go."

"You knew my mother?" Ch'en'ya asked, whirling on her.

"And your father." Now it was Jackie's turn to look away. Her eyes
stung. "You can stand down, *se* Ch'en'ya. He's already dead."

"How—?"

"*esGa'u*'s wing," Jackie said. "He died to help save me. And as for your mother, her *hsi* was . . ."

"Was *what*? Why was it not there for *me*?" Her wings rose in frustration and anger, as if she had been waiting all her life for the chance to ask this specific question. "What was so *important,* that my mother gave up her life and left her daughter here in this miserable place?"

Jackie unbelted the *gyaryu* from her waist and laid it down on the ground in front of her.

"She did it for me, *se* Ch'en'ya, and for *that*." She pointed to the sword lying in the grass. "Eleven years ago, *si* Th'an'ya saw *esGa'u*'s wing descending and saw, somehow, that a new *Gyaryu'har* would be sent to retrieve the sword. This person would need her guidance.

"So she gave much of her *hsi* to *si* Ch'k'te—your father, my friend. And in an hour of need it was given to *me*. When I had no one to rely upon, I had your mother's *hsi* here. In my head." She touched her left temple. "And when I recovered the sword I released their *hsi* to *esLi*'s Golden Light."

"You . . ."

"That's right. Do you want to use your *chya* now? The *hsi* that was not there for you, was there for *me*. When I was done with my task, I released it. If I had known you were here—"

Ch'en'ya drew her *chya* in a lightning-fast motion. Jackie forced herself to remain still, though every bit of her being wanted to dive for the *gyaryu* or roll out of the way. She did neither: Ch'en'ya brought her sword out before her, pointed at Jackie's unprotected chest, but did not strike.

"You are not afraid of me," she said at last.

"What do you mean?"

"Everyone else is afraid of me. They call me wild and undisciplined: They say the Strength of Madness is in my wings. Yet you are unafraid."

"Of course I'm afraid." Jackie forced herself to look at Ch'en'ya and not at the menacing blade. The words *Strength of madness* echoed in her mind. "You hold a *chya* twenty centimeters from my chest and you obviously know how to use it.

"I don't know *what* strength is in your wings, but I do know that you should either kill me with the damn sword or put it away. Your choice." She spread her arms wide in a gesture that she hoped Ch'en'ya would understand.

The young zor held the fighting pose for another few moments and then sheathed the *chya*. "Pah. I do not see any need to kill you."

It was said in such a serious way, wing-position and all, that Jackie nearly laughed out loud. "*esLi* be praised," she managed, and picked up her scabbard and belted it around her waist. She looked around then, and saw a half-dozen zor watching them from near the settlement.

"They are waiting to see what you do next," Ch'en'ya explained.

"Let 'em wait." Jackie took the lead and walked toward the edge of the bluff. The view was magnificent: A pristine river cut through a wooded vale forty meters below, the trees dappled by the shadows of low-hanging clouds.

"They will want to know if I have touched your honor."

"You threatened my life. Of course, *I* put the *gyaryu* down." She turned to Ch'en'ya. "Look. This is an *a'Li'e're*. You believe that *es-Ga'u*'s wing brought the *HaChren* to this world, and I believe that *esLi*'s wing brought me here to find the survivors: perhaps even just to find you and return you to Zor'a."

"For what purpose?"

"I don't know. I can't see that far ahead. From the time I started to fly this path I've been making one instinctive move after another; this is just the most recent one."

"You will take me from my home to visit the homeworld I have never seen. Why do you expect me to agree to this?"

Maybe to teach you some manners, Jackie thought to herself, but didn't say aloud. "Make up your own mind. *I'm* following the shadow of *esLi*'s wing as I perceive it. When the homeworld learns of the *L'le*, I am sure that they will arrange transport for anyone who cares to leave. You can remain here if you choose, but you might wind up completely alone." She turned her back on Ch'en'ya and began to walk back toward the settlement.

You do not believe me," Mya'ar said, watching the aircars and shuttles take off and land from the Port of Honolulu.

Randall Boyd looked at the profile of the zor ambassador dappled by the late-afternoon sun, the faint tropical breeze disturbing the edges of his wings.

"I have seen too much and learned too much in the past few years to discount anything. If you say that it's true, then I believe you," Randall countered.

"I am gratified to hear you say so." Mya'ar looked away from the landing-field to his friend. "I would not take you away from your duties if I did not consider it important."

"I appreciate your concern. Now, please tell me why we're here."

Mya'ar took a pocket comp from the sleeve of his robe and gestured over it. Lines of data in zor-script appeared in the air in front of him.

"A servant of the Lord of Despite was here on Oahu late last sun. I felt him pass through and then depart. Early this sun, I sensed something of him here at the port, but could not locate him. Then he was gone."

"What time was that?"

"Around 0900, I would say." Mya'ar swept a claw across the surface of his comp, and an extra set of annotations appeared above the others. "0845. I was here eleven–sixty-fourths of a Standard day—something over four Standard hours."

"You spent four hours here?" Randall couldn't help but smile. The Port of Honolulu was beautifully decorated, but it wasn't anywhere he'd spend any length of time.

"I meditated." Mya'ar's wings rose in surprise. "Is there a problem?"

"Four hours. Please go on."

"*se* Randall, your facial expression indicates amusement—or is it confusion? It could not be amusement, for that would imply you were mocking me."

"I wouldn't think of it." Randall composed his face. "Continue with your description."

"I meditated," Mya'ar repeated. "Eventually I determined that the *gyu'u* of the Servant was no longer here. With no reason to remain, I returned home to rest."

"Until you commed me."

"Indeed, because I felt it again. These—" He gestured toward the data hanging in midair before them. "These are the vessels that departed Honolulu Port between 0800 and a sixteenth of a day later, about 0930."

"There must be more than thirty ships on that list."

"Five-eights and seven. Forty-seven."

"Do you know which one—?"

"*se* Randall, I have already cross-indexed this list with ships arriving from the same destinations and have determined that only *one* is presently inbound. I extended my perceptions as far as I could—"

"Given the distractions," Randall interrupted.

"—as far as I could," Mya'ar continued patiently. "It is *this* one." He pointed to one of the lines of data. "Inbound from SeaTac."

"How far away is it now?"

"According to the comp, it is less than one sixty-fourth of a day away."

"Less than half an hour," Randall said, doing the radix-eight math in his head.

"Two-eights and one—seventeen minutes."

"You sense the presence of—" Randall lowered his voice as a trio of People walked by on the concourse. "—the presence of a servant of *es-Ga'u* on an incoming shuttle from SeaTac?"

"Yes." Mya'ar's wings raised themselves in a position of guard. His taloned hand ventured near his *chya*.

A stray cloud occluded the sun for a moment.

"You're sure."

"Yes."

"There it is," Randall said, pointing eastward. A shiny sliver of metal caught the sunlight as it approached from the south: All civilian craft had to avoid the Imperial airspace around Molokai, adding a few dozen kilometers to ships coming in from the east.

"What . . . do you feel?"

"It is hard to describe." Mya'ar tucked the comp away and the data disappeared. "There is a feeling of . . . something at work. Like the trail the shuttle leaves behind." He gestured toward the contrails that marked the sky in the wake of the vessel.

"Will you know which passenger is the Servant?"

"I believe so."

"And when you identify him—or her—what do you expect to do?"

Mya'ar let his wings rise slightly in amusement and gestured across the terminal. Randall let his gaze follow the motion and noticed People scattered throughout the busy hall; as his glance fell on them, several nodded to him.

"It depends on what he does."

The shuttle began its descent. Mya'ar's wings changed position again.

Randall turned his attention to the shuttle, its landing-gear now extended and visible.

A minute ticked away. A group was beginning to gather near the gate, ready to meet arriving passengers.

"Something's wrong," Randall said. "It's not slowing down."

The shuttle continued to descend. It was clearly moving far too fast to make a safe landing. The crowd near the gate had seen it as well, and was murmuring.

"It is not turning aside," Mya'ar said. "It is on a collision course."

He said it quietly, but the others at the gate also seemed to know. It was clear that port security had caught sight of the shuttle, and they were moving in to clear the area. Mya'ar took Randall Boyd by the elbow, and several zor took up positions nearby, as they moved away from the concourse.

Mya'ar pulled his comp from his sleeve and displayed an image of the incoming shuttle.

Minutes ahead of schedule, the doomed vessel overshot Honolulu Port and slammed into the Koolau peaks near Waianae.

chapter 25

Jackie hadn't had much of a chance yet to use the *Gyaryu'har*'s official residence in esYen. When she last had been on the zor homeworld, Sergei had just recently died; the abode was still full of his possessions and she hadn't been comfortable with it. Most of those things had gone into storage or had been distributed or returned, leaving the place largely empty.

After arriving in Zor'a System, Jackie had arranged for Elar and Ch'en'ya to go to Sanctuary by shuttle. Dan had put *Fair Damsel* in at the merchanter port, and Jackie had arranged her own transport to the surface. At the High Nest, T'te'e had greeted her warmly, expressing the hope that she might remain for the next convening of the Council of Eleven; then she had found her way to her own residence, and found herself alone for the first time in months.

It didn't last long. As she sat in a comfortable armchair in the house's contemplation chamber, the house told her that someone had arrived at the entryway and was asking to see her.

She touched the controller of the house comp, easily in reach of the armchair, and displayed a view of the entryway. A single rashk, clad in a garish orange robe, stood with both pairs of arms folded in front of him.

"M'm'e'e Sha'kan," she said to herself. "What are *you* doing here?"

She thought about refusing him or making him wait, but her curiosity was too great. She signaled to the house to admit him and made her way to the front part of the residence to receive him.

"*se Gyaryu'har,*" M'm'e'e said, when she came into the front anteroom. "Glad is M'm'e'e, you to see, by the Three. That you safe are, glad M'm'e'e is."

"May the Three shine upon your waters," Jackie replied formally.

M'm'e'e's arms waved expressively. "Our own culture have you studied. May your scales moist remain, we say would, but know do I not, whether this expression you offend could, ha ha ha."

"No offense. May I offer you refreshment?" She gestured to a sitting-room through an archway. M'm'e'e located a low settee capable of supporting him, and Jackie sat in a carved wooden chair nearby.

"Hospitality appreciated is. M'm'c'e does not refreshment require, information only."

"What sort of information?"

"*Hesya* met by Admiral Laperriere was, not correct?"

The directness of his inquiry caught Jackie somewhat by surprise; but she took a few breaths before answering.

"Come now, M'm'e'e Sha'kan. That's not how the game is played. 'Take and give, give and take.' A very wise person told me that."

"*se Gyaryu'har* certainly correct is, ha ha ha," M'm'e'e replied. He waved his upper arms for a moment, then folded both across his chest and leaned back in the settee. "To hear one's own word from another's mouth, curiously amusing is.

"Perhaps M'm'e'e explain should, why he to Zor'a come has."

"That would be a good start."

"Study and research," he said. "Your admonition to Laura Ibarra received was. Deduced, did M'm'e'e, you thought him Hesya HeGa'u to be. Time and research taken has it, to learn identity of this Hesya. This information not in Sol System available was; a long swim from there only, found could it be.

"Thus here has M'm'e'e come, legends to study. In your wake has M'm'e'e come. A different legend do you follow now, friend Jackie, *Gyaryu'har.*"

"Sound reasoning," Jackie acknowledged. "But why are you *here*, visiting me?"

"To M'm'e'e news came, that you returned to zor homeworld had. A social call appropriate was, think you not?"

"I'm honored."

"Honored, perhaps—pleased, not. Hesya HeGa'u, M'm'e'e is not." His arms moved rhythmically for a few moments. "Still believe you M'm'e'e, servant of Army of Sunset, to be?"

"No, I guess not." She settled herself in the chair. *I'd probably know, or the* gyaryu *would,* she thought. "I suppose I owe you an apology, but it was too strong a coincidence, given what I'd learned. I assumed that you were behind the request for me to bring the *gyaryu* to New Chicago."

"Indeed yes," M'm'e'e said. "Understandings are, why friend Jackie conclusion might reach. M'm'e'e, Hesya is not."

"And Zor'a isn't Shr'e'a, either."

"Stated purpose was and still valid is: Use sword could you, train Sensitives."

"The only problem with that scenario is that the *gyaryu* can't *do* that." A gentle breeze passed through an eleven-tone windchime outside, as if confirming her remark.

"Cannot Sensitives make," M'm'e'e said—more a comment than a question. "Yet *you* it a Sensitive made."

"Not exactly. My . . . abilities derive from a peculiar set of circumstances, only some of which have to do with the sword. It isn't a matter of just grasping the hilt."

"Explaining, might *Gyaryu'har*?" He shifted his body forward on the settee, as if eager for the answer. "A matter of, what might be it?"

"The High Nest and the *gyaryu* both tested me. I passed. I'm not really interested in discussing the details."

" 'Interested' or forbidden, wonders M'm'e'e."

"Keep wondering."

"Offense to give, meant M'm'e'e not."

"And none taken. Perhaps we can discuss something else."

"Legends, perhaps," M'm'e'e said. His lower arms folded, then moved rhythmically, one over the other, then folded again. "A new one, *Gyaryu'har* now following is," he added. "*seLi'e'Yan,* pre-Unification, thinkings of M'm'e'e suggest."

Well informed, Jackie thought to herself.

"I'm not sure *what* legend I'm following at this point. Certainly I'm being pointed toward that one, though. But I didn't let the sword be taken from Shr'e'a. He tried—"

"Hesya. At Josephson."

"That's right. He tried to take it there: He played his best card. While he showed me the city of Shr'e'a, bone-tiled towers and all, his brother attacked me, in the form of a crewmember of *Fair Damsel*. It wasn't the first time it had been tried, but this time I fundamentally put a stop to it.

"In fact, Shrnu'u's—Sharnu's—attacks are what put me on to the earlier form of the legend in the first place."

"Connection does M'm'e'e not make."

"Let me clarify it for you, then. You know *how* I obtained the *gyaryu*, M'm'e'e Sha'kan: In keeping with *The Legend of Qu'u*, and the plans of the High Nest, I went to Center—to the Plain of Despite—and Stone presented me with it. Then he let me escape—*helped* me escape, in fact, giving me a way to travel all the way back to Zor'a.

"Now, here's the part I *didn't* understand: *If* I was following the Qu'u legend, and Stone was supposed to represent Shrnu'u HeGa'u, then why did he give me back the sword without a fight? And why would he then attack me to get it back? There had to be something else. Some*one* else. I followed some earlier lines of speculation to learn that, in earlier versions of zor legend, Sharnu was one of *two*. Hesya was the other one. The legend was revised."

"After Unification, revised was. But who this did, and why?"

Jackie shrugged; she knew the answer, but she wasn't ready to tell M'm'e'e that she'd heard it from Qu'u personally.

"In any case, my understanding of the older legend played directly into Hesya's hands. You see, at Josephson I had a talk with him directly: with Hesya—with Stone."

"Talked, did you."

"We were at Shr'e'a. It all made sense—in fact, it's interesting that he arranged this little scene *after* I learned about the older legend, so it *could* make sense."

"Stone a manipulator is. Of humans, of zor."

"And of vuhls," she said. "Whatever part they have to play in this game, I believe that he's manipulated them as well."

"Assuredly?"

"He . . . showed me. Seems that they've killed their Great Queen and replaced her with another one. They thought they had us beat, but now they've got a fight on their hands.

"And they've got something new to worry about: someone they call the Destroyer. The impression I received is that they're petrified."

"Friend Jackie, Destroyer is?"

"No. The Destroyer is yet to come." *Maybe sooner than I think,* she thought, as an image of Ch'en'ya came to mind.

"A zor, Destroyer will be, think you?"

"I don't know. No zor would've guessed that *esHu'ur* would have been human. Who the hell knows what the vuhls think."

"A rashk will it unlikely be, by the Three, ha ha ha."

"No, I expect it won't be a rashk." She smiled, not sure whether M'm'e'e could read the expression. "I don't think even *I* think of rashk as 'destroyer' types."

"Not even M'm'e'e Sha'kan?"

"No. Not even *you,* M'm'e'e Sha'kan. In the final analysis I don't bear any ill will toward you, or toward the Solar Empire, even in view of all that's happened in the last several months."

"To be hoped it is, that Jackie a friend to M'm'e'e Sha'kan and also to the Solar Empire is, and remains."

"I hope I might also consider *you* a friend."

"Most certainly yes!"

"Then I'd like to ask you, as a friend, for *your* help with something. I would've approached you about it eventually, but since you're here, it seems like a good time to bring it up."

"How may M'm'e'e Sha'kan of assistance be?"

"It's in connection with your original objective regarding the sword. I can't train Sensitives, but Sanctuary *can,* and in the coming months and years the Empire is going to need them to deal with every-thing the vuhls can throw at us. In addition to defending the fleet against attacks like we saw at Josephson, Sensitives will have to be able to recognize enemies in disguise such as we saw at Cicero.

"I discussed this plan with Master Byar, and he has agreed to make the facilities at Sanctuary available to non-zor Sensitives-in-training. With Admiral Hsien's permission, I've invited several Sensitives presently under his command to come here to Zor'a and begin the pro-cess. If they're able to succeed, they can become teachers."

"How M'm'e'e help can?"

"As you understand the significance of the zor legends more than most, it would be a great help if you would advocate this program to His Majesty's Government. I realize that many people in the Empire don't believe in the commitment of the People in this war—this is a way that we can truly work together."

"Heard this also, has M'm'e'e Sha'kan. But the depth of the ocean from the surface be easily measured cannot. Help will M'm'e'e, both human and zor friends."

"Thank you. That should shut up even old Hansie Sharpe," she added, smiling.

"Sharpe?" M'm'e'e sat forward again. "Sharpe, Sir Johannes Xavier, means friend Jackie, *Gyaryu'har*?"

"Yes, that's right. He's a courtier, a minor aristocrat. I met him on Cle'eru."

"The same, then," M'm'e'e said. His lower arms moved, while his upper arms hung loosely. "*Gyaryu'har* liked him not?"

"I've only met him a few times—what do you mean, 'liked'?"

"Killed was he. Three-threes of days past, a shuttle from SeaTac to Honolulu malfunction suffered—aboard was he. Surprised is M'm'e'e, that heard of this have you not."

"No." *Poor bastard,* she thought. "I mean, I wasn't a close friend—why would I hear of it?"

"Inquiries being made are, by Office of Envoy. Interested in this crash are they, particularly in death of Sharpe."

"Was it suspicious? Why would the Envoy's Office be interested?"

"Many thinkings has M'm'e'e had; no answer to this question to find. Knows he not."

"Was he the only—celebrity—on board?"

"Shuttle only half-full was. Tourists, bureaucrats, courtiers—and Sir Johannes Xavier Sharpe. Why crashed, wishes to know Envoy's Office. Why of interest, curious is M'm'e'e."

The question bothered her even after the rashk spymaster left. A shuttle crash hundreds of light-years away, even one happening close to the Imperial residence in the Hawaiian Islands, wasn't something that would normally attract the attention of the High Nest. Since it hadn't reached her ears through official channels, the investigation had to be at an extremely high level.

I would have preferred to make this flight on my own," High Lord Sa'a said, gazing out the window of the aircar from her perch. "But *se* T't'e'e and the rest of the High Nest do not wish to have me fly halfway around the globe. Security risk, they say. Who would attack the High Lord?"

"An *esGa'uYe*," Jackie answered. She sat opposite, in a seat that had altered to accommodate the *gyaryu*. "It would be more difficult for me to protect you if you flew on your own."

"I am unaccustomed to having you present to protect me."

"I hope to remedy that." Jackie knew that Sa'a hadn't intended to be hurtful, but the comment stung.

"What is more, *si* Sergei did not feel it to be his responsibility to personally protect my honored father *hi'i* Ke'erl. It was beyond his capacity in any case."

"Our flight is different now."

"Is it?" Sa'a's wings rose in some wing-pattern Jackie did not recognize. "The last part of my honored father's life was a flight which he undertook alone. He did not suffer from *naGa'Sse*, the Sensitive's blindness, which had been the curse of his own honored father: Quite the opposite—he saw far too much, far too well. This flight is now mine. Believe me, *se* Jackie: You do not wish to see what I see."

"Do you question my bravery, or my loyalty?"

"I ask eight thousand pardons if I have touched your honor. I did not intend to do so. There are just some things from which I would shield you."

"Like the Plane of Sleep, for instance."

"And now you question *my* judgment?"

"Regarding that flight, I do. With all respect," she added, as Sa'a's wings moved into a posture of slight affront. "I realize the exigencies of the situation, and that you could not wait for me to be present. The Eight Winds blew us apart and I was unable to stand by you . . . though I would have advised against it in any case."

"We needed to know what *si* S'reth had to tell us."

"And the *esGa'uYe* as well."

"*se* Byar had little trouble dispatching him."

"I have the greatest respect for Master Byar, *hi* Sa'a," Jackie replied, "but I'm beginning to believe that no *esGa'uYe* can be slain that easily unless he intends to be. The *gyaryu might* be able to terminate a servant of the Deceiver, but I wouldn't even be sure of that.

"By risking your life on the Plane of Sleep you placed both *se* Byar and myself in danger of becoming *idju*, had something happened to you."

"I will not stay in my *esTle'e* and feed berries to *S'r'can'u*, *se* Jackie. I am a warrior and I will take the warrior's part."

Jackie had no answer for this, but instead looked out the window at the clouds dappled by the orange sun of Antares.

"You did not accompany me on this flight to take me to task, *se* Jackie, or to demonstrate your loyalty to my person. Why have you chosen to visit Sharia'a?"

"I think I may be looking for the same thing you are: anything that will give me a clue as to what's coming. Hesya took me to Shr'e'a to try and get me to give him the *gyaryu*—I'd like to see the city in person. I've actually seen it twice, both times as Shr'e'a—first during Owen Garrett's *Dsen'yen'ch'a,* and second, during the battle at Josephson.

"Maybe we can combine what we've learned to get some idea of what our enemies plan: either the aliens we're at war with . . . or the *real* enemies, Stone and his crew.

"He told me that the vuhls were afraid of the coming of someone called the Destroyer. It was a myth among them, and now it's become more than a myth—it's becoming real."

"As *esHu'ur* did many turns ago, when he was embodied in *si* Marais."

"Right. The previous Great Queen was impaled because she didn't believe in it, but the new Great Queen certainly does."

"This was in the vision that the *esGa'uYe* Stone gave to you," Sa'a said, her wings rising to a position of guard. "How do you know that it is true?"

"As far as I can tell, he's never lied to me." Jackie thought about it, pyramiding her fingers. "No, I think he's told me the truth each time we've met—never all of the truth, and never quite what I thought was true, but he's never lied.

"It's almost as if he has a set of marching orders. For a century he's been trying to nudge humans and zor in a certain direction; *esLi* alone knows how long he's been doing the same thing with the vuhls."

"You are basing your Inner Peace and your honor on this assumption. Your actions are directed by the conjecture that a servant of *esGa'u,* that Hesya HeGa'u—the One Who Weaves—is telling you the truth."

"It seems so," Jackie agreed.

"This is madness, but I can offer no alternative."

The two fell silent for a time, each lost in her own thoughts.

"I had a visit from M'm'e'e Sha'kan," Jackie said at last.

"The rashk spymaster." Sa'a did not add anything to her comment, but her wings conveyed dislike, or even disgust. "What did he want of you?"

"He wanted to know about Hesya." She described their conversation: M'm'e'e's questions about the legend of Shr'e'a, the vuhls' fear of the Destroyer, and finally, the information about the destruction of the SeaTac shuttle and the death of Hansie Sharpe.

"Why is the High Nest taking an interest in the crash?"

Sa'a's wings were extended in slight amusement. "Perhaps I owe you a few eights of pardons, *se* Jackie," the High Lord continued. "I criticize your decision to trust your instincts—and then must inform you that the High Nest is listening to *se* Mya'ar's instincts. He sensed the *gyu'u* of an *esGa'uYe* on Oahu, and then sensed the hand of *esGa'u* when the shuttle was inbound later that day."

"When it crashed."

"Yes."

"What about Hansie Sharpe? M'm'e'e Sha'kan seemed to focus in on his presence on that shuttle, and his death. I'd run into him a few times . . . on Cle'eru, and then at a reception just before I left for Dieron—"

"Some of the persons in this room are not human: they are servants of the Deceiver."

It was Sergei's voice, or the memory of it, that she heard. "The first time was before the *Fair Damsel* went to Crossover and someone was waiting for me. The second time was before I went to Dieron—"

"And you encountered Shrnu'u HeGa'u there. Could this Sharpe person have been a servant of *esGa'u*?"

"Hansie?" She thought about him—a mousy little man, pretentious and bigoted. Poor old Hansie: She'd taken a look at the vid of the crash.

The gyu'u *of an* esGa'uYe: *a talon of the Lord of Despite. Maybe Hansie was a servant of* esGa'u—*but hadn't he had a couple of opportunities to kill her before she'd gotten the sword?*

Of course, Stone had wanted her to get the sword at the time, so maybe he had been under orders to leave her alone . . . Then why kill Hansie?

"No," she finally said. "It's a puzzle-piece that doesn't fit. I don't have an answer."

The High Lord's aircar was guided to a pad atop an eighty-story building near the outskirts of Sharia'a. Jackie hadn't been sure what to expect, but she knew it wasn't going to be the low, bone-sheathed towers Hesya had shown her in the vision: That was Shr'e'a, pre-Unification, more than eight thousand years ago. It was ancient history, like a vid or a sim that had been created for her benefit . . . or to scare her.

She had no doubt that the vision of Shr'e'a had been accurate in every detail, though even the most learned scholar at Sanctuary couldn't know that for sure.

The modern Sharia'a was home to more than ten million. Almost one in twenty were human, but the vast majority were People. The architecture was modern and made few concessions to flightlessness: no railings on platforms, open-air lifts on the outside of buildings, access doors eights of floors above ground level. Though the airspace was empty where the High Lord's transport had flown, Jackie could see People (and humans with flight-belts or airbikes) sharing the air with vehicles of all kinds.

With the reality of Sharia'a staring her in the face, the vision of the ancient city seemed like a remote dream.

Why am I here? she thought to herself, as they descended to the platform. *Sergei,* she asked the *gyaryu: Why are we here?*

We go where you go, Sergei answered from within the sword. *You said that you were looking for a clue to your next flight.*

This isn't Shr'e'a. I won't find it here.

If you were convinced of that, Sergei answered, *you would not have come. There might be a* sSurch'a *waiting for you here.*

Did you ever come here?

si S'reth *and I visited here when he was Speaker for the Young Ones.* She felt the slightest twinge of emotion as Sergei said this: a shadow discussing a shade.

T he High Lord honors us," the mayor of Sharia'a said, extending his wings in honorific greeting. After a suitable pause, he bowed toward Jackie, arranging his wings in a posture of honor to *esLi.*

"I am pleased to be in the City of Warriors," *hi* Sa'a answered. The delegation from the city inclined their wings, as one, to the compliment. "My companions and I would be honored to be shown the wonders of your city."

Further pleasantries were exchanged. The Sharia'a'i made arrangements for the High Lord's party: They provided Jackie and the two other humans with airbikes, permitting the group to travel together. Presently, all were airborne, with the mayor in the lead. Jackie noted the presence of eleven guards in the air around them, their claws near their sides, in reach of their *chya'i*.

se Jackie— Sergei's voice came from within the *gyaryu* as they flew. *Take care.*

What's up?

An esGa'uYe, he answered. *Very close by.*

She could feel it, too: It was subtle, masked somewhat by the *hsi* of the People and humans nearby.

Jackie guided her airbike near the High Lord.

"*hi* Sa'a—"

"I know," she said quietly, neither raising her voice nor altering the position of her wings. "You can feel him as well."

"It's not Hesya or Sharnu." Jackie was fairly sure of this: She assumed the aura of their *hsi* would be obvious by now.

"I know this one," Sa'a said. "I have . . . encountered him before."

Jackie's hand was on the hilt of her sword. Several of the escorts immediately moved closer, perhaps sensing danger. Sa'a's wings moved subtly, and they retreated a bit but remained closer than they had been.

"Where?" Jackie asked her.

"On the Plane of Sleep." Somehow, it seemed logical. "He was the one at the Stone of Remembrance. He was waiting for us when we contacted *si* S'reth. Now we are at the place of *seLi'e'Yan* and he appears again."

"Maybe we should get out of here. I realize that this could be awkward—"

"I will take the warrior's part, *se* Jackie, as I told you. There is no honor in retreating. If the Eight Winds blow me to *esLi*'s Golden Circle, it is as it must be."

When Jackie tried to interrupt, she inclined her wings. "We must learn why this *esGa'uYe* is here. Perhaps he has a message of some sort."

"Perhaps the message is, 'I want you dead,' " said Jackie.

"I leave it to you to prevent this from happening." The High Lord looked away and flew onward.

The feeling was much stronger when they reached the central square. The party landed near the center, which was separated from the ground walkways by a low fence. Jackie took her usual position behind and to the right of the High Lord, a wingspan away, the *gyaryu* unsheathed and in her hands, but pointed toward the ground at an angle.

A series of ritual exchanges were given and received by the High Lord in the Highspeech. Jackie recognized the story: It was the common version of *seLi'e'Yan*—with but one villain and the usual outcome.

The central square seemed disturbingly familar. Even with hundreds of the People around her, she felt alone. The orange sun beat down from a cloudless sky; dust swirled in the breeze. The ritual phrases spoken by the city officials of Sharia'a and the High Lord seemed distant, as if they were happening somewhere else and she was only a remote spectator.

Abruptly, beyond the square, she could feel something terribly wrong that twisted her insides.

You wanted to know, a voice said in her head.

The dust began to swirl around her, though it didn't seem to be affecting anyone else in the party.

You wanted to know.

The *gyaryu* was in her hands but the dust was stinging her eyes and clouding her vision. The scene was changing: Instead of a crowded city square, she could see a hill strewn with bodies—vuhls, many of them dismembered or maimed, a bright sun reflecting off their exoskeletons. In the midst of this scene of destruction was a man dressed in some sort of battle-armor; he seemed calm and detached as if the carnage didn't affect him at all.

Next to him stood Ch'en'ya, her *chya* in her hands, her wings showing something like satisfaction—recognition of a task well done. She was older, fully grown, but clearly identifiable. She did not seem surprised by the death all around her. It wasn't clear that she was even interested.

The man's gaze was directed away from Jackie, but he began, slowly, to turn to face her. His expression held *enGa'e'li,* the Strength of Madness. She'd seen it once before: in the eyes of Owen Garrett. The stranger's anger seemed barely leashed, as if he were ready to turn it upon her.

He extended his hand toward her as he looked directly at where she was standing: a signal, a command or perhaps an invitation—

You wanted to know, the voice said again. It trailed off into a laugh—

•   •   •

ѕе Jackie." The vision had disappeared. Sa'a's face was before her; her wings were held in a position conveying concern.

Jackie looked at her hands and the scabbard of the *gyaryu*. The sword was sheathed. The ceremony seemed to be over; four zor dignitaries stood with Sa'a, all communicating concern.

"You have had a *sSurch'a*," Sa'a said. "What did you see?"

"The Destroyer," Jackie answered quietly, hoping that only Sa'a could hear her. "I've seen the Destroyer. The *esGa'uYe* showed him to me."

ou saw the daughter of *si* Ch'k'te," the High Lord said. She held a fragile goblet with *h'geRu* in it. They were in the aircar, a few hundred kilometers away from Sharia'a.

"She was with him."

"The Destroyer."

"I believe so. She was next to him, part of his entourage. She was older."

"A *sSurch'a* of the future, then. *esLi* has given you an indication of what is to come."

"Or *esGa'u*—" Sa'a's wings moved to a posture of honor to *esLi*. "Or the Deceiver has given me a vision for his own purposes."

"That is a possibility. But an *esGa'uYe* led you to Ch'en'ya in the first instance, correct? After the battle at Josephson, you received the co-ordinates that led you to the place where *si* Th'an'ya's ship crashed."

"Then this is just a continuation of that?"

"*This*," Sa'a said, setting the goblet aside and shifting positions on her perch, "is likely more than simply a *sSurch'a*: It is a *shNa'es'ri*, a crossroads. 'A step away—or a step forward.' It is up to you to choose."

Jackie was up out of her seat and took two steps toward the High Lord, who was reaching for her *hi'chya*. She made herself stop, keeping her hands at her sides. Sa'a, alarmed, seemed to be forcing herself to relax as well.

"What did you say?" Jackie asked.

"A *shNa'es'ri*," Sa'a repeated. "I believe that this is a crossroads, and you will have to decide which flight to take."

"No," Jackie said. "The part about 'a step away—or a step forward.'"

"A quote. From 'The Flight Over Mountains.' I apologize—it came to mind."

"Someone said that to me. At the base of the Perilous Stair, before I went to Center. He—it—told me that I would have to make the journey alone. That I would have to climb the Perilous Stair alone."

Sa'a did not answer.

"I assumed that I was climbing the Perilous Stair when I went to Center, to get this." She placed her hand on the *gyaryu.* "I assumed that when Stone arranged for me to get it, I'd reached the Fortress."

Sa'a's wing-position changed again. She swirled them through a complex pattern, one Jackie had never seen before. It felt as if a breeze was suddenly blowing against her, almost sending her off-balance.

"No," Sa'a whispered. "You have not reached the Fortress, and pray to *esLi* that you never do."

"I'm still on the Stair." Jackie looked down at her hands, and then back at Sa'a. "I'm still on the Perilous Stair."

On the way to Zor'a, Jackie had had a discussion with Ch'en'ya that she'd dismissed as mere anger. Now, having seen what the *es-Ga'uYe* had to show her, she considered it in a different light.

"Why are we going to Zor'a?" Ch'en'ya had asked, looking out through the bridge viewscreen at the darkness of jump. It was a quiet watch; Pyotr Ngo was in the pilot's seat, ignoring Jackie and their zor passenger.

"We are returning to Zor'a to train you as a Sensitive."

"What will the purpose of this training be?"

"To fight the aliens and protect the fleet. Believe me, we need all the help we can get."

"And we will kill all of the aliens we meet."

"That isn't necessary." Jackie looked at the young zor: Every line in her body, every articulation in her wings, connoted rage. "We may have to fight them with anger, but it's not necessary that we seek to kill them all."

"No, you are wrong. We must fight them with hatred. Not just anger: *hatred.* And what *is* hatred, *se Gyaryu'har,* but the desire for the destruction of the enemy?"

"There's nothing to be gained by seeking destruction and nothing else. Nothing."

"There is *everything* to be gained! This is 'The Flight Over Mountains'—it is about the survival of the Light." Her wings formed a posture of reverence, and then shifted to something else—*enGa'e'Li,* the Strength of Madness.

"Look. We fought the People for sixty years because we didn't *understand.* Isn't it possible that we don't understand *them?* Couldn't we be making some sort of horrible mistake?"

"There is no mistake." Ch'en'ya looked at Jackie, her hands clenched at her sides. "*esGa'u* slew my father and led my mother to her own death. You have climbed the Perilous Stair and cannot see the hand of the Deceiver?"

"I know the whole story, *se* Ch'en'ya. I have been through the entire tale. I have pierced the Icewall, goddamn it! I see the hand—but not the heart. The vuhls are not *esGa'uYal.* They are *esHara'y.*"

"Pah." She looked away again. "You are trapped in *Ur'ta leHssa.* You cannot look up."

Now it was Jackie's turn to be angry.

"I've seen the Valley and returned. You don't know anything but rhetoric. What do you wish—to challenge me?"

A tiny movement toward her *chya.* Jackie's hands didn't move: If Ch'en'ya was ready to draw a sword against her, she'd deal with it then.

"Why did you not kill me when you found me?" Ch'en'ya asked.

"I thought you might grow to be a warrior."

"I see. How am I not a warrior *now?*" Her hands relaxed ever so slightly. Jackie still tried her best not to move.

Pyotr was now watching the scene, Jackie noticed. He hadn't said anything, and even if he didn't know the Highspeech, he seemed to have an idea of what the conversation was about.

"A warrior knows Inner Peace," Jackie stated.

"I see. Do you know it, then? Or are you excused, as a *naZora'e?*" Ch'en'ya had not let go of a single gram of anger.

"Why do you think I don't know Inner Peace?"

"A Sensitive's Sight," she answered sarcastically.

"Don't give me that. The Deceiver can confuse the High Lord. In *esHu'ur's* time, *hi'i* Sse'e realized that the People had been pulled into a war—by the Deceiver."

"This is different," Ch'en'ya protested.

"No. This is the *same.* The Deceiver wanted humans and the People to fight each other. The Deceiver wants you and me to fight each other as well. I won't have it."

Jackie turned her back on Ch'en'ya then, and stalked off the bridge. She didn't feel a blade, but she felt Ch'en'ya's eyes following her all the way to the lift.

In Sanctuary's practice yard below, Ch'en'ya moved slowly through the practice forms, her *chya* held before her, paying no heed to her fellow students or to those watching the exercises from the balcony above.

"She is undisciplined and full of anger," Byar said, his wings moving to indicate patience. "But that is only to be expected." He turned away from the balcony to look at Jackie. "Yet she learns every lesson and does not need to be reminded. Her Sensitive powers . . ." He spread his arms wide. "She is the daughter of her mother," he finished.

"*esLi* grant that she inherits other things from her as well," Jackie said.

"Such as?"

"A civil tongue. Patience."

"I have not noted either of these as problems, *se* Jackie. She speaks politely to me and to the instructors, and seems willing to learn at the pace we have set. She seems very . . . determined."

"She is full of the Strength of Madness."

"Yes, of course." They began to walk toward the inner compound of Sanctuary. "That is also to be expected. But her skills can be put to use."

"That's what I'm afraid of."

"We are at *war, se* Jackie. I do not need to remind you of that." They passed under an archway and out of the bright-orange sunlight, into a dim and cool hallway. "We cannot afford to ignore any source of help."

" 'Beggars can't be choosers.' "

"If I understand the aphorism correctly, yes. We will be training humans here soon, in accordance with your plans; some of the staff of Sanctuary consider this to be a flawed approach, but none is prepared to gainsay you."

"But they're not happy about it."

"They will not gainsay you," he repeated. They passed through a wide rotunda dotted with perches and causeways above her head, and still more on levels below the path they now walked.

They entered an alcove that looked out toward the sunset. Jackie leaned against a low table that held an ornate flask, delicate cups and a few books; Byar fluttered up to a perch.

She stood up straight and crossed her arms in front of herself. "While we were at Sharia'a, *se* Byar," she said, "I believe I saw the Destroyer."

"The nemesis of the *esHara'y*?"

"That's right. It was . . . a vision of the future. The Destroyer was surrounded by alien corpses. I saw something in his eyes: *enGa'e'Li,* the Strength of Madness. As much as *I'd* like to see them all dead, it was a disturbing image."

"Did it somehow touch your honor?" Byar's wings betrayed only curiosity, as if a corpse-strewn scene wouldn't disturb him—which, perhaps, it might not.

"No. It affected my Inner Peace, though. It was sent to me by an *es-Ga'uYe.*"

"It could have been a false seeming," Byar said, his wings assuming the Posture of Guard.

"I don't think so. They've tried to deceive and distract me, but they've never directly lied to me." *Yet,* she added to herself.

"I see. Then how did you know it to be a *future* vision?"

"Ch'en'ya was in it. She was an adult, perhaps twenty-five or thirty turns older than now. She was with *him.*"

"With the Destroyer." He seemed thoughtful for a moment. "A servant? An ally?"

"An ally, I think. She seemed . . . content. It was as if—she saw all the destruction as a job well done. It gave her pleasure."

"A warrior's task is to destroy. You carry the *gyaryu* and I carry a *chya*—but their ultimate purpose is clear: They were forged to taste the blood of enemies."

"Not like *that.*"

"This is a *human* sensibility, *se* Jackie, if I may be permitted to say so. Even now, we are training warriors and Sensitives to fight a war—a destructive war—for the survival of the People and the Solar Empire. We will even fight on behalf of the creatures who will not fight for themselves."

He altered his stance to convey distaste—it was a wing-position that usually went with discussion of the rashk, whom most zor disliked.

"If I were not human, I might be offended at that."

"Eight thousand pardons, *se* Jackie, but if you were *not* human, it might not be necessary for me to clarify the point."

"I—" She bit back a retort, thinking. "I suppose there's some merit in that," she said, after a moment. "But it bothers me all the same, to see this as her future."

"There is no guarantee that this is a *true* future, *se* Jackie. It is likely only a possible future. *esLi* Himself"—he re-formed his wings in a posture of honor to *esLi*—"only knows what lies ahead in anyone's flight."

"So it might not happen, after all."

"The *esGa'uYe* has shown it to you for a reason. He wishes to push you in a particular direction—either toward that result, or away from it. What we do not know, is which result he prefers."

"I don't particularly *like* the outcome he showed me. Was that meant to push me away from it, or just to scare me into thinking that it might come to pass? Damn." She put her hand on the *gyaryu* and walked to the window, where Antares, Zor'a's primary, was lowering toward the horizon.

A cold breeze suddenly came from nowhere, interrupting the sultry, sweaty air outside. It seemed to ruffle the hairs on the back of her neck.

"He's here," she said, without turning around.

"I know him," Byar acknowledged. "This is the one we met on the Plane of Sleep."

He was already moving. Jackie turned and ran after him. Byar seemed to be following his own instincts—he had his *chya* in his hand and was flying at high speed through the corridor. Students were dodging out of the way, and at least two instructors had already joined him.

The snarl from the *gyaryu* was like a bell ringing in her head.

Such a pity to be wingless, she heard in her mind.

Shut the hell up, she said to the voice, running with her hand on her sword. She wasn't confident that she could run very fast with the *gyaryu* in hand, and wasn't sure what she'd be doing with the blade when she got to their destination.

They burst out of the building with Byar in the lead. They were on the parapet now, and the wind was kicking up dust all around them. Below, in the practice yard, most of the students had fled, but there were two zor in the middle of the field, blades drawn, circling for advantage.

"*esLi*," Byar said under his breath. He rose a meter in the air, but then paused, as if hesitant to fly down and join the fight. One of the combatants was an adult zor, and clearly the source of the disturbing feeling that had moved them all into action.

The other was Ch'en'ya.

She held her wings in the Cloak of Challenge, which explained why no one else had entered into the area or joined in the combat: She had declared, in effect, that this was her fight to win or lose.

"You little arrogant—" Jackie began, but felt Byar grasp her wrist gently. He had not looked away from the combat.

"You have had a *sSurch'a*. What is it?"

"This is a *shNa'es'ri*," she said. "The *esGa'uYe* has presented me with a dilemma."

"What are your choices?" Byar asked.

Ch'en'ya was feinting, trying to get in a blow against the other zor-who-was-no-zor.

"If I stand by and do nothing and she is victorious, it will make her even more sure of her destiny and push her closer to the Destroyer. If I stand by and do nothing and she is killed, I will lose her, though I will know that my vision was false.

"And if I intervene in a challenge of honor, we are both *idju*."

"That is *three* choices," Byar said levelly, still not looking away from the fight. He let himself descend to the ground again and let go of her wrist. "What is the fourth?"

"*What?*"

The two zor charged, clashed and separated. *chya* and *e'chya* snarled and hissed. There was a distant rumble of thunder and the air held the metallic tang of an oncoming storm.

"*Four* choices. This is a *shNa'es'ri*: two choices, or four. Not three. *What is the fourth choice?*"

"I don't have time for Socratic bullshit, *se* Byar. What are you trying to say?"

"*se* Jackie." Byar glanced at her for just a moment, as the *esGa'uYe* advanced quickly, swinging his *e'chya* in great arcs that Ch'en'ya was hard-pressed to dodge. "This is not a teaching. If there is a *sSurch'a* for this occasion, you must find it yourself. The *esGa'uYe* has left you one more choice and you must determine what it is."

The alien was beginning to press now, executing fantastically acrobatic maneuvers, slashing at Ch'en'ya. The young zor was clearly skillful with her *chya*, but still was no match for her alien opponent. In a way, she seemed to be unable to look away, as if the entire universe was narrowing her vision down to the *e'chya* that waved and danced before her.

"She's being mesmerized," Jackie said. "He's stepping beyond the boundaries of the duel. He's—"

Help! she shouted to the *gyaryu*. *I can't stop the fight, but—*

Suddenly the combatants parted and the *esGa'uYe* retreated, guard up, *e'chya* held before him. Another figure had appeared on the field, *gyaryu* in hand, half-opaque and half-transparent. His wing-markings made him recognizable to every zor present.

"*esLi,*" Byar uttered quietly.

"I am Qu'u," the figure announced. It didn't need to be said; the *e'chya* snarled, making Jackie's stomach churn. "Your sorceries have no place here, creature of Despite."

"This is not your fight!" Ch'en'ya shouted, looking from the *es-Ga'uYe* to Qu'u, to the balcony above. "By *esLi,* this is *my* fight! This is a challenge of honor and I will fight it or be *idju*! How *dare* you deny me this?"

"No," Qu'u said. "No, Younger Sister, you will not be denied this challenge. But you will fight in a clear sky."

As if in answer, the thunder rumbled, closer now. The sultry afternoon had given way to dark clouds in a matter of minutes.

"It shall be a battle of blades—no more and no less. None shall take this honor or this duty from you, since you have chosen it. But no deceit of the Enemy will be used. I swear this by the *gyaryu.*"

"I swear this by the *gyaryu,*" Jackie repeated, under her breath.

Qu'u looked at the blade held before him and then up at Jackie. He arranged his wings in the Stance of Honor to *esLi.*

"The Crawler would interrupt a challenge? How do I know you will not intervene, Servant?"

"My oath," Qu'u replied. "If that is insufficient for you, then you have no place in a field of challenge. Choose now."

"I choose to fight," the Servant said immediately. Qu'u nodded, and moved the *gyaryu* to rest position.

The battle was now truly joined. Without sorcerous aid, the *es-Ga'uYe* seemed to be diminished, while Ch'en'ya's confidence grew with every volley. She radiated hatred. It was more than just a challenge of honor: This foe was a scion of the race that had killed her father, deceived her mother and made her an exile.

She had had the mold of her life shattered and re-formed by an alien race. Ch'en'ya understood that while the current of events was beyond her ability to control, she could affect the outcome of *this* battle, at this moment.

It was insanity. It was a terrible, fierce, emotion-driven power. It was *enGa'e'Li*: the Strength of Madness in full force. Blow after blow, heedless of counterattack, Ch'en'ya drove her opponent farther and farther off-guard.

The rain began to pelt down and the fight continued, combatants and onlookers heedless of the weather. Qu'u's image remained, observing all that had happened, while Jackie maintained her concentration to keep him there.

At last the alien stumbled, landing on his side, his *e'chya* flying from his grasp. Ch'en'ya was on him in a moment, her *chya* poised for the kill. He was nearly unconscious, bleeding heavily, his image starting to waver.

"Will you spare him?" Qu'u asked.

Ch'en'ya looked away from the prone figure, drifting from zor-form to vuhl-form to human-form, to look at Jackie and Byar and then back to Qu'u.

"No," she said, and drove the *chya* through the creature's midsection.

chapter 26

The great naval base at Zor'a was teeming with activity. More than two dozen ships were insystem, assembling in preparation for action against the aliens.

Jackie had taken a shuttle from the surface earlier in the day. It had been a busy few weeks at Sanctuary, since Ch'en'ya had killed the intruder in the challenge; she had been impossible to live with since then—bloodied and wounded, she had still been absolutely triumphant, insisting that killing the creature outright had been the *right* thing to do. It was her right, but it was still nothing more than killing a body—just as when Jackie had killed the Drew Sabah creature; just as when the intelligence agent had killed Stone more than eighty-five years ago. It was no more than an inconvenience for the *esGa'uYal*.

They should have spared the alien, but Ch'en'ya was stubborn in this, as in all things.

She had wanted to accompany Jackie to the naval base, but Jackie wouldn't hear of it. Putting some distance between the two of them might be the best thing at this stage, Destroyer or no Destroyer.

She had told Ch'en'ya that, and her response had been, "Pah." It was her favorite word.

•   •   •

As ever, her status as *Gyaryu'har* commanded deference and perhaps some fear among those Jackie passed on the station. She walked (actually, she *stalked*) through the corridors, making her way toward the naval docks. As she approached, she picked out a familiar figure in a familiar setting. She could hear the voice before she could see its owner, but it stopped when she came around the curve of the dock.

"Now, *there's* a sight," Barbara MacEwan said, interrupting her angry conversation with another human naval officer. She walked toward Jackie, stopped and smiled. Barbara executed a perfect salute and then extended her hand; Jackie took it warmly and smiled back.

"Are those commodore's bars on your uniform?" Jackie asked.

"Seems so," she answered. "I guess that's the standard award in His Majesty's Navy for crippling a ship. Wonder what I have to do to get an admiral's flag?"

"Abandon a naval base," Jackie shot back, and Barbara's face fell. "And get roped into a zor legend," Jackie added.

"I'm sorry, I didn't mean—"

"No, and I didn't interpret it that way. Alvarez promoted me to admiral so he could retire me. Remember, a few months ago I was facing a general court-martial for giving up Cicero. Who knew where that would lead?"

"I remember," Barbara said. They walked along the corridor together. "And the last time we talked, you were on your way into some kind of trap. Looks like you got out of it."

"Or *into* it." Jackie ran a hand through her hair. She suddenly felt tired, as if all the events of the past several weeks were descending on her shoulders. "We were pointed at an unexplored system and found some zor who had been stranded there. One of them was Ch'k'te's daughter."

"Ch'k'te? *Our* Ch'k'te?"

"Yes, *our* Ch'k'te. Apparently, Th'an'ya, his teacher and . . . mate . . . was pregnant when she went off with the expedition. She apparently knew, or had some premonition, that they'd never see home again . . . but she left most of her *hsi,* her life-energy, with Ch'k'te so that he could pass it on to me.

"Th'an'ya was my guide"—she tapped her temple—"and advisor during the entire time I was looking for the sword. She arranged it so that she would be available to whoever turned up to recover it."

"How'd she know?"

"They *knew.*" Jackie stopped, hands on hips, and looked at Barbara.

"It's complicated, but it looks like the High Nest intentionally placed Sergei and the sword in harm's way because they'd foreseen the invasion. At some point I was picked out as the person to go and get it back. And here we are."

"And what does—Ch'en'ya?—have to do with all of this?"

"I'm not sure. She's self-willed, uncooperative and full of anger. She wants the aliens dead—every one of them—and is willing to do it with her own sword if necessary. A few weeks ago she fought a duel with an alien at Sanctuary—"

"A vuhl?"

". . . Not exactly." They began to walk again. "No, it's even more complicated than *that*. The vuhls *are* our enemy, but they're not the most dangerous participants in this game. There's another group out there, scheming and manipulating. They've been involved with us for a long time, nudging us toward some conclusion."

"When you say 'a long time' . . ."

"At least since before we encountered the zor. Likely, longer than that." *A lot longer,* she thought to herself. *Hesya and Sharnu. What else have they done? Who else have they been?*

"How do you fight an enemy like that? The vuhls, I can understand—more than most, which explains these." Barbara pointed to the bars on her shoulders. "Josephson cost us a lot of fine officers; those of us who survived have to pick up the slack."

"What's your mission? Or can you tell me?"

"I haven't been ordered not to. I've still got *Mauritius*—I'd rather have *Duc,* but she's in dry-dock for a few months more—and my squadron's going to take some more of your trained Sensitives and jump to Cicero."

"Whose crazy idea is *that*?"

"Hsien's. And the First Lord's. Just like at Adrianople, we have orders to jump in and make a quick decision about the feasibility of taking back the base, and to get the hell out if we can't. It's only a mildly crazy mission—and they found someone mildly crazy enough to lead it."

"It's suicide."

"No, damn it, it's *not*." Barbara's face took on a serious look. "We don't know how to win this war yet. We don't even know if it can be won. But we have to start somewhere. At Thon's Well we destroyed the invaders, and it cost us plenty; at Josephson, the same. At Adrianople we actually took the war *to* the enemy—"

"There were no hive-ships there, and they blew up whatever tech would have let them use their mental powers on your ships. They've had Cicero ever since we left it behind."

"I know all that, but it's got to be done anyway. How badly did we hurt them there? I don't know. You don't know, either, unless you've held back information. All I know is that we can't possibly win if we shy away from fighting. We can't retreat forever."

"I know that, but we won't win by squandering our resources, either. *You've* been in combat against the vuhls: You know what they can do."

"And what they *can't* do. We can't have *you* everywhere; we have to see if we can win a battle without the secret weapon." She pointed at the *gyaryu;* from within, Jackie heard something that might have been a faint chuckle. "We MacEwans have always been soldiers; it's my job, and it's got to be done."

"You want to die in battle."

"No, I want to die during *sex.* I just want to have an Empire survive long enough for me to have shore leave in it." Barbara smiled and took Jackie's hand, then offered her another salute.

"I'll get us home again. Count on it."

"You'd better," Jackie said, returning the salute. "That's an order."

"Aye-aye, Admiral." Barbara turned on her heel then, and walked back along the docks, singing some old Earth-tune to herself, something about the "Highland Brigade."

Jackie watched her go, wondering if she'd see Barbara MacEwan again. It was true that they were better-equipped to fight this war than they had been a few months ago, when Adrianople was first taken; but there was still no way of telling what their chances might be if they went up against the vuhls in combat.

At Josephson, Hesya and Sharnu—Stone and Drew Sabah—had nearly killed her, and nearly cost them the battle. And that was a battle where she'd had the *gyaryu* in hand and had been able to protect most of the ships in the fleet with its help. What chance did Barbara Mac-Ewan have without it?

A fighting chance, she answered herself. It wasn't much to count on, but with Barbara in command, it was at least something to hope for.

More than a thousand light-years away, in a very different, very alien place that no human or zor had ever seen firsthand, an insectoid creature was making her way through a smooth, dimly lit corridor. It was a part of a huge, hivelike structure that extended for kilometers in every direction—up several levels, downward below the surface of the planet, and outward to every point of the compass. It grew constantly and irregularly, with regular renovations and alterations in its structure. Only smell- and taste-markers provided any clue as to the arrangement and function of its thousands of chambers, corridors and passageways, for no overall map existed.

It was brighter than zor or even human eyes would find comfortable, and even the most well-adjusted person of those two races would find it claustrophobic. The acrid, damp smells and the constant noise would be unnerving to any but the members of the race that inhabited the place, but for them it was quite comforting.

The corridor along which the creature was moving was quite near the center of the hive, below the ground and approximately the same distance from all of the outlying areas where her servants labored to extend it. Unlike most passages, this one was nearly empty; she could only see the occasional servant. Even these lesser-beings opened side-portals and removed themselves from her path as she passed; her great size made it almost impossible for them to remain, in any case. None even dared to extend a feeler or a mandible to touch the warm fluid that glistened on her hide: What might be socially permissible between equals, or even a mark of obsequious deference from a lesser to a greater, was tantamount to sacrilege in this case. No one dared touch the body, or the bodily fluids, of the Great Queen without leave.

If she had wished, the Great Queen could have commanded that some of these servants convey her in state through this corridor, but she had chosen not to bother with this ceremony. Among her chief Drones and other officials of First Hive, this queen was considered somewhat unusual: In her brief time upon the Seat of Majesty, Great Queen K'da had been diligent in making sure she was unpredictable.

The best way to avoid an impalement stake, K'da mused to herself, as she moved through the corridor. In the back of her mind she remembered the faintest taste of one of her predecessor's vital organs, brought to her by a loyal Drone.

After a few dozen meters, she had reached a part of the complex where there were no servants to get out of her way. Even the fierce, fanatical *P'cn* Deathguard that kept posts at regular intervals anywhere the Great Queen went, were nowhere to be seen. This was a part of the hive-complex where only Great Queens went. As hard as it was to imagine, this was a place where Deathguard—even her own *P'cn*—feared to tread.

A seam appeared at the end of the corridor and the Great Queen moved through it, the sides of the opening caressing her slightly as she passed between them. As the seam closed after her passage, the sounds of the hive became suddenly muffled. That, along with the spaciousness of the chamber in which she now stood, were as unnerving as the sight of the object that stood in its center.

It was a transparent cube, filled with swirling, sparkling luminescent mist that caught the light in the chamber and reflected it in weird rainbow patterns on the curving walls. The mist did not completely fill the cube; there was a space of about twenty *u'n'klii* below the top of the cube that was clear. Half-submerged, half-visible above the swirling mist, was a silver sphere. It moved slowly up and down, changing its position gradually with the eddies in the mist.

=Great Queen,= the Ór said, in her mind. She tasted the faintest bit of obeisance, but the mind-voice was impossibly distant, completely alien. There was nothing to read but what was being spoken.

"You have counsel to offer," K'da said. "We are ready to receive it."

=I have news for you,= the Ór answered. =The thing has happened that you most fear.=

"The Destroyer?"

=Yes.= The sphere answered from inside the Ór—or was it the Ór itself? No one knew. =The Destroyer has been spawned by the meat-creatures.=

K'da could not help but exude nervous fluid. It ran off her carapace and pooled around her. She would have to clean it up herself: No service 'bots or lesser-creatures entered this chamber, and it would not do to leave it behind.

=You are afraid.=

"Our legends say that the Destroyer will come in fire, and bring chaos and pain. Should I be unafraid?"

=What have I promised you?= the Ór answered, the mind-voice level and untroubled. =Have you forgotten, Great Queen?=

"You promised us that while you lived, we would conquer," K'da responded. "But, the Destroyer—"

=Yes?= the Ór asked.

"The legend of the Destroyer is much older than your promise,"

K'da said at last. She felt fear in her pores, and thought it might leak out between the plates of her hide once again; but she willed it into submission, replacing it with anger at the presumption of this . . . this *thing*.

=If it means so little to you, perhaps I should give my assistance to the meat-creatures,= the Ór said. Within the swirling fog, K'da could see shadowy tendrils begin to form, as if the mist were being drawn away to somewhere else. Within the tank, the silver sphere began to descend.

"No! No, I did not mean to offend. Please forgive me." She was angrier still, but forced that emotion below the surface.

The shadows faded to nothing. The mist began to move again, and the sphere bobbed to the surface. =Three twelve-twelves of cycles ago, I arrived on this world and offered you my assistance,= the Ór said at last. =Your near-ancestor, N'th, accepted my offer for herself and her hive-descendants.=

A portion of the wall of the room dissolved to show a sight familiar even to members of the worker caste: the night sky of Homeworld, filled with rainbow light, shooting stars of every hue descending from heaven to earth.

The arrival of the Ór: the beginning of the war of conquest for First Hive, first on Homeworld, then across the colonies, and then beyond.

=Every enemy, every opponent, every race. While I live, all shall be conquered. Do you doubt my word, Great Queen K'da?=

"No, no, of course not." *Curse you for forcing me onto my hind feet*, K'da thought, suspecting that the Ór might be able to hear this thought, but not caring. "But . . . with the recent defeat of our forces, and this news of the Destroyer—"

=I care nothing for the weakness of your commanders. Your race is stronger and possesses *k'th's's* to consume your enemies. Why else were you chosen? Do you now think yourselves unworthy, because of minor setbacks?=

"Eight hive-ships is *not* a minor setback," she answered angrily. "It was all executed by the plan—*your* plan. The meat-creature fleet was lured together to be destroyed. But they had the talisman . . . and the Harbinger."

=The Harbinger knows nothing,= the Ór replied, its mind-voice sounding like a sneer. =You took the threat too lightly. These meat-creatures are many and they are cunning. You thought them easy and ripe for conquest, and now, because of your people's failures, *e'e'ch'n* has brought about the Destroyer. Now you must deal with it.=

"With your help."

=If you wish it.=

"I do," she answered, though it angered her to say these words. "I wish your help."

=Very well. But know this: The meat-creature who will be the Destroyer is now an infant. It will be protected by its very anonymity and it will not be mature for many cycles. You must use all of your force while the Destroyer is not yet a threat. More forces must be sent through the *r'r's'kn* to the meat-creatures' space while they are still at a disadvantage.

=There are worse fates than impalement, Great Queen K'da.=

K'da turned away from the Ór to look at the wall, where *the thing*'s arrival was still being depicted. A shower of fiery rain, coruscating in every visible color, as if the Homeworld were passing through a cosmic veil. Somewhere among the hurtling particles was the web-wrapped package that had landed in what would become First Hive. Somewhere in the picture was the Ór.

The task before K'da and First Hive was clearly laid out: But as she watched, and felt the faint mind-touch of the Ór upon her, K'da felt a new, more deeply seated fear.

There are worse fates, she thought, *than impalement.*